Angus Donald was born in China in 1965 and educated at Marlborough College and Edinburgh University. For over twenty years he was a journalist in Hong Kong, India, Afghanistan and London. He now works and lives in Kent with his wife and two children.

www.angus-donald.com

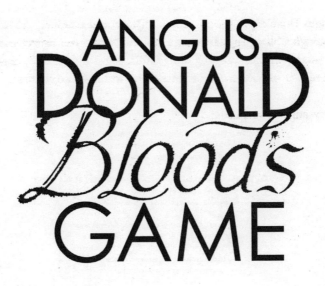

ANGUS
DONALD
Blood's
GAME

ZAFFRE

First published in Great Britain in 2017
This paperback edition published in 2018 by

ZAFFRE PUBLISHING
80–81 Wimpole St, London W1G 9RE
www.zaffrebooks.co.uk

A CIP catalogue record for this book is
available from the British Library.

ISBN: 978-1-78576-218-5

Also available as an eBook

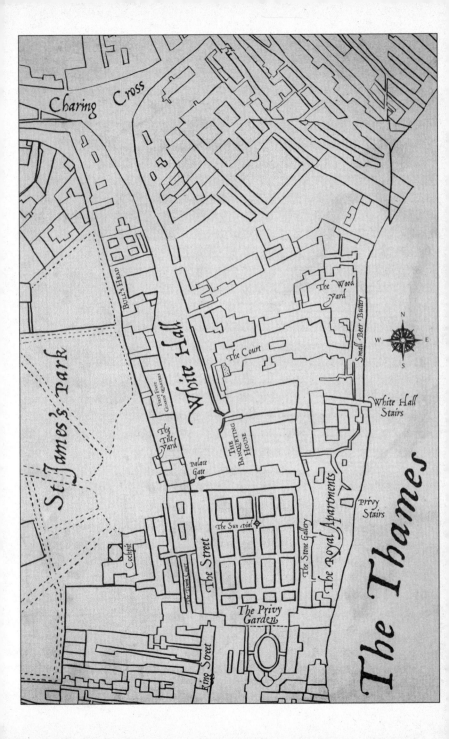

Part One

Wednesday 23 November, 1670

As he picked his way through the muck and puddles of Cock Lane, Holcroft Blood found himself thinking about the queen of diamonds. She was the best-loved of all the fifty-two hand-painted Parisian playing cards that lay, dog-eared, grubby and tied up with a piece of string, in the pocket of his threadbare coat. She was his favourite; more than that, she was his friend.

She was not as dark-eyed and daring as the queen of spades, nor as honey-sweet as the queen of hearts, but she had an air of amused tolerance on her painted face that Holcroft found particularly appealing. She was attractive, he thought, without being sluttish: tall, slender, with brown eyes and a pile of blonde curls under an enormous black hat. An elegant black velvet choker with a large single diamond at the front enclosed her slim neck. Holcroft felt that she understood him, that she already liked and admired him, that, if only she were a real, flesh-and-blood person, she would truly be his friend – someone he could share his secrets with, someone to laugh with, talk with, walk with, someone who was always at his side.

Holcroft did not have friends – at least none who were not constructed out of card, linen, lacquer and lead paints. There was a stray dog that lived in the Shambles of which he was warily fond. He had a large number of noisy brothers and sisters, some of them living with him and his mother and the baby in the little cottage at the end of Cock Lane, Shoreditch, a village just north of the City of London. But he had managed, somehow, after fifteen years of life, to be completely without companions. He knew that he was different to other boys and girls – his mother had told him early on that he was special; his oldest brother Tom just called him a buffle-head. He did not like to look other people directly in the eye, for example, it made him feel they were challenging him; he disliked change of any kind and surprises in particular, and he liked things to be neat and ordered at all times. Mess, even the smallest amount of chaos, was frightening and when he was scared the dizziness would threaten to overwhelm him. As a child, when this had happened, he had sometimes screamed and lashed out at those around him.

It seemed to Holcroft that being special made it impossible for other people to be friends with him, although God knows he had tried. They were not interested in the things he liked doing – counting all the visible bricks in the walls of the houses in Cock Lane, or recording the number and colour of the horses that passed by in the street in a single hour – and they drifted away, looking at him out of the side of their eyes or, worse, called him names and laughed at him. But Holcroft told himself he did not care: he had the queen, who was just as good as a real friend, right there in his pocket. He would talk to her later, when he had completed this errand for his mother and tell her about his day and what he had seen. She would be interested.

The pack of cards had been a gift from his father, Colonel Thomas Blood, on the occasion of one of his rare visits to the Cock Lane cottage. He usually came after dark, heavily cloaked and with his big black hat with the beautiful ostrich feather plume pulled down low. There were bad people, powerful people who wished him harm, he said, and who were best avoided. That was why he did not live with them and only came to visit on special occasions. When he did, the children would be evicted for the night from the big four-poster bed in the cottage's only upstairs chamber and had to sleep curled together like dogs by the hearth-fire on the floor in the parlour.

Holcroft did not mind. He enjoyed his father's visits. The colonel would drink his brandy and tell them stories of his adventures in the wars, when he had ridden at the head of his troop of gallant men in the cause of Parliament, fighting bravely to end the tyranny of evil men – so many adventures, so many glorious battles, so many narrow escapes from death. Once, when he had come back from a trip abroad, he had given Holcroft the Parisian pack and showed him the four suits, the numbers on each card, and the interesting people painted on the royal cards. His father had introduced him to the queen of diamonds: she was a tough lady, he told him gravely, kind and clever but a little bit dangerous, too. Holcroft liked her immediately.

The Wheatsheaf was surprisingly full that Wednesday morning, when Holcroft pushed in through the door and made his way up to the counter. It smelled of tobacco smoke, old sweat and fresh-brewed ale and a whiff of urine in the mix as well. He stood on the stone flag before the counter, making sure to keep his shoes inside the mortar lines, and waited till the harassed tavern-keeper was ready to serve him. He put his mother's pewter pint pot on the wooden boards and passed the time by counting the small shiny blue-and-white tiles on the wall behind, and had just got to sixty-eight when . . .

'Your ma's usual order, is it, young Holcroft?'

'Three gills of Barbados rum, if you please, sir.'

'As I said, the usual.' The man dipped a measuring ladle into the rum barrel and carefully poured the brown liquor into the pint pot, three-quarters filling it. The sweet, pungent smell of alcohol burned in Holcroft's nose.

'And she's keeping well, is she, your ma?'

'She says she feels a little poorly today, sir. She says she just needs a drop of good Barbados to make her right.'

The tavern-keeper said: 'I'll wager she does. I saw her in here last night,' and gave a nasty little snorting laugh. 'She wasn't poorly then. In very high spirits, she was! Very cheerful. Cheerful as a lord, you might say.'

Holcroft said nothing. He stared at the counter. The man was chuckling.

'Just a joke, youngling – don't take offence.'

A joke – Holcroft wasn't good with jokes. They made no sense to him. The man had not said anything funny yet he was grunting like a madman.

Holcroft had his penny ready, held out in his open palm, and the tavern-keeper, taking his continued silence for a rebuke, took the coin without another word. Holcroft then placed his left hand flat over the top of the pot, grasped the vessel's handle with his right, turned and walked to the door.

'You should try a drop of rum yourself, lad. Do you good. Might put a smile on your face for once.'

Holcroft ignored the tavern-keeper and pushed out through the door and into the bright street. He turned right and began to make his way home. He had not gone more than twenty yards, carefully carrying the pewter pot in both hands to make sure it did not spill, while stepping round the brimming potholes in the unpaved street, when he heard the first cat-calls.

'Hey, jingle-brains, what you got there?'

Holcroft ignored the voice. He stepped over a dead dog and carried on walking down the street. It was only another hundred yards to his home.

'A tot for your cup-shot mummy, is it? Give us a sip, mummy's boy.'

Holcroft lowered his head and kept walking.

'I'm talking to you, blockhead. What you got in the pot?'

Holcroft finally looked round. There were three of them. Tough, lean, raggedy boys about the same age as he was, or a little younger, on the far side of the road. He knew their faces but not their names. It did not matter. He knew the type. He knew what would happen next. He looked ahead to the end of the street where his cottage was. He could run, but that would almost certainly mean spilling the rum. If that happened his mother would scream and weep and pull her hair out. He knew that they did not have another penny to replace the liquor if it was spilt.

One of the raggedy boys, the smallest one, ran ahead of Holcroft, and crossed the road barring his path. The two behind him were closing in. Holcroft heard the litany of familiar taunts about his stupidity: 'Tom-noddy . . . buffle-head . . . ninnyhammer . . . nump-son . . .'

He could see a pair of squat, red-faced women, standing outside their front doors, strong arms folded, looking on with amusement as the predatory boys closed in around Holcroft. He did not like this. These boys were going to spoil his errand. His mother had given him strict instructions: go to the Wheatsheaf, buy the rum and come straight home. And he had tried his best to do just that. But these three were going to ruin everything. He felt sick and dizzy. By the side of the street he saw a mounting block, a waist-high cube of stone, with three steps cut into one side. He walked over to it and carefully placed the pewter on the top step.

Then he turned to face his tormentors.

The leader was clearly the biggest one – as tall as Holcroft, but thicker in the chest, and he moved with the rangy grace of a street cat. He had a shock of ginger hair, a wide grin and a black gap where his two front teeth should have been. The little blond one to Holcroft's left, the one who'd run ahead to cut him off, was of no account. He was a follower, and younger than the others by some years. The redhead's other companion, dark, bull-necked and vicious-looking, might be even more dangerous than the red.

Holcroft was no stranger to bullies. All his life people had objected to him in one way or another. And he had taken beatings with regularity until his older brother Tom, at his mother's tearful pleading, had reluctantly taken him aside and taught him the rudiments of pugilism and Cornish wrestling. Tom had then taken pleasure in knocking him down again and again, day after day, while he lectured his brother in the finer points of the fighting arts.

Holcroft did not think there was any point in saying anything to these three, so he merely jumped forward and pumped a straight left into the redhead's nose, smashing his head back. Then he dipped a shoulder and buried his right fist into his enemy's now-open belly. He hit him a third time, again with his left, and with all his weight behind it, smack on the right cheekbone. The boy went down. Holcroft whirled, saw the dark boy nearly on him, fist raised. He blocked the punch and seized the boy by the lapels of his coat, pulled him in and crashed his forehead hard into the bridge of his opponent's nose. He felt the crunch of cartilage, and the boy's weight as he staggered, but Holcroft kept hold of him, shifting his position slightly as he brought his knee up smartly into the fellow's groin. Holcroft released him and the boy slid bonelessly to the ground.

The tall redhead was gasping and spitting blood, back up on his feet but tottering. Holcroft took his time and clubbed him on the join of the jaw with his right fist, hard as he could, then followed in with a left uppercut to the chin that cracked his teeth together and hurled him on his back into the mud.

He looked at the third one: the blond child. Both Holcroft's hands were hurting now, and he felt as if he were about to burst into tears, as he always did after a bout. He screamed, 'Haaaaa!' pushing his face right forward and scowling like a gargoyle, and the urchin gave a squeak and took to his heels. Holcroft looked at his two foes, now both curled in the mud, coughing, spewing, writhing feebly. He had nothing to say to them. He turned his back and went over to the stone mounting block to collect the pewter pot of rum. He looked, looked again and saw that the pot had disappeared.

The burly women spectators had vanished, too.

Holcroft's heart sank into his shoes. No rum for Mother now. He felt cold and tearful. He would never hear the end of this.

One eye cracked open: the iris blue as innocence, the white curdled and veined with decades of debauchery. It focused slowly on a fat black beam set in a lime-plastered ceiling. There had been a noise. Raised voices from the parlour beneath the bedroom: anger, a denial, insistence.

The second eye opened. The shaggy grey-brown head lifted from the damp pillow. Full-blooded shouting billowed up from below. Thomas Blood was fully awake now; he swung his long legs off the bed and stood, naked, a little dizzy, swaying, listening to the rumble of feet on the wooden stairs. Two fast strides and Blood stood beside the door, a flimsy thing of elm boards and ash laths. He slid the iron bolt home but knew it would not hold. He looked round the room. There was an empty wine jug and smeared glasses on the dresser; the dismembered carcass of a bird squatting in its own jelly and a basket of torn bread on the table by the window. The stale bedroom air reeked of chicken gravy, sour wine and sex. The girl was still asleep, her bright-auburn hair spread across the sheets like a splash of heart's blood, one pink breast lolling sideways against the ridges of her bare ribs.

He scooped a pair of mouse-coloured breeches from under the bed and was struggling to get one leg inside, his damp skin making the wool cling, when the pounding on the elm began.

'Blood! Colonel Thomas Blood – open up this damned door!' It was an educated voice for all its crude bawling, the voice of a man who was born to command.

Blood's head was encased in his linen shirt. He could smell the rancid funk of a dozen days' wear. But his arms were through now. He shoved the tails roughly into his breeches. *Where in the name of God were his boots?*

'Thomas Blood, open this door or we will break it down. Open up this very instant!'

'What? Who is it? We're trying to sleep in here!' Blood mumbled the words like a man still gripped by Morpheus. But he had found one of his boots and, hopping ludicrously, he managed to get it over his bare foot and stamp it into its proper fit. The girl was awake now, sitting up with the sheet clutched to her bosom, the back of one wrist rubbing her eye. Blood winked at her, gave her his best grin, equal parts big white teeth, lust and mischief.

'I order you in the name of my father, His Grace the Duke of Ormonde, Lord Steward of the Household, to open this door. Open the door by the time I count to three, or I swear I shall break it down.'

So it's Ossory, thought Blood, *Thomas Butler, Earl of Ossory. Ormonde's eldest. How did that arrogant pup track me down?*

'One moment, sir, the merest instant, if you please. Let me find a gown to cover my nakedness and I shall be with you directly!'

Blood strode over to the bed, swooped down and kissed the girl hard. He snatched up his silver-topped cane and his blue coat from the side table, jammed the black broad-brimmed hat with the white ostrich plume on his head, walked to the window and flung wide the shutters. Golden sunlight streamed into the room. He winced at the brightness of the morning.

'One!'

'I'm coming, sirs – have a little patience for the love of God.'

'Two!'

Blood jerked the sash window up and got one leg out. He blew the girl a kiss.

The girl gave him a languid wave.

'Three!' The elm boards shuddered as the weight of a man was hurled against them. But, astoundingly, the fragile door held.

'I've borrowed a shilling or two from your purse,' Blood told her.

'What! Hey . . .' The girl sat fully up in her bed, dropping the sheet to expose her sleep-pink torso, naked to the waist.

'Knew you wouldn't mind, Jenny-girl.'

The door burst open. Three large young men in moss-green coats tumbled into the room, followed by a hatchet-faced man of some thirty-five years wearing a fine black periwig and an even finer scarlet cloak. The men froze, staring at the half-naked girl in bed.

'Keep the faith, my darling, we'll all come up smiling yet,' said Blood – and dropped from sight.

Blood landed awkwardly in the muck of the street and a shaft of pain lanced up his left leg. He was a big man, fifteen stones and an inch over six foot, but he was no longer as young as he had once been. There were threads of grey now in his shoulder-length chestnut locks, and his belly was no longer greyhound lean – too many years of drinking and fucking, too many years of fighting and running from the law had taken a toll on his once-endless strength. He felt old, and not for the first time.

He limped down Southwark Street towards the stables, shrugging on his long blue coat as he walked and, looking over his shoulder, he saw a thin angry face thrust out of the bedroom window he'd just exited.

'Halt in the name of the lord steward!' bellowed the Earl of Ossory. 'Halt or I shall give fire!'

Blood caught a glimpse of a pistol, a gleam of silver and polished brown wood. He gave the nobleman a cheery wave and hobbled onwards at his best speed. There was a bang and a splash from a long horse trough a yard to his right. *No one can shoot straight any more,* Blood thought. *If that over-bred dandyprat had been in my troop during the war, I'd have had him flogged bloody for wasting a bullet.* But the war had ended nearly twenty years ago and, despite a victory for Parliament, a King was now back on the throne of England and Royalist lickspittles like Ossory and his thief of a father were once more the most powerful men in the land – even if they couldn't shoot to save their souls.

Nevertheless, the worst shots did sometimes hit the target by accident and Blood did not care to be pistolled in the back by an incompetent lordling on a lucky day, so he limped onward a little faster and rounded the corner of the street with a sigh of gratitude.

Once safely out of sight, he paused for a moment to take stock, then plunged into a wide yard off the main thoroughfare tucked around the back of the tavern where a pair of horses were tied up to the rail and a short bald man in a leather jerkin was brushing the mud from their coats. He touched the silver wolf's head of his cane to his hat at the startled ostler, gave him a wide easy smile, and walked on past without a word. A dozen steps later he pushed open the half door of a horse stall and called out: 'Up and at 'em, boys. Rise and shine. Barbarians at the gate!'

Two men, one small with a scarred face and a squint in his left eye, the other a great shaven-headed lump of bone, muscle and blubber half a head taller even than Blood, emerged from separate mounds of hay brushing strands from their sleep-creased faces.

'Ormonde's boy got wind of us somehow,' said Blood, reaching out a hand to the smaller of the two, a Yorkshire man who called himself William Hunt, hauling him upright. 'Some grubby little informer, I have no doubt, looking to earn a shilling or two. So, no time to dally.'

The other man, Joshua Parrot by name, lumbered past Blood and peered out of the open half of the stable door.

He said, 'What about the girl?'

'Oh, she'll be just fine. Ormonde might give her a lick or two, but Jenny can stand that; he won't be too savage. The old fool thinks he's in love with her. Jen will have him eating out of her hand by dinnertime.'

A moment later, Blood poked his head around the door of the stables. The ostler was gone. The muddy street was empty but for a burly fellow slowly rolling a vast barrel of beer towards the tavern's open trap door, a square hole in the street, and a scabrous urchin squatting by the wall and drawing patterns in the mud with a stick. The big wooden sign on the corner of the street displayed the gorily severed head of a turbaned Saracen creaking in the foul breeze that blew up the street off the River Thames.

'All clear,' Blood called and stepped out, his two mismatched lieutenants following, one at each shoulder. They had not gone more than five paces when they heard the sound of clattering boot-nails on granite cobbles. Five different men but in the same gorgeous moss-green coats as the tavern intruders came hurtling around the corner. Blood stopped short. William Hunt barged into his broad back and cursed, 'Jesu!'

'Watch that blasphemy, Will,' Blood murmured. He saw cudgels, a sword or two, in the gang of Ormonde footmen in front of him. A thin pink-faced young footman in a white wig at the back was waving a horse pistol.

'Colonel, sir,' said Parrot, laying a meaty hand on Blood's right shoulder. He turned and saw three more men in moss-green coats come running around the corner that led to the tavern. A heartbeat later and the glossy black periwig of the Earl of Ossory could be seen behind them.

Five in front, four behind. Blood had faced worse odds and won.

'There!' said Will, pointing at a narrow alleyway on the other side of the street; a dark stinking tunnel, the upper storeys of the houses almost meeting above, blocking out the sunlight. The three fugitives ran across and dived into the square opening, sprinting into darkness. Their pursuers were no more than ten paces behind and hallooing like huntsmen in sight of their fox.

With every step Blood's ankle sent a lightning bolt of pain up into his groin. He caught his foot on something and went sprawling, splashing into filth. Parrot's massive hand seized him by the scruff of his coat and lifted him upright. There was light up ahead, the alley's end, and William Hunt's small frame was outlined in the white square, his arm outstretched towards them. There was a spark, a fizz and crack, then a spear of flame lashed out towards Blood. He could have sworn he felt the wind of the ball as it passed his cheek. A man cried out in pain from behind him, he heard shouts of outrage from the pursuing pack. A horse pistol fired in reply to William's shot, a deeper report, but Blood and Parrot were already out of the alley and following their companion who was running on ahead through the busy streets of Southwark, his head darting from side to side, questing for an escape route.

There were shouts of 'Murderers!' and 'Stop them!' from behind. But the crowds were thicker here, nearer the bridge. They jinked left into a quieter street, then right into an empty road. And right again. A dead end. Not a street or alley, but a short bay next to a large warehouse beside the river, fenced off from the slow brown ooze of the Thames, a place for carts to load cargo from the river barges before beginning the long journey down the Old Kent Road to the port of Dover. Parrot seized the iron-barred fence between them and the river and shook it with his full, colossal strength. It was like trying to shake a mountain. He looked at Blood and shrugged.

'Didn't fancy a swim much anyway,' said Blood

The various cries of 'Stop! Murderers!' and 'They went down here' and 'Watch your feet, you clumsy whoreson' were very close now.

'They will hang us for sure if they take us alive,' said William, looking up pitiably into Blood's face. He was more than halfway through loading his small pocket pistol, about to shove the wadded lead ball down the barrel with the slim wooden rammer.

'But they're not going to take us alive,' said Blood, smiling boldly at the small man. 'Not now. Not ever. So – as usual, lads, it's *sauve qui peut*, God speed, and rendezvous at Romford tonight, yes?'

The two other men nodded: William Hunt miserably, Joshua Parrot wearing a mad, piratical grin. He had a five-foot-length of thick, rounded timber in his hands, a snapped-off wherry oar by the looks of it.

'Keep the faith, boys, and we'll all come up smiling yet.'

Blood twisted the silver wolf's head of his cane, pulled off the black-lacquered wooden sheath and revealed a yard of slim shining steel blade concealed inside. He strode quickly to the exit of the loading bay and walked out and straight into the path of the surging mob.

'Who wants to die first?' he enquired mildly.

The crowd of men and women – now swelled to at least thirty strong – was momentarily checked by the sight of Blood's naked blade. At the back of the throng, Ossory called out: 'Seize them, you cowardly swine!' But no one leaped forward at his lordly word of command. They stared at Blood and the yard of needle-sharp steel twitching in his right hand.

It was Parrot's unexpected, roaring charge that scattered them. The big man came barrelling out of the loading bay past his comrade, the broken oar swinging. He smashed the wooden club into the head of a bald man in the moss-green livery, knocking him instantly to the floor. Parrot's second swipe knocked two tradesmen flying, sending a half dozen more members of the crowd leaping backwards. His third blow smacked into the belly of a fat, flour-dusted woman and she doubled over coughing. The compact mass had been broken apart; now Parrot was the focus of a semi-circle of terrified onlookers, kept at bay by the sweeps of his oar. Blood slipped in behind his comrade, his sword-stick licking out to skewer the right shoulder of the pink-faced young man with the horse pistol, just as he was about to fire into Parrot's broad back. The man howled and dropped the weapon with a clatter to the cobbles. He heard Hunt's pocket pistol crack behind him and another duke's man fell to his knees to his right, clutching his bloodied chest. Blood slashed at another fellow's face, a tradesman with a cudgel, cutting a flap of bloody flesh from his jaw. The man ducked aside moaning, gore spewing through his fingers. Blood dodged a flung fist, kicked a man in the groin. Now in the general melee, Blood took a hard shove to the back and found himself face to face with Ossory on the edge of the circle. The earl had an unsheathed rapier in his hand.

Blood lunged with the sword-stick at Ossory's right forearm, hoping to pink him and make him drop the weapon, but his opponent danced nimbly away from the steel. He came forward step-stepping and then went into the full lunge. Blood parried, driving the rapier high and wide, and attacked again. Ossory turned sideways, letting the sword-stick slide past his chest. Then the nobleman countered, the longer blade lifting and lancing towards his opponent's heart. Blood cracked the rapier away to his left with the lacquered ebony haft of the cane, and stepped inside its reach. Ossory was wide open. A dead man if Blood lunged. An easy kill. But Blood hesitated for a split instant, sword-stick poised to skewer, then pushed the blade wide and barged forward, his shoulder and full fifteen-stone weight crashing into the slender earl's chest, knocking him to the cobbles.

Blood took a deep, gasping breath, wondering at his own mercy. He saw no one ahead of him, and no one on either side. He began hobbling as fast as his ankle would allow, back down the way he had come. He snatched a fast look behind him and saw Parrot still swatting petulantly with the broken oar at the few remaining members of the mob, but they were clearly beaten, backing into doorways to evade the swinging wood, others actually running down the street in the opposite direction. Two men in green were on their knees, bleeding busily on the cobbles. The fat woman lay curled around herself, vomiting and spitting. Ossory had lost his beautiful periwig and was sitting spraddle-legged on his cloak gaping at Blood. The rapier was four yards away from his right hand. There was no sign of William Hunt.

Blood saluted Ossory with his sword-stick, a flamboyant, sweeping gesture, then wheeled and hobbled onwards. He turned a corner, then another. There was no pursuit. He sheathed his blade. Pulled his wide-brimmed hat lower over his eyes, buttoned his coat up and strolled into the heavy traffic of the Borough High Street, allowing the press of the crowds, carts and horses to sweep him north towards the bridge. He glanced left at the yellow bulk of Southwark Cathedral, then right through the open gates of a coaching inn, and casually spun full circle to look behind him, going up on his toes and using his full height to scan over the bobbing heads. But there was no one – green-coated or otherwise – who seemed at all interested in his movements. As he came onto the bridge itself, under the grim row of rotting traitors' heads and the ever-present flock of feasting, shrieking seagulls, he looked back one last time. No one following. He prepared himself to cross the brown water and enter the City of London.

His ankle hurt like ungreased buggery, his shirt was sweat-soaked and there were splashes of wet mud and bright gore on the turned-back sleeves of his big blue woollen coat, but the blood sizzled in his veins from the morning's exertions. He felt good. Damn good. His head felt clear and sharp. Which was just as well: he had a deal of business to conduct this day.

His Majesty Charles the Second, by the grace of God, King of England, Scotland, Ireland and (in deference to the long-defunct claims of his ancestors) France, Defender of the Faith, Knight of the Garter, etc., etc., gave another mighty strain. His face glowed, the fat veins in his temple swelled. His abdominal muscles clenched, unclenched, clenched again. Nothing.

'It's no use, Grenville,' he said to the groom of the close stool, a greyish, careworn courtier who stood beside him in the closet, proffering a large wooden box stuffed with lambs' wool. 'I'm locked up as tight as a pair of Cornish wrestlers.'

Sir John Grenville grimaced. As a Cornishman, he did not much like his compatriots being compared to blocked bowels, even royal blocked bowels. He took a tiny step backwards – there was not a lot of room to spare in the closet – and eyed the King, who was sitting naked from the waist down on a large, ornately carved oak box with padded velvet seat, a generous oval hole cut in it and a wide porcelain bowl hidden in the darkness beneath. Outside the closet the King's new mistress, that smart-mouthed whore Nell Gwyn, should be dressing herself after her morning's exertions and preparing for her discreet departure. Indeed, Grenville hoped that she had left the royal apartments in the Palace of White Hall and was already back in her own lavish rooms. He did not want the King to be enticed into another noisy and prolonged bout once he'd finished his business in here.

'Sire,' he said. 'Perhaps we should abandon this most gallant attempt. The duke has been awaiting your pleasure in the red audience chamber this past hour or more.'

'Let him wait. Which one is it again?'

'Which one, sire?'

'Which duke, blockhead. There are only two who constantly seem to delight in robbing me of what little leisure I am granted: Buckingham and Ormonde. Which one is it?'

'It's His Grace the Duke of Buckingham who seeks an audience with you, sire. He has been waiting more than an hour.'

The groom of the close stool was indulged certain liberties with the King. As well as his more odoriferous duties, or perhaps because of them, he was the King's closest advisor. A man who was privy – in all senses – to His Majesty's most intimate secrets.

'I don't much care if he waits all morning. Buckingham, eh? So what does he want? Tell me honestly, Grenville.'

'Honestly, sire? Honestly, he wants power, as Your Majesty knows very well. He wants to enrich himself at Your Majesty's and the country's expense. He wants more influence and more money. So does the Duke of Ormonde, for that matter. So do the whole pack of them: Arlington, Clifford, Lauderdale and Ashley. They all want the same thing. Every man in your ministry. But what His Grace the Duke of Buckingham *says* that he wants, is to discuss the current, uh, grave situation with regard to the royal finances.'

'Sounds terribly boring.'

'Indeed, sire, I doubt it will be overly stimulating, but it might be wise not to irritate him more than is necessary. He now has considerable sway in both Houses and his influence is growing.'

Charles had returned from exile in the Low Countries ten years ago in a state of near-beggary and Parliament had been obliged to vote him an annual sum from the Treasury, more than a million pounds sterling, to allow him to live in a suitably regal state. Both Houses considered the amount generous, princely even. The King himself – and his many courtiers, servants, ministers, mistresses, friends, relations and dependants – entirely disagreed.

'Sire, perhaps we should abandon the struggle for today.'

'Wait, wait a moment! I think I might have something.'

The groom of the close stool shut his eyes. The proffered box of lamb's wool was beginning to feel as if it were filled with lead.

After a painful stretched-out silence, the King let out a long, trembling, eerily high-pitched trumpet-blast.

'Sire? May we now agree that we are done for today?'

'Wait, wait, wait. Yes, there is more. Yes, by God!' He groaned like an exhausted heifer trying to give birth.

There was a tinny sound – a ping like a spent pistol bullet hitting a steel breastplate. Sir John Grenville jerked with surprise.

'That will do, by God. Pass me the wool box, Grenville, and let's go and see about this damned impatient, importunate and grasping duke.'

The Duke of Buckingham stared at a huge tapestry that occupied the entire side of the red audience chamber. It must be thirty-feet long and twenty-feet high and by the look of its quality it had been made in Flanders, probably Oudenaarde. It depicted Julius Caesar returning in triumph to Rome having subdued the barbarians of Gaul. The *Imperator* was mounted, his hand raised flamboyantly in the air, as if he were in the midst of declaiming, his officers, all on foot, clustered round gazing up adoringly. In the background a pack of deer hounds gambolled in a forest.

Buckingham hated it. He had seen it a score of times before at audiences with the King and at meetings with his ministers in this very room, but he had never noticed until now that Caesar had a marked resemblance to His Majesty – the same long nose in a long horsey face, thin moustache and long luxuriant chestnut hair; although he seemed to remember from his long-ago schooling that Caesar had famously been bald, and he knew for certain that Charles's own sparse hair was covered by a shockingly expensive chestnut periwig – a cost of 800 shillings, one of his spies had told him!

Buckingham found himself surprised by his own lack of perspicacity. The tapestry was a metaphor, of course, for King Charles's restoration to the throne. How could he not have seen it before? And how typically crass it was of this beggarly monarch to compare himself to mighty Caesar. The Roman had conquered swathes of the world, had made himself master of the greatest city on Earth. In contrast, Charles had lost a bloody civil war, fled into exile, and scurried back to London nearly a decade later when England had grown sick of the Protectorate's joyless, iron-fisted governance.

The man was a mere popinjay, a mountebank who couldn't keep his prick in his breeches for five minutes, who thought that scattering grand titles, pensions and perquisites to his toadies, mistresses and bastard children was the same as governing his kingdoms. Caesar had always known the value of money, which could scarcely be said of Old Rowley, as the wits called Charles behind his back because of his resemblance to the racehorse of that name. He spent money like a boatswain in a brothel – and would he listen to his closest friends, men who had been childhood companions, on grave financial matters? No, he humiliated them by making them wait for him to finish tupping his latest whore – that actress chit who was no doubt soon to be ennobled as the Countess of Lift-My-Skirts. Or whatever the hell the King was doing that morning besides wasting the duke's precious time.

Buckingham's vitriolic thoughts were interrupted by a door on the far side of the room banging open and the sight of the King striding long-legged into the room dressed in a vast purple silk robe, matching purple silk slippers with huge purple silk bows and accompanied, as ever, by the dour Sir John Grenville and a dozen floppy-haired, yapping spaniels. A pair of young white-wigged footmen, splendid in scarlet and gold, held the doors wide open to allow the boisterous dog pack to tumble into the room.

'Hail, Caesar,' muttered the duke as he made his low and elegant bow. As he straightened, he unconsciously adjusted his long grey silk waistcoat. He said, much louder, over the sounds of the excitedly barking animals: 'Your Majesty, how gracious it is of you to favour me with your presence this morning. May I say how extraordinarily well you are looking today, magnificently regal, 'pon my word of honour.'

The King merely nodded at him and muttered 'Buckingham' before turning to one of the footmen and saying: 'Bring me wine, and some of those almond biscuits. Oh, and see if there is any of that honeyed pork left from last night – my darlings love it. Yes you do, don't you? Yes, you do!'

The King knelt among the leaping throng of dogs, stroking heads and allowing the eager animals to lick his hands and face. Buckingham struggled to conceal his rising disgust – as usual, he failed.

Finally the King rose and said: 'A little cheese too. A pair of roast ducklings. And oranges. I must have at least a dozen of those sweet "China" oranges! Nell tells me they are particularly good for my bow—' He stopped.

'Sire, pray do not forget, you are dining with the First Lord of the Treasury in less than an hour,' said Grenville.

'I am hungry now – don't you see? Not in an hour. Now. And my little darlings deserve a treat. They have been ever so patient today.'

Sir John Grenville held his tongue and one of the scarlet footman padded away silently to convey the royal command to the kitchens. The King turned to Buckingham, clapped his hands briskly, then rubbed them together in anticipation of the food. He had not been idle this morning: he had barely broken his fast with a slice of bread and cheese, and then had swum across the Thames and back, twice, before taking his new mare Titania for a hard gallop in St James's Park and returning for a delightfully energetic encounter with little Nell in the royal bedchamber. She was a demanding minx, if ever he had known one. He had earned a snack, he thought to himself, even if there were a tedious dinner to attend afterwards. It was not as if he was overweight. For a man of forty years he was as wiry as a stripling and tall with it, six foot three inches in his stockings, and the royal prick, with a little loving encouragement, could still make itself as stiff and as splendid as the golden sceptre of state.

'As Sir John reminds us, I have a dinner engagement soon and so I regret, Your Grace, that our conversation must be distressingly brief.'

'It is an honour to have even a moment of your time, sire.'

'If you say so, well, then, yes . . . So what was it that you wanted? And, as I say, do please try to be brief.'

'As your loyal Master of the Horse, sire, I have some limited purview over the expenditure of the royal household. And it has come to my attention, sire, that you recently purchased a pretty sea-going vessel for your private use . . .' Buckingham drew a piece of yellow paper from his wide coat pocket '. . . a ship of eighty-six tonnes, measuring fifty feet in length, designated His Majesty's yacht *Saudades*. And coming in at a cost of . . .'

'What of it?' The King cut him off. 'Did you come here to waste my time with this? I bought a pleasure boat. So what? I prefer to travel by water, if it is at all possible. Is that such a terrible crime?'

'No crime, sire, certainly no crime but . . .'

'What is it? Spit it out, man.'

The dogs were still milling around the King's feet, occasionally a black one would bounce up and lick at his hand.

'Down, duchess, down,' said the King. 'Your little treat is coming soon. Daddy promises. It will be here very, very soon, my love.'

'Since you already own *eleven* royal yachts, sire,' Buckingham continued, 'do you really feel that this purchase was absolutely necessary given the many and varied calls upon the royal purse?'

The King glared at the duke. 'It is to be a gift – a special gift for the queen, if you must know. *Saudades* means home-sickness or sadness or some such nonsense in her native tongue. She wishes to use it when she travels to Portugal to see her family. You surely cannot object to me buying a small token for my beloved Catherine?'

'Sire, I would that you could buy a hundred yachts, even a thousand. But as we have discussed before, there is a lamentable shortfall in the royal accounts. There is a limit to the amount of money that you can spend. The well is not inexhaustible. For example, I have here a receipt for £2,800 for a jewel, another present for the queen, and here I see you spent £6,000 on a pair of diamonds for one of her ladies-in-waiting. There was a banquet last month in which you spent £1,000 on French pastries . . .'

'And they were perfectly delicious. I must eat, must I not? Otherwise I would starve. And I must entertain my friends.'

The King and his minister looked at each other in silence.

'He does have a point, sire,' murmured Grenville.

'Oh, be quiet, you. You're supposed to be on my side.'

'It is not about sides or factions,' said Buckingham. 'You must at least attempt to curb your wild spending, sire, or disaster will surely follow. If you were to return the yacht to the boatyard . . .'

'No, Buckingham, by God, no. I am the King. I must be seen to be generous. Largesse, man, largesse is the mark of a great King. A certain carelessness with his finances befits a monarch. I absolutely refuse to scrimp and snivel like some damned pauper. I did enough of that abroad.'

The footman returned at that moment with a dozen more servants and began to lay out a large table with food and drink.

'I must speak plainly, sire. There is no more money to be had. This year's parliamentary subsidy is spent. We cannot borrow any more against the next. Your expenditure far exceeds your revenue, and has done every year since ... for every year of your glorious reign so far. Even the richest men in the country are balking at making any more advances to the Crown. But, sire, I do have a simple solution. Perhaps if you were to appoint me to the position of Lord Steward of the Household, I might be able to overhaul the royal expenditure and find some—'

'Now we get to the nub,' said Charles. 'Now the meaning of all this nonsense becomes plain. Are you not rich enough already, my lord, that you would seek to mulct me of more? I have forgiven your many crimes, I have forgiven your spying on my every move, your prying into my private affairs, for the comradeship we shared as children. I have raised you up to be among the highest in the land, and this is how you repay me? No, Buckingham, no, I will not make you lord steward. I have one already. His Grace the Duke of Ormonde has the white staff – not that he does me much good in that post. And no, I will not count my pennies like some beggar in the street. You say there is no money – and in the same breath you seek a plum post worth tens of thousands of pounds a year. If you wish to be the lord steward of my household, then you must prove yourself worthy. Find me some money.'

One of the spaniels, reacting to the King's angry tone, stood at Buckingham's feet and yapped sharply up at him. The rest of the pack was distributed around the room, sniffing in the corners and behind the chairs. One red-and-white animal by the window was managing with ease the defecatory act that had so troubled the King earlier that day. The duke ignored the bouncing dog at his feet. He scratched his smooth chin, pretending to think. 'We could go back to Parliament, sire. I have a good many friends there. If we put the facts before them, if we pleaded, if I dropped a word in certain ears then maybe something might be arranged.'

'No, Buckingham, we tried that at the last session. I went to them cap in hand, as you told me to, whining like a workhouse orphan, and they rebuffed me, a parcel of bloated shire knights, greasy small-town merchants, fox-hunting farmers – and the rogues had the gall to say nay to me. I was humiliated. No, sir, we shall not go again to the Commons. Those fellows, or men just like them, murdered my father. Never forget that. You may be sure they have not. I must have money – very good, I accept that as the bald truth – but you must find it for me. I do not care from under which rock you find it. But find it. And quickly!'

When the Duke of Buckingham had left the chamber, the King turned to Grenville. 'And you, sir, for your he-has-a-point-sire treachery, you can peel me a pair of God-damned oranges for my poor solid bowels.'

Monday 28 November, 1670

Mary Blood sat at the small, well-scrubbed table in the parlour of the cottage in Cock Lane, Shoreditch, and wept. She made almost no sound, the tears running silently down her pale cheeks. She could not afford to sob out loud, the baby in her arms had only recently fallen asleep. It was sick again and its outraged bawling had denied her rest these past three nights. By God's mercy, it had finally stopped its noise and allowed her a few moments to sit rocking it gently against her bosom, closing her eyes and indulging her own sense of despair. If only there was a drop of rum left to ease her pains, or a splash of brandy; anything to dull her hopelessness.

The room was sparsely furnished. An ash-wood table, two chairs, two benches, an upright cedar dresser containing a few mismatched bowls, plates and cups, all neatly organized in descending order of size, and half of a penny loaf sat on a wooden board beside a long, sharp knife, whittled thin by hard use. The bare plaster walls were painted with limewash but large areas were discoloured into strange shapes and patterns by damp. A tiny fireplace was swept clean of ashes, the metal grate scrubbed, blacked and laid with an unlit pyramid of dry sticks and wood shavings. From the flung-open window shutter the grey light of a late-autumn afternoon eased into the room along with the sounds and smells of the street: the cries of a pie-seller, the rattle and squeak of a heavy wooden cart, the occasional clop of a passing horseman, and the scents of fresh dung.

Her son Holcroft sat at the table, cleaning a pair of candlesticks with a rag. The cheap pewter sticks were already as shiny as they were ever going to be, yet the boy continued to rub at one of them, holding it gently in his left hand and caressing it with long, even strokes of the cloth. He was absorbed in his task and counting the swipes against the shiny metal under his breath: 'eighty-six, eighty-seven, eighty-eight . . .'

'Holly,' whispered Mary, opening her blood-shot eyes. 'I think it is clean enough now. They both are quite gleaming.'

He ignored her. 'Ninety-one, ninety-two, ninety-three, ninety-four . . .'

'Holly!' She kept her voice low for the baby's sake but there was unmistakable frustration sewn into her words. 'I know how you like to do your polishing, my honey child, but you will wear the sticks away to nothing – and then where will we all be?'

' . . . ninety-six, ninety-seven, ninety-eight . . .'

'Holcroft!' It was a full-bodied scream now. The baby opened its milky eyes and began, immediately, to express its discomfort.

'Now look what you've done!' Mary began to sob without restraint now, her wet gasps creating a weird counterpoint with the baby's cries.

The boy said: 'Ninety-nine, one hundred.' He placed the shining candlestick on the table next to its twin, aligning their square bases exactly with the edge of the wood. Then looked across at his mother and smiled: a beam of such beauty that it squeezed her heart. She began to sob all the more wretchedly. A drink, a drink – God, what would she do for a drink.

Holcroft stood up, his thick brown hair brushing the low plastered ceiling, and he walked round the table and plucked the baby out of his mother's arms. She did not protest but sagged back against the chair, as if a burden had been lifted from her soul as well as her arms. The boy began to pace across the flagstones of the parlour floor, even measured steps, turning at the wall and crossing again, crooning softly to the squalling child. Within three turns the baby stopped wailing and began to gurgle happily.

The door of the house banged open and two grubby children ran in – a boy, Charles, and a girl, Elizabeth, eight and ten years of age: 'Mama, mama, guess who is coming!' cried the girl.

'Guess! Guess!' echoed her younger brother.

'It's Tom,' shouted Elizabeth. 'Tom has come home!'

At that moment the doorway was darkened by the form of a grown man of about twenty years in a sombre grey coat and a broad-brimmed grey hat. Holcroft stopped his pacing and stared at the newcomer's chin, not lifting his eyes to meet the other man's.

'Good day, buffle-head; still playing nursemaid?'

Without waiting for an answer from Holcroft – and none would be forthcoming – Tom went over to his mother and kissed her on the cheek. She clutched at him, pressing her tear-stained cheek against his dirty yellow waistcoat. 'Tom, welcome, it is so good to have you home,' she said, sniffing. 'Have you been with your father – have you news of him?'

The baby stared at the strange man in grey.

'None to speak of. I saw him a sennight past, up Romford Market way, though he could barely see me. He was blind drunk in the Lamb, celebrating with Hunt and Parrot the fact that one of his quacksalver cures had actually worked. He cured a parson of his shivering sickness, or so he told me, and had been paid handsomely.'

'He has money, then?' She tried to keep the desperation from her tone.

'I doubt he has now. Is there anything to eat, Mother? I'm clammed.'

'There is some bread on the board. Is there any of that nice mutton pie left, Holly?'

The boy shook his head.

'I'm sure there is still a little well water in the jug,' his mother said.

'Bread and Adam's ale it is, then,' said Tom. He strode to the dresser and, ignoring the knife, tore off a hunk of bread with his big, dirty hands. He sat at the table to eat. Holcroft narrowed his blue eyes but said nothing.

Mary returned from the pantry with a mug of water and handed it to Tom. 'Staying long, son? You know you're welcome and we could sorely use a man around here.'

Mary walked over to Holcroft and accepted the quiet baby from his arms. The boy stood with his arms hanging by his sides and stared silently at the floor. His lips moved silently: *We could sorely use a man around here.*

He had another older brother called William and another younger called Edmund, but both had been sent to sea as soon as their father could find anyone who would take them. No sea captain had wanted to take Holcroft aboard his ship: his strange silences, sudden violence and general oddness of manner made folk nervous around him. Most of the family considered him dull, little better than a simpleton. But his elder sister Mary had not. Like his mother, she had recognized that his mind turned in a different way to the common run of humanity, that he was special, and that in some narrow respects he could be astoundingly perceptive. But she was gone now too, married off to a prosperous man named Corbett and was raising a large, noisy family of her own in Northamptonshire.

'I'm not staying long,' said Tom. 'I have business in Surrey tonight. I've just come to collect a few of my things.'

He crammed the last of the bread into his mouth and sank the rest of the water in a single swallow. The table before him was scattered with crumbs. The mug had left a wet ring on the pale, hard-scrubbed wood.

His mother's face fell. The baby began to grizzle once more.

'Is my chest still upstairs?'

Mary nodded; even more wretched than before. She looked down at her free hand as it rested on the table: it was quivering gently. Tom rose. He handed his mother the empty mug and clomped over to the staircase in the corner of the room. As the sound of his heavy boots echoed up towards the house's only bedroom, Holcroft glided forward and swept the crumbs from the table carefully into his hand. He tugged the candlestick rag from his belt and wiped the wooden table clean of the water ring.

When Tom came downstairs a few moments later, he had a large, elderly horse pistol in his hand, and a small sword a little less than a yard long in a battered sheath tucked under his left arm.

'Tom . . .' said Holcroft suddenly. 'Tom – if you . . . if you were to sell those things we could buy food for everyone.'

The whole family stared at him in amazement. Holcroft was no mute but he rarely spoke unless spoken to – and often not even then.

'We're certainly not selling these,' Tom told him. 'They're the tools of my trade, brother. A workman never parts with his tools.'

Every hungry eye in the parlour was fixed on Tom's face. He looked warily at Holcroft. He had grown some since Tom's last visit, thickened in the shoulder, and his long arms now ended in large fists. It had been some time since Tom had easily been able to knock him down. Not that he was afeared of his little brother, of course. He could beat the silly buffle-head any time he chose.

'If all goes well tonight, Mother, I will try to bring you some money. I promise. All right? A shilling, God's blood, ten shillings, if things go to plan. Not enough? A sack of gold then – why not! You can eat and drink like lords and ladies for a year and a day. A barrel of rum just for you, Mother!'

The dull silence in the parlour was painful to the ear. Holcroft turned away, picking up one of the candlesticks as he pulled the rag from his belt.

'Anyway, I must be away. I have an appointment to keep.'

'But, Tom, you have only just arrived!'

'Fortune calls, Mother, fortune calls!' said Tom, brandishing the horse pistol heroically in the air. And then he was gone.

'Brandy!' said Blood, rapping the counter with his silver wolf's head cane and shaking the rain from his ostrich feather hat onto the grimy, sand-strewn floor of the Bull's Head. He looked round the low, dingy room, surveying its inhabitants and noting the usual collection of drabs and drunks: a stained clergyman slumped over a pint of wine, a trio of unshaven watchmen huddled over a barrel table, a slut giggling in the lap of a long-legged servant in scarlet from one of the big houses on Pall Mall. Blood's eye lingered on an incongruent pair of gentlemen in long snuff-coloured coats adorned with golden buttons, lace at their throats and glossy periwigs, who were sitting by the fire, nursing ale pots and looking uncomfortable.

They were too close to home to be feeling this much discomfort, thought Blood. Something was clearly making them nervous. The Bull's Head backed on to the Spring Gardens, a bedraggled patch of greenery just south of Charing Cross, which was a notorious haunt of prostitutes and pick-pockets. But that was not it. The Palace of White Hall was only a few hundred yards from here. And these were palace men, through and through. They should feel quite at home in this tavern, it was in no way foreign territory. Their nervousness did not bode well for Blood.

'Brandy!' he called again. 'For the love of God, Suzy, something to wet my weasand before I fall down dead of thirst.'

'Nothing for you, colonel. Nothing for you without the chink to pay for it. You still owe me for last week's carouse, and Red Peggy says she went out into the gardens with you on a kiss and a promise and had not so much as a farthing to show for her kindness.'

Suzy, the tavern-keeper's wife, looked as sour as month-old milk, a square yellow slab of a face, small eyes like raisins in raw dough, grubby breasts almost spilling out of her stained, half-unlaced bodice, strands of grey greasy hair straggling down from under her once-white linen coif.

'Suzy, my dove, I swear you get more comely with every passing day. Matthew is surely the luckiest man in Christendom. You surely wouldn't begrudge an old friend a nip or two of the good French stuff to keep out the rain, come now, my dear.'

'No brass, no bingo – those is Matt's strict orders: he mentioned you specifically. And he'd beat me black if I disobeyed his word.'

'Who says I have no money?' Blood dipped a hand into the pocket of his coat and a round silver shilling winked delightfully between his fingers.

She stared at him, half-disbelieving. Blood's hand had disappeared back into his pocket. 'So, my darling, a measure of your best brandy – and tip me a nice gage of fogus, if you please.'

When the pewter mug had been set before him on the counter and a white clay pipe stuffed with Virginia tobacco had been delivered, lit and a cloud of fragrant tobacco smoke had added its note to the general fug, Blood walked over to the two sober gentlemen by the fire and, pulling out a stool with his foot, he set himself down between them.

'Blood,' muttered the man to his left.

'Good day to you, Littleton,' said Blood cheerily, 'and good day to you, Osborne. I trust you are both in bounding good health – no black plague, no purple scurvy, no Cupid's measles, I trust?'

Both men ignored his rude pleasantry.

'Do we have to meet in this . . . this awful place?' said Sir Thomas Osborne, looking around the Bull's Head with a shudder. He was a tall, brisk man, broad-shouldered with black moustaches.

'We couldn't very well meet him at the palace, could we?' said Sir Thomas Littleton, a younger, blonder figure but rounder and dowdier too, with large eyes and a faint resemblance to an owl. 'With peepers in every gallery and ears at every door. We'd be the talk of all London, indeed all England before nightfall. And I would not care to receive him in my own house – would you, sir?'

'So charming,' said Blood. 'You make me feel so valued, so beloved, so warm inside.' He drained his mug, turned to the counter and called loudly for another tot of brandy.

'I do not wish to be unduly discourteous, colonel,' Osborne said. 'But, as you well know, there is a fat price on your head after that business at Dublin Castle – and the Duke of Ormonde has let it be known that he will pay it whether you are brought to him dead or alive. He cares not which. Lord Ossory is determined to win his father's favour by capturing you – he is afire with zeal, or so I'm told. You are – how shall I put it? – an undesirable connection, very much *persona non grata* in London society.'

When Suzy had brought over the brandy jug and refilled his pewter, Blood said: 'If I had succeeded in Dublin, if I had captured the castle and held it, if I had not been betrayed, if that foul-mouthed knave Ormonde had been knocked from the summit of the dung heap and swept into the gutter with the rest of the turds, you would be showing me a deal more respect.'

Littleton shrugged. 'If.'

Blood blew a plume of blue smoke directly into Littleton's face. While the fat man coughed and spluttered and mopped his huge eyes with a scarlet-spotted kerchief, Blood said, 'Tell me, sirs, was there any particular reason why you asked me to meet you in this fine establishment today or was it just to remind me of my past humiliations and my present social shortcomings?'

Osborne said, 'We have another commission for you, sir. And, perhaps by no coincidence, it concerns your old Irish adversary.'

'Ormonde?' Blood lifted an eyebrow.

'The same.'

'I don't suppose you want me to cut his fat throat, do you?'

Neither of the two gentlemen said anything. Osborne stared into his nearly empty ale pot. Littleton considered the wisdom of the crackling fire.

'Jesu – I was jesting. Are you in earnest?' Blood looked back and forth between the two. 'You came to ask me to kill a man?'

'Keep your voice down,' growled Osborne.

Blood turned around to survey the room. The long-limbed servant and the slut had disappeared. The watchmen were deep in their own dark business. The clergyman was snoring loudly with his mouth wide open, drool glistening upon his black coat. Matthew Pretty, the tavern-keeper, who despite his name was as ill-favoured as his wife, was out of earshot, wiping the counter with a rag and shooting distrustful glares in Blood's direction.

Littleton said, 'Our master feels that Ormonde's, uh, removal from the court would best serve His Majesty's true interests . . .'

'You don't have to tell me why Buckingham wants it done. The reason is as plain – and quite as ugly – as the nose on your face.'

'You do not say his name. You do not say it in this place . . .'

Littleton's plump round face had grown red.

'What? Buckingham? George Villiers, His Grace the Second Duke of Buckingham?' Blood's voice was now loud. 'That is the name I should not dare to say? Why not? You know it. I know it. The world knows it. I know too why he wants to rid himself of Ormonde; he wants to rid himself of the only man who stands between him and the full gale of the King's favour.'

'You're no better than a child, Blood. It will not do. This is a deadly serious matter and while His Grace might indulge you out of respect for your long association, I'll have you know that I . . .'

Blood leaned into Littleton's fat, round face. He said quietly, 'You come here and insult me, tell me I am undesirable, not someone you would care to entertain in your own house, yet in the same breath beg me to commit black murder for your master. Is that it?'

'This has been a mistake,' said Osborne, rising to his feet. Littleton too was struggling to lever his soft body out of the deep leather chair. Blood reached out a long arm, gripped his fat-padded shoulder and shoved the younger man back into his seat.

'There are some small conditions that I have to which His Grace must readily agree before we can proceed,' said Blood calmly. 'And I will need a goodly sum of money, too. In gold, as usual, if you please.'

'So you will do it?' Littleton looked at him with renewed hope. 'You really will? My brother James at the Pay Office can certainly provide you with whatever sums you need – within reason—'

'Wait, Littleton! Wait! What conditions, Blood? Tell us what the conditions are.' Osborne stared down at Blood, stroking his black whiskers, frowning, wary, almost frightened by Blood's volte face.

'Sit yourself down, Sir Thomas, whistle up some more of that very fine French bingo, another gage of Virginian too, if you please, and I'll lay out for you what I want in return for doing this dark and dangerous deed.'

Tuesday 6 December, 1670

Holcroft waited outside the arch of the gatehouse that marked the entrance to the Palace of White Hall. He stared up at the massive structure: with its four soaring octagonal towers, narrow arched windows and thick walls in a chequered pattern of flint and stone, it looked like a knight's castle from the olden days. And this was just the gatehouse to the palace. But then everything seemed huge here in this royal enclave on the outskirts of Westminster, at least to Holcroft's eyes. The road behind him that led back to London was at least five times as wide as the muddy lane in Shoreditch where he lived. The building to his left, he had been told, was the King's banqueting house, and it was as big as a palace all on its own and that was only one building in this enormous royal complex. Here, the King, his wife, his servants, his soldiers, his ministers and mistresses all lived together, higgledy-piggledy, in sprawling splendour.

Holcroft was clutching a bundled rag, his fardel, which contained all his worldly possessions: a clean shirt that his mother had washed and ironed for him the night before, two copper farthings rubbed almost smooth by age and usage, a piece of hard bread rubbed with onion and, of course, his pack of beloved French playing cards.

Part of him had been secretly glad to leave that squalid dwelling in Cock Lane and his mother's endless weeping. Change was bad, of course; he liked things to be regular, orderly, predictable; routine was ever his friend. But the Shoreditch house was distressingly chaotic. People came and went at all hours, meals were scanty and infrequent and Tom had sometimes brought his friends back from the alehouse at midnight and drank rum and laughed and sang. His younger brother and sister tracked mud up the stairs; the poor, sickly baby would never cease in its crying unless he walked him.

No, change was bad, it made him feel dizzy and sick, but he was feeling something else besides as he stood waiting to be met – a quickening of his heart, a clamminess of his palms – that was not wholly unpleasant. A new life awaited him, Mother had said. And it was all Father's doing.

Blood had turned up at Cock Lane a week ago, the night of Tom's brief visit, arriving in a whirlwind of enthusiasm, jests and more than a whiff of brandy. He had kissed his weeping wife, presented her with a sunny bouquet of daisies and a pair of bright-silver shillings and had told her the wonderful news: Holcroft was to serve as a page to a rich man, a duke no less, and was to go away and live in a palace – the Palace of White Hall, indeed, with the King himself. Holcroft's master was to be one of His Majesty's chief ministers, a magnificent nobleman, one of England's greatest gentlemen.

The next morning, Blood had taken Holcroft's chin in his hand as they stood together by the parlour table and had forced him to look into his eyes; something that made the boy feel most uncomfortable. 'You'd better serve His Grace well, boy, or you'll feel my belt on your bare arse.'

'I will, Father.'

'I mean it, son. This is a great opportunity for you. Serve him well.'

Holcroft said nothing. He twitched his jaw out of his father's hand and stared at the table. His mother was moving heavily about upstairs, already three-parts drunk on the little money Blood had brought, and he could hear the baby whining fitfully up there too. His younger brother and sister were out playing in the street. He was alone with his father.

'Son, I'm not always going to be here to look after you and your poor mother,' said Blood, pulling out a chair and sitting down at the table. 'I know I have not been the perfect husband – or father, for that matter. But you know that I care for you all, don't you? It's just that I've got to do something for somebody, and it might well be . . . Well, it might be dangerous for me. And, anyway, I'll not live for ever. One day, when I'm in my grave, you and Tom will have to care for your mother and the children. I won't be able to do even the little I do now. So I want you to listen to me, really listen, about this plum I have secured for you. Are you listening, son?'

Holcroft remained silent, staring at the table.

'Well, I'm going to say my piece anyway. And if you're wise you will pay heed. The duke, your new master, is a powerful man – an extremely powerful man, Holcroft, maybe the most powerful in the land after the King. You will serve him, live with him, learn from him, stand by his side day and night, maybe for years. You will dis-cover a great deal about power – how to get it, how to wield it. For example: what do you think it is, son, that makes him so strong? What do you think the duke's true strength is?'

'Money. All that chink makes him powerful.'

'Half right, son, but only half right. His Grace has all the money in the world, sure, but what makes him powerful is knowledge, information. The duke knows everything there is to know. He has eyes and ears everywhere – and I mean *everywhere* – and he pays them well to keep him informed. Knowledge is power. Remember that when you get to the palace. This is the true cur-rency of the corridors of White Hall: gossip, rumours and, best of all, real, solid intelligence. The right kind of information can make a man rich, the wrong kind can leave him bleeding in the gutter. If you know something that another man doesn't then you've got one up on him. You have power over him. Do you understand me, boy?'

Holcroft said nothing but he pulled out a chair and sat down care-fully on the far side of the table from his father, eyes lowered, his broad, clumsy hands resting before him on the pale-scrubbed ash.

Blood reached out his own right paw and covered Holcroft's left hand. 'This position will be good for you, son. I promise. Serve His Grace well, don't cross him, be faithful and obedient and you will rise in his service. Maybe one day you too will be a great man. There will be opportunities for advancement. You'll know 'em when they present themselves. Seek them. Seize them. Use them to get ahead. Make me proud of you, son. Keep the faith, my boy, and we'll all come up smiling yet.'

Blood got up from his chair and walked round to Holcroft. He embraced the sitting boy clumsily but hard, his arm reaching over to squeeze Holcroft's shoulders. He kissed the boy roughly on the cheek, a rasp of bristles, a final blast of last night's brandy fumes. Then Blood slapped Holcroft's back, picked up his hat and walked out the door into the street.

That had been a week ago. And now here Holcroft was, waiting for admittance to the Palace of White Hall. The home of the King. The late-autumn sun beat down on his bare head. His empty stomach gurgled. His eye caught the movement of the sentries at the gate. After a quarter of an hour of statue-like immobility, they were stamping, saluting, presenting their muskets: an officer was approaching.

As a general rule, Holcroft did not look at people directly but he had hardly been able to stop himself from gazing in wonder at these two men standing guard on either side of the main arch of the gatehouse. They were the most beautiful things he had ever seen, resplendent in scarlet woollen coats with a multitude of silver buttons, big turned-back light-blue cuffs and wide skirts that hung almost to the knee. The blue of the cuffs was pleasingly echoed, to Holcroft's tidy mind, by their blue breeches and blue worsted stockings. Their shoes, however, were black and very, very shiny but they were tied with blue laces. And a broad blue sash was wrapped raffishly around their waists, nipping the big red coats in to make them look exaggeratedly slim. Their muskets were polished and oiled until they gleamed, their broad chests crossed by a bandolier from one side and a baldric on the other, from which hung a curved sword. They looked both ferocious and very fine. Holcroft was half-terrified of them, half-entranced.

The two sentries were not oblivious to the tall, hatless, raggedy young man gazing at them from a dozen yards away. The man on the left scowled. He seemed ready to say something to Holcroft, to tell him to be on his way, when someone said: 'Got a message. God's teeth! You're the new page?'

Holcroft turned quickly to find himself staring at a stranger of about the same age as himself but cast from an infinitely superior mould. He was dressed in a tightly fitted silk coat the blinding colour of pure gold with rich-scarlet breeches and waistcoat, white stockings and black shoes. Holcroft could scarcely imagine the King himself looking more splendid. The golden boy made even the soldiers guarding the gatehouse look a little drab.

'You are Mister Blood? Damn it, man, you might have made an effort in your dress. This is the King's residence, you know. You look like a street beggar. Most of the new chicks come in their very best clothes.'

'These are my best clothes,' said Holcroft in a small voice. He had spent most of the night before mending the tears in his shirt and sewing a patch on the elbow of his brown fustian coat where it had worn through. His breeches had been scrubbed until they were pale grey, indeed almost back to their original white. His brown woollen stockings had been lumpily darned by his mother and he had polished his shoes with goose fat until they shone.

'Best clothes ... Oh ha-ha-ha-ha-hah. Best clothes.' The golden boy was convulsed with mirth. Holcroft caught a glimpse of the nearest soldier's face. There were definitely signs of a smirk there.

Holcroft felt ashamed and a little angry, but mostly confused. 'Why does that make you laugh so much? My best clothes?'

'Oh stop it. Stop it! I will split my waistcoat, beggar-boy.'

Holcroft looked at the fellow, who was now laughing harder than ever. 'My mother told me I should try to conduct myself well . . .' he began.

'Oh, oh, oh . . . your beggarly mother told you to behave yourself, did she? Oh, you are going to be my death. Hahaha—'

Holcroft hit him. He bunched his right fist and, giving it his full shoulder, smashed it into the laughing boy's face, following through, and hurling the boy flat on to his back.

The boy in the golden coat looked up at him in shock. Blood began to well from his crushed nose. He scrambled to his feet and rushed at Holcroft, who sidestepped quickly and gave him a two-knuckle downward chop on the side of the jaw as he passed, knocking him to the dirt once more. The boy got to his feet and dived at Holcroft's legs – and received one hard, jarring knee to the cheekbone. *This boy doesn't know how to fight at all*, thought Holcroft. *Why has nobody ever taught him?* Yet the golden boy was game, if not gifted; he dived forward again with his arms wide, and Holcroft, trying to sidestep the lunge, found his legs tangled in the boy's flailing arms and the two of them tumbled into the dust together. The boy crawled forward over Holcroft's sprawled body, fingers clawing. He blocked one scrabbling hand, sweeping it aside with his left, and popped a short, hard right into the golden boy's already bloodied nose.

'Sergeant, would you mind awfully helping me put a stop to this unseemly scuffling.'

Holcroft was dimly aware of someone speaking above him, a refined, musical voice. He looked up. The golden boy crashed a painful fist into his shoulder. He felt strong hands seize his neck and arm and pull him away from his opponent. He was glad to see the golden coat was torn and daubed with blood. The other boy was held around the neck by one of the guards, glaring at Holcroft as he spat out a red thread of drool.

'If I release you, will you swear to desist from further warlike acts?' said the voice in his ear. Holcroft nodded and felt himself released. The boy had clearly made a similar undertaking and the sergeant released him.

'You are the Earl of Westbury's youngest boy, Robert, isn't it? You are senior page to His Grace the Duke of Buckingham, is that right?' The golden boy nodded but didn't cease from glaring murder at Holcroft.

'Ensign John Churchill of the First Regiment of the King's Foot Guards, at your service – and these are my men,' said the young man, who was dressed in a similar red coat and blue trimmings as the other soldiers but with a good deal of silver embroidery and a delicate lace cravat at his neck. He wore fine black leather boots that came up beyond his knees and had a pistol shoved casually into his sash and a slim sword hanging at his left side.

'Now, would you care to explain why you have been brawling at the gates of the King's palace like a pair of drunken costermongers?'

'He assaulted me, the little guttersnipe. Knocked me down with a sneak punch when I wasn't expecting it. If he were a gentleman, I would certainly challenge him and run him through.'

'Well, it is your good fortune that he is not, for the King has issued a proclamation against duelling, as I'm sure you know. You, sir, what's your business here and why did you assault this young gentleman?'

Holcroft said nothing. He stared at his now badly scuffed shoes.

'Speak up, lad.'

'I was sent here to be a page to the Duke of Buckingham, sir. I waited here while a message was sent to the duke and then this rude fellow came over and made mock of me, of my clothing and of my mother. So I hit him.'

'Well then, it seems that we have all the facts of the case. You, sir, what is your name by the way?'

Holcroft told him.

'Very good. You will apologise to the young gentleman here for bloodying his nose and soiling his pretty coat. And you, Robert Westbury, you will gracefully accept his apology. Come along, both of you.'

Holcroft fixed his eyes on a streak of blood on Westbury's chin. 'I offer you my apology, sir, for striking you without warning.'

Westbury grunted something foul under his breath.

'Excellent. All is forgiven then. Now you cut along, Mister Westbury, and get yourself cleaned up. I will escort Mister Blood to his new situation in due course. Off you go.'

Westbury gave Holcroft a final look of hatred, then turned and passed through the arch into the wide street beyond.

Jack Churchill turned to Holcroft. 'I'm sure he will be his sunny, happy-go-lucky self once more when he has had time to cool down. In the meantime, why don't you and I share a restorative glass of sack in the guardhouse, then I will take you along to see the Duke of Buckingham.'

'Do you serve him too, then, sir?' asked Holcroft.

'Not I. My patron is the King's brother, James, Duke of York. Not so very long ago I was a page in his service, just as you will be shortly for my Lord Buckingham. So I will offer you a few pointers, if you will listen to them, while we restore ourselves with a whet.'

The young officer led Holcroft across the road, through a narrow entrance guarded by another red-coated soldier, and into a broad cobbled courtyard. They turned right and walked a dozen yards to a little wooden building, not much more than a hut, in front of a wide palatial structure that spanned the whole width of the courtyard with a row of Grecian stone columns making a shady colonnade outside the stone front. Jack seated him at a rough wooden table outside the hut, went inside and came out with a green bottle and glasses on a tray. He poured a measure of the dry white wine, known as secco or sack, into a crystal glass.

Holcroft had never drunk from a glass before and he feared that he would crush its delicate beauty in his big hands. He remembered visiting his mother's parents' big house in Lancashire some years back, after the family had fled Dublin and his father had been obliged to take refuge in Holland, and he had seen his grandfather drinking from one. But Holcroft had always drunk from pewter, leather or earthenware in Shoreditch. He sipped carefully from the glass – it made the wine taste delicious, crisp and fresh. He held the glass up to the weak autumn sunlight steaming across the empty courtyard and admired the colours: the yellow wine, the sparkles of blue and orange as the sunshine struck the crystal.

'Do you like the wine, Mister Blood?'

He nodded, aware that his companion was observing him closely. He forced himself to look fully into the young officer's face. It was a beautiful face, almost girlish in its delicacy, very lean but strong-jawed and tanned by some harsh foreign sun.

'Do you think my clothes are risible, sir?' Holcroft asked.

Jack laughed. 'I would never dare to say so having witnessed how you served young Westbury with your fists.'

Holcroft stared at him. Jack smothered his smile. 'His Grace will clothe you well enough, my friend, in good time. But you *are* poorly dressed, it cannot be denied. There is no crime in beginning in poverty – why, my own family has little in the way of wealth – but a man should strive hard to escape it. Poverty should be the spur to rise in the world and, in your new position, well, if you play your cards right . . .'

'I do like to play cards, sir. I have a set, here in my fardel. They are all extremely beautiful. But the queen of diamonds is my favourite.'

Holcroft began to rummage in his belongings then; after a moment or two he triumphantly removed his treasured Parisian pack and flourished them before the other man's amused smile.

Jack looked fondly at him, the way one might at a clumsy kitten that had found its way into a riding boot.

'Take care, youngster, that you do not lose whatever wealth you may acquire in the duke's service. More than one promising young man has come to ruin by putting his trust in the turn of a card.'

Jack poured Holcroft some more of the wine.

'Oh, I would never lose money that way.' The sack and this fellow's kindness were making him feel unusually talkative. 'My father says that all our wealth was lost when His Majesty was restored to the throne. We had lands in Ireland, you know, but the Duke of Ormonde took them in the King's name, father says, and gave them to another family.'

'I would keep that under your hat here, if I were you.'

'I have no hat, sir . . .'

'It is only a figure of speech.'

'What is that?

'It is a saying, a light-hearted saying . . . like a joke. I meant only that I would not speak of that if I were you. Who is your father?'

'He is Colonel Thomas Blood, sir.'

Jack sat back in his chair. 'Indeed! I now see where you get your fire.'

Holcroft said nothing. *Fire?*

'Listen to me, my young friend, I have some advice for you. There will be opportunity for you here at the palace. Attend to the duke and serve him well but be bold, too. You might find yourself a generous patron, or even a patroness, eh? You are a handsome fellow, if a little unusual in your manner, and if you were to catch the eye of a fine lady, who knows what favours she might bestow on you.' The young soldier winked at Holcroft.

Holcroft frowned. He did not fully understand what this genial fellow was suggesting. Perhaps he was making another joke. Holcroft could not tell. However, he did seem friendly and Holcroft was in that moment feeling even more than usually friendless.

'Would you be my patron, sir?'

Jack laughed: the same happy note, quite without malice.

'I am not, alas, in that position, Mister Blood. You and I are almost in the same sad, impoverished state here. We are two young men trying to make our way in the world with nothing but our wits and charm to support us. But I wish you all the luck in the world. And I'll give you a final piece of advice before we go. The ladies love a soldier and, having seen you fight, I think you might have the makings of one. You are quick and strong and evidently do not lack for courage. Keep it in mind. It is a fine life and can be most rewarding. Assuming that you live long enough to enjoy it. Now we must away – it would not do to keep your new master waiting too long on your first day. I shall conduct you to the Cockpit and we'll part there as friends.'

Holcroft had never been inside a room that was quite this sumptuous. It was enormous, three times the height of a man, the walls papered from floor to ceiling in striped blue and gold. Three vast windows were flanked by tied-back curtains of watered blue silk and the thick blue carpet, wondrously spongy beneath his shoes, depicted fantastical beasts of the Orient – tigers and elephants and dragons on a background of intricate geometrical design. Through the windows Holcroft could see St James's Park and a fine tall gentleman in a deep-purple robe with a towering pyramid of a black wig was promenading with a grand lady in a vast pink dress across the immaculate grass. *Could that be the King himself?* Holcroft almost did not dare to look. He stood stiff and still, as he had been instructed to do, and waited until His Grace the Duke of Buckingham, his new master, deigned to notice him.

The duke was seated behind a huge wooden desk covered in thick piles of papers, conferring with two men – one thin and dark with a fine moustache, the other younger, plump and fussy – in low, urgent tones. In the vast room, Holcroft could not quite make out what they were saying. His new master spoke more loudly than the other two, and the boy heard the King mentioned more than once and he thought he heard the dark man say something about France being their only hope. His mind wandered a little. He thought about the mocking golden boy who didn't know how to fight and wondered whether he would make trouble.

His stomach rumbled. The wine was strong in his blood but the glow he had enjoyed with the soldier Jack Churchill – his new friend – was fading. Perhaps he would be punished for brawling with Robert Westbury. He did not know the rules here. A scuffle in the street was nothing in Shoreditch, almost a daily occurrence, but everything here seemed to be different. He must try to please these great men. If he lost his position because of a brawl he would disappoint his father. And he would be sent back to Shoreditch.

The short plump man twisted in his seat, his elbow gently knocking a pile of the papers and sending the top sheet wafting down and along, caught by a stray gust, to the carpet a yard from Holcroft's shoes. He bent quickly to pick it up, glanced briefly at it and stopped.

It was a square of yellow paper and he had expected to see lines of words on it, a letter, perhaps, or a receipt from some tradesman. A friend of his father's had taken particular care to teach him his ABCs in Dublin, and he had enjoyed reading anything from pamphlets to passages from the Holy Bible from the minute he had mastered the art. But on the piece of paper in his hand, instead of familiar Roman letters, he saw a block of figures, in no particular order, the numbers one to nine written out and repeating themselves in seemingly random order, sometimes with little marks, asterisks and quotations beside particular numbers and dashes between little clumps of them. Holcroft was fascinated. He glanced up from the piece of paper. The three men were still very deep in their talk, oblivious to him. He looked back down and read:

1* 6' – 3 2' 1' 5* – 9 3' 7* 7* 9 2' 7* 4' 2* – 3' – 6 1' 5' 2' – 1 2'
2' 2* – 6* 7* 5* 3' 5' 3' 2* 5 . . .

It was clearly a code of some sort, probably with the numbers and symbols indicating letters of the alphabet. But only the numbers one to nine were used, in which case the marks must indicate a secondary use of them . . .

'Give me that!' The tall dark man was coming round the table towards Holcroft, his face pale with rage. He tore the letter from the boy's hand and gave him a resounding slap on the side of the face.

Holcroft stepped back and raised his fists.

'You would strike me!' The man's face was now only inches from Holcroft's; he could smell coffee on his breath overlaying the rot of teeth. 'Touch me and I'll have you whipped bloody, by God.'

'Steady, Osborne,' said the plump one. 'Sure he meant you no harm.'

Buckingham looked on with amusement from his chair behind the desk. He steepled his fingers, cocked his head and seemed to be examining the boy for the first time.

'Littleton, you fool, it's an old letter from our . . .' Osborne stopped suddenly. Then he finished lamely, '. . . from Versailles.'

'Then the boy would scarcely be able to read it,' Littleton told him.

Osborne glared at Holcroft, who had the sense to lower his hands.

'But I can read it, sir,' Holcroft blurted out, 'at least I think I can. Although I meant no harm by looking at it, I merely meant to return it to your table, quiet like, but it was so interesting. Beg pardon, sirs.'

'Hold hard, boy,' said the duke, standing up from his seat behind the desk. 'You say you can read it – from only one swift glance.'

'Nonsense – the boy's little better than a half-wit, an imbecile,' said Osborne. 'Blood admitted it himself. He spends most of the time cleaning and sweeping and straightening things up at home. Making things neat. Doesn't speak much but might be useful around the place to keep it in order, that's what Blood said. He doesn't understand half of what is said to him.'

The duke gave Holcroft a long, slow look. He came out from behind the desk and took three steps towards him. 'You are Colonel Blood's son, yes? The new page that has been foisted on me?'

Holcroft nodded. He examined his new master with lowered eyes: a long pearl-grey silk coat with emerald collar and cuffs, a matching waistcoat with a gold chain elegantly draped over the gold buttons at the front.

'You say you can read the message on this paper, yes?'

Holcroft nodded.

The duke said: 'Give him the paper, Osborne, let us see if the boy has inherited a drop of Blood's cunning.'

'Your Grace, I don't think . . .'

'Just give him the damned paper, man.'

Holcroft took the paper, and quickly scanned the figures and symbols.

'Read it then, boy, if you can,' growled Osborne.

'I would guess that the Us and Vs are the same number, and I suppose the double Us are just two Us but the rest is perfectly straightforward . . .'

'Read it,' said the duke.

Holcroft began: 'My dear Littleton . . .'

'He could easily have guessed that part,' said the fat man behind the desk. 'My name is hardly unknown about the palace – or even in the gutters of St Giles. Or whatever foul slum he hails from.'

'Be silent, sir. Now read on, boy,' commanded the duke.

Holcroft cleared his throat: 'My dear Littleton, I have been striving hard in the service of our cause here at court but a shortage of funds is preventing me from fulfilling my duties. As you well know, I encountered this same problem in Antwerp with disastrous results and I cannot stress enough the importance of ample amounts of ready money in this sort of undertaking. There are certain inducements I must make in order to open the right doors if you wish me to continue my investigation of Madame's—'

'Stop! Stop! That is enough, I believe you,' said Osborne, snatching the paper once again from Holcroft's hands.

Holcroft was aware that all three men were staring at him with their mouths open. He looked down at the geometrical designs of the carpet, trying to find comfort in the regular shapes.

'It's like witchcraft,' Littleton finally said. 'It takes one of our trained clerks half a morning to encrypt one of these letters and yet the boy reads it as easily as if it were *The London Gazette*.'

'How does he do it?' asked Osborne. 'How do you do it, Mister Blood, tell me?'

'I do not know, sir, I see it and the pattern becomes clear.'

'Well, well,' said the duke. 'He might look like a raggedy-arsed link-boy but he clearly has a brain like a counting-house comptroller. At last I have had something of value from that rascal Blood.'

Holcroft continued to stare at the carpet.

'You've done well, boy! You will render me good service, of that I have no doubt.' The duke reached into his waistcoat pocket and flicked something towards Holcroft. It glittered as it arced through the air and, as Holcroft caught it, he saw it was a silver half-crown. It felt warm, heavy and slightly greasy in his hand.

'Now leave us to our labours, Mister Blood. The page will show you your quarters and instruct you in your duties though I believe we can make better use of you than tidying up my chambers and sweeping the floors.'

'I never want to go back to that terrible place, Father, never. I would rather die,' said Tom.

Blood sat back and took a long pull at his pint of white wine. 'And you never shall go back, son, not while my old limbs still have a little strength.'

The four men – Blood, Tom, Joshua Parrot and William Hunt – were seated in a small room off the main tap of the Bull's Head in Charing Cross. Tom was still in his prison rags and, after a week in the Marshalsea, the most notorious gaol in England, he had lost more than a stone in weight and taken on a pallor that was almost ethereal.

The boy is weak, Blood thought, *and stupid. Just like the other one. What possessed Tom to think that he could become a gentleman of the road? What a childish notion. He had neither the wit nor the dash to carry it off – and nor was it a task for one man to attempt alone. Madness!*

It was no wonder that the militia had picked him up on the Portsmouth road after his ham-fisted attempt to stop a carriage and six at the point of a horse pistol. The grizzled carriage-driver had simply refused to stop, swept past at the gallop and had immediately alerted a passing militia troop to Tom's presence on the road. The soldiers caught up with him an hour later, and by dawn they had him chained and bloody in the notorious Southwark gaol. Why, Blood wondered, was he cursed with such useless sons?

'I am serious, Father. I don't want to do this thing – tonight or any other night. I can't go back into the pit. And they will put me back in there – put all of us in there if we are caught. You have no idea how terrible it was. They chained a man to a rotting corpse all night because he would not pay his gaolers a small bribe. There were thirty prisoners in a cell no bigger than this snug, no room to lie down, barely room to breathe. The rats there gnaw on men's feet at night and some of them are bigger than—'

'Oh, I do know all about it, son, believe me I do. But we are bound to do this dark deed – I have given my sacred word of honour.'

William Hunt stifled a snigger. But Blood fixed him with a hard blue eye and the small man looked away. If his grown sons were weak and stupid, thought Blood, his men were little better: Parrot could obey orders but only if they were spelled out to him in the simplest terms; his chief assets were his strength and ferocity. Hunt was sly and reasonably smart – but since the war he had lost his nerve and developed a wide yellow streak down the centre of his backbone that meant he could no longer be trusted to stand his ground if things went awry. But Blood was stuck with them, these old comrades, the last of his irregular cavalry troop to survive the bloodshed of the brutal civil wars and stay with him in the intervening years.

They had had some high old times together back in the day. They had raided homes of known and suspected Cavaliers, hanged all the men of fighting age, made free with the women, pocketed the valuables, dug up the buried coin and driven off the livestock to feed the army. It had been a time of war and, as always, much was forgiven fighting men in the heat of battle, and after it. But even the iron-hard troopers of Parliament's New Model Army considered the company commanded by Captain Blood – he had awarded himself the promotion to colonel long after the end of hostilities – to be a little hard to stomach. Many swore that they were not much better than bandits. Some said they were a lot worse. Nevertheless, powerful bonds between the men of Blood's troop had been formed in that time of death and chaos. And these two had stuck with him, when the others had faded away, died or grown fat and peaceable. He needed them. He needed his eldest son too, for the difficult task at hand, weak and stupid though he might be.

'The only reason you are out of the Marshalsea – free and clear of that hell on Earth – is because of the man to whom I gave my sacred word,' said Blood. 'And because of a stack of *his* bright gold that I paid over to the warden. You were the one who wanted to play at being Claude Du Vall, the dashing rank-rider, and look how it served you. Arrested by the troopers, and slung in the pit to await trial. You'd still be there were it not for me – and no doubt hanging by the neck at Tyburn in a week or two. So you will cease your whining, son, and listen to what I have to say. We will take Ormonde tonight and send him to Hell where he belongs. It will go smooth as silk, no one is going to be caught – I guarantee it – and no one is going to be gaoled. Our vengeance will be served and a great power in the land, a duke no less with the ear of the King, will be in our debt.'

'I don't want to do it, Father, please. I don't want to kill anyone.'

'Hush your mewling mouth now, youngling,' said Parrot, a looming shape seated on the bench beside Tom. 'We need four men for the job – at least – why else did we hand over the colonel's good money to free you from the pit? Earn your freedom, boy. And show a little gratitude.'

Blood looked intently at his eldest son. He doubted that he would feel much gratitude to his father for extricating him from the Marshalsea. It was a quality much harped upon by the old but seldom practised by the young. And yet true gratitude did exist in the world and could create an iron fetter between men. Blood owed a debt of gratitude to Hunt – who had taken a sword cut meant for him in a melee outside Kingston upon Thames, when his captain had been helpless. The little man, brave as a rooster in those days, had deliberately ridden his horse between Blood – who had been dismounted – and a huge, roaring Cavalier who seemed determined to cut him into pieces. Hunt had taken the blow meant for Blood and then Parrot, riding up belatedly, had split the enemy's skull with his sabre. Blood remembered Hunt's actions and honoured him for them. And Parrot's too. And he remembered their conduct in a dozen similar escapades besides. Gratitude. It meant that, despite their obvious shortcomings, he could never disown either Hunt or Parrot as long as they lived.

It was gratitude, too, that bound Blood and Buckingham together. Not long after the melee in which Hunt had taken his wound, Blood and five of his men had cornered a richly dressed

Royalist stripling against an oak tree in a meadow by the Thames. The boy had defied them with a drawn sword, and had told the six enemies he faced that he meant to sell his life dearly and take at least one of them with him. Blood had teasingly asked the handsome young Cavalier if he had any money on him with which to buy his life. The boy had said no but had added that, if Blood would give his word to let him go unharmed, he would write out a note of hand for five hundred pounds, to be redeemed in person after the war. In an uncharacteristic fit of mercy, or possibly just good old-fashioned greed, Blood had agreed, accepted the note, and let the boy go. He was startled to find, when he looked at it later, that the note was signed George Villiers, Second Duke of Buckingham.

It was not until the Restoration of King Charles – when Blood's fortunes were in a sad state of disarray – that he was able to redeem the note from the now-prominent duke. As well as the five hundred pounds – paid immediately and without the slightest quibble – Buckingham had asked Blood to undertake a delicate task on his behalf. A former servant was attempting to blackmail the duke, falsely accusing him of the vile crime of buggery. Blood and his men had paid the servant a visit in the dead of night and, after administering a savage beating, and threats of a more permanent punishment, had persuaded the man to desist. Buckingham was grateful. More commissions had followed. And Blood, now landless, soon penniless again and on the run from the law, was grateful for the paid employment.

Tom took a deep draft of his wine, finishing the pot. 'Gratitude, you say. All right. You got me out of that stew and I'm grateful. But I'll put a pistol ball in my own head if things go wrong. Better death than gaol again. Far better. I'll help you kill Ormonde. But at least give me a decent drink to fire my belly. A pint of hot spiced Barbados, or good French bingo, if they have it. If I must do this foul deed, I need a proper drink inside me.'

'You take after your mother, boy. No – no hard stuff till it's done. You can have one more pot of wine and that is it. We do it tonight, we do it sober, and when it's over you can drink your fill for a week at my expense.'

Holcroft was led away from his first encounter with his master by the duty page, a fellow named Albert St John. The page was a year or two younger than him but wore a similarly blinding coat to Holcroft's adversary of that morning. He was, however, a good deal more cordial and while he showed Holcroft around the duke's sprawling apartments he kept up a stream of cheerful but inconsequential chatter.

The duke's rooms were at the very western edge of the Palace of White Hall, on the far side of the huge, square Privy Garden, and even beyond The Street, the wide thoroughfare that led due south from the castle-like gatehouse. Buckingham's establishment might have been a little removed from the centre of power – it was, for example, a good three hundred yards west of the King's bedchamber, Albert informed him – but it happily allowed His Grace to avoid any tedious nocturnal encounters with the King's several mistresses. It was more than comfortable, indeed quite lavish, and looked out over the soothing greenery of St James's Park. There were a dozen large staterooms for the duke's use clustered around a small courtyard with a rectangular patch of neatly trimmed lawn and a joyously crowded tulip bed at its southern end. A warren of passages, galleries and cubbyholes that linked the staterooms were for the use of the servants and the ducal staff, including the four or five pages who permanently resided with the duke. The Cockpit-in-the-Court, an old-fashioned octagonal wooden theatre, now used only rarely for masques and other entertainments, formed the northernmost limit of the duke's domain and gave it its name.

Beyond the Cockpit, and slightly to the east, was the realm of James Butler, Duke of Ormonde in the Irish peerage, and Buckingham's bitterest foe.

The Irish duke's apartments, much to Buckingham's pleasure, were less extensive than his own and considerably less well appointed. They were also cheek by jowl with the Tilt Yard, the barracks of the First Regiment of the King's Foot Guards and the quarters of that bold company's officers beyond, which were on the other side of the gatehouse that marked the entrance to the palace. It was noisy late at night when the soldiers caroused and, during the day, there was a constant stream of traffic in and out of the gate.

Last year Ormonde had protested to the King that, in view of his long and loyal service to the Crown, it befitted him to have a larger, more opulent set of lodgings, perhaps in the eastern part of the palace nearer the King on the banks of the Thames, but Buckingham had blocked him by claiming that the renovation of a set of new apartments beside the King's, to a standard that befitted the dignity of a nobleman of Ormonde's standing, would be prohibitively expensive. He also whispered to the King that Ormonde disapproved of his constant philandering and sought to restrict access to his mistresses by setting his servants to stand guard at night in the corridors. It was an outright lie, of course, but the King had been moved by this second argument far more than the first; indeed, he was incensed. Buckingham had triumphed. Ormonde was forced to rent a more suitable and spacious palace, at considerable expense, from the exiled Lord Clarendon in Piccadilly.

'You should have heard our dear old duke laugh,' said Albert, as the two of them walked up a narrow set of stairs. 'He called it the merriest jest.'

'He lied to the King and considered that a joke?' said Holcroft.

Albert looked at him. 'Yes, it was very funny.'

Nevertheless, Ormonde remained a close confidant and trusted advisor of the King, Albert continued, despite being housed so far away. He was still Lord Steward of the Household and his word on affairs of state was heeded more than any other man's, save perhaps Sir John Grenville's.

All this Holcroft learned as he was conducted through the long corridors that snaked between the great rooms of state in the Cock-pit. Albert chattered away as he trotted along and Holcroft's head swam as he tried to take in all the new information: 'There are two pages attending the duke at all times during the day, to run messages or errands, and one page on duty at night. That's the worst! You have to try to stay awake when the whole world is asleep, and if the duke rings the bedroom bell you have to be at his side, alert and awake, in an instant if he wants to send someone a message or whatever. The senior page Robert Westbury does the rota. He does it most efficiently, I must say, as he shares out the night duties fairly, so we only have to do it once a week at most – unless he's punishing us for some terrible sin. He's always happy to accommodate you if you need time away to see your family or if you're feeling unwell or something.'

Holcroft's heart sank at the mention of his enemy's name. Clearly there could be no escaping the fellow in the Cockpit and he wondered if he had made the biggest blunder of his life when he had started the fight with him.

'The one you have to watch is the steward – Matlock. He has overall charge of the whole household, including the pages. He doesn't like us much and he has the authority to beat you, if he sees fit. But we don't see all that much of him as Westbury does all the day-to-day organization. If you have any problems, you can always go to him and he'll surely find a solution.'

Holcroft did not think that very likely. But he said nothing.

'This is where we all roost.' Albert opened a door and showed Holcroft into a long, narrow room, painted white with a sloping wall on one side to match the pitch of the roof. It was almost trian-gular in section and divided roughly in two, with a wooden table and four chairs by a small window cut into the sloping wall near the door, and half a dozen narrow beds in a line down the vertical wall. One of the chairs had fallen onto its back and, without thinking, Holcroft stepped forward and picked it up, setting it with its three mates straight at the table, the seats tucked neatly under the wooden surface. A small boy was sound asleep in the nearest bed, wrapped up tight in his blankets with only his sharp pink nose and a few wisps of red hair poking out from the bedclothes.

'That's Fox Cub,' said Albert. 'His real name is Henri, Comte d'Erloncourt, and he's French and a Papist.' Holcroft stared at the sleeping boy with horror. A Papist! He had heard his father and his Presbyterian cronies talk about these foul creatures who bowed down before the Whore of Rome, and he was slightly disappointed to discover that the boy did not possess a pair of horns and a tail, at least none that Holcroft could see. But Albert was still chattering away: ' . . . we call him Foxy or Fox Cub because he looks like one. He's been on night duty, which is why he's asleep in the daytime – Westbury gave him three nights in a row because he dozed in his chair outside the duke's chamber on the first night and had to be shaken awake by His Grace himself when he wanted a bite from the kitchens. He was lucky not to be sent to Matlock for a whipping.'

Albert led Holcroft down the row of narrow cots until he came to the end one. A pair of linen sheets and two thick woollen blankets were folded and piled on top of the bare mattress, with a plump goose-feather-stuffed pillow beside it. As the boy helped Holcroft to make up the bed, he marvelled at the luxury of having a bed all to himself and clean linen sheets, to boot. Holcroft had just smoothed the top blanket to his satisfaction, when the door of the pages' dormitory opened and a tall figure in a gold coat stepped into the room. The boy sleeping in the bed nearest the door jerked awake, sat up in bed and immediately began babbling manically, 'I wasn't asleep, Robert, I wasn't, honestly. I was just resting my eyes for a moment.'

Robert Westbury's nose was dark red and conspicuously swollen, he had a cut on his cheek and two black lines under his eyes. He had a big sheet of paper in his hand. He stared at Holcroft who was frozen in place, bent over by the bed with his hands flat on the blanket.

Westbury kept his eyes locked on Holcroft but he addressed the redhead. 'It's all right, Fox Cub. Go back to sleep.'

Holcroft said nothing; he kept his eyes fixed on the golden buttons of Westbury's coat. It occurred to him that the boy had changed his coat for another exactly the same, for it was no longer torn or stained with blood and dirt. That the boy owned two such items quite stole his breath away.

'Good day to you, Bertie, I see you've met the new chick.'

'What on earth has happened to your face, Robert?' said Albert, clearly appalled by the obvious marks of the fight.

'I fell down some stairs. Clumsy of me. Won't happen again. I'm appointing you the chick's daddy until he finds his feet in the Cockpit. Make sure he knows everything he needs to by nightfall.'

Westbury turned away and Holcroft watched him pin the big sheet of paper to a board on the wall at the far end of the room.

Without turning his head, Westbury said: 'You can start by telling him that he's on night duty for the rest of the week. You're off the hook, Foxy.'

With that, the golden boy walked over to the door, yanked it open and left the room.

'Thank you, Robert, thank you so much. I won't forget this!' burbled the red-headed boy happily to the swiftly closing door.

'Well, I don't know what you've done to deserve it,' said Albert, 'but you must have done something. I have never heard of Westbury giving someone night duty on their first day, and for the rest of the week, too. He seems to have taken against you. Have you done something to upset him?'

Holcroft shrugged but held his tongue. *So he had to stay up all night, so what? He done that many times before. How bad could night duty be?*

With a little grunt of effort James Butler, Duke of Ormonde, swung his right leg up and dumped it into the silk-covered lap of the young lady who sat opposite him in the carriage. Miss Jenny Blaine, a bracken-haired beauty who had yet to see her twenty-fifth birthday, slipped off the tight silver-buckled shoe and began to gently massage the swollen foot of her elderly protector as the carriage rattled along the Strand, heading west to the duke's rented home at Clarendon House on Piccadilly.

She might be more than half his age and about a third of his weight, but to the duke's expert eye she showed no signs of revulsion as she gently worked the knotted flesh through the sheer white silk stocking. Over the drumming of the rain on the roof of the carriage, he could hear the footsteps of his six footmen, running alongside the slow-moving vehicle and crying out for all to make way for its passage. Ormonde gave a tiny grunt of pleasure and closed his eyes as the pain from his aching feet gradually began to recede. He put his right hand on the loaded pistol on the padded seat beside him, the cold metal of the barrel and the warm walnut wood of the grip comforting him. He let out a lungful of air, lowered his shoulders and let the girl's ministrations soothe away his discomfort.

It was no surprise that his feet were playing up now; it had been a hellish month all told. A state visit from William, Prince of Orange, the King's nephew and youthful head of the first family of the United Provinces of the Netherlands, had occupied all of his time and kept him busy day and night, and the lavish banquet he had just attended in the young prince's honour at Guildhall had been the high point in a long and tedious diplomatic process. But it had been a success, the duke considered, a great success. The visit had passed so far without any major embarrassments, which was surprising considering the Dutch had been at war with England until three years ago. The war had ended when the bold Dutch admiral Michiel de Ruyter had sailed up the Medway and burned much of the English fleet at its moorings at Chatham. He towed away the flagship HMS *Royal Charles* along with a very large slice of English national pride. After that humiliating catastrophe, a peace treaty had been cobbled together by the Earl of Clarendon's disaster-prone ministry and hastily signed by King Charles, while the rest of Europe looked on with amused contempt.

And if being trounced in a naval war were not embarrassing enough, the prince's mission to England was guaranteed to gall: he came to collect on a debt of two hundred and eighty thousand pounds that his royal uncle had incurred with the House of Orange over a number of years. Charles couldn't pay it, of course, he could barely afford to keep his own household in bread and beer, and it had been Ormonde's task to try to soothe the Prince of Orange's ire at this uncomfortable truth. He had spent many long hours in the prince's company – a rather delicate and solemn young man, but also endowed with considerable strength of character and a keen intelligence. Ormonde had finally persuaded him to accept that the repayment must be postponed – and, in a moment of quiet triumph, he had cajoled the young prince into agreeing to write off more than one-third of the debt, a hundred thousand pounds, for the sake of future amity between England and the United Provinces. Charles was at a crossroads, Ormonde had told the prince in confidence. The King had scant financial means of support within England and he must have money from somewhere: he could either look to Catholic France for funds, something that many of his most senior advisors were urging, not least that viper Buckingham, or he could look to the Protestant

Dutch Republic. If Buckingham's faction won the day, and Charles sided with France, it meant war once more with the Dutch – and, with the combined might of France and England against them, the small republic must fall. On the other hand, if Ormonde could sway Charles towards an agreement with the United Provinces, both of these proud Protestant nations could better withstand the ever-growing ambitions of mighty France and the unquenchable thirst for *la gloire* of its absolute ruler Louis XIV.

The prince had grasped the reasoning instantly and, in truth, it had not been too difficult a task to persuade him to grant a remission of a large portion of the royal debt. The young man must have suspected that Charles could not pay before he set sail for England, and it was obvious that it pleased the young prince to appear magnanimous in the eyes of the world. But Ormonde was still well satisfied with the outcome of the visit and his role in it. Valuable bonds of friendship had been strengthened, and perhaps in time there might be the prospect of a royal marriage – Charles's niece Lady Mary Stuart, perhaps, to this eligible young Dutchman, to draw the wealthy Protestant republic closer into the English orbit. The duke devoutly hoped that the King would understand just how well he had been served by his Lord Steward in this affair, yet, in his heart of hearts, Ormonde knew that Old Rowley would merely look bored when the new deal was explained to him, play with his damned dogs and ask plaintively whether the Prince of Orange could possibly be induced to advance yet another massive loan.

The duke let out a long, frustrated sigh.

'Too hard?' said the girl, looking up from her manipulation of his huge misshapen foot.

'No, my sweet, that's perfect. But perhaps the other one now.'

As the duke rearranged his limbs, he contemplated the girl on the seat opposite him. She was breath-taking – there was no denying it; pale skin, soft brown eyes that were almost amber in hue, and that glorious mane of bright hair. He would have her tonight, a little present to himself for the triumph of the House of Orange's state visit. After a light supper and a bath, he would sample her young body at his leisure. He had been harsh with her; he had beaten her with a dog whip after that humiliating incident with that Blood fellow, a roughneck who had seduced her and led her into his dirty world of Presbyterian rebels, French spies and Fifth Monarchists, all of them scum who sought the fall of the King and his loyal ministers. But it was time to show her his forgiveness. She was a good girl at heart, just easily led astray, and as she had been so pleasingly repentant after her fall, perhaps she ought to be rewarded with a full return to his favour.

Jenny sneaked a glance at the duke from under her eyelashes as her fingers worked on the huge foot. He was still, she conceded, a handsome man despite his advancing age and bulk. She particularly liked his commanding beak of a nose; a big, fearless, manly feature that dominated his square ruddy face under the long grey periwig. She could not deny that she felt some measure of tenderness for him. She liked being around him, the way he demanded respect from everyone from the King down; the way he expressed his desires and they were instantly fulfilled. He was wealthy and in another existence she might quite have enjoyed the silk-and-roses life as the *maîtresse-en-titre* to a great man of affairs. She would certainly regret his death – in his off-hand way he had been kind to her – and she hoped that it would be quick. And she would miss the luxury of life at Clarendon House. But she had never been able to refuse Thomas Blood. She had never once said no to him from the day they had first met.

He had accosted her six months ago when she had been out walking with her maid in St James's Park. Blood had been funny and charming and courteous – and when her wide straw hat had blown off her head in a sudden gust of wind, he had dived, fully dressed, into the canal to retrieve it for her. She knew that he wanted her for her young body and she strongly suspected that part of her allure was Blood's desire to cuckold the Duke of Ormonde – for whom he blithely confessed a life-long hatred – but she liked him, he made her laugh, he seemed interested in her likes and dislikes, the minutiae of her daily life. In contrast, Ormonde summoned her with a bell when he felt the urge, rutted like a bull, an angry bull when he could not maintain his manhood, and fell asleep immediately after the act. Sometimes he ignored her for days, leaving her to wander around Clarendon House, bored and alone except for the servants, while he went about his business in White Hall and the City for the King. So when Blood asked her to meet him for a private supper in the upper room of the Bull's Head the next evening, she found herself saying yes. And after supper, when he took her into his arms and kissed her, well, she had not said no to him then either.

Being with Blood made her breathless, his touch still made her shiver, even after half a year of knowing him. Their love-making was as profound and shattering as it had been that first night. When she was away from him he dominated her thoughts. What was he doing? Who was he with? Was he thinking of her? She knew full well that he was using her – that he was married to that drab bitch Mary, who had squeezed out half a dozen brats for him, that he would never divorce that drunken hag and belong wholly to her. But he'd promised that once this dark deed was done they would be together, living together, travelling together, loving together. Just the two of them. And for the promise of that joy she'd do anything. Anything.

She wondered if Blood had got her message. When Ormonde had called for his carriage at Guildhall, she had extricated herself from the glittering melee of Dutch courtiers and wealthy English merchants and stepped outside into the rain to whisper a few words to a waiting street urchin. With a shiny penny, she had dispatched him to the Bull's Head to let Blood know that the carriage was on the way to Clarendon House, and that it would follow its usual route along the Strand, down Pall Mall and then up St James's Street to the palace at the top of the hill on Piccadilly.

She only hoped that she had given them enough warning. Blood had told her that they would be ready and waiting for her signal at the Bull's Head. And she trusted him. Yet now the carriage was already at the end of Pall Mall and shortly it would take the sharp right turn up St James's. There was not a lot of time left. Had Blood changed his mind? By God, he was cutting it fine. They would be at the house in a few minutes, safe behind its gates and walls and surrounded by a host of servants. Then Ormonde would surely want to have her and, given the amount of wine he had taken at the banquet, she would certainly face a long, dreary night using every trick she knew to keep his wilting prick hard enough to achieve his satisfaction.

Jenny peered out of the window into the blackness of the stormy winter evening and she caught a glimpse of a pale, rain-wet face of a running footman and her own reflection superimposed on to his. She looked tired, she thought, and old. The dewy freshness was passing from her face. Ormonde would not want her for much longer – whatever happened tonight. If Blood failed to fulfil his promise, then the slack-bellied old goat would soon throw her into the street anyway. That was the lot of all whores – to be used and then discarded. But Blood was different. Blood said he loved her. He said he would always love her, no matter what. And she believed him. Blood would still love her even when she was a worn-out baggage of thirty.

She felt the carriage turn sharply and begin the short journey up St James's Street towards Piccadilly. She felt the horses slow as they struggled up the hill. She heard vague shouts outside the carriage, something about a dead man lying in the street. The coachman slammed the hand-levered brake on and the carriage crashed to a halt. The duke's bulk was thrown forward directly on to her body, crushing her with his weight. Both the oil lamps that lit the interior went out at the same time, plunging the carriage interior into darkness. She started screaming – for no reason that she could ever explain afterwards. The duke was cursing foully and shoving at her with his strong arms in an attempt to lever himself upright. Outside the carriage she heard the clatter of many hooves, the clash of steel on steel, shouts of rage and the cry of a wounded man. Ormonde snarled, 'Where's my fucking pistol!' and 'Shut your fucking noise, you stupid cunt!' And she heard him scrabbling blindly about on the floor of the carriage. She felt the awkward shape of the flintlock beneath her silk slipper on the carriage's floor, and pressed her foot down hard to hold it in position.

The carriage door opened from the outside and a head, the black hat bedecked with an ostrich feather and jewelled with raindrops and the face masked with a dark kerchief, was thrust inside. The man held a flaming resin torch in one hand and a levelled pistol in the other. Over the top of the kerchief, Jenny looked into a pair of bright dancing eyes, blue as innocence.

'Get out of the carriage, Your Grace, or you die right now,' said the masked man. 'Get out, if you value your life. You too, my lady.'

Holcroft sat on the hard high-backed chair beside the door to the Duke of Buckingham's bed chamber. He was most uncomfortable, his buttocks nearly numb, and the golden coat that he had been issued was scratching his neck. Close up, he had seen the so-called golden cloth was in fact mostly coarse yellow silk with only a few threads of gold woven into the material to give it a metallic sheen. The golden buttons were just well-polished brass. His scarlet woollen waistcoat and breeches were uncomfortably tight and his loose white stockings kept sliding down his shins to puddle at his ankles. But despite his discomfort, he was painfully tired. It had been a long, eventful day and the shock of each discovery about his new life had taken its toll. He could not prevent his eyelids drooping and constantly found himself teetering on the edge of sleep's abyss.

He had heard the tall clock in the hall below strike one some time ago and yet the candles still burned in the duke's chamber behind his back, and the light leaked out under the door to provide some illumination of the dark landing. He dared not sleep. The duke was reading his correspondence and might at any moment call upon him to fetch wine or a slice of bread and cheese. Albert had warned him that Westbury could send him to Matlock for a beating if he were found to be asleep and he did not want to be punished on his very first day. He stared into the darkness, using an effort of will to keep his eyes wide open, and inside his head he imagined he was dealing out his treasured pack of Parisian playing cards. This was a trick he had used before, when the noise and fuss of too many people in the Cock Lane house made him feel bad. He conjured up images of a hand of Slamm being played and watched with his mind's eye as the cards were dealt out, twelve to each of the four players, and the four remaining cards forming the Stock in the middle of the table, with the top card turned over to determine which suit should be trumps. It was the queen of diamonds – his friend. She seemed to understand his predicament exactly. 'You can do it, Holcroft,' she seemed to be saying. 'You can last the night. I'll be with you.' He was just picking up his imaginary hand to examine the cards he'd been dealt, when he heard a voice as if from a vast distance away.

'Boy, hey boy – are you sleeping, you lazy dog?'

Holcroft whipped his head round and looked up briefly at the looming form of the Duke of Buckingham in his nightgown, peering down at him and holding a stub of candle in his right hand.

'Not . . . not asleep, sir,' Holcroft stammered. Then he recovered himself, leaped to his feet, bowed and said, 'How may I serve you, Your Grace? Would you like some food or drink? Shall I fetch you some warm milk from the kitchen? Some wine?'

'I have wine enough for my needs,' the duke said, handing him the candle stub, 'but my eyes ache from reading. Come inside and read to me from my correspondence while I take my ease.'

Holcroft followed the duke into his chamber. And while his master settled himself into the huge curtained bed, Holcroft recharged a three-pronged candlestick with fresh candles from the box and lit them from the burning stub. He set the candlestick on the table by the bed, sat down on a stool and, at a gesture from the duke, he picked up a piece of heavy paper from a pile of documents. Checking with a flick of his eyes to the duke's face that he should begin, looked down at the paper in his hands.

28th November 1670

From Charles Sackville, Palace of Versailles, France

To His Grace the Duke of Buckingham, at the Palace of White Hall, London

Greetings, old friend, it is with a growing delight that I can inform you that matters have been advancing at a swift pace here. To my astonishment and joy, I have encountered little or no opposition from the French court to the basis of the arrangement, nor even its finer details, and I hear nothing but words of encouragement for my endeavours from all sides. The agreement is to be called the Treaty of Dover, as we suggested, and I believe, God willing, that it can be signed and sealed by both sides at that good English port within a few short weeks, even perhaps before Christmas. The original sums we spoke of to the French Treasury, amounts which I personally felt were optimistic, perhaps even preposterous, have been approved with scarcely a quibble. The figures we have now agreed upon are, given in English terms, £200,000 on signing of the treaty and £300,000 a year thereafter during the duration of the prosecution of the war against the United Provinces. I confess I find myself gratified by the ease by which so much has been achieved and —

'Boy, Holcroft is your name, is it not?'

'Yes, Your Grace.'

'You read well, Holcroft, very well. But as a kindness please read a little more slowly. I wish to ponder the exact choice of words that the writer has made and thereby judge his mood at the time of writing. The content of the letter is already familiar to me but I am listening for – uh – any notes that ring discordantly.'

'Yes, sir,' Holcroft began to read from the letter again, this time at a funereal pace.

'Much better, boy, much better. One more thing . . .' the duke looked hard at Holcroft as he lounged on the pillow-strewn bed, the yellow candlelight softening the age-lines on his face ' . . . I trust that I do not have to tell you that anything you learn from my intimate correspondence, indeed anything of a privy nature that you learn while in my service, must never be spoken of or transmitted to any other – no matter who they might be. Any betrayal of my confidence will be dealt with harshly. Is that clear?'

'Yes, sir.'

Holcroft continued to read slowly. From time to time the duke made little appreciative humming noises. The English gentleman at the French court, this Charles Sackville, continued at length about the terms of the treaty, the generosity of the French and finished his missive with some items of gossip about King Louis's new mistress and one or two other personages at the Court of Versailles. When Holcroft had finished reading, he looked up at the duke, who had his eyes closed and appeared to be sleeping.

Holcroft set the letter down on the top of the pile and was about to steal away and resume his position outside the chamber, when the duke opened his eyes. He stared at the boy for a few moments almost with a look of confusion, then sat up abruptly, reached over to the pile of papers, fumbled through them and pulled a small square yellow sheet from the middle of the pack. He handed it to Holcroft. 'Now read this one to me.'

As Holcroft reached across to take the letter, the duke's fingers lightly caressed his skin as he took hold of the paper. It was such a shocking contact, despite being a gentle touch, that Holcroft jerked in surprise. He saw that the duke was watching him, a strange, hungry look on his face.

'Are you quite comfortable on that nasty little stool?' the duke asked softly. 'If you preferred to, you could take your ease here beside me on the bed while you read – see, there is plenty of room.'

Now Holcroft raised his eyes to the duke's face and looked steadily at him for the first time. His pale-blue stare was cold and blank as a field of fresh snow. 'Thank you but I prefer the stool, Your Grace.'

The duke dropped his gaze, pretending to brush at some dust on the coverlet. 'Very well, read on, boy.'

The letter was short, dated to the week before, and it was written in the same strange code of numbers and symbols that Holcroft had first seen the day before in the audience room.

With perfect ease, Holcroft read:

Sir, I write in haste to impart fresh and, I believe, vital knowledge that I have received from one of the men who kept a watch on Madame before her sudden death at the end of June. Two weeks before we began our surveillance, Madame received a secret visit from two grand English noblemen. Our man Jupon only discovered this yesterday by chance from a ladies' maid that he has been cultivating. The two gentlemen came directly from London at the end of April and returned there a little over month later at the beginning of June. She has revealed that these Englishmen had no less than three private meetings with Madame in May of this year in Versailles, each one under a cloak of an extravagant party that the King himself was also attending. The identity of these two Englishmen has not yet been revealed. It may be that the source does not know their true names. I await your orders. Your obedient servant, Astraea.

The Duke of Buckingham was sitting bolt upright in the bed, his earlier lassitude completely discarded. The transformation was astounding. His eyes were bright, his jaw clamped tightly shut. He seemed to be on the edge of a terrible rage. Holcroft did not know what to do. He did not understand quite how the letter he had just read could have angered him so much.

He said, 'Should I read another one, sir?'

The duke looked at him, as if for the very first time that night.

'No. But I have half a mind to send you to knock up those slug-gards Osborne and Littleton and the chief clerk.'

Holcroft got to his feet. 'Is something the matter, sir?'

'Something the matter? No. But I fear I have been made mock of – indeed, that I have been made to look a fool by my enemies, by my friends even, by the King and the whole court.'

'Shall I go directly and wake the gentlemen?'

'Hmm?' The duke was deep in thought. 'No, I have a better idea, boy. Do you think you could write me a message in the same disguised fashion as the one you have just so ably read to me?'

'Certainly, Your Grace. It is but a simple letter transposition.'

'Good boy. Clever boy. Then let us write. Light candles, there are pen, ink, paper, in the desk over there. To work, Mister Blood, to work!'

The Duke of Ormonde felt himself propelled out of the carriage by a strong hand hauling on the collar of his coat. He fell forward into the darkness and splashed wrist-deep into the mire of St James's Street. It was dark, a cloud-cloaked night, only the faint glimmers from the brick gatehouse of St James's Palace at the foot of the hill providing illumination, just enough to make out indistinct shades of grey and black, but no more. A heavy boot crashed into his ribs, flipping him over on to his back. He sat up quickly and swung a fist at the black shape looming above him, connected to hard flesh and heard a yelp. Then there was a sweeping movement above him and a shocking blinding pain above his left eye; he felt the world tilt and slip in strange directions. He was flat on his back in the mud again and for some reason unable to move any of his limbs. He felt the rain pattering against the skin of his cheek. He was aware of horses moving about, the slop of their hooves near his head. There were voices above him, too, fading in and out.

'Shall I do it now, Father?' said one. 'Shall I finish it?'

'I'll fucking do it,' said another deeper, rougher voice.

'Wait, both of you, wait. I have a better idea. This should not be a dark-o'-night murder. Get him up on the back of a horse and we'll take him to Tyburn, 'tis not so far and there're ropes already strung for the business. We'll string him up like the dirty old thief he is.'

The last voice had a slight Irish lilt but Ormonde could not understand the meaning of the words. He was no thief. There was a murmur of agreement and he felt strong hands grip him and lift him upwards. This made no sense at all; his house, his servants, his whole life, were all just forty yards away, somewhere in the blackness at the top of the hill. What had happened to Jenny? He hoped she had had the good sense to run away silently into the darkness.

'Good sirs,' he said, his own voice sounding far away and feeble, 'I have forty guineas in my purse that you shall have this instant – and a thousand pounds in jewellery in my house yonder. You may take it all. Merely escort me there and you shall be rich men.'

A blow leaped out of the darkness, smashing into his jaw and snapping his head back. Pinwheels of light danced in his skull. The night roared and moaned in his ears. He barely comprehended the response to his offer, something about holding his filthy tongue and did he take them for mere footpads? He felt a hand roughly groping at his waistband nonetheless and pulling the heavy purse free.

'Get him up on the back of my horse,' someone said. 'Tie him there with this.'

In his dazed and febrile state, he felt hands lift and tug him up and over the back of an animal, behind a huge rider, and before he knew it a cord was fastened tight around his middle, twisted around both arms and pulled in so that he was roped to the big man in front of him, his arms clasped around his thick waist. His head cleared slightly and, at the same time, there was a growl of thunder. A few moments later there was a lightning flash of pale grey that just gave him enough light to see two men, one tall and slim, the other smaller, both masked and shadowed by broad hats, looking up at him. He was roped tightly behind a giant of a man, hatless, the vast round pate glittering with silver stubble. A fourth man, his back towards him, was in the act of mounting a horse. Three still bodies lay on the ground. The door of the carriage sagged open. Jenny was nowhere to be seen.

'Get the thieving bastard to Tyburn, lads,' said the mounted man, his Irish lilt more pronounced in the gloom. 'I'll go on ahead and make sure the ropes and ladders are readied.'

There were noises of acknowledgement and the duke heard the sound of horse's hooves as he cantered away. He could smell the ancient sweat-soused leather jerkin of the big man. He felt the horse under him begin to move up the hill, it was moving awkwardly, slowly under his considerable weight and that of the other man. The duke could now make out the lights of his own gatehouse, the porter's lodge at the top of the hill. If his arms had been free, he could have hit it from here with a well-thrown stone.

'Help!' he shouted. 'Help me! Murder! I am Ormonde and they have seized me. Help, I say, help!'

Now they were at the junction of the roads, and turning left on the old western road that led to Tyburn Lane. They were moving away from his house. The rain was coming down harder, masking sight and sound; the prospect of safety slipping away with every stride of the labouring beast.

The duke collected his wits. Thunder rumbled and lightning bleached the sky. The house was twenty yards behind now. 'Help me!' he shouted. 'You there, the porter. It is Ormonde and I am to be murdered. Come out from the fucking lodge, you lazy good-for-nothing, or I'll have the flesh off your fucking spine.'

A massive elbow scythed backwards from the big man in front of him and slammed into the side of the duke's head. Ormonde was rocked sideways with the force of the blow. He righted himself on the back of the horse but found that, despite the blow, his head was now strangely clear. He had one chance to escape death. Just one – and it had to be taken now. He put his right foot under the huge rider's right stirrup, brought it up as hard as he could, shoving him off balance, and at the same time threw his whole weight to the left. He felt the rope bite deep into his waist and forearms, but the big man was falling too, and the two of them tumbled from the horse's back and with a combined 'Ooof!' they splashed down into the blackness of the street. He landed on the big man's back, felt the rope part under the strain and, fumbling his arm clear, he struck out, his fist hitting hard flesh. He punched again. But the big man turned under him, seized his shoulder and crashed a hard forearm into his mouth. Ormonde rolled in the darkness, the blood hot on his face and lay still, dazed and spent from his exertions.

The big man was up on his feet and baying for help from his comrades and the duke was aware that the two other horsemen were circling his prone body. And then there! There, by God! At last. A lantern coming out from the porter's lodge and a querulous voice saying, 'Who goes there? Who is it? Who ventures abroad on this foul night!'

Ormonde sat up with a jerk and shouted, 'It's me, Brooks, it's your fucking master, you incompetent old poltroon! It's Ormonde. I am captured. Call the footmen! Get all of them out, all of them, get them out here now.'

The duke heard the big bald villain, the one he had been roped to, running off, sloshing heavily away through the muck. One of the mounted men, still above him, shouted, 'Kill the rogue!' aimed a pistol and fired at Ormonde. He felt the lead ball punch through the thick wool of the coat bunched up at his side, but no pain, just a sharp tug of cloth. The second rider fired, too – and missed, the bullet splashing slurry on to Ormonde's face. The first rider said, 'Run him through!' but the other said, 'It's too late, Tom,' for there were more lights coming from the porter's lodge and cries of alarm and the shapes of men. Ormonde saw the riders turn their mounts and, cursing filthily, canter away west and into the night.

Sunday 11 December, 1670

Holcroft discovered, to his surprise, that he enjoyed his new employment. After reading the letter from Astraea that had so disturbed the duke, he had worked with his master for five consecutive nights when all the rest of the house was asleep, writing letters in the numerical code and handing them over to the yawning chief clerk at dawn to be dispatched by courier to parts of England, France and sometimes Holland, too. There was, mercifully, no repetition of the invitation to join the duke on his bed – Holcroft's refusal was respected and they were, at any rate, both too busy. But Holcroft came to understand gradually that the duke was pleased with his work; that his efforts were valued. It was a novel experience for the new page – being valued. All his life he had either been pitied or despised for his strangeness. But here, in the Cockpit, alone with the duke at midnight, with the curtains drawn, and the candles blazing, his facility with the code, his ability to write a letter out perfectly in numbers and symbols, and to decode an incoming missive as easily as a billet doux was genuinely admired by one of the country's most powerful men, he felt, perhaps for the first time, that he was a person of some small consequence.

Of course, there was a vast gulf of rank between them, not to mention age and wealth, but when they were alone Buckingham treated him as if he were – not a friend, that would be absurd – but not as an ignorant servant or dispensable lackey. Sometimes, after a gruelling late-night session, Holcroft was dispatched to the kitchens to bring back bread and cheese or a little cold roast beef, and they would eat together and even share a bottle of wine.

He did not truly understand all that he wrote at the duke's behest, and he also knew that during the day the chief clerk, John Mullins, and his trio of inky subordinates also made secret communications with the duke's other informants. But he understood enough of the correspondence he saw and wrote to recognize that the King was desperately short of money and the duke was labouring to provide him the necessary funds through the French treaty, which was now revealed somehow to be no good, a false treaty or a sham. He knew too that the two English gentlemen who had been in Versailles in May had somehow hoodwinked the duke in this respect.

Many of the letters that he had drafted concerned the move-ments of the great men of England over the spring and summer months, and the duke seemed to be coming to a conclusion about the identity of the two mysterious travellers. Holcroft, even though he did not wholly grasp what was afoot, felt privileged to be helping the duke unravel this great secret.

If Holcroft's relationship with his master was satisfyingly cordial, the same could not be said for his relationships with the other pages. Unable to catch him out sleeping on night duty, Robert Westbury was still determined to exact his revenge. He sent a succession of pages to wake him 'accidentally' on the hour, every hour during the daytime in the dormitory. Holcroft suffered this for two days and then went and found himself a dusty, disregarded corner of the stables in which to sleep peacefully by day. The other pages did not quite know what to make of him. They knew that Westbury was punishing him, and naturally wished to side with their leader; and yet Holcroft also seemed in high favour with the duke. This meant that sometimes they shunned him and sometimes they treated him as if he were backstairs royalty. Holcroft, who found the behaviour of other people a mystery at the best of times, merely ignored them all. He was too busy or too tired anyway to do much more than sleep in his pile of straw, wash, eat and go and attend to the duke when the clock struck six.

On the fifth night, long after midnight, when Holcroft had been yawning over a letter he was writing in code to the correspond-ent in Versailles, Buckingham suddenly said: 'Why is it that you only wait on me during the dead of night? What do you do in the daytime? I needed you yesterday afternoon and no one seemed to know where you might be found.'

Holcroft had looked at him stupidly: 'I've been allotted night duty by our head page. He has allocated me seven nights in a row.'

The moment the words were out, Holcroft realized with horror that they might well come under the description of 'peaching', talking about another fellow's activities to the authorities, a sin that his brother Tom held to be the worst of them all. He blushed and looked down at the sheet in front of him.

'The head page is the Westbury boy, is it not?' said the duke. 'Hmm. He does not love you, I collect.'

Holcroft said nothing.

'Well, all that stops now. You are to tell Mister Westbury that you are to attend me at all hours in the new capacity of my confidential clerk. You will sleep when I sleep. I want you available at all times, not whenever Robert Westbury determines. Have Matlock make up a bed for you in my dressing room until further notice and you will send to the kitchens for your food. Now, back to work. Write this to Astraea:'

Holcroft had dipped his quill in the ink pot and began to write:

'We believe that our mysterious visitors can be narrowed down to the three men we have agreed to call A, B and C. I suspect that it is A and C because they often come as a pair and because, in my experience, B would prefer to make the running alone, however I could be wrong . . .'

5'5' 2' – 1 2' 9 3' 2' 5' 2' – 7* 6 1' 7* – 4' 5' 5* . . .

Sunday 18 December, 1670

After nearly two weeks in his new home – and that time spent almost continually in the presence of the duke – Holcroft was granted a half-holiday by his master one Sunday afternoon and, joyfully, he determined to go and visit his mother in Shoreditch.

As he walked up Cock Lane, avoiding the mud and puddles lest he mar his new shiny black leather shoes and white stockings, he initially enjoyed that warm feeling of someone about to do someone else a very good turn; for in his pocket, tightly gripped in his hand, was the silver half-crown that the duke had given him on his first day and he was very much looking forward to presenting it to his mother and seeing her face light up when he did so.

However, that was not the only feeling in his breast – he felt a growing sense of unease, too, as he walked though the mean thoroughfare to his former home. He saw the dead dogs and the gangs of starveling, half-wild children, the shabby, hopeless men, the tough, squat women standing like guardsmen outside their front doors – he saw all of them with fresh eyes. He forced himself to lift his gaze and nod hello to a few, tipped his new black felt hat once or twice, but in his golden coat and fine palace togs they only stared back at him suspiciously and soon he dropped his eyes and focused only on avoiding the potholes. *I have changed*, he thought. *In only two weeks I am become wholly another person*. He saw the trio of boys he had fought on his errand to the Wheatsheaf for his mother and braced himself for another encounter. But they ignored him as he plodded by, perhaps not even recognizing him, and carried on with their day's amusement – the tormenting of a cornered cat, by pelting it with stones of increasing size.

If Holcroft had changed, he was surprised to see that the cottage had changed too, and that made him feel even more uncomfortable. Its door was wide open, which in of itself was not so terribly unusual given that Charles and Elizabeth ran in and out from the street all day long. But Holcroft could see immediately when he put his head inside that the house was in turmoil. There were three wooden packing cases on the kitchen floor, spilling wood shavings, and inside he could see the few possessions of the family wrapped in protective rags. The table had disappeared. The dresser had been stripped bare of its crockery, the row of pans hanging on the wall was also gone, and his mother was on her knees before a large leather-covered trunk laying a pile of folded clothes inside. She jumped up when she saw Holcroft's shape in the door and rushed over to enfold him in her arms.

Holcroft felt such a wave of dizziness come over him that he could scarcely return his mother's embrace.

'Oh, Holly, you look so fine!' His mother put her hands on his shoulders and admired his new golden coat. 'You look like a prince of the blood. A prince of the Bloods perhaps.' And she laughed in a slightly manic way. He caught the sweet stench of raw spirits on her breath and realized that she was drunk.

'This page's coat? Oh, I'll soon be changing it for a better one. I'll soon be wearing the black of a confidential clerk. I've been elevated, Mother. The duke says I may visit his personal tailor for a new suit when I can find the time.'

'The duke's own tailor, my goodness!'

Holcroft looked at his feet. He realized that he had been boasting crassly. He felt ashamed and did not know what to say next.

His mother did not seem to notice. 'As you can see we are all at sixes and sevens here,' she told him, 'but there is a bite of pie left if you are hungry. But I have such a deal to do: I daren't join you. The carter is coming at dawn tomorrow and I must be ready for him. So much to pack – so little time to accomplish it in! Where are those scrapegrace children?'

She looked owlishly around the tiny room as if they might be lurking somewhere among the packing cases. 'Charlie!' she cried. 'Where are you? Come: I need you to help me with the linens.'

'I can help you and . . . I brought this for you,' said Holcroft, and he stepped forward and offered her the half-crown, holding it out flat on his palm like a man feeding a horse a slice of apple.

'Oh, you are a good boy,' said Mary, seizing the coin and slipping it into a pocket of her apron. 'I'm so pleased you're doing well. Rising in the world. You'll be a proper gentleman soon!'

'Where is the baby?' asked Holcroft. Mary stared at him. Her face, so animated a moment before, suddenly froze, then fell and she said with a weird calmness: 'He died. He died on Wednesday last. We baptised him Neptune, for your father's uncle, and just in time because, well, the next day I buried him . . . I buried my poorly little boy in St Leonard's churchyard.'

Holcroft embraced her properly now, felt her melt into his chest and begin to weep bitter tears on his golden coat. He was dry-eyed himself; somehow he had known that the infant was not long for this world and if what the minister said was true, the mite would now be with the angels. So what was there to cry about? The baby was with God in Heaven, surely a better fate than enduring a miserable existence here in Cock Lane.

After a while he gently pushed his mother away from his chest, offered her a clean kerchief from his pocket and said: 'Why are you packing, Mother? Where are you going? Has the landlord lost patience with us?'

His mother half-laughed through her snot and tears as she wiped her red eyes: 'That lustful hound lost patience with us months ago but . . . but I came to an, ah, accommodation with him. No, it is my mother in Lancashire – you remember your Granny Maggie? We stayed there after – after Dublin. Well, she has been kind enough to invite us to come and bide with her for Christmas and the new year, Charles, Elizabeth and me. I didn't ask for you or Tom; you're almost full grown now and I thought you'd much rather stay with your nice duke. And Tom, well, as you know, we don't see much of Tom these days; he's always up to something with your father.'

She was composed by now and almost cheerful. 'Your father came to see us a few days ago, did I tell you? In the dead of night like some creeping house-breaker. He's had to go back into hiding, some bad business with that cruel old devil Ormonde, the man who had us tossed out from our lands in County Meath. You remember Sarney, Holly, and our lovely old house there? Or were you too young to recall?'

Holcroft remembered Sarney perfectly: a high, square, stone-built house, draughty and damp even in summer but surrounded by bright fields and clumps of shady woodland where he had spent hours at play with Tom, his other brothers or the local boys, or sometimes escaping from his noisy peers and wandering his father's lands all alone and perfectly content.

He had been happy there but, at the age of seven, it had all been rudely swept away. They had all left the country house and moved into a low, cramped, wood-panelled set of rooms above a coffee house in the stinking and crowded streets of Dublin. It had been a shocking fall from grace. The Dublin apartments belonged to a grim Presbyterian schoolmaster who, while he could be terrifying when he flew into a rage about the new laws benefiting Catholics, or if he heard anyone speaking well of the recently restored King, had at least laid down a sound basis for Holcroft's education during the year or so they had all lodged there. He and his brothers had been taught to read, mostly from the Bible, but also from numerous anti-Catholic tracts. The schoolmaster, William Leckie was his name, had instilled the basics of mathematics in Holcroft too and given him a smattering of French, law, philosophy and rhetoric – not that he would ever be much of a public speaker. It had taken a month of daily lessons before he had found the courage to speak a single word aloud to Leckie.

'Will Father go with you to Granny Maggie's house?'

'Not him,' Mary replied. 'He's got to stay out of sight, by which he means away from me, until all the fuss dies down. He'll lie low for a few weeks; then he promises he'll join us. But he can't be too badly off – he gave me a golden guinea to pay the carter and fetch the children some decent victuals. Wasn't that lovely of him? He's such a good man at heart.'

Holcroft felt punctured. He had hoped that the half-crown he had given his mother would have made her bloom with happiness, but the knowledge that his father had given her eight times as much cast a shadow over his own generosity, made it seem paltry and, worse, an unnecessary sacrifice.

For the first time in his life Holcroft felt a flash of hatred for the old man. All those years of poverty and hunger, all those times when his mother had been humiliated not only by her lack of a visible spouse but also by the lack of means to buy a loaf of bread or a cup of milk for her children, when the dashing Colonel Blood had been absent, getting into scrapes, having to lie low again for a few weeks or months, challenging the law, the government, the world – and inevitably, constantly, losing to them – all that, and now he swooped in and presented his bedraggled wife with a gold coin and an empty promise, and Holcroft's gesture was rendered meaningless.

Suddenly Holcroft hated his mother, too. Why did she allow herself to suffer this indignity? He was fairly sure that his father had other women, his two villainous friends had even made comments about it in his presence, yet his mother sat patiently at home, stomach empty, cupboard bare, shaking for lack of a drink, children wandering shoeless in the street, waiting for his father to come, waiting for him to love her again and make everything right.

'I have to go,' he said.

Mary Blood clutched his arm. 'You said you would help me.'

'I have to be some other place,' he lied. Then he knew that what he said was strictly true. If he stayed a moment longer in this hovel, this place of silent desperation, with this haggard, drunken casualty of his father's lust and lies, he would scream. Or hit someone. Maybe even his mother.

'I will find Charles wherever he is and send him in to help you,' he told her. Then he turned his back on his mother and walked out of the door.

Careless now of the street mud that splattered his shiny black shoes, white stockings and the hem of his golden coat, Holcroft ran the whole four miles from Shoreditch back to White Hall. After locating his younger brother and directing him homeward, he felt compelled to get back to his own home before dusk, and the December day was short. But more than that, it was an instinctive running, a running away from his mother's misery as if it were a disease that might spread to him. He also had a longing, a craving almost, to sit in the Privy Garden – the King's elegant pleasure ground, which was situated between The Street and the royal apartments – before it got dark.

The Privy Garden was a place of imposing bronze and marble statues and neat squares of mown grass. It was a place of order and quiet, which had once been reserved for His Majesty's personal use, but now was frequented by many of the grandees of the court and a favourite location for lovers' trysts – even more scandalously, it was occasionally used as a place to hang drying laundry. Holcroft had no desire for either of these activities. He merely wanted to sit alone as the dusk gathered, in the security of its neat geometrical layout and gaze upon the King's new sundial, a marvellous candelabra-like contraption nearly ten foot high made of brass, stone, wood and gilded ironwork.

The sundial held nine glass spheres on extending arms that depicted the earth, moon and the planets and had two hundred and seventy different dials – Holcroft had counted every one of them. It showed not only the hours of the day but many other things devoted to astronomy and astrology, that Holcroft did not fully understand. He loved it nonetheless. It did not lie. Or weep. It did not tell jokes. It merely told you what hour it was and whether the moon would be full and which constellations might be seen in the night sky.

Holcroft arrived at the sundial, hot and breathless, his side aching from the unaccustomed exertion. He had devoutly hoped that he would be alone there – for all its semi-public status the Privy Garden was often deserted, particularly in winter – but he was to be disappointed. There were more than a few solitary people walking in the gardens in the last hour of sunlight and, worse than that, a young man and an older woman were seated on a stone bench before the majesty of the sundial, both rapt in contemplation of its mechanical beauty. Holcroft approached cautiously, unwilling to break the spell of their intimacy, but equally unwilling to cede his usual place on the stone bench to these interlopers. He stopped about ten yards away and contented himself with glaring at their backs.

Then the man turned, as if he sensed that he was being watched, and Holcroft saw that it was the soldier from the gatehouse from his first day: his friend Jack Churchill.

If the ensign of the King's Foot Guards objected to being gawped at by a lowly page while he enjoyed a private hour with his ladyfriend, he did not show it. Indeed, on seeing the boy he rose gracefully from the seat and said, 'Good evening, Holcroft, I wondered when I'd run into you again. I trust you are quite well?'

Holcroft smiled at him, his former pique quite forgotten in the pleasure of seeing Jack again. 'Very well, sir, as I hope are you.'

'May I present to you my cousin Barbara Villiers, the newly made Baroness Nonsuch, Countess of Southampton and Duchess of Cleveland.' Holcroft saw that the lady grasped a short white stick that held up a vizard, a small black velvet mask decorated with clusters of emeralds, before her face. He had seen ladies of fashion about London toying with these devices to hide their identity and add an air of coquettish mystery.

'This is my young friend Mister Holcroft Blood, who is a new page in the Duke of Buckingham's service.'

'No longer a page,' said Holcroft proudly. 'I am now His Grace's confidential clerk.'

'So, you begin to rise already. Bravo, my young friend, you will finish up a duke yourself one day, just like your master!'

'How do you like the Duke of Buckingham's service?' asked the lady, casually sweeping the vizard away to one side to reveal her face. 'My Cousin Georgie can be a taskmaster, I fear, and brusque when he is out of humour.'

With the mask gone, Holcroft saw that she was quite as beautiful as her male companion: a great pile of luxuriant chestnut hair under a broad straw hat, the violet shade of which perfectly matched her slightly slanting, heavy-lidded eyes. She had a black diamond-shaped beauty spot below her left eye and an elaborate spot in the shape of a tiny coach and horses under her right cheekbone, which seemed to be dashing down towards the corner of her mouth. She was very tall, yet her long body was also voluptuous, perfectly in proportion and clad in a shimmering silvery-gold silk gown and a blue silk mantle. She smiled at him and Holcroft was instantly smitten. He had never been so close to someone with so much power over the onlooker. And while she must have been nearly thirty, she still had the effortless ability to command a young man's full attention. By the time Holcroft had recovered from the shock of her beauty he had almost forgotten her question.

'It is . . . it is not at all what I expected,' he said. 'I had thought that I would be fetching and carrying, delivering messages about the town, perhaps tidying his apartments. But instead, I spend most of my time writing letters for His Grace, or copying his rough notes out into . . .' He stopped. He had been about to speak of the code but a part of his mind told him that the duke would take this ill. '. . . a fair copy,' he finished lamely and looked down at his mud-splashed shoes, suddenly overcome with a raw shyness.

He knew who she was, of course. Albert St John had told him all about the King's legendary mistress: Barbara Villiers, the woman who had given him five bastards, all of whom the King had graciously acknowledged as his own. Yet Holcroft had also heard rumours that she was being supplanted in the King's affections by the actress Nell Gwyn, a woman ten years younger.

'I am sure he must be pleased to have such a diligent and, dare I say, handsome young man to serve him,' said Barbara. 'No wonder he has made you his confidential clerk.' Holcroft looked up at her and smiled.

'You look as if you have travelled far today,' said Jack.

'I went to see my mother at Shoreditch. I had not seen her once since I came here.'

'I trust she is flourishing – and proud of you.'

'She was drunk again.'

There was a slightly uncomfortable pause.

'We have been abroad today, too,' said the lady. 'Jack and I went to see the unicorn at the Tower.'

Holcroft looked up at her in wonder. 'Did you truly see a unicorn?'

'It was no true unicorn,' snorted Jack. 'It was merely a grumpy old rhinoceros – I saw a similar beast in Tangiers in the sultan's menagerie. We did see a lion, a mangy brute and toothless, but definitely a lion, and a huge white bear from Norway half-mad from boredom. A very sad creature.'

'I believe it was a true unicorn,' said Barbara firmly and Holcroft felt a little shaft of envy when he saw how Jack smiled lovingly at her and she returned the look. They were more than mere cousins, no doubt about that.

'We also saw the jewels,' said Barbara, fingering a string of fat pearls around her own slim neck. 'They are locked up tight in the Irish Tower, of course, but Jack slipped the keeper a shilling or two and we were allowed to view them privily. Quite magnificent! The crown of Saint Edward, the Imperial State Crown, which contains the Black Prince's Ruby – it really is the size of a hen's egg, you know' She held up a her thumb and index finger two inches apart to show him. 'We saw the golden orb of state, the royal sceptre, too, golden salt cellars, golden plates and cups, diamonds, rubies, jewel-encrusted swords and spurs. And so much more besides, I felt quite overwhelmed by the presence of so much royal splendour.'

'This is the King's treasure?' asked Holcroft.

'Oh yes. The Crown Jewels of England,' she replied, her eyes glowing with pleasure.

'Does the King ever put them on?'

'Not since his coronation nine years ago,' Jack told him.

'Then what is the use of them?'

'They are very beautiful,' said Barbara, 'and some shallow souls might see that as a great virtue all in itself . . .'

'Oh yes indeed,' said Jack, smiling. 'I most certainly do.'

'. . . and they are also worth a great deal of money – as much as a hundred thousand pounds, some say.'

Holcroft said nothing. *Just like you*, he thought, *beautiful and useless and worth a great deal of money*. Despite his exposure to the duke's secret letters and their talk of vast subsidies, his mind could not readily encompass a set of ceremonial baubles worth a hundred thousand pounds; a sum that it would take him five *thousand* years to earn on his present – and very generous – clerk's salary.

A church bell began to toll from the chapel to the northeast of the Privy Garden. 'I am sorry,' said Barbara, 'but I must go. I promised Father William that I'd attend a Mass this evening – for the good of my soul.'

Holcroft had not known she was a Catholic and the shock must have shown on his face. She gave him an amused look under her heavy eyelids and another little smile that hollowed out his heart. 'But I am not always so pious, you know, sir. Quite the opposite, in fact. Indeed, I have private apartments off the Stone Gallery yonder, the white door at the end of the yellow gallery, and the King does not choose take up so much of my time these days. Perhaps, when you are at leisure, you might come and pay me a visit – for a dish of tea. You could tell me all about yourself.'

'I shall escort you to your Romish rite, my dear,' said Jack, 'before you put your soul at risk with any more sinful ideas than a dish of tea.' He grinned crookedly at Holcroft, and raised one eyebrow. It was a jokily conspiratorial look that irritated the boy. He wished the young soldier was a little more jealous about the invitation that this lady had extended to him.

'I'll bid you good evening, my friend,' said Jack as he and Barbara, vizard once more in place in front of her beautiful face, glided away towards the Stone Gallery on the eastern side of the court. 'I hope to see you about the palace again soon,' Jack called over his shoulder and gave a little wave.

When they had disappeared into the gloaming, Holcroft felt strangely bereft. He *was* a buffle-head, he told himself. She was the King's mistress and probably Jack's too, and not for the likes of him. He would *not* visit her – not for a dish of tea or for any other reason. To calm his mind, he sat down on the bench, let out a breath and began to contemplate the perfect sundial.

Holcroft looked approvingly at the fir-tree-shaped device, admiring the planetary spheres of glass on their moveable arms, decreasing regularly and pleasingly in size as they rose higher up towards the apex. After a while he got up and walked around the dial, and studied the enamel panels on four sides that depicted the King and Queen Catherine on the front and the Duke of York, the Queen Mother Henrietta-Maria and Prince Rupert of the Rhine, the King's war-hero cousin, on the other three sides.

Albert St John had told him that this magnificent object was a symbol of royalty, of the King's family, of their place at the centre of his realms, and of the world itself, but Holcroft did not see how a structure of brass and steel, no matter how elegant, could be the same as a living family of flesh, blood and bone. Nevertheless, he knew that it was due a certain reverence, so he carefully examined the pictures, bending down to peer at them in the gloom, noting that the King looked rightly magisterial with his golden sceptre in his right hand and his queen perfect and lovely. He studied the intricate gilt-work on moveable arms, admired the glass planets and, of course, the dials themselves – although it was now too dark to tell the hour.

He sat back down again on the stone bench and pondered some more and the view had its usual soothing, almost soporific, effect. The sundial showed the clockwork-like turnings of the universe, regular, timely, predictable: order created by a divine plan. Holcroft approved. Order was what he craved most. After the upsets of leaving his home and arriving at the Cockpit, the shock of meeting his new employer and taking on his new role and having to adapt to his new strange life, he needed this physical symbol of certainty, this symbol of the unchanging patterns in the world created by God. The sundial represented a universal truth – the truth of God.

He thought about his dead baby brother Neptune, took a deep breath, let it out, and allowed his poor infant soul to fly away, far, far away and up to the heavens. He thought about his mother, soon heading north to Lancashire: well, it was better than alternately starving and drinking herself insensible in Cock Lane. She would be cared for at Granny Maggie's house, and so would Charles and Elizabeth – they would be far better off roaming in the fresh air of Lancashire than the dank, dangerous, soot-encrusted alleys of Shoreditch.

All would be well.

Sixteen miles to the northwest of the Privy Garden, in the little town of Romford, the bells of the church of St Edward the Confessor rang out for Evensong. Yet their chiming could scarcely be heard by the three men sitting on a bench by the wall inside the Lamb Inn that lay almost in the church's shadow, due to the noise of the cattle and sheep lowing outside in the market and the cacophony of conversation inside the packed alehouse. It was market day, when the local farmers streamed in to Romford bringing their flocks and surplus produce for sale, buying the necessities of life, listening to the news, and indulging in a good deal of eating and drinking with their friends and neighbours. It was also on these days, if they felt the need of his counsel, that these stout Essex men and women paid a visit to that eminent physician, apothecary and surgeon, that man of parts, Dr Thomas Allen.

In looks and bearing, Dr Allen bore an extraordinary resemblance to that notorious rogue and outlaw Colonel Thomas Blood, except that he wore a long, sober black coat and high-crowned black hat with a buckle on the front and a pair of gold-rimmed spectacles on his long nose. It was through these that a pair of bright, innocent blue eyes now looked at his patient.

Mistress Harris, sitting on the other side of the table from Dr Allen and his two associates, had been speaking for some time now, listing her many and varied complaints, which ranged from earache to bunions, and passing through various distressing conditions of her chest, bowels and limbs. Dr Allen confined himself to nodding, tutting and murmuring expressions of mild dismay. He kept his eyes fixed on her round brown wrinkled face, his chin supported in his hand and the elbow plonked on the ale-splashed table, but his mind was entirely elsewhere. He was thinking about the girl Jenny Blaine and wondering if it would be possible to sell her. He had heard that some women, if they were as pretty as she, could be traded for as much as five pounds in the remoter parts of Yorkshire, which lacked a sufficient number of available females for marriage.

Since the debacle with the Duke of Ormonde in Piccadilly twelve days before, Jenny had been living with Blood, William Hunt and Joshua Parrot in one tiny, grimy room above the parlour of the Lamb. Blood had promised that they would be together if she fulfilled her side of the bargain in the Ormonde business – and she had. She had sent a note the next day to the bruised and battered duke, telling him that, after the terrifying violence of that rainy night in St James, she no longer wished to reside in London, nor to accept his protection, and while she was grateful for his many kindnesses, she was determined to return to her family's remote village in Lincolnshire.

She had not consulted Blood about her decision to break with Ormonde. And it seemed that the duke was content to let her go, for he had made no reply to her note nor any effort to track her down. And so she was now all Blood's, body and soul. Yet Blood, if he was completely honest with himself, was finding her constant presence a little irksome.

Neither did Jenny relish her new circumstances as much as she had believed she would. She was used to ducal splendour, to space and the best of everything at the pull of a bell rope, and Blood, who had long since spent all the money he had been advanced for the attempt on Ormonde, was barely able to pay for the room and board for the four of them. She made her displeasures well known. In short, she complained loudly and ceaselessly about everything. She complained about Blood's drinking; she complained about the bed that she shared with him – apparently it was infested with a greater number, or a livelier species of bedbug than she was used to; she complained about Parrot's thunderous snoring, about Hunt's sly attempts to glimpse her naked body when she made her toilet in the small wash basin in the corner of the room. How much sweeter it had been, thought Blood, when he'd merely been fucking Ormonde's whore and gleefully setting a pair of cuckold's horns upon his greatest enemy's head.

He was fond of her, no doubt about it. But the idea of selling her had its attractions, too. He did not plan to abandon her to the caresses of some love-starved Yorkshire clod; his plan was to sell her and then, once he had been paid in full, to rescue her from her new home after a day or so, ride to the next town and repeat the process. However, he did not relish explaining the scheme to her. He doubted she would see it in a sensible light.

Dr Allen was suddenly aware that a heavy silence hung over the table between him and his patient. Mistress Harris was looking at him expectantly and he wondered how long it had been since she had ceased speaking. He nodded his head. He looked to his right and saw that Hunt had fallen asleep, his head hanging back, mouth open. Joshua Parrot was over by the tap, deep in conversation with the Lamb's landlord, Nathaniel Borrell.

'Mistress Harris, this is without a doubt one of the most interesting cases I have ever come across,' said Dr Allen, in his gravest voice. 'Truly fascinating. I have not had a patient with such a distressing array of ailments since I treated the Great Cham of Tartary a year or two back. But you will be relieved to know that I cured that noble personage entirely and he presented me with this solid silver pistol as a gesture of his gratitude.' He tapped the gleaming steel stock of the weapon shoved into his belt.

Mistress Harris looked suitably gratified to be linked in misfortune to such an evidently important foreign gentleman, even if she did not know exactly – or indeed at all – who he was.

'Did this Cham also suffer from shooting pains in his knees?'

'Indeed he did,' said Dr Allen, stroking his chin, 'although I don't believe they were as severe as those in your own poor limbs.'

She beamed at him.

'However,' he continued, 'I do believe that I have the remedy for your ailments – for all your ailments.'

Blood groped in his pocket and pulled out a small waxed linen pouch, which he gently pushed across the table to the old woman.

'Only this extremely rare powder has the strength to cure your many distressing and unusual conditions, Mistress Harris. If you sprinkle the exact amount that will cover a shilling piece into warmed ale, and drink it down at dawn, noon and midnight, your problems will soon be completely cured—'

'Horse shit,' interrupted Mistress Harris, who had opened the pouch and, wrinkling her nose, taken out a pinch of the brown, strong-smelling and somewhat grassy dust that it contained. 'It looks like dried horse shit.'

'It is the roasted excrement of the Nazareen Gryphon – a terrible beast that is part lion and part eagle. I purchased it in the Holy Land, where it had been collected up, dried in the ovens where the Host is made and blessed by the High Abbot of the monks in the Holy Sepulchre in Jerusalem itself. It is worth far, far more than its weight in solid gold but, because I have a kindness for you and you remind me of my own saintly mother – may she rest in peace, poor soul – I will let you have the packet for only two shillings. Plus, of course, a one shilling fee for the private consultation.'

As the old lady passed over the coins, and got up to go, Blood saw that Parrot was making his way through the crowded parlour towards the table.

'Osborne sent a rider with a message. He says: "The Bull's Head. Next Saturday. At noon." The fellow is awaiting your reply.'

Blood let out a hiss of dissatisfaction. 'Next Saturday? That's Christmas Eve. I'm not traipsing all the way into London. It would be almost blasphemous, surely. Besides it's too dangerous now. Tell him no. Tell the rider to tell Osborne that if he wants to deliver a rebuke for the Piccadilly business, fine, but let him come here to do it. Tell him I'm not running my head into a London noose just so he can have the pleasure of scolding me.'

Parrot leaned even closer in. 'He supposed that you might say that. The second message is this: "He says if he does not see you at the appointed time and place, he will tell the House of Lords commission, which is at this very moment sitting to investigate the Ormonde affair, that if they were to send a troop of the King's cavalry to the Lamb Inn, in the town of Romford, Essex, they may find the perpetrator residing there with his rascally confederates."'

Holcroft sat on the stone bench until it was too dark to see the sundial at all. He was only roused from his thoughts by the arrival of Fox Cub bearing a brass lantern and a summons from the duke himself. The boy seemed overly pleased that he had managed to locate Holcroft: 'The duke is in such a taking, Holly. He has been asking everywhere for you.'

The little boy skipped along beside Holcroft's long-legged stride as they made their way out of the gate at the north-western corner of the Privy Garden, crossed The Street, and ducked into the filthy alleyway that led to the duke's apartments in the Cockpit.

'Do you think he might make me a confidential clerk one day,' piped the boy in his charming accent. 'I have been here a year and he has yet to take the slightest notice of me.'

'I very much doubt it,' said Holcroft. 'Unless you have some skill at the reading and writing of ciphers.'

The boy went silent. Holcroft was aware that he had said something out of turn. He looked down at the boy and, although he was not skilled at reading the facial expressions of his fellow men, he did perceive that the boy now looked particularly downcast. It dawned on him belatedly that he had upset his companion. And something his mother often repeated to him rose in his mind: 'Remember that other people have feelings too, Holly, and they're as easily bruised as yours. Have a care what you say.'

'I am sure that the duke has something in mind for you that is much better than mere confidential clerk,' he said, after a moment's consideration. 'I am sure that he recognises your quality and will shortly reward it.'

Fox Cub brightened immediately, his little pink face shining once more, but Holcroft felt a weight on his heart: he had just told a lie. And that was a sin. Or was he merely making a joke? He didn't know.

The Duke of Buckingham was in a fine temper. He stalked up and down the edge of the carpet by the big windows in the blue audience room letting out a stream of foul-mouthed abuse about the character of the King's mistress and quaffing from a large glass of wine that a servant, following him about the room at a discreet distance, refilled at every opportunity.

'. . . as if it wasn't bad enough that she inveigles a new title almost every month from our lust-fuddled King, either for her or for her growing brood of royal bastards, I'm told that Charles has just granted her an income worth four thousand seven hundred pounds a year from the Post Office. He doesn't have enough money to feed his filthy pack of spaniels and he's giving her Post Office funds to squander on parties and new hats and God know what else. She must be the greediest woman in England!'

The duke's audience was Sir Thomas Littleton, who sat glumly in a vast armchair, his arms tucked in around his belly and looking even more like a vast owl than usual. As the duke paced up and down, Littleton tried to think of something to say that would soothe him. Holcroft, who had been admitted by Fox Cub some ten minutes earlier, stood silently beside Littleton's chair and tried to comprehend why his master found the fortunes of the Duchess of Cleveland, Baroness Nonsuch, etc., so enervating.

'Why does this affect us?' asked Littleton finally.

Buckingham rounded on him. 'It affects us, you goggle-eyed dunce, because I am trying my hardest to put the King's finances back into some kind of order and, despite my efforts, this bloody woman is merrily stripping him bare on an almost daily basis. She "borrowed" – borrowed, ha! I should say helped herself to – ten thousand pounds from the privy purse last month.' The duke took a gulp of wine. 'She told the King about it afterwards and he forgave her – he just forgave her! And she gave half of it – five thousand pounds – to her new lover Jack Churchill. And do you know what he did? Do you know, Littleton? Did he spend it on fine new clothes, old wine, any kind of debauchery? No, sir, he did not. He had the barefaced cheek to convert it straightaway into an annuity, bought from the Marquis of Halifax and worth a cool five hundred pounds a year. That Churchill boy will go far – you mark my words. Cousin Barbara steals the King's money and gives it to her lover and he *invests* it! In this dissolute day and age – can you imagine? Are you listening to this, young Holcroft! There's an important lesson to be learned here.'

Holcroft inclined his head but said nothing. He could see his master was drunk.

'Nice of you to make an appearance, by the way,' said the duke sarcastically. 'I've been asking for you all afternoon.'

'You granted me a half-day holiday, Your Grace!'

'Did I? Well, that doesn't mean I don't need you. Now to work – an anonymous letter for *The London Gazette*, I think, listing all the reasons why my grasping cousin Barbara Villiers should be exiled from the court forthwith. It will be in the form of a petition to the King from his concerned subjects. We will mention every rumour, every scrap of tittle-tattle about her money-grubbing ways; see if we can't make a decent case for her dismissal. Or at least get her to curb her greed for a while. Fetch pen and ink, Holcroft. You, Littleton, can marshal some arguments too. Ready? Right, young Holcroft take this down: To Mister Henry Muddiman, editor of *The London Gazette*. Sir, I feel compelled to write to you on a most serious matter . . .'

Thursday 22 December, 1670

What the editor of *The London Gazette* made of the duke's drunken and vitriolic letter denouncing the Duchess of Cleveland, Holcroft never discovered, for he heard no more about it, either from Buckingham or from anyone else. It was certainly never published in the *Gazette*. He had continued in his usual duties in the Cockpit in the days approaching Christmas and occasionally accompanied the duke to meetings with other members of the Ministry, carrying important papers for him, and sometimes jotting down notes at the duke's command for future reference.

On one such excursion, Buckingham had asked Holcroft to accompany him to an audience with the King in his apartments on the other side of White Hall and carry some documents necessary for the conference. Holcroft had naturally been excited at the thought of making his first acquaintance with King Charles, but, in the event, he had been disappointed, and left outside in the Stone Gallery to kick his heels on a bench while his betters discussed weighty affairs of state in the King's red audience room.

As was his practice, Holcroft pulled the Parisian pack of cards from his pocket and, after dealing them out and playing a game of Slamm with imaginary opponents, he settled down to commune with the queen of diamonds. He was just revealing to her his disappointment at not seeing so much as a glimpse of the King, when he was aware that he was not alone in the Stone Gallery. Jack Churchill was striding down the narrow alley towards him, with a smile on his face and a cheery greeting on his lips.

'Holcroft, how good to see you,' said the soldier. 'All alone again, I see. Do you mind if I join you? I have been invited to dine with a friend who has her apartments here – but you know Barbara Villiers, of course – and I am fearfully early. And it does not do to arrive before the appointed time with Barbara. She gets into the most awful rage if you disturb her before she is ready to receive you. She is not an early riser by habit and she always takes an age over her toilet. May I sit for a while?'

Holcroft happily made way for his friend on the bench. And they chatted companionably for a while about inconsequential things: the weather, which had turned cold, and the rebuilding works after the Great Fire in the City of London, much of which was nearly completed.

After a while, Jack said: 'Tell me, Hol – may I call you Hol? Holcroft is such a mouthful – do you see much of your parents these days? Or does the duke keep you too busy for such mundane family matters?'

Holcroft frowned at him. It seemed an odd question.

'I recall that you said you had visited your mother when we met last time. And I wondered if you also regularly saw your father?'

'My mother has gone to Lancashire. But I expect I will be seeing something of my father at Christmas – at least I hope so. The duke has granted me a full day's holiday.'

'It is just that I have always wanted to meet him – I have heard much of his exploits during the wars. Such a colourful character. Do you think you might be able to introduce me? Is he in London now, for instance?'

'I don't know exactly where he is.' Holcroft was not absolutely sure, but it seemed to him that his friend Jack was behaving a little strangely. His face was slightly flushed and his eyes were darting all over the place. Finally they fixed on the pile of cards that lay on the bench between them.

'Ah-ha! Your famous Parisian pack – I trust you have not lost a great fortune at the tables recently!'

'I do not have a great fortune to lose, Jack.'

'I know. I was joking.'

'Oh. I see. Well, in truth, I have not played cards with anyone since I came here.'

'Truly? Then we must have a game or two while we wait here.'

Jack Churchill picked up the cards and shuffled them expertly. Holcroft felt a twinge of disquiet at an alien hand touching his beloved deck but he managed, with some difficulty, to quell it and when Jack had dealt, they fell to playing a simple two-handed game in a companionable silence.

Jack was rather surprised to discover after only a couple of hands that Holcroft had an extraordinary ability to remember which cards had been played in what exact order. It seemed as if he could anticipate the exact card that would come next before it was dealt. It was almost uncanny. He tested Holcroft – it was only a friendly game after all – asking him to predict which card would be played and, nine times out of ten, Holcroft was able to say correctly what his opponent would throw down next. For the first time in their acquaintance, Jack found himself genuinely impressed with his friend.

'Tell me, Hol, have you ever played cards for money?'

Holcroft shook his head.

'Hmm. Then I wonder if you might like to meet some friends of mine at Christmastide. We could have a light supper, perhaps play a hand or two afterwards. Would you enjoy that?'

Holcroft thought that sounded marvellous. He had received no social invitations of any kind in the weeks he had been in White Hall – not that he had received any at Cock Lane either – but he was aware that the people here often gathered with their friends and colleagues and ate and drank and amused themselves, and he could scarcely contain his delight at the thought of a convivial evening with Jack Churchill and a party of his intimates.

'Yes. I would have to ask my master the duke but I'm sure . . .'

Their conversation was interrupted just then by the loud banging of a pair of heavy oak doors and the arrival of the Duke of Buckingham, who was muttering, 'That bloody idiot . . . that thick-skinned, stubborn, damned incompetent spendthrift . . .'

under his breath but quite loud enough for both Holcroft and Jack to hear, which allowed them to exchange a quick smile.

Then Holcroft was bundling up the pack of cards and his master's papers, nodding farewell to Jack and half-running to keep up with the duke as the great man swept away up the Stone Gallery without another word.

'Was that young Jack Churchill I saw you with earlier today,' said the duke an hour or two later. 'Playing at cards with you in the Stone Gallery?' Buckingham had finished his dinner and was sitting back in his chair in his private study in the Cockpit, his face glowing with good food and wine.

Holcroft, who had been crouched down attending to the smouldering coal fire, stood up straight and admitted that it was.

'He's a friend of yours then, is he?'

'Yes, sir.'

Buckingham beamed at him.

'You know also, don't you, that Jack Churchill is the lover of that grasping bitch Barbara Villiers – my cousin, the Duchess of Cleveland?'

Holcroft said, 'She is his cousin, too.'

'Only distantly. Which is a shame – a charge of incest would have been a delightful bonus.'

Holcroft said nothing.

'Tell me, Mister Blood, do you enjoy serving me? Do you like the Cockpit? Are you happy in your employment as my confidential clerk?'

He nodded.

'And do you consider yourself a loyal fellow? Are you loyal to me?'

'Yes, indeed, Your Grace.'

'I should damn well hope so. When your father begged me to, I gave you a position as a page in my service, out of the kindness of my heart. Then I raised you up to be my confidential clerk. I have been good to you, no?'

'Yes, sir,' said Holcroft, uncertainly. He had no idea where this conversation was leading but he knew he did not like its tone.

'Well then, sir, I shall give you a chance to show me your loyalty, and repay some of the boundless kindness I have shown you.'

Holcroft frowned and then, a little too late, said: 'Thank you, sir.'

'You do wish to repay some of the kindness I have shown, don't you?'

'Yes, sir.'

'Good. Now, listen closely. This is what you will do for me. You will continue your friendship with Jack Churchill, deepen it; play cards with him as often as you like, get closer to him, become his intimate – and you will befriend the Duchess of Cleveland, too, if you can. These are my orders, Mister Blood. You will become the greatest of friends with Mister Churchill and his whore Barbara Villiers. You will insinuate yourself. Am I making myself clear?'

'Sir.'

'You will hear things, naturally, about their relationship from time to time, Holcroft. Private things. You will gain their confidence. You will ask them about their motions – discreetly, of course. And next time you hear that they have made a rendezvous, an assignation – the next time you know for certain that they will be together, you will come to me. Do you understand?'

Holcroft felt as if he had been kicked in the stomach.

'You wish me to betray the confidences of my friend Jack?'

'I wish you, Mister Blood, to demonstrate your faithfulness and loyalty to me. I seek the downfall of Barbara Villiers. Purely for his own good, the King must be made to see that she is making a fool of him. You will help me achieve this goal. You will worm your way into the good graces of Jack Churchill and Barbara Villiers; it may take a few weeks, but do not let that concern you – what is most important is that you come directly to me and tell me when you know that they will be together. There will be a hundred pounds in gold for you if you will do it. Think of that, boy – a hundred pounds! All for you. On the other hand, and you must surely know this already: I can have no place in my service, no place in my household, for one who is not completely loyal to me. Am I quite clear?'

Until this moment, Holcroft's feelings for the duke had been entirely of respect, even admiration. He was a great man and Holcroft had been proud to serve him. At a stroke all that was wiped away. Holcroft looked at his master's face with growing horror as the man's explicit orders sank in. He understood perfectly what the duke wanted – nothing less than that he spy on his only friend in White Hall, the only man, apart from the duke, who had shown him any kindness in this strange new place. And not only that, not only was he to play the informer, to 'peach', as his brother Tom would have it, on his new friend and his friend's lover, but he was also expected to be directly responsible for the couple's exposure and downfall.

Holcroft had never heard anything so repugnant in his life. And yet what could he do? If he refused his master's orders he would be expelled from the Cockpit and have to return to – what? His mother was gone, off to the north. Where would he live? How would he live? What would his father say? He could picture the old man's disappointment – what had he said repeatedly to him in the parlour at Cock Street: 'Serve him well. Serve the duke well or you will feel my belt . . .'

Holcroft did not truly fear a beating from his father – he had suffered many in his childhood and would not allow himself to be swayed by the threat of temporary pain – but he did not want to disappoint the old man. He could not disappoint him. He did not want to fail at the task he had been given: to serve the duke well. He did not want to spoil the plum that his father had arranged for him.

And at the back of his mind, in a dark place that Holcroft did not like to even acknowledge, he heard the soft clink of gold coins and the whispered words: 'A hundred pounds! All for you.'

'So you understand me, boy?' the duke said, an ugly tone twisting his voice. 'You understand what you must do?'

'Yes, sir,' Holcroft said quietly.

Friday 23 December, 1670

King Charles smothered a yawn. He knew this was a good play, everybody said so, and on the advice of his groom of the close stool he had attended this performance of it by the Duke's Company in their theatre in Lincoln's Inn Fields. But if it was such a good play, why was it so damned tedious? Sir John Grenville, who was now sitting beside him in the royal box, was leaning forward, hands gripping the rail, rapt by the performance of England's leading actor Thomas Betterton as the soldier Alcippus telling his friend that he feared his love Erminia has been unfaithful to him. Charles felt like shouting: 'Of course she has been unfaithful to you, you idiot! They all are!' but he knew this would make him look ridiculous.

Nevertheless, the play was failing to grip. It was billed as a tragi-comedy but the King found it neither comic nor particularly tragic. It had all the usual shenanigans of star-crossed lovers, darling Nell Gywn looking adorable in a dangerously low-cut gown, and a rather clever parody of Lord Arlington as a dishonest spymaster, which the King knew would enrage the man most satisfactorily. The message of the play was that royal authority should be respected, which was all well and good, but still he found his mind wandering: he had hoped it would be a touch more risqué, a little broader in its humour; a few more bare-breasted dancing girls waving giant dildos. A dwarf or two. Something *funny*. Was that too much to ask?

Charles looked down at the pit where the common run of humanity sat on their benches and saw that about half the audience was absorbed by the play and half talking with friends or munching oranges and sweetmeats. It was full, anyway. Not a bad turnout, he thought, for a play by an unknown woman playwright. He looked around the half-circle of boxes kept by the richest theatre-goers. He saw that Lord Arlington had already left the theatre – typical of the bloody man, such a prig, couldn't take a joke – leaving the candles still burning in the sconces but taking with him his ally, indeed his chief toady, Sir Thomas Clifford. In the next box along, the Duke of Buckingham was deep in conversation with his hatchet-man Sir Thomas Osborne. Why did everyone christen their children Thomas these days? After Doubting Thomas? Was this an age of religious doubt? Of course it was. He had more than a few doubts himself.

A tall servant stood behind the duke's chair, a handsome lad with an unruly mop of brown hair, who was frowning at the stage as if perplexed by the theatrical goings-on. The Duke of Buckingham saw the King looking over at him and made an elaborate gesture with his hand and a bob of the head, indicating that he would have bowed had he not been comfortably sitting down. The King nodded back. He's scheming again, he thought, I can tell by the eager look on his face. But who is he plotting against this time?

The next box belonged to the King's younger brother, James. The Duke of York looked just as bored as the King felt and when he sensed the royal gaze, he smiled back at Charles and raised an ironic eyebrow. On a chair to his left was that good-looking young guards officer that all the ladies twittered and sighed about, James's protégé Jack Churchill. His father, Sir Winston Churchill, had been a staunch man during the wars and the son seemed a loyal chap, too, although too girlishly pretty for the King's taste.

The Earl of Lauderdale's box was dark and empty, as expected. Lauderdale rarely came to London these days: as secretary of state for Scotland his powerbase was north of the border and he resided there and ruled that kingdom very much like a viceroy; not that Charles minded too much, Lauderdale was loyal to the Stuart line and while the man debauched himself and lined his pockets as much as any of the others, the King trusted him not to go too far and, more importantly, he knew that Buckingham had several spies in his household who kept a constant eye on him.

He expected the last box in the row to be empty. It belonged to the Duke of Ormonde who, after the shocking attack on his person in the street outside his home a couple of weeks ago, was known to be recovering in Clarendon House, a bruised recluse behind barred gates and surrounded by a score of burly footmen. The House of Lords committee that the King convened to investigate the attack had discovered nothing except that there had been an attack by four persons unknown and that Ormonde had been the victim. Ormonde had testified that one of the men who attacked him had been called Tom – as if that narrowed the field at all!

The Ormonde box was, however, far from empty. A sconce of candles fixed to the side illuminated the sharp face of Thomas Butler – another Thomas! – the Earl of Ossory, the Duke of Ormonde's eldest son. He was not paying the slightest attention to the play. He was glaring with malice at the back of Buckingham's head three boxes along.

The King well knew that there was bad blood between the two families: Buckingham and Ormonde had been locking horns for years, struggling for mastery as the second man in the land after the King. But while the two older men seemed to recognize that this was a contest with certain rules and codes of conduct, Lord Ossory seemed to take each move in the struggle for power as a personal slight, a slur on his father's honour. The King had been obliged, at different times, to send both Buckingham and Ossory to the Tower of London to cool them off, and he wondered that night whether he had been foolish to release either man. Perhaps he ought to banish one of them. Or both. But he could not face the disruption to the peace and order of the kingdoms that would unleash: the petitions, the grovelling requests for more titles and posts, the jostling of new men for influence. It had been bad enough after Clarendon had been brought down and sent packing three years ago. Maybe it was a case of better the Devil you know. Maybe. But what a parcel of grasping, small-minded, self-important rogues they were: all of them. These are the greatest men in the land, the King thought, my closest advisors. God save us all.

The applause at the close of the final scene was no more than politely enthusiastic. But the King himself rose from his seat in the royal box, his wig brushing the ceiling, and made a point of clapping loudly and calling, 'Bravo, my dear!' to the diminutive creature in the lemon gown on the stage. As Nell Gwyn made her curtsey to the King, she winked at him and cheekily pulled down the top of her dress to allow him – and the rest of the audience – a swift glimpse of her perfect globular breasts and their pink rosebud nipples. The audience roared in appreciation and Nell, her charms now safely tucked away again, blew kisses to all and danced off the stage.

Holcroft was stunned. It was not the first time he had seen a woman show off her bosoms – but he had never seen a woman do it who was not a drunken street whore offering her saggy wares to passers-by.

'See that woman there,' said a voice below him, 'blonde, curly hair, short, clasping her hands, wearing those dreary widow's weeds.'

Holcroft looked where the Duke of Buckingham was pointing and saw a smiling woman with sad brown eyes under a high pale forehead standing by the curtain just off stage. She reminded him strongly of someone, a relative or family friend, perhaps, but he could not quite think of who it was.

'Her name is Mistress Behn and she wrote this nonsense. Take her these flowers and this note. Then come and find me in the dining hall: the King has ordered a light supper for all the players and his friends.'

Holcroft took the flowers from Buckingham's hand, a bunch of tired white hellebores, and a note of thick yellow paper sealed with the duke's wax insignia. He walked out of the box and began to make his way along the corridor behind towards the stairs. He became lost for a few moments in the darkness behind the stage, bumping into half-dressed men and women, who stank of cheap scent, face powder and old sweat and called out to each other with extraordinarily lavish endearments and a feverish excitement.

He followed the light coming from the stage and found Mistress Behn in the same spot the duke had indicated, looking out at the wide arena where a dozen actors and their courtly admirers were mingling, talking, laughing and eyeing each other lasciviously.

'Yes?' she said, catching sight of Holcroft standing awkwardly a yard behind her in the half darkness. 'Are those for me?' She took the flowers from the boy's hands and eyed them critically. Holcroft could see that it was a rather miserly gift, a gesture and not a grand one. He handed over the note.

'The Duke of Buckingham's compliments, ma'am.'

'He is casting me off,' she said, still looking at the limp flowers; the note unopened in her hand. 'He has no more use for me.' She said the words with no self-pity, merely as a statement of fact. Then she looked at Holcroft. 'Tell him I still need the money. All of it. Tell him – what is your name?'

'Holcroft Blood, ma'am.'

'Tell him, Holcroft Blood, he must make good on the money. Tell him I will not go back to debtors' prison.' Her voice was calm despite her words.

'I will tell him, Mistress Behn,' said Holcroft. He turned to go.

'Wait a moment!' She stopped him and cracked open the seal on the letter. She read it quickly, bobbed her head and said: 'As I thought.'

Then she paused before looking up and saying: 'So, Mister Blood, tell me now, did you enjoy the play?'

'No.'

She looked a little surprised. 'You know that I wrote it?'

'Yes.'

'And you did not find it the slightest bit amusing?'

'No, not at all.'

She laughed then, a cheerful, natural bubbling up, entirely and truthfully mirthful. He studied her closely. He could not tell if she was upset by what he had said about the play or by the message that he had brought her. But his reason told him that if the duke was truly casting her off, she might well be exhibiting some sort of strong emotion. If she was, he could not detect it at all in her face. She merely seemed to be slightly amused.

'I thought as much. The King did not care for it either, and Lord Arlington left after the second act. And I saw you up there, standing grim as the reaper behind his lordship's chair and you did not smile or laugh once. What was it about my poor little play that you disliked so intensely?'

'It is an idiotic story,' said Holcroft without hesitation. 'This one is in love with that one but she can't be with him because she is to be married off to another. He is in love with her but dare not tell her. Everyone in love with the wrong person. It's just silly.'

'You think the agony of unfulfilled love is silly?'

'Of course. It makes people stupid; even sensible men and women become fools in love.'

'You may well be right. But perhaps that's why I find it so interesting: it is an elemental force that turns sensible people into fools. I would venture to guess that you have never been in love, Mister Blood. Is that correct?'

'I have never been in love and I devoutly hope that I am never cursed with such misfortune.'

'What an interesting young man you are, Mister Blood. Almost everybody seems to take for granted that love is a wonderful boon to mankind. You do not. I must confess that I do not agree with you but I have never before heard the counter-argument put so passionately by one so young. Unfortunately, since your master has no more use for me, I must depend for my living on writing these silly plays and I can only hope that others do not find them as objectionable as you. However, I hope that our paths will cross again, sir. I find your directness, as painful as it is to hear, refreshing. Honesty such as yours is a rare quality in this deceitful world.'

Holcroft rejoined the duke in the dining hall adjacent to the theatre. He fetched the duke a plate of pastries and a glass of iced sack and waited quietly while his master finished his whispered conversation with Sir Thomas Osborne. The actors, many still in their costumes, circulated among the throng, flirting with the King's guests who were all at this moment standing. The King himself had been provided with a chair and was conversing with his brother James while he fed an overweight black-and-white spaniel that was sitting on his lap from a large bowl of liver pâté.

The dining room, a long, dark wood-panelled space, was decorated for the feast of Christmas, with holly sprigs and ivy adorning the walls and entwined through the candle sconces that bathed the space in a warm yellow light. Across the other side of the room, over the heads of the other revellers, Holcroft saw his friend Jack Churchill, and flinched. He could barely look at him. The conversation he had had with the Duke of Buckingham the day before echoed in his head, and his cowardly acceptance of the disgusting plan proposed by his master made him feel deeply ashamed. All he could hope for was that the duke would forget his scheme to use Jack to bring down Barbara Villiers. Perhaps, if he did nothing, it would all blow over.

The duke finished speaking to Osborne, handed his plate to a passing footman and walked over to the King. Holcroft dutifully followed him.

'Ah, Buckingham, there you are,' said the King, shooing the fat dog from his lap. 'I must offer you my congratulations on your wonderful success in negotiating the treaty. All has been most satisfactorily agreed, signed and sealed at Dover Castle and I am told by the Treasury that the first tranche of the French money has been delivered. A most dexterous piece of work, upon my soul, most dexterous. I am to make the proclamation of the treaty tomorrow morning – something for our people to celebrate at Christmastide – and I must say, my dear fellow, that you have managed things absolutely marvellously. Bravo! You have my most heartfelt thanks.'

Buckingham forced a smile onto his lips. 'You are most gracious, sire. Your appreciation makes all my efforts worthwhile. However, I must warn you that the bulk of the money is already spoken for, to settle outstanding debts and so forth, and I fear the rest will not lie long in the royal coffers.'

The King frowned. 'There is no need to spoil a such joyous occasion with your cheese-paring, Buckingham. We have agreed a peace with France and very soon we shall deliver our part of the bargain and take the fight to those contumelious Dutch dogs. You have achieved a notable success, Your Grace, a triumph even, let us try to savour it at little, at least for tonight.'

He lies so well, Buckingham thought, *it comes as a gift of God, I suppose. If I did not know he had played me false I would never know it from his face.* He said, 'Indeed, sire. But while I have your ear, may I tell you that the other financial matter, the delicate affair we discussed yesterday in the *blood*-red audience chamber—' At this Buckingham raised his eyebrows meaningfully, and the King nodded, his brow knotted in displeasure. 'I may tell you that this matter is progressing satisfactorily and I expect to have the agreement of the party involved very shortly.'

That rattled Old Rowley's gilded cage, Buckingham thought, *and serve the dissembling old spendthrift right.*

The King leaned forward in his chair. He suddenly looked cold and very angry. 'I do not require to be appraised of the proceedings of *that* matter every time we meet, Your Grace, in fact I will thank you not to mention it to me again until the affair is concluded. Do you understand me?'

Before Buckingham could reply, a voice rang out behind him: 'You, sir, my Lord Buckingham. I would speak with you!' The duke turned to see Lord Ossory's sharp and furious face emerging from the chattering throng of players and courtiers.

The young man stopped three yards from Buckingham, who was now standing behind the King's chair. Ossory put his right hand on the stock of the duelling pistol thrust into his belt. The left he pointed at Buckingham, a long index finger extended as if it were an unsheathed rapier.

'My lord, I know well that you are at the bottom of this late attempt upon my father Ormonde's life. And therefore I give you fair warning: if my father comes to a violent end by sword or pistol, or if he dies by the hand of some paid ruffian, or by the more secret way of poison, I shall not be at a loss to know the first author of it. I shall consider you the assassin. I shall treat you as such and wherever I meet you I shall pistol you – even though you stand behind the King's chair.'

Buckingham could see big men in the red-and-blue colours of the King's Foot Guards, and the young ensign, Churchill, converging on Lord Ossory at speed, shoving their way brutally through the crowd.

But the angry nobleman was still speaking: 'I tell you this in His Majesty's presence that you may be sure I shall keep my word.'

As the Earl of Ossory was bundled out of the dinning room by a trio of powerful soldiers, he was still shouting: 'Do not forget my words, my lord. I meant them, every one!' Holcroft looked at the Duke of Buckingham's face. He saw that its normally healthy ruddy hue had turned quite grey.

Saturday 24 December, 1670

Sir Thomas Osborne sat beside the fire in the Bull's Head tavern in Charing Cross and sipped a pint of port wine. He had heard the bells of St Martin's chime for noon, a quarter past the hour and half past. *He's deliberately late*, he thought, *how typical of the man. He has to show that he is not ruled by any other – a childish notion. We all have masters; the trick of life is to choose them, not have them imposed on us. I'm his master, even if he will not own it, mine is Buckingham, for the moment anyway. The duke serves the King, the King answers only to God. But no man is truly masterless.*

He heard Blood come though the door but did not look up from the fire. He heard his jaunty confident step, the rap-a-tap-tap of his silver-topped cane on the counter, the awful badinage with the foul-tempered Matthew Pretty, a bawdy jest aimed at his hideous wife and, finally, the weight of a big man sinking into the leather armchair to his left and the words: 'Good day, Sir Thomas. What joy to see your shining face once again!'

He looked at Blood, his coat rain-damp and mud-splattered from the ride down from Romford, tankard in his hand, his cheeks rosy – he guessed the man had fortified himself more than once during the sixteen-mile ride.

'Well, sir,' he said, 'what have you to say for yourself?'

If Sir Thomas Osborne had hoped to put Blood out of countenance with his schoolmasterish opening, he was to be sorely disappointed.

'Oh, I always have plenty to say for myself, Tommy-boy. Was there any topic in particular that you wanted to discuss?'

'You know perfectly well what I want to discuss,' growled Osborne. 'Ormonde – what have you to say on that matter?'

'Oh *that*. Well, what can I say? We failed. It was a bold effort though sadly unsuccessful.'

'I know that, fool. Why did it fail? I heard you stopped the coach. You had him out in the dark street, alone, unarmed: three of your murderous ruffians all about him, all well furnished with sharp blades and loaded pistols and – what? What happened?'

'The thing is, Tommy-boy, whatever you think of me, I'm not such a straightforward villain as you might imagine. I'm not really an ice-hearted murderer, at least not by nature. I'm an ordinary man seeking justice for the wrongs that have been done to me. Ormonde stole my lands; he and his cronies in the government in Dublin dispossessed me, and many of my friends, when the King returned, and for no other crime than backing the wrong side in the damn wars. He stole my lands, my livelihood and he deserved to be properly punished. I deemed it right that he should hang like a common thief at Tyburn – it came to me just like that, when my pistol was pointed at his fat head. Not murder, but justice – that was what I wanted. It would have made no odds to you – he'd still be dead – but it would have made all the world of difference to me. Unfortunately, the slippery old bugger managed to wriggle free as we were carrying him off to Tyburn.'

'So he escaped, free and clear with nothing but a few bruises.'

'We'll get him next time, don't you worry. Keep the faith, Tommy-boy, and we'll all come up smiling yet!'

'You won't.'

'We will, Tommy-boy, just you get the rest of that promised pile of gold together and in a few weeks we'll do the complete business for you.'

'You won't, because that arrangement is null and void. Ormonde is barricaded in Clarendon House and is not likely to venture out any time soon. You have botched it once again. So there will be no more money for you, not for this business, at least. And if you dare to call me Tommy-boy one more time, I will use that promised gold to pay someone with even fewer scruples than you, and who is far less of a cack-handed bungler, to make a slow and painful end of you.'

Blood looked at him sorrowfully. 'I'm hurt. How could you? I thought I was the only unscrupulous cack-handed bungler that you loved! No? Ah well, I can see that you are not in a festive mood, T— I mean, Sir Thomas. It is Christmas Eve. Are you not looking forward to celebrating the birth of Our Saviour with the customary orgy of food, drink and jollity?'

'I just want to complete my tiresome business with you and go home to Yorkshire.'

'So go, then. I've had my scolding; I'm a naughty boy. And it's hands off Ormonde for now. I understand. Go home to your wife and bairns and don't keep me any longer from my own Christmas carouse.'

'I wish it were that simple. But, entirely against my advice, our master wants you to undertake another task for him. This one being a little more complicated than the last. I told the duke it was a bad idea, that you would doubtless make your usual God-awful cock-up of it again, but he insisted. He says that you have proved capable in the past and will do so again.'

'I'm gratified to hear I have the duke's confidence – if not yours. So what is it that His Grace wants me to cock up God-awfully this time?'

Sunday 25 December, 1670

Colonel Thomas Blood stood up at the head of the groaning table in the snug of the Lamb Inn, Romford, a dripping goose leg in his right hand, a brimming glass of wine in his left. Before him sat the remains of the noble bird, still majestic even half demolished and glistening with its own grease, and platters of bread and butter and turnips, carrots and cabbage, a herring pie, a veal pie, mince pies, round yellow cheeses, bowls of fruit, jugs of gravy and many bottles of wine. Around the table sat his nearest and dearest: his two elder sons; Holcroft, in a finely cut new black wool coat and Thomas, in sombre grey; his lady-friend Jenny Blaine, ravishing in a new blue-green taffeta dress dripping with lace; and his old comrades from the war, scarred, squint-eyed William Hunt in plain fustian and huge, bald-headed Joshua Parrot in his customary leather jerkin.

The feast had been lavish, even by Blood's extravagant standards, for a sudden and unexpected influx of bright gold had made any stinting in the celebration of Our Lord's nativity seem like unchristian parsimony. The food sat comfortably in his extended stomach, the wine sang in his veins, his face glowed with seasonal joy; he looked benevolently and a little tipsily at all those gathered around him, all of whom he loved so very much.

He raised his wine glass, burped softly, and said, 'My good lady and honoured gentlemen, friends and family, on this blessed day I give you a toast: to the Crown Jewels – may they bring us fame and fortune! May God Almighty, and his son Our Lord Jesus Christ, and the Holy Spirit all bless us and guide us in the bold endeavour upon which we must soon embark.'

Part Two

Tuesday 21 March, 1671

It was the first day of spring and, like the sun, Talbot Edwards, Assistant Keeper of the Jewels, had decided to show his shining countenance abroad that day – something he liked to do less frequently now that he had attained the grand age of seventy-seven. However, after weeks of rain-bound inactivity in his home in the Irish Tower in the northeast corner of the Tower of London, he felt he owed himself an excursion. And, since his wife's fiftieth birthday was approaching, he had decided to take himself to the Royal Exchange in Cornhill to purchase a gift for her.

He walked out of the Byward Tower gate, in the southwest corner of the fortress, across the wooden bridge over the stinking moat, turned right and began to walk up the gentle hill along the left flank of the Tower. He did not notice a figure of a small, lean man in a fustian coat with an old hat pulled down low over his scarred face, who emerged from the row of thronging public houses that lined the other side of the street and sauntered along about forty paces behind him.

Edwards walked slowly along Tower Street and continued on into the crowded market at Little Eastcheap. There he stopped at one of the many butchers' stalls and briefly examined a brace of hanging hares, conversing in a familiar fashion with the stall-holder. He continued his journey west and north, lifting his hat to a pair of fine ladies, their faces covered by blank golden vizards. He still had no notion that he was being shadowed when he turned right up Gracechurch Street, past the meeting house of the Society of Friends, where a lay preacher, bravely flouting the laws on uniformity of religion, was haranguing a sparse crowd gathered outside the doorway. He made a left on Lombard Street – and today some of the goldsmiths, in honour of a day of actual sunshine, had set out their benches outside their shops. He nodded to an Italian money-lender bent over his table with its charming little stacks of golden guineas on offer, then turned right, cutting through Birchin Lane past several humming coffee shops and up to Cornhill.

Edwards paused next to the empty pillory on the south side of the road to admire the new Royal Exchange. It had been destroyed in the Great Fire and was now rebuilt as a huge block-like stone building with a majestic archway at the main entrance, noble columns, and topped with a tall square belfry with clock faces on all four sides and a gilded grasshopper winking in the sunlight from the tip of the spire. The fire, following on as it did from the devastating outbreak of Black Death the year before, had seemed like the coming of the End of Days to many Londoners and, indeed, vast swathes of the City had been totally destroyed in the conflagration. Some said it was surely a judgment of God on the many sins of the City: but, chiefly, greed. Yet a mere five years after the holocaust almost all the City had been rebuilt as good as new and, in some cases, such as the Royal Exchange, rather better. The new building pleased Edwards enormously. It had a sense of optimism, of energy and confidence: a grand bazaar in the heart of his city where anything from peppercorns to priceless jewels, from sacks of coffee beans to joint-stock in the East India Company, could be bought and sold by men speaking a score of languages from a hundred diverse nations.

After a last admiring look, Edwards crossed the street, nimbly avoiding a coach and four and plunging into the bustle of the Exchange.

Talbot Edwards had been a soldier in his youth, serving in the regiment of Sir John Talbot at several bloody engagements during the late wars. Since those conflicts he had been in service in the household of Sir Gilbert Talbot, another Royalist soldier of the same illustrious family, and it was this gentleman who, on being appointed master of the Jewel House after the King's restoration, had secured the post of assistant keeper for the ageing family retainer. Edwards was immensely proud that his only living son Wythe had been serving under his old colonel in Flanders these past ten years and had managed at last to purchase himself a captaincy in the regiment.

Edwards might once have been a soldier jealous in honour, sudden and quick in quarrel, as the playwright put it, but his post as assistant keeper did not demand much in the way of either suddenness or quickness. He made sure that the Crown Jewels were kept securely behind their bars in the ground-floor room in the Irish Tower, checking them at dawn and dusk, and once a month he unlocked the grille and brought them out and carefully gave the precious metal and the jewels a light polish with a cloth and a little sweet oil. It was not a well-remunerated employment: his cramped rooms above the Jewel House were in a disgraceful state of disrepair and his monthly stipend barely covered his bills for meat and drink. However, one of its perquisites was the showing of the jewels to gentlemanly visitors to the Tower for a small fee. In this way, Edwards was able to supplement his meagre income and to be accorded a measure of respect that he believed his long years of service to the Talbot family – after whom he had been named – more than warranted. It also gave him the means, perhaps, to purchase the gift he had in mind for his wife Sarah.

He turned right after entering the Exchange and climbed the wide stone stairs to the first storey and once there, panting slightly and with his slight follower only ten yards behind him, he began to walk slowly down the gallery on the eastern side. This first-storey gallery held the stalls and small shops of the great guilds of London and of particular interest to Talbot Edwards, the glovers. While his follower loitered behind a huge square pillar, Edwards examined pair after pair of fine white gloves on the counter outside a glover's shop. He spent the most time examining four pairs of beautiful white ladies' gloves fashioned from the softest kidskin, with seed pearl buttons and gold edging at the wrists. He seemed deeply enamoured of them. However, finally, after returning to finger them several times, holding them up to allow the sunlight to play on the pearls, Edwards had a brief exchange with the glover's apprentice, a gawky red-headed lad, then he weighed his slim purse in his palm, sighed, and with evident reluctance moved on to the next stall along where a selection of bright silk scarves had caught his eye.

It was enough for the man who watched him. William Hunt allowed Edwards to wander away further down the gallery and stationed himself two stalls along, outside a shop selling dishes of sweet curds and cream, ostentatiously reading the large placard that advertised the provender. Then, choosing his moment, when the glover's apprentice was occupied with some matter in the recesses of the shop, Hunt glided forward, seized the stack of white gloves from the counter, thrust them swiftly into the bosom of his coat and, turning, walked briskly away, heading for the stairs.

Monday 17 April, 1671

Holcroft looked at the remaining cards in his hand. Four trumps, the ace, king, knave and four of spades – three trick winners, the four had to be discarded against the missing queen, which he was almost certain Captain George Fellowes sitting on his left was holding. He also held the ten of clubs – a winner, once the trumps were out, as all the other clubs had been played. Fellowes' partner James Pratt, sitting to Holcroft's right and sweating gently in his heavy moss-green coat, the livery of his master the Duke of Ormonde, had nothing much in his hand to speak of except for the queen of hearts and had unconsciously indicated this quite clearly by putting his cards face-down on the table, sitting back in his chair and pulling on a long-stemmed pipe of sweet Virginian tobacco.

Across the table from him Jack Churchill, his partner, was smiling calmly, but Holcroft could see a large drop of sweat on his clean-shaven upper lip. It was not only the heat that was making his friend perspire – although the weather was unusually hot for mid-April – the stakes in this game of cards were extremely high; more than twenty pounds in gold was riding on this last hand of the game, a sum greater than all the money that either Jack or he possessed; indeed, it was a year's salary for Holcroft.

Holcroft, however, was discomforted neither by the unseasonal heat nor the deep play. He looked down at the tricks already won: three for himself and Jack and four for Pratt and Fellowes. With the winners in his hand and the honours that he would accrue from holding three of the four face-card trumps, they would just gain the necessary points to win both the game and the match; there could be no other outcome. He longed to tell Jack that there was no case for concern but the strict etiquette of the game forbade such a conversation and so Holcroft waited patiently, staring down at the table, while Fellowes played his queen of spades, Jack discarded a diamond, Pratt played the seven and he played his losing four.

As Fellowes, chuckling to himself, collected the trick and added it to their array on the table top, now five strong out of the twelve tricks in this game, Holcroft murmured: 'All the rest are mine, I do believe.' And to the frankly disbelieving faces around the table he quietly laid down the three trumps one after the other and finally the ten of clubs.

'I believe this game and therefore the match is ours.'

Jack exploded in laughter while their opponents glumly scratched their heads and slowly reached for their purses. As his opponents began to count out the fat golden guineas on to the tablecloth, Holcroft slowly gathered up his playing cards.

'Another match, gentlemen?' he asked.

Fellowes, a corpulent, purple-faced man of thirty-five or so muttered something foul under his breath. Jack looked at him sharply. 'Would you care to repeat that, sir?' he said, pushing back his chair and standing up in one movement, a hand on his sword hilt.

Fellowes ignored him. He looked hard at Holcroft. 'You swore to us that you had never played Ruff and Honours before, sir. But by your slick play today I would suggest that that is not entirely the God's-honest truth.'

'I have *not* played it before,' Holcroft told him.

'Yet you have fleeced us of a little over twenty pounds in less than two hours – how do you explain that, sir?'

'Take very great care with your language, sir,' said Jack, his hand still on his hilt. 'You have been bested fair and square in this game but, if you continue in this line of talk, I shall be most happy to give you satisfaction at any time of your choosing.'

'I have never played Ruff and Honours before, sir, on my soul,' said Holcroft, 'but I have played a game we call Slamm since I was a child and it is similar. I have not lied to you, sir, neither has there been sharp practice. But I too would be most happy to fight you, if you require it.'

'Gentlemen, please,' said Pratt, an amiable fellow, frequently drunk and not especially sharp-witted even when sober. 'I am sure there's been no impropriety. We are all friends here. Don't be a sore loser, George, there's a good chap. Pay up with a smile and take your lumps like a gentleman.'

Grumbling but making no comment that might call for bloodshed, Captain Fellowes did so, and he and his friend left the guardhouse with as much dignity as they could muster. As Holcroft listened to the sound of their boots on the cobbles of the Tilt Yard outside the hut, he gave a sigh of relief.

'Well, now,' said Jack, reaching for the bottle of secco and pouring them both a glass. 'That has been a most satisfactory afternoon, my friend, most satisfactory indeed. I thought we were sunk for sure when Fellowes flashed out that queen of spades; and in the previous game when Pratt produced that ace of hearts at the last moment. I don't know how you do it but it's as if you can see their cards through the linen. Like a kind of magic.'

'It is merely observation, Jack. I see my own cards, and by the cards that the other fellows play you can pretty soon see where their strengths and weaknesses lie. And as I've told you several times before, I always keep a running tally in my head of all the cards played—'

'And that is beyond me, too, Hol. I am too busy thinking of my own poor play to reckon up the other side's cards.'

Holcroft said nothing. He did not see how one could *not* know almost precisely where the important cards were after a trick or two had been played. The distribution of the cards among the four players dictated the play. All you had to do was remember who played what card at each trick.

Since their meeting in the Stone Gallery just before Christmas, Jack had persuaded Holcroft to join him on several evenings in a game called Trump against some of his friends. And the Duke of Buckingham had always been more than pleased to grant Holcroft the time off to play cards with Jack. Trump was a simple trick-taking game, Holcroft soon discovered, but it was very popular in White Hall and always played for money. Within a month or so, Holcroft and Jack were an established partnership, taking on all-comers at Trump and other card games and almost always coming away the victors.

Until now they had played for small stakes, just shillings, a pound or two at most, but since Churchill's expenditure far out-stripped his income, and he had no family money to fall back on, he had talked his young friend into attempting this high stakes game of Ruff and Honours, a gentleman's game, as he had put it, with George Fellowes, a wealthy officer in the King's Foot Guard, and James Pratt, the Duke of Ormonde's senior page.

'I salute you nevertheless,' said Jack, raising his glass.

Holcroft was aware that he had missed his dinner to play this match, and looking now at the small pile of gold on the green cloth in front of him, he said: 'I'm clammed, Jack, would you care to come with me to Pettigrew's chophouse for a bite? I'd be honoured to treat you for once.'

Jack laughed and shook his head. 'The honour would be mine, Hol, but I have an engagement with a certain noble lady of our acquaintance and I must not keep her waiting. As you know, she has something of a temper.'

Holcroft felt a sudden leaden feeling in his stomach, quite over-laying his nagging hunger. He knew exactly whom Jack meant. And what it meant for him, too. He kept his eyes lowered as the soldier headed for the door.

'I shall give her your love; she often asks after you, Hol, you know. She thinks you are avoiding her – that you do not care for her.'

'It's not that,' said Holcroft, unable to look at his friend.

'Well, go and see her sometime. She won't eat you.' And with that Jack walked out of the door and into the sunlight.

Holcroft sat alone at the table for a few minutes. He felt cold and a little angry, knowing what he now had to do, and absurdly resenting his friend for presenting him with the perfect opportunity for betrayal: an opportunity that he could not ignore. The weight of the duke's unwanted commission lay heavy on his shoulders. He had done nothing about it for months now and recently Buckingham had been asking pointed questions about all the card games he played, about the movements of Jack Churchill and the Duchess of Cleveland and demanding to know when Holcroft would bring him the information he required. The duke had repeated the threat of dismissal and the promise of the hundred pounds. He had given him a week to fulfil his mission or face exile from the Cockpit. And Holcroft knew he could not resist him any longer. Eventually, with a heavy heart, he got up, swept the small pile of gold into his hand and followed Jack out of the door.

Holcroft located his master without too much difficulty. The duke was in his habitual seat in the gallery of the royal tennis court watching a game between the King, a vigorous player despite the affliction of his forty years, and John Wilmot, Earl of Rochester, a notorious poet, wit and wastrel.

Holcroft sat down next to the duke and watched through the netting as the King in the service end, dressed only in a white shirt and breeches, thrashed the ball again and again past a scarlet-faced Wilmot at the hazard end of the chamber. The Earl of Rochester was clearly the worse for drink, and between points he kept turning to the gallery to declaim snatches of his scabrous poetry to the sparse crowd of White Hall idlers, which taunted his royal opponent for his lack of youth:

> On thy withered lips and dry,
> Which like barren furrows lie,
> Brooding kisses I will pour,
> Shall thy youthful heart restore,

Such kind show'rs in autumn fall,
And a second spring recall;
Nor from thee will ever part,
Ancient Person of my heart.

'It is my turn to serve, I believe, Your Majesty!'

At the end of the match, the King was visibly furious, despite his crushing victory over the younger man – he had won all six sets, and Wilmot had barely made a point in any of them – and he stomped to the side of the court to towel himself dry and drink a long draft of ale.

'Your Grace,' said Holcroft quietly to Buckingham. 'I have the information you require.'

'What?' said the duke.

'Ensign Churchill is at this very moment paying a call on the Duchess of Cleveland.'

The duke stared at him. 'Now? Now? I've told you several times to give me timely warning. Very well, it will do, I suppose, it will do. And you will be wanting your hundred pounds blood money, I make no doubt.'

In fact, Holcroft was far less concerned about the money than the threat of dismissal but in the black self-hatred and misery of his betrayal, it did offer a gleam of comfort. It was a great deal of money. His mother had written to him in February and told him that she had been ill, nothing serious, but her own aged mother, whose fortunes were also in sad repair, could not afford a physician to treat to her. Holcroft consoled himself with the thought that the money could be forwarded to Lancashire, a physician might be hired and some small good might come of his treachery after all.

Buckingham had left his side and had gone down into the wooden-walled court to speak to the King. Holcroft watched as the King laughed, made a jest and slapped Buckingham on the back, his earlier irritation forgotten. Then it occurred to Holcroft that there was a way in which he might salvage his honour, nullify the betrayal, and still earn the hundred pounds for his mother, too, as long as he was quick. He got up, climbed up the ranks of gallery benches, went down the back stairs and slipped quietly out of the side entrance of the tennis court. Then he began to run.

Parson Ayliffe was rather more well set up than most men of the cloth. He was tall and broad-shouldered, heavy in the chest and, despite the gold-rimmed spectacles perched on his long nose, not the slightest bit bookish. Beneath his black high-crowned hat his innocent blue eyes gleamed with excitement. Neither did he walk like a parson. He strode through the Middle Tower on the western side of London's greatest fortress, crossed the moat by the bridge and continued on through the Byward Tower as if he were the owner of this ancient royal palace, his high black boots clicking on the cobbles, and moving so fast that his companion, a slender, heart-stopping girl with bright-red hair under a straw hat with a green silk ribbon almost had to break into a trot to keep up.

They walked along the walled street that ran parallel with the river known as the Water Lane, stopped to admire Traitor's Gate, a barred archway rising out of emerald water that led out to the Thames where for hundreds of years the enemies of the Crown had been admitted to the Tower of London to meet their fate, and caught a glimpse of the busy wharf beyond. Then they turned left and plunged through the gateway at the Bloody Tower, under the menacing teeth of its portcullis, and into the Inner Ward.

Parson Ayliffe nodded at a passing Yeoman Warder in his embroidered red tunic and old-fashioned hat and received a respectful salute at the sight of his broad white collar and clergyman's black coat. To his left was Tower Green, where a dozen well-dressed ladies and gentlemen, some prisoners of His Majesty and others friends and visitors, were taking the air. The 'unicorn', a huge sullen grey-white beast caged in iron, snored in the northwest corner of the inner ward. To his right loomed the stone mass of the White Tower, the thick walls freshly painted with whitewash and seeming to gleam in the sun. He ran smartly up the steps and waited at the top for the breathless girl, Jenny Blaine, to catch up with him.

'You are quite clear about the signal,' said Ayliffe in a quiet voice, offering his strong black-clad arm for her to take.

'For God's sake, we've been over it often enough,' she whispered crossly, and then smiled radiantly at an aged gentleman who was passing. He gave her an admiring leer and a courtly bow.

They crossed the ward by the row of trees in front of the Grand Stone House at the tower's northern side, their branches thick with bright-green spring leaves, and passed through the gap between the Stone House and the barracks of the guard, heading to where a small three-storey building known as the Irish Tower stood. A mangy brown lion sat yawning in an iron cage by the wall. The reek of rotten meat and the big cat's dung filled the air.

Up a short but steep flight of stairs they found themselves at an oak door painted a cheerful blue. Jenny pinched her both cheeks hard between finger and thumb, then slapped them lightly to add a little colour to her face.

'Ready, my love?'

Jenny nodded. She looked more than a little terrified.

'Keep the faith, Jenny-girl,' said Parson Ayliffe, with a most unclerical grin, 'and we'll all come up smiling yet!'

And he rapped loudly and confidently at the door.

Holcroft ran as fast as he could along The Street, turned right into the Privy Garden, sprinted along a row of houses and dived into the warren of apartments at the entrance of the Stone Gallery.

He turned right, then left . . . then realized he was hopelessly lost and begged directions from a passing footman, a supercilious fellow who declined to speak to the gasping boy in the black clerk's coat but merely pointed to a white-painted door at the end of a long passageway. Holcroft jogged down the corridor, took a moment to catch his breath, squared his shoulders and knocked.

There was no reply. He knocked again, banging his knuckles urgently against the white wood. Eventually, a long, long minute later, the door opened a crack and a pinched-faced, dark-haired maid in a white cap peered out and enquired crossly what he wanted.

'I must speak to Her Grace, the Duchess of Cleveland, it is a most urgent and delicate matter.'

'Her Grace is not receiving any callers today. She is indisposed; come back again tomorrow.'

Holcroft put his shoulder to the door with considerable force and barged it open, knocking the squawking maid flying. He stood for the moment in a hallway, suddenly indecisive, then seized the handles of the first pair of doors he saw and flung them open. Inside was a small but rather pretty bedroom, with a large brown oak wardrobe, a side table covered with pots of unguents and bottles of scent, a fragile gilded chair, a wash basin and jug decorated with pink roses on an iron stand and a large four-poster bed on which, among the tangled sheets, lay the entirely naked form of his friend Jack Churchill and, beneath him with her legs splayed, the long white body of Barbara Villiers. Both of the lovers stared at him with mouths wide open.

'What the Devil do you mean by this, Hol,' Jack demanded angrily. 'Have you gone completely mad?'

'Why, it's your adorable page boy, Jack,' said Barbara, smiling. 'He's come at last!' Then to Holcroft, 'Have you come to join us at our sport?'

Holcroft's face was bright red. He tried to tear his eyes from the duchess's superb naked body but found that it could not easily be done.

'The . . . the King . . .' he managed to stutter. 'The King is coming here. Now. The King is coming to see you *now*.'

Then he turned and flung himself from the room.

Edwards opened the blue door and found himself looking out at a tall middle-aged man dressed in a parson's black coat and square white collar and a charming flame-headed girl who was smiling nervously up at him.

'Good morrow to you,' he said. 'How can I be of service?'

'Might I have the honour of addressing the esteemed Mister Talbot Edwards, the master of the Jewel House?'

'Merely the assistant keeper, in truth; the master is Sir Gilbert Talbot, and he lives at White Hall – but yes, I'm Edwards, if that's whom you seek.' His tone was gruff but he was clearly pleased by the parson's mistake.

'Sir, I do hope you will forgive us for bursting in on you unannounced. My name is Thomas Ayliffe. I have a small parish in Essex, a very humble benefice, and this is my wife, Jennifer. We are visiting friends in London and we were advised that we must not leave the City until we have had a glimpse of the royal jewels; the very crown, insignia and vestments worn by His Majesty at the glorious occasion of his coronation. I was naturally astounded and protested that surely the King would never allow such a thing. However we were earnestly assured that were we to address ourselves to a most distinguished gentleman by the name of Talbot Edwards at the Tower we might be afforded a brief visit to the Jewel House under his supervision. We would be happy, of course, to pay the appropriate fee, or emolument, if that is not too impertinent. And if you could spare us your valuable time.'

'Oh yes, and who was it who told you this?' asked Edwards.

'It was none other than the Duchess of Cleveland, a connection of my cousin Sir Aubrey Villiers; the lady has proved a most generous patron of our little church of St Christopher's in Dunwich-by-the-sea, though she has not yet, alas, paid us the honour of a visit. She has, however, been a great help to me and my wife these past few days in our exploration of the City, a most noble lady, most wonderfully condescending; she accompanied us to the Royal Exchange. It was she who suggested we apply ourselves to you.'

'We really would be most awfully grateful,' purred Jenny, giving the assistant keeper her most lustrous, widest-eyed smile.

'I know Her Grace well,' said Edwards, beaming at them. 'A delightful lady, so gracious. An intimate of the King, I am told. She is, in fact, a frequent visitor to the Jewel House, oh she has been here many and many a time. Indeed, she has become more of a friend than a visitor. Come in, and I will find the keys, although I am afraid I must trouble you for six shillings as a contribution to the upkeep of the house, the candles, and so on.'

Inside the entrance, Edwards lifted a set of large iron keys off the hook behind the door and watched closely as Ayliffe pulled a heavy purse from his pocket and carefully counted out the silver coins into his waiting hand.

I'm a fool for not asking more, he thought, as he saw the glint of bright gold among the folds of the leather. *This Essex parson is not so humble as he makes out. How else did he snare such a wife?*

The assistant keeper took a taper from a box on the wall, lit it at a sconce, and by its small, flickering flame led the clergyman and his wife down a short, dark and winding set of stairs and, at the bottom, he unlocked a narrow black door, reinforced with thick bands of ancient iron.

He pushed open the door, and began to light a series of candles set in the walls at strategic points around the small, dank and musty-smelling room. Ayliffe observed that there were no windows or furniture, save for a single table and chair, nothing really in the room except a large iron grille on the far side that stretched from floor to the low ceiling and from one wall to the other. The grille was hinged on the left-hand side and evidently could be opened at need but was secured by a large iron padlock on the right near the stone wall. As the candles were lit and the dark room began to lighten, he could make out through the bars of the grille the enticing gleam of yellow metal, the rich glow of red velvet and the intriguing flashes of gemstones of every shade and colour under the sun.

'Oh,' said Jenny, 'how splendid, how perfectly lovely!' She stepped forward towards the grille, as if propelled by an invisible hand, walking towards the greatest collection of portable wealth in the Three Kingdoms.

As the three of them drew reverentially closer to the bars, Edwards in a low, husky, almost conspiratorial voice, went into his well-worn patter.

The King marched down the long corridor, still in his sweat-stained tennis attire, and attended only by a pair of scarlet-clad footmen and Sir John Grenville. He scarcely noticed the tall, gangling clerk who bowed low as he approached, and kept his head far down as Charles swept past. *Yes,* he thought, *Barbara. It has been far too long since I tasted her. Nell has the wit and her own fresh and outrageous cheek, but Barbara is a riper fruit and all the sweeter for it. Won't she be surprised and gratified to see me. It's just as that lewd dog Buckingham said, I have neglected her delights far too long.*

As he reached the white door, one of the footmen darted ahead and pounded on the wood. 'Open in the name of the King,' he thundered. There was a short pause and then the portal was flung open and Barbara, Duchess of Cleveland, pink-cheeked and slightly breathless, stood in the doorway, with a peach-coloured silk robe clasped around her under which she was quite obviously wearing nothing at all. She looked adorable, as if she had only just emerged from her bed, yet the hour was past four in the afternoon, which was a late lying-in even by her louche standards.

'Your Majesty,' she said, dropping an awkward curtsey, one hand still holding her robe together, 'I am deeply honoured by your visit. Won't you come in and take some refreshment?' She indicated the withdrawing room to her right, easily glimpsed from the door, where the pinched-faced maid was muttering angrily under her breath and hastily laying out bottles and glasses and a little plate of seed cakes on an elegant gilded table.

'You have caught me quite by surprise,' the duchess continued, 'I am most disgracefully déshabillé, but if you give me a few moments I shall make myself more presentable to Your Majesty.'

'There is no need for that, Babs, you look perfect just the way you are.' The King moved forward and took her into his arms, kissing her full mouth passionately, sliding his hands over the peach silk.

'Charles,' said the duchess, pushing him gently away, 'why, you are as eager as a schoolboy! At least let me catch my breath.'

'Into the bedroom with you, hussy,' growled the King, steering her backwards, away from the withdrawing room and towards the other door. His victory over Johnny Wilmot in the tennis court had made him feel unexpectedly virile, like a young buck once more – ancient person indeed! – and he intended to prove the matter of his potency without further delay.

The pair stumbled into the bedchamber, falling onto the bed, and as the footman exited and solemnly closed the double doors behind them, the King kissed her hungrily, fondling her buttocks with his right hand. Her robe fell open and she returned his kiss and her small hands began to tug at the white linen shirt, untucking it from his breeches. The King's spare hand swept away a rumpled coverlet on the bed, clearing it for action, and his fingers caught on something, a long, silky strip of material. He glanced at it, looked twice and saw that he was holding a stock between his fingers, a long, thin strip of cloth edged with lace and rather like a delicate scarf that was used by the more fashionable military gentlemen to cover their necks. The King stared dumfounded at the stock in his hand, his excitement now utterly forgotten. How could this item be in the lady's bed? Barbara took the King's face in both hands and eagerly began to kiss his lips and cheeks.

'Get off me!' he snarled.

He stepped back from the bed, his erection softening in his breeches, still holding the lacy silk stock. A monstrous notion was blooming in his mind. He looked around the bedroom; there on the table were two glasses both stained with wine at the bottom. The notion became a hard certainty.

'Where is he? Where is the scoundrel?'

'Whatever can you mean, my love?' said Barbara, recoiling on the bed and pulling the robe instinctively around her naked body. The King looked at her and, although she seemed outwardly unconcerned, nonchalant, even, he saw a flicker of fear in her eyes.

'Your lover, slut. Where is he?' His eyes ranged round the room. He bent down and peered under the bed. Then he looked at the big brown oak wardrobe in the corner of the room. He took two strides and stood in front of the double door. 'Come out, sir, and face me like a man. If ye dare!'

The wooden doors swung open slowly and a naked, shamefaced Jack Churchill stepped out, his bundled clothes clutched in his hands at his chest.

'Sire,' he said, 'I most humbly beg your pardon. I was quite overwhelmed by the lady's charms. And she said you had cast her aside, were finished with her. Yet it is truly no fault of hers . . .'

'Silence!' roared the King. Sir John Grenville poked his grey head through the double doors and frowned when he saw the naked young man standing in front of the King.

'Sire,' he said, 'Should you like me to—'

'Get out, you imbecile, this is a private matter,' bawled the King. The groom of the close stool hastily withdrew.

'Your Majesty, he speaks the truth,' said Barbara. 'You have not honoured me with a visit these many months past, and not pleasured me for a year or more, and I could only conclude—'

'Silence,' said the King again, this time in a quieter tone. 'You, sir, on your knees!'

'Your Majesty, if I could but explain—'

The King cut him off. 'I should have you thrown in the deepest, coldest dungeon in the Tower. I should have you hanged at Tyburn. No, by God, hanged, drawn and quartered—'

'And have the world know that your mistress of these past ten years must now seek satisfaction from a younger man?' The duchess's words held a crackle of real anger. She was sitting up on the bed now, arms wrapped tightly around her chest, her eyes blazing. 'You storm in here after months of neglect, without a moment's warning, without a gift or a single flower, and disturb the mother of your children at her leisure. Bawling threats and stamping your feet like an infant. Over what? A little afternoon dalliance? Am I not to have friends? While you flaunt your actress whore at every public gathering in London. For shame, sir, for shame!'

Not a word was spoken for a long, long while. The King stared at the duchess, then at Churchill kneeling naked on the floor. Then to the surprise of all three of them, not least himself, he laughed.

'Oh, Barbara,' he said, chuckling, 'I have sorely missed your spirit. I swear your fire would singe my wig at twenty paces.'

He turned back to Jack, who was now looking up at him, the first gleam of hope in his eyes.

'You, sir, are Jack Churchill, if I am not mistaken. The man who sets the hearts of half the court a-flutter – the women and the men, I'm told. I even heard that you also bought an annuity from Halifax – five hundred a year, was it? And I wonder where you got that ready money from, eh? I know your gallant old father has precious little.'

Churchill wisely said nothing. The King sighed. 'Well, you are a rascal, sir. But I forgive you – I forgive you because I know you only do it for your daily bread. Now dress yourself and be gone from here. I shall await my lady's pleasure in the other room. I do believe that we have some unfinished business between us, my dear.'

The King paused at the door and looked back at Jack who was now struggling into his breeches. He briefly examined his lean and muscled white torso. 'A younger man, forsooth,' he muttered.

'One last thing, Mister Churchill,' the King said, his hand on the handle of the door. 'Do you play tennis?'

Jack, astounded by the question, managed to admit that he had played the game once before.

'Then you and I shall try a match – tomorrow at noon.' And with that the King opened the door and stalked out.

'You had better make sure you manage to lose to him, Jack,' said Barbara, coming off the bed to help Churchill with his shirt.

'Do not worry, I shall have no difficulty at all in managing that.'

' . . . now *this* is the great orb of state,' said Edwards, poking a finger through the grille at a golden object the size of a large cannon ball and decorated with a band of pearls and gemstones around the middle, with a half band running vertically across the top. 'It was carried by His Majesty at his coronation, and that fine jewelled cross on the top symbolizes our Blessed Sovereign's position as Defender of the Faith, something that might be of interest to you, parson, in your line of work.'

'God bless His Majesty,' said Ayliffe reverentially. 'But tell me, sir, would it be possible to open the grille just for a moment and examine the orb more closely? I confess I find it strangely fascinating.'

'Oh, no, sir, the jewels must always stay safely behind bars. I cannot open the cage for casual visitors. It wouldn't be right.'

'Oh no, indeed, but surely they must trust you, sir, with the key, with your unblemished, even exemplary, record of loyal service to the Crown?'

'They do, sir, but I am on the strictest orders not to open the grille in the presence of any man save the Master of the Jewels, Sir Gilbert Talbot himself. We wouldn't want to tempt any rascally filching cove into trying to pocket a ruby or two, would we, sir? It's all right taking a little peek through the bars, sir, no harm in that, but it mustn't be opened up, no indeed.'

'Very wise, sir, very wise indeed. We live in times of sin and lawlessness and it would not do to foster temptation.' Ayliffe touched his nose, laying his finger flat against the side of it. Behind him, there was a small female gasp then a thump, and when Ayliffe and Edwards both spun around, they saw Jenny lying on the floor, seemingly lifeless.

'Oh, Jenny, oh Jennifer, my love,' cried Ayliffe, immediately crouching by her head and peering into her pale face. 'I should have known the excitement of this day would prove too much!'

Edwards, too, knelt down beside her and, seizing her fine-boned hand in his meaty grip, he began to pat it gently.

'What ails her, sir? D'ye know? Tell me 'tis not the plague returned.'

'God forbid! No, sir, like all women she is a weak and fragile creature and, now that I come to recollect it, she did complain of feeling a little queasy this morning. I believe it was merely the joy of seeing the jewels, that and a lack of air in this chamber, perhaps. Do you have any spirits about the place? A drop of brandy? That might be just the thing to revive her.'

Between them, and with some awkwardness, Edwards and Ayliffe carried the apparently unconscious girl up the narrow winding stairs to Edwards's apartments, with the assistant keeper calling out on the way for his wife and daughter to come to their aid. They settled her on a mouldy chaise longue in the withdrawing room and Mistress Edwards, a cheerful matron with a certain bulldog quality to her square, ruddy face and sagging jowls, sponged her brow with lavender water. Her daughter Elizabeth, a singularly ill-favoured girl of eighteen, with sallow, pockmarked cheeks and one long furry eyebrow, brought in a bottle and several glasses on a tray.

Ayliffe accepted a large glass of brandy from Elizabeth and, gently easing Mistress Edwards away from the couch, he knelt and trickled a few drops between the unconscious girl's lips, then took a healthy swallow for himself. 'My dear,' he said, lightly patting her cheeks, 'can you hear me?'

Jenny fluttered her eyelashes, slowly opened her eyes and tried feebly to raise her head. 'Where am I?' she said.

'You are in the apartments of Mister Talbot Edwards,' Ayliffe told her. 'In the Irish Tower. You were taken ill while we were viewing the King's jewels. How do you feel, my dear?'

'Oh,' she said, putting a wrist to her brow, 'I feel so horribly faint.' She gave a little moan of anguish. 'I am sorry, so terribly sorry for putting you to all this trouble.'

It was a performance not dissimilar to that of an actress dying slowly but flamboyantly of unrequited love at the end of a play – which, indeed, was no coincidence since this was the profession Jenny pursued whenever she found herself without the protection of a wealthy gentleman friend.

'That's quite all right, you poor duck,' said Mistress Edwards, shouldering Ayliffe roughly out of her way and continuing to apply the lavender water to Jenny's temples. 'You rest here as long as you like.'

Edwards and Ayliffe withdrew to the far side of the room where they amused themselves for a while with the brandy bottle, while Mistress Edwards fussed and clucked over Jenny, finally allowing her to sit up on the chaise longue. An hour later, on a gushing tide of thanks and mutual good wishes, Ayliffe and Jenny, still admirably pale and playing the invalid for all she was worth, took their leave of the Jewel House and its occupants and tottered down the steps of the Irish Tower to rejoin the rest of mankind.

Wednesday 19 April, 1671

Mistress Aphra Behn passed through the imposing gatehouse of the Palace of White Hall and stepped into the wide thoroughfare of The Street. Under her black woollen hood, her face was just as pale as any invalid, but her brown eyes sparkled with something very close to anger and her jaw was set with a firmness unusual even in the strongest-willed individual.

She wore her habitual plain black dress in memory of her dead husband Johannes Behn – an unfortunate Dutch merchant who traded with Surinam and had died at sea seven years previously, the ship sinking in a storm with all hands and his valuable cargo of African slaves – and who had left her with nothing but his name. In a basket over her arm, she carried a thick sheaf of papers, the manuscript of her latest play *The Amorous Prince*, which was the ostensible reason for her visit to the Duke of Buckingham's apartments that day – if questioned about her visit, she planned to say that she hoped to acquire his patronage for a run of the play to be performed by the Duke's Company. It was unlikely that anyone would question her; the guards at the gatehouse had allowed her through without a word, but it had long been her habit always to have a plausible reason for anything she did when she did not wish to reveal the true nature of her task or destination.

It *was* money that she sought from Buckingham, a great deal of money, but not for the production of the play, and she knew from long experience of the bloody man that the duke, rich as he was, would be most unwilling to part with it. Nevertheless, she felt reasonably confident that she could persuade him to hand over a decent amount, if not the whole sum – enough for her present needs anyway. The alternative did not bear thinking about.

Halfway down The Street, she turned right into the narrow alley-way that led up to the Cockpit, keeping to the side to keep her high-buttoned boots out of the river of brown filth that trickled down the centre of the cobbles. She passed the tennis court and heard the excited voices of the players and spectators echoing against the panelled walls and the thwack of ball on wood. At the top of the alley, she turned left, and was stopped at the gate into the duke's private garden by a surly porter, a scarred oaf with grease-matted hair in an ancient military coat with a half-pike in his hand and a sword at his belt, who demanded that she state her business.

'I have come to pay a courtesy call on His Grace the Duke of Buckingham. He is a very old and dear friend of mine.'

The porter looked her up and down in a most offensive manner, eyeing her pretty face, blonde curls, her slim waist and the swell of her gauze-covered bosom at the top of her widow's weeds. 'A dear friend, you say. I wager you are,' he muttered and rang a brass bell to summon the duty page.

Five minutes passed while Aphra sat on the dirty bench in the lodge, staring into space and ignoring the open leers of the porter, and then a small ginger-haired child of about ten years in a golden coat and a red waistcoat and breeches came running across the garden from the western side and skidded to a halt by the lodge.

'What's doing, Arnold?' piped the child in a French-tinged accent, wiping a few breadcrumbs and a smear of butter from his pink cheeks with the back of his hand. 'We were just sitting down to our dinner.'

'It's a *lady*, Fox Cub,' said the porter, making the word sound almost exactly like *whore*, 'come here on her own two feet, no horse or carriage, no chair, no lady's maid or escort, and come to see our own dear duke.'

'He's very busy, ma'am; he has a moil of paper work to attend to; he ain't put a nose out of doors all day, just scratch, scratch,

scratch with his quill. But I'll tell him you've come to visit. What name shall I give?'

'Mistress Aphra Behn. Tell him I urgently need to speak to him about a most delicate and private matter.'

Arnold sniggered. 'Make sure you tell him she's a rare looker, Foxy. And say it's a very dear friend.'

'He forgave him!' said the duke. 'He found him in a cupboard in my lady's chamber, naked as the day he was born and he just laughed and said he forgave him because he did it for his daily bread. The luck of that devil. Then the King stayed to pleasure her himself. Has the man *no* self-respect?'

Holcroft had nothing to say, and indeed no words were required of him. He just stood like a statue beside the duke's overflowing desk and tried to look as grave as Solomon in judgment.

'I know what you are thinking, you greedy rascal – you are thinking, *What about my hundred pounds?* Well, you can forget about that! That money was conditional on the downfall of that lustful bitch, and has she fallen, no! She is back in the King's affections, more so now than ever, I'm told, and even better placed to pillage the royal coffers at her leisure.'

Holcroft had in fact been thinking that the duke's information was surprisingly accurate. He had been told the full story by Jack the day before, his friend thanking him handsomely for his warning – *that* had made Holcroft squirm – and telling him word for word what the King had said. The maid, Holcroft thought, it could be no one else, and his respect for the duke's information-gathering system increased tenfold; his fear of it, too.

Had the maid told Buckingham about his abrupt entrance and warning of the King's imminent arrival? He assumed not, for he would surely have been dismissed by now, if not worse. He should make her a present of some kind, a golden guinea to stop her mouth, perhaps. The loss of the hundred pounds was no great tragedy. His winnings from the card tables meant that he could afford to send an adequate sum of money to his mother. But he had learned two things today: firstly that the duke's promises were not to be trusted; secondly, that what his father had told him was true: his master had spies *everywhere*. He would step more carefully in future.

Just then the russet head of Fox Cub poked through the door, and he waggled his eyebrows up and down at Holcroft until he went over to speak to the young French page.

'There is a lady to see you, Your Grace,' Holcroft said, when he had conferred with Fox Cub and returned to his master's side. 'It is Mistress Behn from the theatre. Apparently she has something urgent to communicate to you: a delicate and private matter.'

The duke gave Holcroft a thoughtful look. 'I do not care to wait upon the lady today. Indeed, I do not foresee a situation in which I shall ever be pleased to welcome her into my presence. You know her, Holcroft, go out and see her and tell her that I am otherwise engaged; tell her that if she has anything to communicate to me, particularly if it is delicate and private, she should set it down in a letter. A nice long letter and I shall reply to it or not as I see fit. Although best you don't tell her that last part.'

'As you command, Your Grace,' he said, and left the room.

Holcroft went directly to the porter's lodge and rescued Mistress Behn from the attentions of Arnold Smith – who had been regaling her at tedious length with descriptions of his sexual conquests, hinting not too subtly that he would be happy to add her name to that illustrious list.

As a denizen of the theatre, Aphra was entirely used to the motions of lecherous, self-deluding old men and she let his words slide over her without paying them too much heed. What old Arnold did not know was that she had a blade, a short but wide and extremely sharp double-edged weapon in a leather sheath secured to her thigh and she was quite prepared to discourage him with force if necessary. Her long skirts had a discreet slit known as a placket cut into them on the right-hand side so that she could easily gain access to the weapon. It would not have been the first time she had been forced to use that razor-edged blade on an importunate man.

But she was relieved to see Holcroft, nonetheless. She remembered him vividly from the theatre and, although she still recalled his merciless words when she had moments of self-doubt about her craft, she gladly agreed to his suggestion that they take a turn in the small garden together.

'He won't see you,' said Holcroft without preamble after they had walked a dozen yards in the sunshine. 'He says you're to write him a letter.'

'How very cowardly of him.'

'Yes, isn't it? What was it that you wanted with him anyway?'

'Oh the usual thing. I wanted some money. The duke owes me a great deal and without it I shall be put in an awkward position with my creditors.'

They paused to inspect the tulip bed, which was in full and glorious bloom, a sea of waving purple and white.

'Why does he owe you money? Did he borrow it from you?'

Aphra laughed. 'I don't have the kind of money to lend to great men like the Duke of Buckingham. No, I was in his service, you might say, and I ran up debts in my name while engaged in his affairs, which he promised faithfully to settle. He has not settled them.'

'I don't think he is a man of his word,' said Holcroft, as they walked away from the flowerbed. 'I don't think you will ever see your money. He promised me a goodly sum too, and I don't think he ever means to pay me.'

'You mean your wages?'

'No, he promised me a hundred pounds for . . . for something, for a special service.'

'Was it a betrayal? Did he ask you to betray somebody?'

Holcroft stopped dead. For the first time in their walk he looked directly into her brown eyes. How could she possibly have known?

'You don't have to tell me. He did it to me, too, asked me to betray somebody, a dear friend, to prove my absolute loyalty to him. I think he likes to do it. It demonstrates his power. He likes to make you forsake those whom you love, to break those bonds, so that you belong only to him.'

Holcroft said nothing.

Aphra said, 'So he owes each of us a goodly sum – how shall we make the noble Duke of Buckingham pay his debts?'

They continued their walk around the garden, following the stone-flagged path, neither saying anything, but Holcroft was aware that they had fallen exactly into step with each other, like the soldiers of the King's Foot Guards when they paraded in The Street in all their pomp. Together, they began a slow second circuit of the tulip garden. It seemed entirely natural that they should be walking together, talking together like this. Once again Holcroft was aware of the strange sensation that he already knew Mistress Behn from somewhere and they were more than acquaintances. In fact, he had the strongest feeling that they were already good, even intimate, friends.

'I know that if you want money from someone you must offer them something that they want in exchange,' said Holcroft.

'What do people want these days? I have no any idea any more. Love. Power. Revenge. What do you want?'

'I want to be a soldier,' said Holcroft immediately. He had no idea where the answer came from but he immediately knew it to be entirely true.

'If you had your money you could buy yourself a commission. I know a soldier, Colonel John Russell is his name, who could make you an ensign in his regiment for a hundred pounds.'

Holcroft thought about that for a while. He could scarcely imagine anything more wonderful.

'What do you want?' he asked.

'I want to stay out of the Marshalsea. I want to write wonderful plays, and maybe a wonderful romance or two as well, I want to be the toast of London. I want money and fame, and ease and contentment, and the love of a good man and a large house with servants, a fine carriage and horses and a lovely garden like this one. I want everything.' She kicked a stone in the path, which rattled across the paving stones. 'But what does our duke want? He is rich and powerful already. What can he really desire?'

They walked on a few more steps.

'I know what he wants,' Holcroft finally said. 'I know what he wants above all else.'

'And what is that?'

'He wants to destroy the Duke of Ormonde. He wants to be Lord Steward of the Household. He wants to be the most powerful man in the Three Kingdoms after the King. That's what my master truly wants.'

'Then that is what we shall offer him.'

In the booth in the corner of the Lamb Inn, Romford, the Thomas Bloods senior and junior, William Hunt, Joshua Parrot and Jenny Blaine were squashed around the ale-wet table and the remains of a goose pie. Blood had just finished giving a description of their reconnaissance of the Jewel House and their first encounter with Talbot Edwards and his family.

Parrot said: 'You say the bars are too thick to cut through?'

'They are an inch thick and made of hardened iron and mortared into the wall,' Blood said, shaking his head. 'And you could not saw or file through just one bar, you would need to cut half a dozen to be able to lift the cage away and get to all the jewels. Even cutting through the steel of the padlock would take hours of work – maybe half a night. This needs to be a quick in-and-out affair before Edwards is missed.'

'What about powder?' asked Parrot. 'A small charge attached to the bars against one wall?'

'The noise would bring the Tower guards running. And black powder is chancy stuff: too much and you'd blow the jewels to worthless fragments, too little and it doesn't shift the bars in the slightest. No, gentlemen, it has to be the key. We must take the key from him or persuade Edwards to open the cage door himself. It is the only way.'

'I could dally with him while you steal the key,' said Jenny.

'You are a good lass. But Mistress Edwards would never let you get anywhere near him alone. And I'm not sure the old man still has that much inclination for red-blooded adultery.'

They all sat in silence for a while. Blood cut himself a slice of pie and chewed meditatively for a while. Then he said, 'I do believe there is a way whereby we can get him to open that cage of his own free will: the essential element is his daughter. I never saw an uglier creature in my life, and of marriageable age with nary a suitor in sight. That, I believe, is his greatest weakness. The girl is the key that unlocks the treasure.'

Thursday 20 April, 1671

'The Lord High Admiral, His Grace the Duke of York,' intoned the footman, holding open the door to allow a tall, austere man in a golden periwig to march into the room.

'Your Majesty,' he said, bowing low to the figure in a plain blue robe seated at a small table drinking a cup of coffee and nibbling a tiny almond biscuit. 'You honour me with an audience.'

'Good day to you, James,' said the King, nodding affably to his brother. 'I don't think you really have to call me Majesty when we're alone. No need to stand on ceremony. Come, sit, have a cup of this most refreshing Arabian brew. It will set you up like nothing else.'

James frowned at him. 'Really, Charles, if we two do not observe the traditional forms of respect due to a monarch, how can we expect the rest of your subjects to do so?'

'The rest of my subjects are not with us, thank God. And if you don't sit down, take your wig off and have a hot cup of coffee and a biscuit, I'm going to issue you with a royal command to do so.'

James, Duke of York, looked around the Rose Room, so called because it looked out on to a private rose garden, which was decorated in salmon pink and scarlet with touches of gold, and saw that it was completely empty of life save for the King, looking faintly dishevelled as if he had just risen from somebody's bed, and two fat spaniels who were snoozing by the fire. He pulled off his wig and hung it on the back of his chair, sat down next to his brother, and scratched with happy relief at his thinning scalp while the King poured him out a cup of dark, fragrant liquid.

'How goes it at Chatham?' asked the King once they had both had a sip and he saw that James's shoulders had begun to drop. 'How go things with the rebuilding of my Royal Navy?'

'Slowly. Damnably slowly. In fact, it has almost come to a stand. The shipwrights have said they will do no more work on the new hulls this month until they are paid in full the wages owed them. The chandlers will no longer accept my notes of hand and half the seamen I had collected have returned to their fishing smacks and merchant vessels. The fleet will not put to sea this year, brother. Perhaps not the next either.'

'Is it just the money? Or is there another reason for the delay – a certain reluctance for this Dutch war?'

'It is mostly the lack of money. And from what I hear from Westminster, Parliament is in no mood to grant you any more subsidies. But it is true, my Chatham people do not truly want to wage another war against the Dutch. They call them our Protestant brothers and say they cannot be beaten at sea. After the Dutch raid on the Medway, that foul humiliation, I thought they would be eager for revenge but no – the men claim that France is our true foe and we should be at war with His Most Catholic Majesty not with these contumelious, heretical, God-damned cheese-mongers.'

'Calm yourself, brother, the delay is no matter anyway. We cannot go to war until the French are ready, and they are not. They must make their concordats with Munster and Cologne, for Louis gave his solemn word to the Holy Roman Emperor that he would not invade north through the Spanish Netherlands, and so he must take his armies around the side and attack from the east, and that means going through Liège, a fief of the Archbishop of Cologne. We have time, James, plenty of time to prepare. We can proceed just as slowly as we must. And I am sure you are clever enough to find a way to drive the ship-building forward.'

'There is no hope of any more money, then?'

'I can let you have a few thousand to quiet the worst of your creditors but no more. I mean to ask the East India Company for a loan of twenty thousand pounds specifically for the Navy but, in truth, I'm not hopeful.'

'What about the French money from the treaty?'

'It is gone, brother, all gone. My own creditors had it all.'

James stared gloomily into his coffee cup. 'I prayed for divine help this morning. I took the Eucharist from Father Simon and made my confession. I beseeched God Almighty to help us in this struggle . . .'

'Have a care, brother. It is not for me to dictate to you on private matters of the soul but you know as well as I do the mood of the people. If it were generally known that you adhere to the old faith, and that you regularly attend Mass and avoid the Anglican ceremony, you would make things far more difficult for me. England is a Protestant nation. It has been this last age or more. And I am the head of the Church of England, the Defender of the Faith, as you well know.'

'And you know too that the Protestant faith is a false, damned, heretical creed. You know in your heart that here is only one true Christian faith, one holy Catholic Church. Only Rome has the authority of the succession of St Peter: "On this rock, I shall build my Church," said Our Lord Jesus Christ.'

The King said nothing for a few moments. 'I invited you to be at your ease with me, brother, so I shall ignore your last remarks. But I give you warning that you must keep your faith to yourself. I might well be compelled to send you from me – to France, say – quite against my wishes, if you do not govern your tongue in this regard. I say this not as a threat but as an expression of the realities of this realm. In their current mood, the English will not have a King who is sympathetic to the old faith – after Queen Mary and the Oxford Martyrs and Guido Fawkes and all of the bloody wrangling over their souls for the past hundred years. They will not stand for it. Not now. Perhaps one day, if God wills it, but not this year, nor the next. If, by your indiscretions, I am forced to choose between the preservation of my throne or my brother's position at court I know which I shall choose.'

Holcroft sat on the hard stone bench in the Privy Garden and contemplated the sundial. He had a thick slice of bread and a piece of cheese in his hand in lieu of dinner – he had fled the more substantial cooked dinner laid out in the clerks' hall, pleading an engagement, and begged the kitchens for this simple meal instead – and he chewed slowly as he admired the spheres of coloured glass gleaming in the sunlight on their moveable arms. The gilt-work on the dials themselves was particularly brilliant today and he knew that it was almost exactly two of the clock even before the church bells of St Martin's confirmed his knowledge. Yet today, for once, the sundial was failing in its duty to soothe his soul.

The sundial represented the natural order of things in the heavens and on earth: the sun at the centre of things, like the King, and the planets in motion around the sun, like the King's ministers and all the great men of England. There was a natural hierarchy in the affairs of men, at least to Holcroft's mind. The King was served by his lords, the lords were served by their attendants, who in turn also had their own servants. England had been governed like this for a thousand years – save for the dozen years after the last King had been executed and replaced by the lord protector, who was merely a King by another name. Each man owed loyalty up the chain to the very top, where the King owed his own loyalty to God, who had anointed him sovereign. Loyalty flowed up the chain, and justice flowed down from the powerful to those who served them. And yet what happened if those with power were unjust? What happened when those in authority did not keep their word, when they promised rewards for service but did not honour those promises? Was it right for the servant to withhold his loyalty if he did not receive justice?

Holcroft knew what his father would have said. Blood had often argued that his chains of loyal service had been broken, that the age-old agreement between master and man was voided if injustice were done – as was the case when they lost their lands at Sarney – and moreover that it was a man's right under God to take suitable recompense from those who wronged him.

Holcroft was not so sure. He wanted to serve the duke with all his heart and to be compensated fairly for that loyal service. But Buckingham had made him betray his friend Jack – between the promise of money and the threat of dismissal, His Grace had forced Holcroft into soiling the bond of loyalty between friends. And when he had refused Holcroft his promised reward he had shown himself to be unjust. If the duke was unjust, did that mean that Holcroft had no further obligation to be loyal to him?

Holcroft looked at the sundial anew. He saw that some of the gilt was peeling from the steel arms; several of the glass spheres were clouding on the inside. The enamel plaques that depicted the King and Queen were speckled with bird excrement. The sundial was imperfect. It was designed, he now saw, to show how the universe ought to be, not as it truly was.

Holcroft made up his mind. He got up from the stone seat, stretched his arms to the sky, turned his back on the sundial and started walking towards the Cockpit. He would meet Aphra Behn again. She was a good woman; he could sense it. She was a friend. He would do whatever she asked of him.

The chain of his loyalty to the duke was broken.

Tuesday 25 April, 1671

At a little after noon, Parson Ayliffe, once more in his black coat, white collar and golden spectacles, knocked at the cheerful blue door at the top of the steps leading up to the Irish Tower. It was about the time a well-to-do gentleman might be sitting down to his dinner, as Ayliffe well knew. The door swung open and Elizabeth Edwards stood on the threshold, drying her wet, red hands on a pinafore, blushing and curtseying all at the same time, and finally ushering the tall, handsome man of the cloth into her home.

Ayliffe had a parcel in his hand, a bulky item wrapped in brown paper and tied neatly with a piece of string. He bore his parcel up the stairs and into the parlour where he shook hands cordially with the assistant keeper and enthusiastically accepted his grudging offer of a small glass of brandy.

It must be noted that Edwards had a reserved tone in his voice as he greeted Ayliffe – he had not expected to see the parson again, assuming that in the six days which had passed since his last visit he had returned to whatever that village-by-the-sea in Essex was called, perhaps never to be seen again. It could not be said that he was glad to see this man of God – the last visit had been somewhat alarming. He had fretted afterwards about the sudden illness that Ayliffe's lovely wife seemed to have contracted in the Jewel House and, while he was fairly sure it was not the plague, one could not be too careful. It might very well be some other kind of pestilence. The last thing he needed was paying guests who came to view the jewels dying of a mysterious malaise shortly afterwards. So Edwards looked carefully at Ayliffe, trying to detect any signs of ill health.

It was also nearly time for his dinner and he had had acquaintances in the past who showed up at his door a few minutes before the time for the meal in the expectation of being invited to join in the repast. So his greeting for Ayliffe was more warily cordial than genuinely joyful.

The tall parson seemed not to notice the chilliness of his welcome. He spoke happily and at some length about his previous visit, praising Edwards's knowledge about the jewels and regalia and marvelling at his command of their history. When he finally allowed himself to notice that Edwards was becoming restive, glancing at the door that led into his dining room more and more frequently, he said, 'But I must not prattle away all day, sir. You will be wanting your dinner soon, I am sure, and I do not wish to intrude. So let me tell you that I am come to you merely to express my sincere gratitude at the help that you and your lady wife were able to afford my Jennifer – she is quite recovered, I'm sure you will be glad to know – and to give you this small token of my esteem; to wit, a small gift for Mistress Edwards from two grateful gentlefolk. We feel that you and your good lady preserved Jennifer's life and we are both deeply thankful.'

Edwards mumbled his own thanks and said there was really no need, no need at all, while he fumbled with the knotted string. When he eventually opened the brown paper parcel, he was genuinely lost for words – for inside were four pairs of beautiful white kidskin ladies' gloves, with tiny seed pearl buttons and delicate gold edging.

'Sarah, Sarah, come and see this. What an extraordinary coincidence. I was looking at some pairs just like this only a couple of weeks ago. Sir, you are most kind. Most kind!'

As his wife came into the room, he showed her the gloves and as she admired them, making little coos of delight, Ayliffe said: 'Well, I really must be about my business. My thanks to you and your good lady once more. But might I ask a final boon, one last favour? Could you direct me to a nearby chophouse, not too expensive, somewhere clean and God-fearing. It has been a vexing morning and I feel badly in need of some refreshment.

'A chophouse, oh no! No, no, no!' cried Mistress Edwards. 'You must dine with us, if only to allow us to thank you for your most generous gift. Elizabeth, go tell the maid to lay another place at the table. The Reverend Ayliffe will be joining us for dinner.'

'Such honest Christian kindness,' said Ayliffe. 'It fair touches my heart. Perhaps I might be allowed to say grace?'

Holcroft and Aphra Behn met at Pettigrew's chophouse on the Strand, which was convenient for both of them being about equal distance from White Hall and Aphra's lodgings in St Thomas Street. Aphra's draughty garret was at the top of a narrow, decrepit house just off Drury Lane and perilously close to the slums of St Giles – a collection of nameless alleys and slumped, sullen hovels, which housed some of the poorest inhabitants of London. St Giles was a lawless place of poverty and despair, of casual murder, rape and thievery; a place that no respectable person would dream of entering and few would even dare to live on its doorstep unless, like Aphra, they were driven there by a lack of money and the necessity to be close to the playhouse in Lincoln's Inn Fields, half a mile to the east.

It was the second time they had met at this venue since their walk in the tulip garden of the Cockpit six days ago. This time Aphra had left Betterton and his troupe rehearsing *Twelfth Night*; Holcroft was making his usual daily delivery of the duke's letters to the General Letter Office in the City, where he also collected any incoming mail addressed to His Grace.

The Duke of Buckingham was perfectly happy to send his everyday, common-or-garden correspondence through the offices of the Royal Mail – but anything confidential, which was usually written in his personal code anyway, he had his own well-mounted private couriers deliver. He knew that the postmaster general, Lord Arlington, perhaps his nearest rival for power after the Duke of Ormonde, had his post office clerks open and read his correspondence and he made sure that he often included snippets of information that would seriously mislead or just plain baffle them.

Holcroft arrived later than the appointed hour, slightly breathless as he had run all the way from the City, but Aphra was sanguine about his tardiness. She had been regaling herself with mutton chops and mint sauce, buttered parsnips and a jug of claret while she waited. She was just finishing her meal when Holcroft sat down and, after dabbing the mutton grease from her lips with a napkin, she smiled prettily and asked him politely how he did.

Holcroft had no time for pleasantries. He was expected back at the Cockpit within the hour and he ignored her question and said: 'I've found the man who will serve as our letter seller – as you asked me to. Someone in the Duke of Ormonde's circle, you said. I still don't understand why. But I can arrange for him to deliver a note to me at the Cockpit, and to be seen doing so. That's what you wanted, wasn't it?'

'Yes. That's perfect,' said Aphra, pouring Holcroft a glass of wine. 'And who is this helpful fellow, may I ask?'

'He's called James Pratt. He is Ormonde's senior page and he owes me a sum that he cannot pay. It is four pounds, twelve shillings and sixpence. He lost it to me at Trump yesterday evening.'

'Very good – he can bring the note to you but that should be the extent of his involvement, I think. Tell him if he delivers the note, his debt is cleared but do not tell him any more than that. From then on we shall say to Buckingham that Pratt insists that he will deal only with you. Agreed?'

'Yes.' Holcroft took a sip of his wine. His stomach growled at the wafting scents of cooked meat that filled the dim, wood-panelled room.

'Do you have time for a plate of chops?'

'No.' He took a piece of dry bread from the basket on the table and began to chew it.

Aphra watched him eat for a moment then said, 'Tell me, Holly, have you had time to read the copy of *The Amorous Prince* that I left with you?'

'I read it.'

'And did you like it?'

'Not much. It is filled with the same preposterous goings-on as the last one. If anything, it is worse.'

Aphra laughed, again it was a genuine eruption of amusement. 'That is a relief. Much as it wounds me to hear you say it, I'm glad you did not care for it. If you'd said that you liked it, if you'd tried to please me, to flatter me, I'd have known you were playing me false. Now I know I can trust you.'

'Did you not trust me before?'

'I hope you will forgive me. But my former occupation has made me distrustful of nearly everyone, even my friends.'

Holcroft said nothing for a while. Then his strange mind, as it often did, made one of those long bounds of intuition.

'You were the Duke of Buckingham's spy in Versailles. You are the confidential agent who signs herself Astraea.'

'Well done. I wondered if you would make the link. But I am no longer Astraea. His Grace dispensed with my services – remember? He was dissatisfied with my work, he said. My erstwhile assistant, a most unsavoury fellow called Jupon, now has that dubious honour. I am certain that he will do a far better job than I ever did.'

'The duke wanted you to identify two Englishmen who paid a visit to someone called Madame this time last year,' said Holcroft, very pleased with himself for making the Versailles connection. 'I wrote those messages to you myself.'

'Did you now? Then you might like to know that I did identify the two men for our master: they were Lord Arlington and Sir Thomas

Clifford. I was dismissed because I could not discover exactly *why* they had so many secret meetings with Madame – who you should know was the King's sister Henrietta, Duchess of Orleans. She died last summer. Some say she was poisoned. I do not believe that was the case. Her stomach had troubled her for many months. But I still don't know why they met with her.'

'It has something to do with the Treaty of Dover and our promise to go to war with the Dutch in exchange for a vast sum from King Louis.'

'Undoubtedly. And that brings me to the point I wish to discuss with you concerning our own scheme to extract our due from Buckingham.'

Holcroft looked attentively at Aphra.

'The Duke of Ormonde is out of favour because he backed the wrong horse,' she told him. 'He tried to influence the King to abide by the previous treaty with the Protestant Dutch and the Swedes and ally against the French. He lost – and Buckingham and the French camp won. And, as far as we know, all of Ormonde's dealings with the Dutch, with young Prince William of Orange and the Grand Pensionary Johan de Witt have been regular and honest, no hint of treason, no skulduggery, he was just loyally exploring different avenues of policy for his King.'

'What is a grand pensionary? He sounds like a very ancient gentleman.'

'It means the most important official of the Dutch Republic, the chief minister of its government, if you like. The equivalent of our Buckingham, or perhaps the Duke of Ormonde, in England.'

Holcroft took another piece of bread and nodded to indicate that she should resume. Aphra looked around the semi-empty room and lowered her voice to a whisper: 'Ostensibly, Ormonde did nothing wrong in his dealings with the Dutch. But what if we were to suggest that he did do something very bad, something secret, something treasonous, and that your friend James Pratt, his senior but very much indebted page, had the letter to prove it? Do you not think that His Grace the Duke of Buckingham would wish to possess that letter, spend a few hundred pounds, a thousand even, to have in his hands the means to destroy his greatest rival?'

Parson Ayliffe had just finished enjoying a lavish dinner at the table of Talbot Edwards and his family in the Irish Tower. A soup of wild grouse and one of leeks and cream had been served and then removed and replaced with a fricassee of rabbits and chickens, a small barrel of oysters, a cold ox tongue and a dish of roasted pigeons and one of boiled lobsters. Finally they had eaten an apple tart, a gooseberry tart and a big round yellow cheese. They had drunk ale, sack and claret and now, comfortably full, but without the company of Mistress Edwards and the ill-favoured Elizabeth, who had withdrawn to the other room, Ayliffe was sipping a glass of port conversing amiably with Edwards on subjects of mutual interest and concern.

They had discussed the extraordinary rise of the value of the stock of the East India Company, but both agreed that it was bound to come thumping down any day now. The future, they felt, lay with those bold adventurers of the Royal African Company: such enormous profits to be made in slaves, and a seemingly endless demand from the plantations in the Americas! With a certain frisson of illicit excitement they discussed rumours of secret Catholics in high places – Edwards suggesting, somewhat disloyally, there were men of evil design and Popish persuasion very near the King himself, even in his own family. But he drew back from naming names. Then they spent a happy half-hour disparaging the morals and habits of the young: something close to Edward's heart – although he did make an exception of his son Wythe, who was a good and dutiful fellow and a fine brave soldier.

'I wish the young men of my own family were such noble paragons,' said Ayliffe, drawing on his pipe and releasing a cloud of fragrant smoke. 'My nephew, Thomas, for instance, is a very sad example of that generation. He cannot stick to anything at all. No bottom – that is his problem; although he is a very engaging and amiable soul and an honest Christian. He is a great one for his books, loves to read more than any fellow I ever met. However, when I arranged a position for him as a clerk in William Scott's emporium in Charing Cross Road, he left after a week saying that reading the columns of figures all day made his head ache. Next, and at considerable outlay of emoluments and so forth, I arranged a place for him with the Duke of Buckingham as a confidential clerk – but he did not find that quite congenial either. I do not know what to do with him. I am quite at my wits' end.'

'Could you not do something for him in the Church? I should have thought that, his being so clever and bookish, he might make a scholar at one of the universities and that might lead to ordination and a parish of his own, perhaps.'

'It might, if I could induce him to attend the university and submit to their laws and practices. He can be a lazy devil. If neither my wife nor I rouse him, we have sometimes found him still abed at noon. The problem is that his late father, my brother Edwin, God rest his soul, left him a decent sum of money in his will, which yields him an income of two or even three hundred a year. This is under my guardianship for now, and that of two of his father's friends, and I give him only a small allowance at present. But he knows well that when he turns twenty-five the whole sum will be his unequivocally, and that if he can wait out a few years he need never toil for his living again. I understand his point of view. He was born to a gentleman's estate and there is no use my trying to force him to undertake some enterprise if he does not choose to do so. But I do wish he would choose to do something. Anything. I worry so about him. Jennifer says that he should find a nice young gentlewoman and get married. And, on the whole, I concur with her views. Marriage can have such a salutary effect on a young person, don't you agree, Edwards?'

An image of the delightful Jennifer Ayliffe filled Edwards's mind. Followed by another equally charming thought.

'I worry, too, for my own sweet daughter Elizabeth,' said Edwards. 'She has been very strictly brought up but, now that she is a grown woman, I sometimes catch her giving wanton looks at the young men of the Tower guard, and I greatly fear for her soul . . .'

Edwards let his words tail away, looking at Ayliffe in a speculative manner. But the parson seemed entirely unaware of the bait his companion had laid out so enticingly. He needed a nudge.

'She is a very biddable girl, so very amiable, do you not think so, reverend? Not a looker, no pretensions to beauty, that's for sure. But nice capacious hips and a good girl, well-schooled. A proper Christian, oh very devout, says her prayers good as gold every night and morning, church twice on Sundays. But she needs a good man, a husband – someone who can master her, teach her the world's ways and give her the security she needs.'

Edwards wondered if he had gone too far.

But Ayliffe still seemed determined to be dense about the matter at hand. He sucked on his pipe and blew out a blue plume.

Edwards, never one to spoil a ship for a ha'p'orth of tar, blurted, 'If only my Elizabeth could find a good young gentleman to marry.'

Finally, Ayliffe relented. 'I wonder,' he said slowly, 'hmmm, I wonder if my nephew Thomas might take a fancy to her. What do you think, Edwards? Do you think the boy might take a shine to your Elizabeth? It might be the solution we have both been seeking for our youngsters. I would certainly support the match for my own part, if you and your good lady wife were willing, and I would happily sign over the boy's money to him before he comes of age, that is, if he were safely married off to a young woman of good family such as your Lizzie. What say you, Edwards? Do you think we could arrange a meeting between the two young persons and see whether they find each other at all congenial?'

'What a splendid idea, Ayliffe!' said Edwards, doing his best to feign surprise. 'Do you know, I think that might answer very well indeed. Certainly something might be arranged. Perhaps you would be kind enough to dine with us again in a week or so, and perhaps you might like to bring your nephew with you.'

Wednesday 3 May, 1671

Robert Westbury looked down the length of the long table in the servants' hall and noted the tall figure of Holcroft Blood sitting at the far end, placidly eating a bowl of soup. Perhaps surprisingly, their paths had rarely crossed in the past six months: Holcroft no longer slept in the pages' dormitory, he was quartered with the other clerks in a suite of rooms on the far side of the courtyard and he usually ate in the clerks' hall or alone in the kitchens. Today, it being Albert St John's birthday, Holcroft had condescended to join them in the servants' hall at Albert's request to partake of their meagre feast. Westbury may not have spoken to Holcroft more than once or twice but he had seen the boy many times around the Cockpit and about the palace and he was hardly unaware of his activities.

As he watched the tall boy in the black coat sucking up soup from his spoon like a starving peasant, he was a little shocked by how strong his hatred was for the confidential clerk: his cuts and bruises from the fight outside the gate had healed long ago and he had suffered no discernible loss in status in the household as a result of the fracas. But the very sight of Holcroft set his teeth on edge. The awkward clod had no social graces whatsoever; his family, so far as Westbury could gather, were a set of penniless rogues and ne'er-do-wells. He seemed to care nothing for any other living human being except that pretty-boy soldier Churchill and yet the duke treated him as if he were the son of God himself, making him privy to all his papers, allowing him to speak up at meetings with his superiors.

Westbury had been in the duke's service more than three years now and he had never been shown the marks of favour that Holcroft had been given from the very first day. Westbury ran the pages' dormitory efficiently, keeping order among the boys, making sure they did not disturb the household with their high spirits and that there was always one of them at least to attend to the duke's needs day or night. And his reward was to be ignored, passed over, treated like a mere child. He would be sixteen this year – a grown man – and he had nothing to show for his three years of fetching and carrying. He had not received any significant gratuities or gifts of any kind; he had not been appointed to any remunerative post within the workings of White Hall. The post of assistant cellerer to the King had been vacant for some months, was within the gift of the duke and, despite the many broad hints dropped by Westbury in Buckingham's presence about his knowledge of fine wines, garnered at his father the Earl of Westbury's lavish board, the post had gone to the son of a tavern-keeper who had obliged the duke in his youth in some obscure way during the civil wars of the last generation. And Westbury's father, the fourteenth earl, had not helped him in the slightest. He had secured him the post of page with Buckingham three years ago and then seemed to have forgotten all about him. Robert's misfortune was that he was the third son, and fifth child of his parents. His eldest brother Alan was the heir and lived in Nottinghamshire at the family seat; the second son Thomas stood waiting to inherit should the heir die before his father; and Robert had been banished to London to make his own way in the world. It was time for a change. And Westbury thought he could see a way of bringing down his enemy and advancing his own position within the duke's household at the same time. He had allowed the lack-mannered guttersnipe to roam unchecked for too long now. Everybody had something to hide – from pilfering to outright peculation. It was time to discover what Mister Holcroft Blood was hiding, and make him pay for it.

'Give our guest some more wine, Fox Cub,' he called down the table. 'His glass is nearly empty.'

When the French boy had filled Holcroft's beaker, he lifted his own. 'Here's to your very good health, Mister Blood,' he said, genially, 'we do not often have the pleasure of your company down here in the servants' hall but you are most welcome, sir, most welcome indeed at our humble board.'

Holcroft stared up the length of the table at the blond fellow smiling at him, a raised glass in his hand. He had not forgotten their fight on his first day in White Hall but neither had he thought about it much during the past few months. Westbury was being friendly. Good. He, too, was happy to be friendly. There was no advantage to being enemies, as far as Holcroft could see, when they served the same master. Let bygones be bygones.

'And your good health, too, sir,' he said.

They both smiled and drank.

Thursday 4 May, 1671

Holcroft and Aphra were meeting for a third time in Pettigrew's, but this time partaking of no more than a mid-morning dish of coffee. Once again Holcroft was taking time out from his daily run to the General Letter Office and in his leather satchel he had a sheaf of crackling papers which he had collected for the duke in the City.

'Here it is,' said Aphra, handing him a dirty note, a sheet of cheap blue paper folded twice, but unsealed. 'Don't put it in with the other letters. Give it to Buckingham yourself.'

Then she handed him another folded blue note, identical to the first. 'Give this one to your friend Pratt and have him deliver it to you at the Cockpit when folk are watching. Make sure you don't mix the two up.'

'Can I read it?' asked Holcroft, a little timidly, holding up the first note. Now that he suddenly found himself plunged into this unfamiliar world of intrigue, he felt bashful, unsettled. The physical object in his hand made the crime they were attempting suddenly real. They were truly attempting to steal money from his master, one of the most powerful men in the realm.

'I don't think I shall allow you to. You are such a severe critic of my writing you might bring me to tears.'

Holcroft looked into her face, confused. Her words contained a wholly different message to her expression. She was smiling broadly at him.

'You are making a joke,' he said accusingly.

'I am, forgive me; yes, I was indulging myself at your expense. Please read it and tell me the worst.'

Holcroft opened the first blue note and read silently:

To His Grace, the Duke of Buckingham, greetings.

*I hope you will forgive the grossness of my effrontery in penning this note
to you, sir, given my lowly station in life and your supremely elevated one,
but I do so out of the deepest respect and admiration for your good self and
because I must in all good conscience communicate with you on this matter
which touches on the security of the kingdom and the continued reign of his
most glorious Majesty King Charles the Second.*

'I like the beginning,' said Holcroft, looking up at Aphra. 'Most
respectful and obsequious – the duke will relish that.'

'Read on, it gets better!'

Holcroft read:

In my capacity as assistant secretary to His Grace the Duke of Ormonde . . .

Holcroft stopped. 'He's not assistant secretary, he's the senior page.
Why would he not know his own position in the household?'

'People sometimes like to make themselves sound grander than
they really are. It makes them feel better about their drab lives. And
they sometimes think it makes other people think better of them
too. But don't worry about that, just read on.'

Holcroft lowered his head again.

*. . . assistant secretary to His Grace the Duke of Ormonde, I was privy
to discussions of a very sensitive nature that took place in November of
the year past between His Grace and Prince William of Orange. During
these discussions, which took place in conditions of strictest secrecy, I
happened to be resting on a window seat in the duke's private study, half
asleep and covered by a thick curtain, and I heard every word. I heard
them discuss with the utmost frankness the King of England's lack of
legitimate issue, the unpopularity of his brother and heir James, Duke of
York, and his unsuitability to reign after Charles's death because of his*

secret adherence to the Papist faith. They then talked about the possibility of William marrying James's Protestant daughter Mary Stuart and, with the military assistance of the Duke of Ormonde and his friends in the army, assuming the throne of England on Charles's death! As well as hearing this black treason with my own ears, I have in my possession a signed copy of a letter, written by His Grace to Prince William, which makes open reference to this unnatural arrangement. It is proof of His Grace's treachery towards our gracious King and his royal line and I felt that I must in all conscience share it with you as the Crown's most loyal servant. However, before handing over the letter, I shall require a trifling sum of money, merely a thousand pounds in gold, to be delivered to me or to a place of my choosing. This money is to provide for me in the future, as this duty that I now undertake purely out of loyalty to my King will surely cost me my position in His Grace's household, if it is discovered, if not my very life.

I entrust this note to my good and trusty friend Holcroft Blood, who will act for me in this matter as, for my own personal safety, I wish to have no further communications with Your Grace until the gold is paid and this infamous letter is delivered into your hand.

I remain, sir, your most humble and obedient servant,

James Pratt.

Holcroft looked at Aphra. 'It is prettily written. I could almost hear Pratt speaking those very words. But is it not a little far-fetched? A grand English nobleman plotting to make a young Dutchman King of England?'

'So long as he were a staunch Protestant, there are many people of my acquaintance who would make the Devil himself the King of England before they would accept another Catholic on the throne.'

Holcroft nodded. 'And do you really think the Duke of Buckingham will pay over a thousand pounds for this false letter?'

'We will have to wait and see. This is merely the first step in what may well be a long and difficult game. But, yes, if we keep our nerve, and do not falter in our resolve, I think it stands a very good chance of success.'

From the arched window on the top storey of the Irish Tower, three sets of Edwards' eyes looked west out over the courtyard and watched as two gentlemen approached on foot. One of the gentlemen was long-legged, thick-chested and dressed in the traditional sober black of a man of the cloth, with gold-rimmed spectacles glinting from his long nose; the second was younger, slimmer, not quite as tall but also dressed modestly. Both men wore their own brown hair long, but well combed and clubbed neatly at the back of the neck.

'Oh, he's very handsome,' said Elizabeth. 'Quite the refined young country gentleman.'

'So that is what three hundred pounds a year looks like,' murmured Sarah to her husband. Then: 'Go and shift your dress, Lizzie, that royal blue is far too strong for your first meeting. Go, put on the plain brown one with the high collar and wash all that ceruse and cochineal off your face. He looks like a sensitive, delicate boy and we don't want to frighten him off.'

'The family resemblance is very strong,' said Talbot Edwards. 'I wonder if Ayliffe and his dead brother were twins.'

As Elizabeth ran off to change, Sarah looked at her husband, who was beaming happily. She flicked some stray tobacco ash off his coat lapel and very slightly rearranged the fold of his white silk neckerchief.

'Don't drink too much, dear,' she told him. 'And don't talk about all the Papists at court, you know it makes you quarrelsome.'

Edwards nodded absently. 'Do you think we could manage a June wedding, my dear? I would like Wythe to be here to see his sister married off. He wrote to say he'd be here in a few days, but he only has a month's furlough and must be back with his regiment in Flanders by mid-June.'

'A June wedding – God save us, Talbot, you will spoil the whole thing by counting your chickens. Let us meet the young gentleman and let him get to know Lizzie a little first. Then we'll make our plans.'

It was Holcroft's practice that spring, whenever he found himself with little in the way of duties to perform for the Duke of Buckingham, to visit the small beer buttery in the northeast corner of the palace and avail himself of a mug of good Kentish ale and a honey bun from the bakehouse next door and sit at a table beside the long windows and look out at the river traffic on the wide brown stretch of the Thames. He was rarely troubled there by other members of the duke's household, since the buttery was almost as far from the Cockpit as it was possible to get without leaving White Hall and, after he had rebuffed the initially friendly bletherings of the ale-wife and her crew, they usually took his penny payment and left him at his table in peace.

If he was not totally consumed by his own thoughts, there was always something to see as he sat there, sipping his bitter nutty ale and chewing his sticky bun. Wherries plied to and fro from the White Hall Palace Stairs, fifty yards to his right, their powerful oarsmen bringing brilliantly dressed lords and ladies in bright silks and satins, some of them known to Holcroft, up – or downstream or across from the Surrey side. The Scotland Dock, a narrow channel between high, weed-slimed wooden pilings, was only thirty yards to his left and beyond that was the wharf where goods were unloaded and stacked by gangs of bare-chested, sweating labourers, their thick white arms marked with strange blurry blue tattoos. This was the landing place where White Hall received its provisions, brought by boat and barge from other wharves in London, such as the fresh fish from Billingsgate Dock, down beyond London Bridge, or from further afield, such as the big slow coal barges, with their huge red triangular sails, that had lumbered all the way south from Newcastle.

Today, while the Duke of Buckingham was in conference with Lord Arlington, Sir Thomas Clifford and Lord Ashley, the Chancellor of the Exchequer, and like to be there wrangling over the King's finances for hours, Holcroft watched as a barge piled high with stacked cords of wood was unloaded. He had the private satisfaction of watching as the fat bundles of kindling, used in almost every fireplace in the palace, were lifted out of the ship by a pair of derricks, stacked into wheelbarrows and carts on the wharf and were taken out of sight and round to the Wood Yard. Merely by turning in his chair and looking out of the open door, he could watch the very same bundles arriving in the Wood Yard behind him and being unloaded from the same wheelbarrows and stacked in rows against the wall.

As he turned back to the long window, he saw a small wherry passing not twenty yards from his nose on the other side of the glass, making for the White Hall Palace Stairs. The wherryman stroked his way powerfully along against the flow of the river and Holcroft noticed a fine lady in an enormous sun hat sitting uncomfortably in the bow: it was Barbara Villiers, Duchess of Cleveland, magnificent in scarlet satins under a green boat cloak, and beside her sat the dark, pinched-faced maid. By chance, Holcroft and Barbara each looked directly into the other's eyes as they passed. Holcroft felt a lurch of guilt as he recalled the episode more than two weeks earlier when he had burst into her chambers. But Barbara smiled brilliantly at him, a gleam of near-white teeth in a carmine slash of a mouth, raised a hand and gave him a little waggle of her gloved fingers.

Too late, Holcroft turned away, blushing hotly. And he stared down at the crumbs of his honey bun on the table for several minutes, making patterns in his mind with the individual fragments until he was sure that she must have passed by. Looking up, he just glimpsed her being handed out of the wherry at the Stairs by a squat man in a leather jerkin and being followed by her grim maid, before she disappeared from sight into the Palace.

It was not that he disliked Barbara Villiers, nor was he over-awed by her rank and wealth, but she made him feel distinctly uncomfortable every time they met. She fascinated him: images of her naked body, the languorous violet eyes and slow smile had haunted him since their last awful encounter. He knew that he wanted her and yet he also knew that she was untouchable, both as the lover of Jack Churchill, his friend, and as the mistress of the King. It was not that he was virgin-pure: he had awkwardly tumbled several girls in the back alleys and stables of Shoreditch. But he found love confusing. The girls had been willing enough at first but after the fucking they seemed to want something from him, some token, some change in his behaviour towards them. He had no idea what they wanted and, when the love-making was done with, he was inclined to forget all about them and carry on with whatever he had been doing before. Barbara was different, however. Her soul, or whatever the spirit that animated her, was terrifyingly powerful – it sucked him in and repelled him at the same time. He wanted her but he could never allow himself to have her. But did *she* understand that he could never come into her bed, no matter how much he might want to?

He finished his pint of ale, swept the crumbs into his hand and dumped them into a bucket for the ale-wife's pigs, wiped the table clean for the next drinker and was about to leave the small beer buttery and head back to the Cockpit, when the Duchess of Cleveland walked through the door.

'My dear, don't tell me you were about to leave. I have come here most especially to speak with you.'

The duchess took Holcroft by the elbow and led him to a table in the centre of the room, waving and calling merrily to the ale-wife to bring them sustenance. The maid stayed sullenly by the open door, like the soldiers on guard duty at the White Hall gatehouse, and watched Holcroft across the space between them with dark, suspicious eyes.

'So tell me, my dear Mister Blood, how do you do?'

Holcroft was saved from answering by the arrival of the ale jug. The ale-wife poured out two cups and duchess took a mouthful, grimaced and put the cup back down on the table. Holcroft drank his in a single draft.

'My dear boy, are you quite well?' said Barbara, putting a soft hand on Holcroft's. 'You seem very solemn today?'

He found himself mumbling that he had a lot on his mind.

'I too have been thinking a good deal – I am concerned about our dear friend Jack. Since that unfortunate encounter with the King's visit the day you came to see me – you know all about what happened, yes?'

Holcroft nodded.

'Well, since then, Jack is quite out of favour at court – all over that silly misunderstanding between the King and myself. The King gave Jack an almighty thrashing in the tennis court the next day, quite humiliated him, but it seems that Charles still bears a grudge against the poor boy. He has set his face against giving him any sign of royal favour and, as for advancement – well, he can forget about that for the time being. Charles is behaving badly, and while I have tried to reason with him, he can be quite obstinate. And I have not seen hide nor hair of Jack since. I worry for him. Have you seen him about the palace in recent days?'

Barbara picked up her ale cup, looked at the scummy brown liquid and set it back down on the table.

'I have not seen him since that day either,' Holcroft told her.

'Well, I know that you two are the greatest of friends so, next time you see him, will you give him some advice from me?'

Holcroft said nothing.

'Will you tell him that all avenues are closed to him in White Hall. If he seeks preferment, he must look for it away from the court. There will be war with the Dutch, and while I dread to think of my beautiful Jack charging into the cannon's mouth, there are opportunities for advancement for young officers who prove their mettle on the battlefield. Dead men's boots must be filled, after all. And if he were to come back from the war covered in glory, well, something might be arranged. But, for the moment, there's nothing for him here. Will you tell him?'

'I will tell him if I see him,' said Holcroft, and he managed a smile for the lady. He imagined himself a dashing officer, heading off to war and coming back, scarred and stern, covered in glory. Perhaps then something might be arranged for him too.

'There's my lovely boy,' said Barbara, smiling back at him. 'But enough talk of Jack. Tell me about yourself, tell me when you are going to come and visit me? You know very well where my rooms are.'

'I'm not going to sleep with you.'

Barbara stared at him in shock. 'I wasn't aware that I'd asked you to,' she said. Suddenly she was very angry. It was as if a spark had been struck in a pile of black powder: 'Just who in God's name do you think you are? I did not invite you into my bed. I was merely being friendly. And how dare you say no to me, anyway; you, a servant, a jumped-up page. As if I would sully my body with your greasy touch. Good day, sir. Good day to you, you filthy, gutter-born, importunate poltroon.'

The Duchess of Cleveland rose. She gave him a gorgon's glare and swept both the ale cups off the table with a single blow of her right arm and, while the echoes of the crashing pottery were still dying away, she marched, chin high, back straight, out of the buttery and into Wood Yard.

It had been a magnificent dinner. Thomas Ayliffe had proved to be a most well-bred young man, polite to his seniors, moderate in his speech, and seeming not at all haughty or sensible of his wealth; in fact, quite down to earth. Mistress Edwards approved of his hearty appetite, Mister Edwards applauded his fine, fierce views on the growing numbers of highwaymen that plagued the King's roads – they should all be scragged from the nearest tree the moment they were caught, the thieving bastards – and Lizzie was already half in love with his dark, dangerous looks and air of silent reserve.

Tom had said little after his humorous remarks about highwaymen, as he had received a very painful kick in the shin from his father under the table and a significant warning look. After that he had contented himself with eating until his waistcoat buttons protested and in paying a few compliments to his hosts, drinking their health from time to time. He had been extremely nervous to begin with, knowing that a false slip would bring the wrath of his father down on his head. But after a few glasses of claret, he had unwound and found that, in spite of the circumstances, he was enjoying himself. The girl was perfectly appalling, of course, that long furry eyebrow gave her a distinctly feral look, but he had not been expecting a beauty. And the more he drank, the more he found himself able to smile at her and even to engage her in conversation – or at least try to.

'Are you fond of dancing, Miss Edwards?' he had said to Lizzie as the saddle of mutton was brought in.

'Oh Lizzie is ever such a good dancer, isn't she, Talbot,' said Mistress Edwards, who had taken a good amount of wine herself.

'Such grace and rhythm, such a shapely ankle – ooh, but I shouldn't be saying such things to a young gentleman. Whatever must you think?' Mistress Edwards simpered horribly and mashed her bull-dog lips with her napkin.

The conversation languished for a while until Parson Ayliffe took up the threads of a discussion with Edwards about the scandalous London price of sugar compared with its value in the Caribbean.

After a while, Tom tried again: 'Tell me, Miss Edwards, are you fond of sea air? The air in Essex where we live is bracing, most health-giving.'

Again Mistress Edwards answered for her: 'Oh the sea air always brings out Lizzie's complexion in the most wonderful way. Last year we paid a visit to Plymouth at the invitation of Sir Gilbert Talbot, who is the Member of Parliament there – Lizzie and I were to help with providing the voters of the town with Sir Gilbert's food and drink – and very hungry and thirsty fellows they proved to be! And Lizzie fair blossomed in all that fresh air. Her skin glowed like a peach, a ripe unplucked peach, sir!'

After that Tom gave up. He ate his meat and drank his wine and smiled benevolently at the company.

As Tom and the parson were about to take their leave, Talbot Edwards pulled Ayliffe aside into the pantry and whispered, 'I think that went well, sir, very well. I can tell that Lizzie is fair smitten with the boy. Do you think we might allow them to make an excursion together, properly supervised, of course, to the pleasure gardens at Vauxhall, perhaps. What say you, sir?'

'I think that is an admirable idea, Edwards. But there is one other matter I would like to discuss with you, if I may. I told you that I was not the only man who was made guardian of Thomas after poor Edwin's death.'

'I believe you mentioned two other gentlemen, old friends of your dear departed brother.'

'Yes, well, it grieves me to tell you that they have written to tell me that they utterly oppose the match between Thomas and Elizabeth. They say that they cannot in good conscience sign over to him the fortune he has held in their trust. And, of course, if Thomas has no money he cannot marry.'

Edwards looked at Ayliffe, suddenly appalled. 'You mean these two gentlemen would block the marriage? Why, for God's sake?'

'Language, my dear friend, please moderate your words. Do not take the Lord's name in vain, I beg you. They feel, and I hope you will forgive me if I speak candidly, that he is marrying beneath himself, and that it would be unwise for him to become linked to a lady of little fortune and no prospects of inheritance.'

Edwards glared at him. 'Marrying beneath himself?'

'I beg your pardon, my dear friend, but I think it best to lay out the position as clearly as possible. However, I think that I may have an elegant little solution to the problem.' Ayliffe paused.

Edwards was still scowling, and for a moment the parson wondered if he had gone too far. If the man took the offence too deeply then the whole plan was wrecked. Finally, the assistant keeper unclenched his big jaw and said: 'And what is your solution, sir?'

'Why, it lies beneath our very feet. I have told them of the high esteem in which the noble Talbot family holds you. I have told them that the King himself entrusts you with his royal treasures. I have, if you will forgive this low expression, laid it on thick that you are a gentleman of great influence and responsibility, trusted absolutely by the highest in the land.'

Edwards managed a smile but the muscles around his jaw were tight.

'I think I might persuade Mister Paris and Mister Halliwell – both gentlemen of unimpeachable character and rectitude – that you are a man of consequence if you were to show them the Crown Jewels in your keeping, and particularly if they were to be allowed to see them unencumbered by those ugly iron bars, and perhaps even if they were allowed to handle some of the royal items, under your strict supervision, of course. I think, I truly believe, that might sway them to the opinion that Elizabeth comes from a suitably respectable family and persuade them to agree to the match.'

Ayliffe found he was holding his breath. For a long time Edwards said nothing. Then: 'Well, if it helps convince them to allow the match, I think I can see my way clear to unlocking the treasures just for a few moments. Yes, let them come. I'll show them what kind of family Elizabeth has.'

Saturday 6 May, 1671

James Pratt waited in the porter's lodge of the Cockpit feeling a little nervous but mostly confused. Holcroft Blood, the Cardinal of the Card Table, the Tyrant of Trump, as Pratt privately thought of him, had told him that he was to come to the lodge on this day at this hour and ask to see Holcroft. He was to give him the note that now lay in the pocket of his moss-green coat, and if he rendered Holcroft this small service his debt of four pounds, twelve shillings and sixpence would be wiped out.

He had, of course, opened the folded piece of blue paper in the privacy of his tiny room in Clarendon House but was astounded to find that it was blank. He wondered if there had been some mistake. He could not for the life of him understand why Holcroft would give him an unmarked piece of paper, for Pratt to deliver back to him. He had held it over a candle to see if there was any secret writing on the paper but no. Nothing. It made no sense at all but Pratt could see no harm in it – and there was also the matter of the four pounds, twelve shillings and sixpence.

The porter, Arnold Smith, had entertained him while he waited, if entertained was right word, with items of gossip that he had heard about the attack the year before on the Duke of Ormonde, Pratt's master, who, while no longer bed-ridden and perfectly healed of the hurts that he had suffered, was still a virtual recluse in his borrowed mansion. Ormonde had become an old man since the event, feeling every one of his sixty years, and the family business was now managed by his hot-headed son Lord Ossory.

'They say it was a gang of wild Scotch Presbyterians who done it, Covenanties, they call themselves,' said Arnold, with a nod and a wink. 'Ruthless bastards; heathens who will have no truck with bishops. A fellow at the Bull's Head said he heard a gang of rogues in the snug talking murder and rebellion in Scotch accents afore the wicked assault on His Grace.'

'I heard it was the Papists,' said Pratt. 'Jesuit agents of the King of Spain who want to force good English Protestants to bow down to the Whore of Rome. They'll stop at nothing, I've heard. Murder people in their beds if it suits their foul purposes.'

'You'd best lock up all the doors and windows at night, son, if you want to keep your duke safe. Catholics or Covenanties, makes no difference – both creatures of the Devil and that's for sure.'

Into this edifying exchanged stepped Holcroft Blood. 'Good day to you, Pratt. You wanted to see me?'

Pratt stood up, nodded to his new friend, and followed Holcroft out into the tulip garden. He handed over the note with a curt: 'Well, here it is.'

Holcroft held the blue paper in his hand for a moment. He saw that Arnold was watching the pair of them from the lodge, his index finger mining busily in one dirty ear, and also noticed Fox Cub sauntering past on the far side of the tulip garden and gave him a cheery wave, which was returned.

'That should do it,' he said and put the note in the pocket of his coat.

'Is that all you want?' said Pratt, still mystified by his role in this affair. 'That's enough to clear my debt?'

'That's all. But if you breathe a word about this business I will tell everyone that you welshed on it and you will never play cards again.'

'I'd no doubt be the richer for it,' muttered Pratt. But then seeing Holcroft's look, he said: 'But I'll keep my silence, I swear.'

'Your Grace,' said Holcroft. 'If I might have a moment of your time.'

'Yes, what is it?' The duke was in his bedchamber, seated at the desk and dressed only in a thick, padded silk gown, writing the last few letters of the day by candlelight. Holcroft had brought him soup, bread and wine and had transcribed two of the confidential letters into the usual code but now the duke was yawning, stretching, scratching; it was not far off midnight.

'I was brought this note by a servant of the Duke of Ormonde today, and I think that you ought to read it, sir.' Holcroft passed the grubby blue piece of paper across to his master.

Buckingham opened up its folds and read in silence for a while. Then he looked at the boy: 'Have you read this?'

Holcroft looked most uneasy. He opened his mouth.

'Of course you have. Don't bother to lie. It's not sealed and you'd be a fool not to open it. And, despite all your peculiarities, you're not a fool, are you, Holcroft? So, well, what do you think about it?'

'I think it seems far-fetched,' said Holcroft with absolute sincerity. 'I cannot imagine a noble peer of England inviting a foreign prince to usurp the throne. I just cannot believe it of His Grace.'

'Can't you, though? I can – I know Ormonde of old. He lusts for power. Always has. Now that he has been pushed to the margins of the court, hiding away like a frightened old woman in Clarendon House for fear of assassins, I think he would fix on any scheme – however treasonous – to get his family back into the sunlight.'

Holcroft said nothing.

'Tell me about this Pratt fellow, then, who is he and how did he approach you?'

'He is in the duke's service, a senior page – not assistant secretary, as he claims. He plays cards a great deal – and not very well. I know he has debts. He came to me today and gave me the note and asked me to help him. I said I would take it to you, Your Grace, but only for your consideration.'

'And no doubt he promised you a consideration for your pains – what was it? Ten per cent of the gold?'

Holcroft said nothing. He was determined, if at all possible, not to tell a lie to the duke. His own tangled morality demanded this fig leaf. He might connive to rob his master, but he would not lie to him, if he could help it.

The duke read the letter again. 'So tell me then, did you cook up this little scheme between you? You and Pratt, hoping to nip some chink, as they say, out of your kindly old duke? Did you write this note, Holcroft?'

'No, sir, I did not.'

The duke looked at him sideways. He seemed to be making up his mind. 'Well, it definitely bears investigation. I want you to go and see this Pratt fellow and ask him a little more about this letter he claims to have, written by Ormonde himself. Get him to show it to you. Read it. I want to know what is in it. Oh, and you can tell Pratt that I won't be paying a thousand in gold. That's absurd. I could not possibly go to that. But if the letter is genuine, if, I say, I may slip him a few pounds for his trouble.'

Sunday 7 May, 1671

'He wants me to read the letter,' Holcroft told Aphra. 'A letter that doesn't exist, and tell him word for word what it says. And he says he won't part with a thousand in gold, just a few pounds. It's not going to work, Aphra. We've made a terrible mistake.'

It was just after dawn on the morning after Holcroft's midnight interview with the duke. He had hardly slept, an hour or two at most, and had risen in darkness and made his way north across London to a tall thin house in St Thomas Street, where he had thrown pebbles at the topmost window until Aphra's sleepy head had poked out and answered his rattling summons.

Now they were in her tiny garret and Holcroft was telling her of his night's conversation, with a great deal of agitation. Even at dawn, the air in that tiny space reeked of cabbage boiled for too long, a scent that pervaded the building.

'Steady yourself, Holcroft.' Aphra was heating a tiny pan of water on a spirit burner on the table, making a pot of tea for them to share. 'It's all going just as planned. He's taken the bait; after all, he didn't dismiss the whole thing out of hand, or march straight to the King's bedchamber and denounce Ormonde. He badly wants to believe that such a letter exists.'

'There is no letter. How can I tell him about a letter that has no form? And if he is only going to pay a few pounds, it's not worth the trouble.'

Aphra considered telling Holcroft to use his imagination and then she remembered to whom she was talking. Instead she said: 'First of all, it is too late to go back now – wait! Hear me out. Buckingham thinks the letter exists. If we back off he will go directly to Pratt and attempt to buy or bully it out of him. Pratt will deny all knowledge and will probably spill the information that you approached him and asked him to deliver a blank piece of paper. If we stop now, Buckingham goes to Pratt and you're finished.'

The confidential clerk put his head in his hands and gave a low moan.

'Holcroft!' said Aphra sharply, breaking off from pouring boiling water into the teapot. 'Listen to me now. All is well. There is no cause for alarm. He is merely bargaining with us – he's trying to get the price down. You tell him that Pratt says that it is a thousand in gold or nothing. Tell the duke that Pratt is considering approaching Lord Arlington with the same arrangement, and that will stop his nonsense about a few miserable pounds. Buckingham wants the letter and he can easily afford a thousand. In truth, he could pay ten thousand without noticing the loss.'

Holcroft lifted his head from his hands. He felt sick and dizzy but he was drinking in Aphra's words as if they were the Gospels.

'Now pull yourself together, Holcroft, and look at this piece of paper.' She passed him a large crisp yellowing sheet of thick paper embossed with a crest of three golden cups on a blood-red background. Holcroft scanned the short, badly spelled note: it was a barely polite refusal from the Duke of Ormonde to Thomas Betterton, master of Aphra's theatre company, saying that the duke regretted that he was not inclined to sponsor a production of a new comedy called *The Amorous Prince* at the Lincoln's Inn Theatre.

Holcroft looked at her, frowning.

'Look at the handwriting, look at the way the writer forms his letters,' said Aphra, taking the letter from Holcroft. 'It is from Ormonde's own hand, I guarantee you, not one of his clerk's. I've checked with other letters that I've managed to lay eyes on. Look at the way he spells this word, and that one there. Note the crest at the top, and the flamboyant signature underlined with curlicues at the bottom.'

Aphra put the piece of paper back on the table and selected another. 'Now read this and commit it to memory, if you can do so. I wrote it but you must pretend that you are reading it in the duke's hand.'

Holcroft looked at the second piece of paper attentively. He saw Aphra's neat penmanship and then overlaid the duke's bold, aristocratic scrawl in his mind's eye. He began to feel calmer.

'Pay particular attention to this part here.' Aphra tapped the paper with her finger. Holcroft read the paragraph indicated, then he read it again.

'Got it?'

'Yes,' said Holcroft.

'Have you committed it to memory?'

'Yes.'

'Good, now let's have a drop of this tea before it gets cold. And one more thing, Holcroft. I'm going to need some money. I have very little and none at all to spare. Do you have five pounds that I could take from you?'

Tuesday 9 May, 1671

They breakfasted before dawn at the Blue Boar Inn, a down-at-heel establishment in a small alley just off the White Chapel Street, half a mile north of the Tower of London. They had stayed there the night before after coming down on horseback from Romford Market – Colonel Blood, his son Tom, William Hunt, Joshua Parrot, and an old friend of Blood's called William Smith who was a particular type of nonconformist called a Fifth Monarchist, who hated the King and believed the end of the world was nigh. A decade before, Smith had followed the wine-cooper-turned-revolutionary Thomas Venner in his lunatic attempt to capture the City of London with fifty men in the name of 'King Jesus'. It had been a disastrous venture.

Smith, a stocky, dark-haired man in a threadbare blue coat, had been living badly ever since Venner's doomed insurrection, his name on the list of wanted men with prices on their heads – along with that of Colonel Thomas Blood, naturally – and he now existed in a desperate, brandy-soaked demi-monde inhabited by a mixture of religious rebels and common criminals, holy madmen and vicious murderers, constantly at the risk of betrayal by paid informers and often too poor even to feed himself.

Blood had recruited Smith, whom he had found begging for his bread in Romford Market, with the promise of twenty pounds in gold, partly out of pity and partly because he needed a good, steady man to watch the horses while the business was done in the Irish Tower, and he trusted Smith not to run if things went badly for them. Like Parrot and Hunt, Smith had been part of the ramshackle cavalry troop with a black reputation that Blood had led towards the end of the war. Blood trusted all three men with his life. He was certain that not one of them would ever betray him. However the money was to be paid when the job was done. Gold in the hand changed a man. It invited temptation and, to Blood's mind, was a needless risk.

At a little after six o'clock, the five men set out from the Blue Boar, all mounted, each man armed with at least one discreet blade and a pair of pocket pistols. They headed down White Chapel Street and turned left just before Aldgate into the City, walking their horses down The Minories, quiet and deserted at this early hour except for a few fruit-sellers setting up their stalls, the width of the street allowing them to ride five abreast, four of them advancing like the cavalrymen they had once been, and Tom doing his best to imitate his veteran companions. Directly in front of them the Tower was rising out of the morning mists on the River Thames. They could hear the roaring of the toothless lion from five hundred yards away, a coughing grunt, that set the hairs of Tom's neck on end, and made the horses skitter.

They changed to single file as they passed down the road on the eastern side of the Tower, eyeing the grey-green moat on their right and the high off-white walls. They passed the Irish Tower on their right and saw the curtains drawn and a large figure moving about – breakfast preparing. At the Iron Gate by the Thames they dismounted and all handed their reins to Smith.

Tom looked out at a cutter on the river, dark hulled but with brilliant-white triangular sails that passed by at a reckless speed, heading downstream towards the sea. For a moment he wished he were on it, fleeing the deed he knew he must do this morning. He wondered if his father ever felt fear. He doubted it. Tom most definitely did. He felt cold and clumsy, a little sick, the pistols too heavy in his coat pockets, banging awkwardly against his thighs.

To their newest recruit, who was securing the reins to a pole set up by the rusting remains of the open gate, Blood said: 'Wait here, Smithy. It should not take more than an hour at most. But have the horses untied and ready when we come, we may need to move fast.'

Then to the rest of them: 'This is righteous work we do today, lads. Stay calm; follow my lead. If we get separated we meet back at the Blue Boar. Wait for the others there or leave a message. Does every man know what to do?' There was a chorus of muted assent. Blood looked at his son. He was pale as death. His father put a warm, heavy hand on his shoulder.

'Keep the faith, my boy, and we'll all come up smiling yet.'

They walked on to the wharf, through a double row of dwellings, one on each side, and with the river beyond the houses on their left, past a pair of sleepy sentries at the Water Gate, who merely nodded at the now-familiar figure of Parson Ayliffe and his friends, and entered the Tower itself.

A few minutes later, the affable Reverend Ayliffe, gold spectacles perched on his long nose, his handsome nephew Thomas, the well-to-do country gentleman, and his two other guardians, the huge, lumpish and scowling Mister Paris and the smaller, scarred Mister Halliwell, both eminently respectable gentlemen in well-brushed coats and brand-new beaver-fur hats, stood outside the blue door, while the parson rapped sharply on the wood with his silver wolf's head cane.

Talbot Edwards was not a man who often relished the dewy freshness of the early morning. He preferred to linger over his port wine during long evenings by his fire and he rarely rose before nine o'clock unless it was unavoidable. So, while he had readily agreed to hosting Parson Ayliffe's friends at breakfast, he had been slightly appalled when the man had suggested seven of the clock as an appropriate hour to meet. When he opened his door that morning, at a quarter to seven, it must be said that he looked out at the four men waiting there with bleary eyes and a sourness of mind. He barely managed to utter a civil good morning before blurting out: 'Breakfast ain't ready yet. And Mistress Edwards is still making her toilet.'

Parson Ayliffe smiled. 'Then perhaps we might view the jewels before our repast, if you are willing, Edwards. It would be a shame to disturb your good lady before she is ready to receive us.'

Edwards grunted something, shuffled back inside his house and groped for the big set of iron keys that hung on the wall behind the door. He grumbled slightly under his breath as he led the men down the winding stairs to the Jewel House, pushed open the door, and began to light all the candles in the windowless chamber. With five men in the room, including the enormous Mister Paris, it was rather crowded, but Edwards managed to ease his way through his guests, forward to the grill and, using the key on the smaller ring, he opened the padlock that secured the grill and with something of a flourish he swung open the heavy iron gate.

'These, gentlemen, are the famous Crown Jewels of England,' he began, 'entrusted to me personally by His Majesty and sadly unused these ten years past since the glorious occasion of his coronation . . .'

He got no further. A pair of powerful arms seized him from behind. A black cloth was flung over his head and he found himself hurled painfully to the floor with a great weight sitting on his chest, pinning him to the earth.

'It grieves me to do this, sir,' said Parson Ayliffe in his ear, his voice slightly muffled by the thick, blinding cloth. 'But I am afraid that I shall be obliged to relieve you of all the King's jewels this morning. I have no wish to injure you, for you have been kind to us, and if you submit, and lie quiet without fuss, then no harm at all will come to you. However, if you resist, or call out, or give us the slightest trouble, I shall have no choice but to subdue you with appropriate, and even with deadly force.'

Talbot Edwards, confused, disorientated and half stifled by the folds of the black cloak over his head, lay perfectly still.

Robert Westbury stood with his feet shoulder-width apart, perfectly balanced, his hands behind his back. He kept his chin up, his voice level, and made his report to his master the Duke of Buckingham.

'We know that he got the note from James Pratt, a page in the Duke of Ormonde's service. Pratt actually came here to deliver it three days ago.'

'Did he now?' said Buckingham. 'That is most interesting.'

'But Holcroft Blood has also been meeting with a playwright, a young and pretty widow called Mistress Behn regularly. We don't know why – certainly it is not on any regular business connected with the household. He has met with this Behn person at least four times in the past two weeks, Your Grace, three times at Pettigrew's chophouse in the Strand, while he was supposed to be doing the mail run, and last Sunday, very early, he visited her at her house in a shabby street off Drury Lane, near St Giles. When they're together, Your Grace, they act, well, you might say furtively.'

'And you are sure that they are not simply lovers?'

'There is no sign of any excessive affection, sir, no touching or kissing, and I must say that I do not believe that Blood is carnally inclined towards this woman – or any woman so far as I can tell.'

'Indeed?' said the duke. 'So what do they discuss, then, if not the joyous beating of their twin hearts?'

'Unfortunately, sir, neither d'Erloncourt nor I have been able to determine that. We have both been obliged to remain in the shadows, or at a suitable distance to avoid recognition by the target.'

'Do they plot together? Do they connive at my downfall?'

'I do not know, sir. They just look furtive, as I said, a bit suspicious. Would you like me to find out more? I could make an effort to befriend Blood, get him to trust me. He might then take me into his confidence.'

The duke made no reply. He stared into space, gently stroking his clean-shaven chin. Westbury felt a warm glow of satisfaction – he had known that there was something wrong with Blood, quite apart from his low birth and odd, inhuman manner. He was clearly plotting something disloyal, something against the duke. He was very glad he had taken the time to follow him discreetly when he was at liberty, and persuade Fox Cub to do the same when Westbury had his duties to perform. One advantage of arranging the rota was that it enabled him to ensure that either he or Foxy was always available to conduct their surveillance of the enemy.

'Would you like me to try to find out more, sir?' Westbury repeated. He disliked the sensation of being ignored, particularly after he had rendered the duke such a valuable service.

'What? No. It may be harmless – something theatrical, or a strange kind of love affair. Anyway, I don't believe that Holcroft could ever be brought to trust you. You fought with him once, did you not? And you were cruel when he first came. It is clear he does not like you – who can blame him: you are an odious little sneak. A bully, too, I should imagine. No, keep away from him, behave as you normally would.'

The duke fumbled in his waistcoat pocket, found a gold coin, glanced at it and flicked it at Westbury. As the guinea arced through the air, he said: 'That is for your pains – and I thank you, too, but you need not trouble yourself any further. Oh, and send d'Erloncourt in to me at once.'

Robert Westbury walked slowly from the room, his chin sagging, his feet heavy. This was not how it was supposed to go. He had spent hours following Blood around the byways of White Hall and further afield in London, dodging into stinking alleyways to avoid detection, suffering cold, rain, sore feet and even more painful boredom. It was humiliating to be tipped like a street urchin and casually dismissed with such scant praise. But strangely he did not blame the duke – perhaps His Grace had not grasped the scale of his efforts: he would redouble them, despite what the duke had said, and with Fox Cub's help, he'd discover whatever mischief the addle-brained guttersnipe was up to and bring him to a satisfying ruin.

'Out with you, Will. Keep a good guard and sing out if anyone comes.' Blood clapped Hunt on his narrow back and half-pushed him towards the door of the Jewel House. Hunt snatched one last look over his shoulder at the beguiling glitter of metal and priceless gems stacked on the shelves at the far side of the room, there for the taking, the mesh of iron bars now gaping wide, before dutifully heading up the stairs to take up his place outside.

Tom seized one of the two sceptres of state, a long golden rod with a diamond-encrusted cross at the top. He gazed at it for a moment, and weighed it in his hand. It was surprisingly heavy, a good three pounds, he thought. He shoved it into his riding boot but found it extended out of the top all the way up to his hip. Far too long. But he had come prepared: Tom pulled a steel file from his pocket and began to saw at the middle of the sceptre, golden filings spilling with every stroke. Cut in two, it would be far easier to hide about his person.

The other men were busy, too. Parrot pulled the golden orb of state from its place on the shelf and shoved it roughly into the front of his breeches – then paused to admire his apparently massive endow-ment with a wide grin. Blood seized the Imperial State Crown, one of the lighter headpieces worn by the King for the opening of Parlia-ment. Made from gold and silver, trimmed with ermine and purple velvet, encrusted with rubies and sapphires and diamonds, Blood admired the priceless crown briefly and then pulled a short-handled mallet from the back of his belt and began gently beating the metal, caving in the pearl-lined arches, squashing the circle of gold flat that so that it might fit into his wide pocket.

Talbot Edwards could hear the sounds of wood battering against precious metal and it jerked him out of his terrified torpor. He sat up and tore the black cloak from over his head, staring wildly at the three men who were desecrating the treasures in his charge. He shouted: 'Help! Murder! Thieves in the Jewel House! Summon the guard!' Then, somewhat woozily, he stood fully upright.

Blood leaped across and lashed him around the side of the head with the heavy mallet. Edwards was knocked to his knees. But still he cried out: 'Thieves! Thieves in the Jewel House. Guards!' The mallet crashed once more into the back of his skull and the old man went down, blood spilling from a wide gash in his scalp, and for a moment or two he was silent.

Blood stepped in, leaned over the bleeding septuagenarian and said: 'Another word, old man, and it will be your last.' Edwards looked beyond Blood and saw that the giant Paris had a long, slim dagger in his big hands. But Edwards once had been a brave man. He had faced death at the hands of the massed ranks of the Parliamentarian pikemen and in that moment he remembered his youthful courage. He took a deep breath and shouted with all his might: 'Help! Help me. The Jewel House is being robbed . . .'

Joshua Parrot shoved Blood roughly out of the way. He loomed over Edwards and plunged the long blade into his belly, withdrew and lunged again into the man's chest. A third blow lanced into his shoulder and a fourth lacerated his cheek.

'Enough, Joshua, enough,' said Blood, hauling at the man's massive shoulder. 'He's quiet now.'

Edwards was indeed silenced. He lay still, with his eyes closed in a spreading pool of his own gore. Tom stared at him with vast cow eyes, the two pieces of the gold sceptre still in his hands.

'Get as much as you can into your pockets,' said Blood. 'Fill your boots to the top with gems. There is no more time to waste.'

Outside the Irish Tower, William Hunt felt a chill of fear ripple up his spine. He could clearly hear the shouts of alarm wafting up from below. He looked around him at the empty cobbled courtyard – nothing. The ancient lion farted surprisingly loudly and rolled over to a more comfortable position. Above him he heard a window slam open and a square, shiny, bulldog face under a white cap poked out.

'Good morrow to you, mistress,' said Hunt. 'I am John Halliwell, guardian of young Thomas Ayliffe. Your husband has very kindly been showing us the jewels in the chamber below, but I have just stepped out for a breath of air. It is somewhat stuffy in there.'

'Oh yes, Mr Halliwell, welcome. Is all quite well? I thought I heard something.' Mistress Edwards smiled down at her guest.

'All is well – Mr Paris was just being enthusiastic about the great beauty of the jewels. He can be rather voluble when roused to admiration. But all is well, I assure you.'

'That's good. Be so kind as to tell Mr Edwards that breakfast is on the table whenever it suits the gentlemen's convenience. It should be ate up hot, so tell him not to dilly-dally down there.'

'I shall tell him, madam,' said Hunt and he watched with relief as the window slammed shut.

He closed his eyes and concentrated on breathing in and out, in and out. It would soon be over, he told himself.

'Who are you? And why is my front door wide open?' said a voice from behind Hunt. He opened his eyes and turned to see a man of about thirty years of age in a scarlet coat adorned with a quantity of gold lace, with a gilt-chased pistol shoved in his sash and a leather baldrick over one shoulder from which hung a long, heavy sword.

'I am a guest of Mister Talbot Edwards. He has invited me and my friends for breakfast.'

'Oh, that's my father,' said the soldier. 'Come on, let's go up.'

Hunt was momentarily paralysed. He could call out and warn his friends but that would mean fighting and probably having to kill this fellow, if he could – he was far bigger than Hunt and younger, too. Or he could obediently go up stairs with the man and into the house – that should allay his suspicions. But if the cries for help continued, he would have to deal with him then, and probably Mistress Edwards and the daughter, too. What Hunt most wanted to do was run, but he could not do that. Instead, he stayed where he was and put his hand in his coat pocket and felt the cool, smooth wood of the pistol grip under his fingers.

Hunt was saved from having to make a decision by the appearance at the top of the stairs of Blood, with Parrot looming behind him. He glimpsed Tom coming up from the Jewel House last of all. Blood looked dishevelled, his coat bulged in unexpected places, his white collar was pulled loose, his face was red, the spectacles were gone and his blue eyes glittered.

The soldier, Wythe Edwards, took a step back at the sight of the three big men coming out of his house and down the steps towards him. He put a hand on his sword hilt. 'And you three are?' he said.

'They are also friends of your father,' said Hunt quickly. 'Invited this morning for breakfast.'

'Good morrow to you, sir,' said Blood, coming down the last few steps with something approaching a happy smile on his face and his right hand extended in greeting. 'My name is Ayliffe . . .'

Blood got no further. From behind him, a terrible howl erupted from the open doorway, only slightly resembling the words: 'Help! Murder! The jewels are stolen!'

Blood did not hesitate. Using his downward momentum from the steps, and the full weight of his shoulder, he leaped forward and smashed his right fist into the side of Wythe's face, following that blow with a round-arm from his left to the soldier's temple, which knocked him instantly to the ground.

'Don't run, lads,' he said. 'Whatever you do, don't run now. We walk nice and calm all the way out of the Tower. Just walk, all right.'

Leaving Wythe stunned and bleeding on the cobbles, the four men began to walk casually out of the courtyard in front of the Irish Tower, clanking a little, and with Joshua Parrot swinging his legs wide and still apparently sporting a monstrous erection. They had barely got thirty yards when they heard Edwards senior cry out once more. Tom looked back and saw an awful blood-drenched figure standing at the top of the steps leading to the Irish Tower, shouting his heart out. And below him on the cobbles his soldier son was shaking his head and slowly getting up from his hands and knees. They walked on across the Inner Ward, past the row of trees before the Grand Stone House, four men, casually sauntering in the early morning. They walked on; a dozen measured strides. Another dozen.

Blood could hear the shouting behind, loud and urgent. He stole a glance. Wythe had emerged from the courtyard of the Irish Tower his pistol in hand and was raising the hue and cry – calling for the Tower guards to come from their barracks and prevent a foul treason. One of the sentries outside the door of the barrack dashed inside. The other looked uncertain, but hefted his musket, glancing between the shouting and gesticulating Wythe Edwards and the four men walking casually towards Tower Green.

A dozen men came scrambling out of the barracks door – shrugging on buff-coloured leather coats, tightening straps on their shiny cuirasses. Some had muskets, some swords or half pikes. There were more men behind them.

'Now we run,' said Blood quietly. 'Run, you bastards, run.'

And the four men took to their heels.

When Holcroft pushed open the door to his master's study, the first thing he saw was a pair of pale, heaving buttocks. It checked him. Then he saw the rest of the Duke of Buckingham, his breeches round his ankles, his coat thrown across the desk, waistcoat tails rucked up around his waist, ploughing away on top of another body. A ginger head peered out from under the duke's armpit and looked directly at Holcroft. And, like a bucket of icy water thrown in his face, he saw that the duke's partner was Fox Cub.

BLOOD'S GAME | 201

Holcroft stood stock still, unsure what to do. Then the duke spoke, without breaking his rhythm, or even once looking over in his direction.

'Thank you for coming, Holcroft. I'll be with you directly.'

And he was – after a dozen more thrusts and a grunting sigh, the Duke of Buckingham came off the little boy's body, wiped himself on Fox Cub's shirt tails, and pulled up his own breeches. He picked up the heavy coat and shrugged it on, leaving the waistcoat beneath unbuttoned. Then he searched briefly on the desk, shifting the piles of paper, before seizing on a piece and handing it to Holcroft with an innocent smile.

'I want three copies of this in the usual code; then burn the original. And I want you to give the copies to Mullins for dispatch before sunset, understood? Good. Well, I shall leave you to it. I'm playing at cards with Sir Thomas Littleton – he wants me to try this new game Whisk, the one they're all so excited about, and I'd best not be late. You know how old Littleton mopes like a child if he feels he's been slighted.'

And with that the duke was gone. Holcroft looked down at the piece of paper in his hand. It was addressed to the duke's agents; a request for information about Dutch shipping that had docked at English harbours in the past three months. It was nothing unusual; Holcroft had encoded a dozen similar messages for His Grace in the past six months. He frowned. Had he been summoned from his quarters by Albert St John for this? The duke could perfectly well have given the message directly to Mullins, his chief clerk. There was no need to have Holcroft do the straightforward coding, no need at all, although he knew that he was vastly quicker at it. It occurred to Holcroft that the duke might have intended that he discover him at his gross rutting; that he might be sending him some sort of message by this unnatural summoning. But he had no idea what the message might mean.

'You won't tell, will you?' said a tiny voice by his elbow. Holcroft looked down at a pale, anxious face and russet mop.

'Did he force himself on you?' said Holcroft.

'No, no, nothing like that. He was kind to me. He said he cared for me. But you won't tell anyone, will you? I know it is a sin. But, worse than that, I'd be teased, mocked by Westbury, by everyone. I couldn't bear it. Please don't tell.'

'I won't tell,' said Holcroft softly and he looked down at the piece of paper in his hand, shame running fiery hot in his veins, until he heard the door click closed behind the departing back of little Henri d'Erloncourt.

It did not take Holcroft long to encode the Dutch shipping message, even writing it out three times. When he had finished, he put away the ink and quills and sanded the sheets dry, but instead of taking them to Mullins, he continued sitting at the duke's desk, thinking, trying to puzzle out the duke's message to him. He would have to ask Aphra – or Jack, when he saw him next, if he ever saw him again.

Glancing casually over the desk he saw something that made him pause: it was the end of a gold chain half covered by a sheet of paper. He knew what it was but for a moment he resisted the urge to pick it up. Could he be mistaken? There was only one way to find out. He gently tugged the gold chain out from under the paper and saw that there was a small golden key on a ring at the end of it. He had seen that key a thousand times but had never held it in his hand. It was the key on the end of the chain that the duke wore across his belly, tucked into a pocket on his waistcoat. It was the key that opened the desk's central drawer, where the duke kept his private letters. It must have snapped and fallen off while the duke was on Fox Cub.

Holcroft knew that the duke kept secret papers in that drawer. He knew too, that if the duke kept it locked then he did not have permission to open it. And yet the chain of loyalty, like the little golden chain in his hand, had been broken. He was quite alone in the study, he could hear nobody in the corridor outside and he did not expect the duke back from his card game with Sir Thomas Littleton for many hours yet.

Holcroft inserted the key, turned it and opened the drawer.

Inside the drawer was the blue note written by Aphra, the one that purported to come from James Pratt; there were some confidential reports with which Holcroft was already familiar; a passionate love letter from someone calling himself or herself Narcissus; a heavy leather purse of golden guineas, which Holcroft weighed in his palm but decided not to broach; and, lastly, a single sheet of thick yellow paper written in the usual code. Holcroft looked at the piece of paper in his hand. His eyes jumped to the bottom of the page, to the sign off, and he read:

6' 4' 5' 5* – 4'1 2' 3 3' 2' 2* 7* – 6* 2' 5* 5' 1' 2* 7* – 7 5' 3* 4' 2*

Which he instantly knew to mean: 'Your obedient servant, Jupon'.

His eyes flicked to the top of the page and he read the whole message with a growing sense of wonder, and then with a hot feeling of betrayal and disgust. The paragraph that disturbed him the most, and which he read three times just to be sure, began:

7* 6 2' – 8 3' 2* 5 – 4' 4 – 2' 2* 5 9 1' 2* 3 – 5'5' 3' 9 9 – 1* 1'
8 2' – 1' – 3* 5' 1 9 3* 2 – 3* 5* 4' 4 2' 6* 6* 3' 4' 2* – 4' 4 – 7*
6 2' – 2 1' 7* 6 4' 9 3' 2 – 4 1' 3' 7* 6 . . .

Holcroft took a quill from the stand, cut it carefully, selected a fresh piece of paper, dipped his nib and, very carefully, he began to copy out the letter from Jupon in its coded form.

Tom ran full pelt past the western side of the White Tower. He could hear the pounding feet of his comrades behind him, Hunt on his left shoulder, Parrot panting behind him and his father coming last of all hallooing and shouting: 'They went that way, the dirty traitors – after them. Stop those damned thieves! Stop them!'

They all but jumped down the steps and tore towards the Bloody Gate. A musket cracked behind them and there was more shouting from a distance. The two sentries at the Bloody Gate were standing under the teeth of the portcullis, their muskets at port. They looked confused, scared even. Tom snatched a glance behind him; there were more buff-coated soldiers, a score at least, behind them, with the young scarlet-clad officer from the Irish Tower, blood on his face, waving his pistol and urging them onwards.

'Halt!' shouted the right-hand sentry, pointing his musket. Out of the corner of his eye, Tom saw Hunt level his pocket pistol, still running at full tilt, and fire. The sentry dropped his musket, clapped his shoulder and spun away. Parrot gave an animal-like roar and charged at the remaining sentry. He had a foot-long, needle-tipped dagger in each hand and he came like a falling mountain on the second man, who hurled away his musket, and ran like a rabbit through the Bloody Gate, disappearing into Water Lane beyond.

Once they were all through the gate, Blood said: 'This way!' and pointed left beyond Traitor's Gate to the Water Gate where there were two more sentries – this time alert, sober, braver men, now determined to stop them. They levelled their muskets. One shouted: 'Halt or I give fire!'

Blood said: 'They couldn't hit a barn door. Come on!' But Tom found he couldn't move towards the man with the aimed musket – it looked as big as a cannon to his eye. Blood pulled out one of his pocket pistols, cocked it, aimed and fired at the sentry twenty yards away. He missed. The man fired back, the lead ball cracking into the cobbles behind them. He began to reload his piece. Then the second sentry stepped forward, hefting his musket.

'Just go straight through them,' bellowed Blood. He seized Tom's shoulder, shook him. 'You want to go back to the Marshalsea?' Tom looked at him in horror. 'Then go,' said Blood and pushed his son forward. The second sentry pulled the trigger, the musket spat fire and Parrot gave a wild cry. Tom stumbled forward. But Hunt was within twenty feet now. He lifted his second pocket pistol, aimed and shot the second sentry through the forehead, the lead bullet exploding the back of his skull and splashing the steps of the Water Gate with his blood and brains. The first one abandoned reloading, snatched up his musket, cartridges and rammer and ran through the opening and on to the wharf.

Another musket barked from behind them. Blood whirled and saw a dozen buff-coated men tumbling through the Bloody Gate, Wythe Edwards to the fore. Blood looked back at the Water Gate, saw Hunt disappearing through it, with a bloody Parrot on his heels. Tom was nearly there too.

Blood made it to the Water Gate in a dozen strides, and stopped there. He grabbed Tom by the arm: 'Give me your pistols, son.'

'What?'

'Give them to me! I'll hold these gentlemen for a while.'

He took the heavy horse pistol and the small pocket gun from Tom and pushed him on to the drawbridge. Tom gave him one long look and fled, chasing after Hunt and Parrot, who were already halfway along the wharf.

Blood shoved the horse pistol into his waistband, cocked the other, extended his arm and fired into the crowd of soldiers. He heard the tinny ping as the ball struck a steel breastplate, and the frightened shouts of the enemy. He put his back to the stone wall, pulled out the horse pistol. He could hear the officer bawling at the men to advance. He spun around into full view of the Tower guards, standing in the centre of the Water Gate – a musket exploded, the ball cracking past his ear. He lifted the heavy pistol, aimed carefully at Wythe Edwards, squeezed the trigger. The pistol barked. The soldier beside the young officer screamed and spun away. Edwards had his sword out now and was using it to beat the back of the nearest redcoat.

'It's one man, you cowards, charge him, charge!'

Blood dropped the heavy weapon. Another musket spat fire at him. Blood took out his last remaining pocket pistol. The soldiers were finally advancing. A dozen men only twenty yards away. He cocked the small weapon, extended his arm and shot the foremost soldier through the neck. Then he dodged back into the cover of the Water Gate wall, put his back against the stone and stripped the sheath from his wolf's head walking cane, tossing it away and exposing the slim steel of the three-foot blade beneath. He looked up the wooden decking of the wharf and saw with satisfaction that Tom and the others were nearly at the Iron Gate where, God, Mary and all the saints be willing, Smithy would still be waiting with the horses.

A musket bullet blew a chunk of masonry from the wall beside his ear, the stone chips stinging and cutting his cheek. He counted to three, his back against the stone, then spun round the corner again, the blade of the sword-stick lancing out and punching through the open flaps of the buff coat of the leading soldier and into his groin. The man yelled, flailed and fell. A jet of gore arced through the air. But Blood was already moving away. He sprinted across the bridge to the wharf, and began to run towards the Iron Gate. His comrades were so nearly there. And he had only fifty yards to go. They would make it. They might all actually make it. Once a-horse, they could lose the soldiers in the crowded streets. There was no stopping them now. By God, he felt good. Never felt better. Heart pumping, blood singing.

He heard a series of bangs behind him, felt a blow like a kick from a mule against his thigh and his right leg collapsed under him, dumping him on the wooden decking of the wharf. He looked down at the blood oozing from his leg, looked up at the wall of shouting men in yellow leather, running up the wharf and converging on him. He tried to raise the bloodied sword-stick, tried to say: 'Who wants to die first?' But all that came out was a croak and the word 'Die!'

Someone kicked the blade out of his hand and he found that he was staring into the furious face of the officer Wythe Edwards, who had a pistol pointed directly at his head, inches away, his finger white upon the trigger.

Part Three

Friday 12 May, 1671

'Your Grace,' said Holcroft, clearing his throat noisily and unnecessarily. 'Your Grace, if I might speak with you.'

The duke continued to ignore him. Holcroft was standing stiffly beside Buckingham's desk in his study, hands behind his back, watching his master read *The London Gazette*, turning the pages and gazing at the close lines of print as if utterly absorbed, as if he did not already know far more about what was going on in London than Henry Muddiman, the *Gazette*'s editor.

Finally the Duke of Buckingham laid down the newspaper. 'Would you say your father was a discreet man, Holcroft?' he said, looking up at his confidential clerk. 'A man who knows how to keep his mouth shut when he is in a tight place?'

Holcroft had no idea how to answer and so he said nothing.

'Because, you see,' continued the duke, gesturing at the *Gazette*, 'after his latest high jinks he is in rather a tight spot now, wouldn't you say?'

'He is in the Tower of London, sir, and as I understand it the cells are not cramped, not as you might say tight at all, surprisingly capacious. Fit for a great nobleman, I'm told.'

'I do sometimes wonder, Holcroft, if you are mocking me with your insistence on being so literal in your comprehension of my questions. That would be most unwise, let me tell you. That would lead to a very swift termination of our relationship. So – are you mocking me, Holcroft?'

'Oh no, sir.'

'Then tell me: do you think that your father will tell his inquisitors everything that he knows about this bungled attempt to purloin the Crown Jewels? Will he readily give up the names of his co-conspirators? In the low cant of thieves: is he a blab?'

Holcroft thought about it for a moment or two. Then he said: 'I do not think he will tell them anything at all.'

'Even if they apply the rack, bring out the red-hot pincers, all that?'

Holcroft had never attempted to make an analysis of his father's character before but now he said with complete certainty: 'I think he would resist his questioners with all his strength. I think that the more they abused him, the stronger his resistance would become. I think he would die rather than give up his friends.'

'Good. And, in fact, I agree with your assessment. That is one of the qualities that I most admire about him. He's an incompetent old buffoon, that's for sure, far too arrogant for a man of his station, foolhardy, rash, intemperate, a rake-hell and drunkard. But I would not say that he is a blab. However, I do think that it would be wise for you to pay him a visit just to remind him who his friends are. Go and see him in the Tower, Holcroft, this Sunday – I shall not require your services on the Lord's day – see if he lacks for any comforts, food, wine, money, what have you, tell him that he only has to ask his *friends* and it shall be provided. But tell him also that his friends rely on his absolute discretion and that they are working night and day to have these false charges against him dropped – but they will be successful only if he is discreet. Will you tell him that?'

'Yes, sir.' He cleared his throat again. 'There is one other thing, Your Grace.' Holcroft shifted nervously from one foot to the other. 'The matter of James Pratt and the, ah, the Duke of Ormonde's letter.'

'Oh yes?'

Holcroft swallowed; he could feel a flush suffusing his neck. He said, very quickly: 'I wondered whether you had given the matter any more thought since we last spoke, sir.'

Buckingham stared at him.

Holcroft said: 'As I said to you before, sir, the owner of the letter insists payment must indeed be a thousand in gold and says, if you are not interested, perhaps my Lord Arlington might be prepared to come up with this modest sum. Do you have an answer for him?'

'I remember our conversation perfectly, Master Holcroft. And I believe that I remarked that it was very cunning of your Mister Pratt to arrange an auction between two bidders. Hmmm. So he is eager for an answer, is he? I do like eagerness in an adversary. It leads to rashness. Very well, tell him I will make it five hundred but – and this point I will not concede – I must see the letter, hold it in my hand, before I will make any payment to him at all.'

'I don't think he'll—'

'Just tell him. It's five hundred pounds in gold but I want to see it first. Or there can be no accommodation for him.'

'I could recite the contents of the letter again, sir. I can recall them perfectly clearly.'

'I know the letter's contents: Ormonde to support Prince William in a bid to be the King of England, marriage to Mary, militia commanders keen, members of both Houses secretly in support, blah, blah, blah. It's not so much the content, Holcroft, I want to see the letter itself. I want to study the handwriting, the style of the words, the exact language he used, examine the signature. Tell your Mister Pratt that. I must see the letter itself. You may also tell him that I have eyes in Lord Arlington's household and if I hear that he is offering the letter to him, our arrangement is null and void; furthermore I will send a note immediately to the Duke of Ormonde telling him that his senior page – beg pardon – his assistant secretary is selling off his private correspondence to the highest bidder. See how he likes that.

'Now, enough of this damned Ormonde nonsense. That will be all for now. Go and see your incompetent father in the Tower this Sunday and remind him who his friends are, impress on him the necessity of silence.'

The room on the first floor of the Blue Boar Inn off White Chapel Street was extremely small. Three nights ago, when there had been five big men snoring under their blankets on the straw pallets on the floor, there had barely been the space to walk to the chamber pot under the stool in the corner without treading on a limb. Now, even with only two occupants, Tom Blood and Joshua Parrot, it still seemed cramped and airless. It stank, too, for the window was rarely opened, the chamber pot was almost full and the two men did not leave the room either by night or day. Added to that, Parrot's wound, a musket ball deep in the meat of his right shoulder, was beginning to rot, seeping quantities of a cloudy liquor along with the blood into the bandage and giving off the odd mouse-like odour of corruption.

William Hunt had been the first to the horses at the Iron Gate, followed by Parrot who was staggering along the wharf, bleeding badly and being supported by Tom. Smith had the reins untied and the four of them had thrown themselves into their saddles with no hesitation at all. The Tower guards were firing their muskets, reloading and advancing steadily like the trained troops they were, and lethal missiles flew all around, smashing the windows and brickwork of the houses on either side, pinging from the rusty Iron Gate itself. Tom had his hat blown clean off. The nearest horse to the advancing troopers had its spine broken by one ball, another in its haunch and was screaming horribly. So none of them had waited even a half minute for Blood but, as had been agreed beforehand, each had individually galloped off up the road as soon as they were in the saddle, mingling with the thickening morning crowds and losing themselves within minutes in the hurley-burley of London.

They had all arrived at the Blue Boar less than a half hour later, sweating, shaken, exhausted but, apart from Parrot, all whole and unmarked, and carrying with them tens of thousands of pounds'-worth of the King's jewels, crammed into their pockets, stuffed into boots and, in Joshua Parrot's case, wedged down the front of his breeches. They had dumped the jewellery with the rest of their belongings in their room, hiding the glittering mound under a cloak, then they returned downstairs to the parlour and called for ale, drank it and waited patiently, a pair of eyes at all times on White Chapel Street, for Colonel Blood to make his belated appearance.

No one was certain what had happened to their leader – William Smith thought he had seen someone diving off the wharf and into the river during the confused fighting, and there was another exit at the far end of the wharf, so he might have got away that way – or he might have been captured. The fifth horse, Blood's horse, had been mortally wounded, so there was no possibility of his riding it back to the Blue Boar – but they all knew him as a man of ingenuity and cunning and, even if he had been taken, there was a slim chance that wearing his pastor's black habit he might give his captors the slip or talk his way to freedom. This, anyway, was what the men told themselves as they drank and waited for their captain to come to them.

By the time the third pint of ale was being drained, Hunt had disappeared. One minute he was there, the next gone. Smith, too, took his leave a little after noon; he was heading back to Romford, or so he said, to await the colonel there. So after taking a bite of dinner in the parlour, Parrot and Tom retired to their room – Parrot as pale as a corpse and on the verge of collapse – and saw that the bright pile of royal baubles had been diminished considerably by either Hunt or Smith, or most probably by both, but that there was still a very respectable fortune in assorted jewels and precious metal for them to hold up to the light of the window and savour.

That had all been three days ago, and since then they had waited and waited and there had been no sign of Blood. Tom agonized over what he should do: Parrot was too ill to be moved – not that Tom could have managed his bulk anyway – but neither could he bring himself to abandon the man to die or recover on his own. The innkeeper, Warburton, an old friend of Blood's with only one leg, who owed the colonel some very large favour, was growing increasingly nervous about housing the two fugitives under his roof. He knew they had committed a grave felony – the cry, 'The crown is taken out of the Tower; the crown is stolen' had echoed up and down White Chapel Street – and, while he might have been persuaded to put up with Blood's presence, he had no relationship with his son nor with the huge man who was groaning, bleeding and probably dying up in his room.

On the morning of the second day Warburton had forbidden them the downstairs parlour. They might keep to their room while they waited for the colonel, he said, and take their food there. Tom had not felt able to argue with his landlord and so he had paid over the inflated lodging fee and spent the greater part of the next forty-eight hours sitting on a stool and staring out of the window at the plot of land behind the inn and listening to the grunts, moans and angry delirious babbling of Joshua Parrot.

Behind the inn was a small vegetable garden: rows of asparagus, onions, cabbages and beans neatly tended with nary a weed in sight. A path ran between the two large beds and continued north towards a row of houses, becoming a courtyard where a pair of questing chickens were pecking at the dust, and then evolving into Seven Steps Alley, a narrow path that led towards Gravel Lane, a moderate residential street.

How wonderful it would be, thought Tom, to have a vegetable garden, and perhaps a cow or even a goat, too, and a few fowl or pigs. With his share of the money, perhaps he would buy a small-holding somewhere rural and remote, find a wife and live in happy bucolic comfort, growing his vegetables, making cheese and butter, killing a goose at Christmas and feasting with his neighbours. He'd have a few children, would never speak about the past, of the bad things he had done. He would give himself a new name – Brown, Gray, White, something harmless and nondescript and settle down and just be quiet and happy for the rest of his life.

Then Parrot gave a wild cry, jerking awake, and sat up on his pallet, his blood-shot eyes staring madly, a foot-long naked dagger in his right fist. He stabbed the air repeatedly, striking invisible foes. He shouted incoherently.

Tom slipped off the stool and went to fetch his comrade a cup of cool ale from the jug. If only his father would come. He would know exactly what to do with Parrot, whether they could risk moving him, whether they should give him physic of some kind, or bleed him. If only his father would come, then the rest of his life could finally begin.

With his tongue, Colonel Thomas Blood explored the gap where his left incisor had been. He spat once, a thick gobbet of red splashing on the wooden floor, and looked up at his tormentor. Wythe Edwards loomed over him, shaking a bunched fist in Blood's bruised face: 'You will speak to me, you verminous piece of offal, you will speak. Because I shall make you.'

Blood said nothing. His wrists and ankles were manacled and he was tied to a chair with half a dozen coils of rope for good measure. The prison cell he was in was not exactly as capacious as his son Holcroft had imagined, but it was a good deal larger than the room in the Blue Boar in which his eldest son Tom now sweated so miserably. A small barred window admitted a good deal of light, and there was a large fireplace in which a mean coal fire was smouldering. Blood moved his battered head forward a little, took careful aim and spat again, showering Wythe's ivory silk stockings with a glutinous mixture of blood and phlegm. The soldier went berserk, raining punches down on Blood's unprotected face, smashing his head left and right, left and right, until it lolled quite loose on his neck. Blood was now beyond speech. He had barely uttered a word to his captors since being taken two days ago, except to mutter, 'It was a gallant attempt, boys, however unsuccessful, and 'twas for a crown . . .' before passing out on the wharf.

He had been dragged to the White Tower and slung into one of the prison rooms on the second floor, fully manacled from the start with heavy iron fetters that sheared his skin when he shifted his limbs. A surgeon had been summoned to inspect the wound in the back of his thigh. He'd briskly probed, grasped and removed the musket ball with a pair of forceps, washed the gory hole out with vinegar and bound it with linen. Blood had mercifully remained unconscious throughout the whole operation. Since then he had been given a little bread and ale, been allowed to wash using the jug and bowl on the stand in the cell, then been questioned without violence for several hours by Sir John Robinson, the lieutenant of the Tower, and the man who had responsibility, above Talbot Edwards, even above the Master of the Jewel House Sir Gilbert Talbot, for the safety of the King's treasure. Blood had said next to nothing. He had merely confirmed his own name and admitted that he was guilty of the theft but, having done that, he shut his mouth and refused to say any more.

The Imperial State Crown had been recovered from Blood's coat pocket, although it had been hammered flat and a large number of the smaller jewels had subsequently come loose. Several diamond bracelets, ruby pendants and golden cups had also been found on Blood's person and, on the wooden decking of the wharf, a diamond the size of an acorn, a large pearl and several smaller gemstones had been recovered. However, the two sceptres and the orb of state were still missing, along with a large number of other treasures and, understandably, Sir John was keen to force Blood to reveal the names of his accomplices and their present whereabouts. Deeply frustrated, he had asked Wythe Edwards to come from his father's bedside to aid him with the interrogation.

A bucket of icy well water, hurled by a zealous gaoler, revived Blood and he looked blearily out of his streaming face at Wythe, who was glaring at him with unconcealed hatred. Behind the soldier stood Sir John, looking shocked by the brutality of his companion, but apparently lacking any desire to restrain him.

Wythe massaged the red and swollen knuckles of his right hand with his left. 'My father is like to die because of the way you served him, both gut and lung are punctured, head near stove in, and I should like you to know that as a result of his injuries I do not have any qualms about using the most extreme methods of persuasion. To speak frankly, I do not care if I have to beat you half to death to get to the truth. You hear me?'

The prisoner looked at him and smiled, a thin dribble of blood running out of the corner of his half-open mouth.

'Who were your companions?'

Blood shook his head.

Wythe punched him, a hard jab with his right fist, smashing Blood's head back, but the young man had evidently damaged his own finger bones with repeated blows against the prisoner's hard skull for he grimaced, sucked in a breath and cradled the injured hand against his belly.

'Who was with you when you robbed my father's house? What are the other miscreants' names?' Wythe lashed out with his boot and cracked Blood on the shinbone, his wounded leg sending a bolt of agony up his spine. The prisoner grunted then, incredibly, began to laugh, a horrible wet bubbling sound.

'You *will* talk to me. Do you think we will not make use of the rack, the hot irons, the water torture, if we have to?'

Blood straightened up as far as the ropes and chains would allow him. He said something unintelligible, speaking thickly, gore running from his shattered mouth. Wythe leaned in to hear him. Blood spoke again: 'I will give an account of myself only to the King.' He was gasping with the effort of speaking. 'Bring me before the King . . . in a privy manner . . . and I shall answer anything His Majesty chooses to ask. I shall speak to no other man.'

'You are mad. You are a moon-crazed imbecile if you think His Majesty would sully his eyes with the sight of a wretch like you.' He raised his fist to strike, thought better of it, and lashed out with

ANGUS DONALD | 220

his foot again, catching Blood on the kneecap and knocking the bound man and the wooden chair over. Blood's skull thumped hard against the wooden floor.

'I do not like this; I do not like this at all,' said Holcroft. He was sitting at the rickety table in Aphra Behn's attic, sipping a bowl of lukewarm tea by the light of a single candle. 'If we show him a letter written by you or me, he will know for sure it is false. He must know Ormonde's hand well; they have corresponded often enough – he certainly knows mine. And he will not part with any money at all unless he has the letter in his grasp.'

The playwright was standing at the small window and staring into the darkness below. There were lamps hung outside the bigger houses on Drury Lane and one hanging outside the Red Lion on the corner a hundred yards away but in St Thomas, the battered, rotting dwellings showed nary a glim.

'Are you sure you were not followed here?' she asked.

'Followed? I don't think so. I looked to see if there was anyone behind me several times but I saw no one. Do you think the duke is suspicious?'

'I'd be surprised if he wasn't. He is not a trusting man. I thought I saw something just then. But maybe it's nothing.'

'What are we going to do about the letter?'

Aphra came and sat down at the table next to Holcroft and poured herself a cup of tea from the pot. 'I had hoped we would be able to do this with the minimal amount of expense,' she said. 'Pass Buckingham some little bit of nonsense written by me, take the money and run. But I realized some time ago that this was not going to be possible. So I had an old friend make this up for us. He writes the playbills for the Duke's Company. But he has other less genteel talents, too. I gave him your five pounds for this.'

She reached into a bag and pulled out a piece of thick yellow paper. It was creased both vertically and horizontally as if it had been folded up and sealed, and there were even the remnants of crumbled red wax on the edges of the paper. Holcroft held it in his hand, dumfounded. He tilted the letter to the candle and read:

Monday, April 17ᵗʰ, 1671

Your Highness,

    I write this note in haste for my courier must leave for Harwich within the hour if he is to meet the Elizabeth before the tide turns. I have spoken this past week to a number of influential men in both Houses of Parliament, all good Protestants, and all men whom you encountered when you were visiting our shores last winter – although I prefer not to reveal their names at this time – and the general feeling towards Your Highness is warm. At least two members of the Upper House, men of considerable means as well as high rank, say that they are prepared to back you with force, putting the militias that they command at your disposal, and several officers in the King's regiments are also prepared to bring their troops over to you in the event of an armed struggle. There are more men, however, who are uncertain about this enterprise, despite their abhorrence of the notion of a Papist monarch, but I believe they might be induced to come to our side with certain emoluments in the form of lands and honours. I am preparing a list for you to peruse at your leisure, which I will send under separate cover. The first step, of course, is to move forward with your marriage to York's daughter, Lady Mary Stuart, and I have made strenuous efforts in this direction. However, the French faction, particularly my lords Buckingham and Arlington, will certainly oppose me on this matter and I often hear the name of Louis, the dauphin, mentioned as a potential spouse for the lady, although the French boy is only ten years of age. I'm taking steps to disparage this and to promote your name as a far more suitable match.

I must finish this letter now as the courier is waiting impatiently but I wish you to know that you have many friends in the Three Kingdoms who would offer you a joyous welcome should you choose to embark upon this glorious venture and come again to our shores, including,

Your most obedient servant,

Ormonde

Holcroft had read the text before, of course, and had memorized the words to recite to Buckingham, but it still shocked him with its treasonous nature. Then Aphra passed him the crumpled letter from the Duke of Ormonde to Thomas Betterman declining to support a production of *The Amorous Prince* and Holcroft held both and looked from one to the other.

'It is miraculous. Every stroke of the pen is the same, even the way he signs his name and underlines it. Your friend is a wizard!'

'Worth your five pounds?'

'Every penny. By God, we have him, Aphra. We have the duke!'

'We still have to get him to pay up – and if I know George Villiers that could be the hardest part yet. But would you be willing to agree to five hundred pounds? Or do you want to press him for the full thousand?'

Saturday 13 May, 1671

On the morning of the fourth day, there came the sudden thunder of iron-nailed boots on the stairs, the door was smashed open and men with muskets and swords tumbled into the little room on the first floor of the Blue Boar Inn. Tom was taken completely unawares and reacted lamentably slowly, getting to his feet from the stool by the window and standing gaping at the bawling red-coated intruders. Joshua Parrot, on the other hand, even wounded and sick, was up from his pallet like a cat, with a long dagger in each hand and a window-rattling roar erupting from his throat.

As the first man charged through the shattered door, Parrot disembowelled him with a neat thrust to the belly and twist of his right-hand dagger. He killed the second man a moment later, with his left hand hacking through his neck so deeply that the white of his spine was glimpsed for a second before the man fell. Someone fired a musket and the ball flew past Tom and smashed the smeared glass of the window. Parrot was in the doorway now, snarling and slicing, and Tom could see hands grasped around his thick neck and a jumble of struggling red bodies beyond in the corridor. A sword hacked down at the big man's head, partially severing Parrot's ear. Another blade passed straight through his thick body, the bloody tip emerging between his shoulder blades.

And Tom, at last, moved. He lifted the latch of the shattered window and pushed it open, the remaining glass falling out of the frame onto the vegetable patch below. Tom had one leg out of the sill. He saw Parrot take a musket butt to the chest and falter, drooping in the doorway, then recover and surge up and forward and out of the door, the two daggers carving the air in front of him and clearing the redcoats from his path. The last thing Tom saw before he dropped to the garden below was the side of Parrot's head exploding in a shower of blood and skull fragments as a pistol was fired into his roaring face at point-blank rage.

Tom landed in the soft soil of the vegetable patch, sinking up to his ankles and immediately rolling over and snapping off half a dozen asparagus stalks. He got up fast, recovered his hat and began blundering through the earth to the path, and there running as swiftly as he could to Seven Steps Alley. He whipped his head around to look at the window in the brick wall of the Blue Boar and saw a dark head looking out after him.

He burst out into Gravel Lane, turned left, sprinting for Hounds Ditch, where the road was narrowed by the stalls of the cloth-sellers and jammed with carts and people. Forced to slow, he began pushing his way through the throng, buffeted by tradesmen carrying huge soft bundles. He pulled his hat low over his forehead and, as a result, he did not see his assailant's face. He merely saw that a man on a horse was beside him, the animal's muscular flank jostling him, and noted the thigh-length black leather military boots and silver spurs and the long scarlet wool coat with shiny brass buttons. Something crashed hard against his head and he felt his knees sag, all his strength washed away. He thought: 'Father is going to be so angry with me.' Then another hard blow fetched him into the darkness.

Sunday 14 May, 1671

Blood emerged from his own darkness and into the agony of consciousness. His face felt like a single swollen mass, the stumps of at least two shattered teeth sharp against the inside of his lip. His leg ached from the pulsing wound in his thigh to the shrieking of his shinbones, all the way down to his ankles where the skin had been stripped by the fetters. As he moved, rolling on to his side, he almost screamed from the cramping in his arms and back.

His eyes were swollen shut but he could feel wetness on his face and a gentle movement on the hot, stretched skin. Someone was washing him – he could feel the wet cloth on his forehead now, soft strokes. And whoever it was seemed to be counting, very quietly, just under his breath. 'Twenty-one, twenty-two, twenty-three . . .'

Blood relaxed. He felt the cloth wipe away the clots of blood and dried matter from his swollen eyes, but he did not try to open them. He knew who was with him. He listened to the counting – 'Twenty-eight, twenty-nine, thirty, thirty-one' – and felt its sweet, soporific effect, like the singing of a lullaby. Only the thrum of his pain kept him from falling into slumber.

After a while, he felt the person beside him get up and move away. He half opened an eye then, and saw Holcroft conferring with a gaoler, a short, hunched muscular creature with large, sad eyes and an enormous grey beard, and saw a coin pass between them. Then the gaoler came, knelt beside him and unlocked his manacles, both wrists and ankles, slipping them free and bearing them away. Blood knew that they must be snapped on again and soon, and he dreaded it, but the sudden absence of their weight was blissful. He found that he was weeping, hot tears running down his swollen cheek, and cursed himself for a weakling.

'Father, are you awake?'

Blood tried to sit up, and Holcroft helped him, lifting his father's fifteen stones more easily than he could have imagined, and setting him in the chair. Holcroft brought him water, and Blood swallowed it down. Then Holcroft said: 'I have a small cask of brandy, if you are strong enough to take some.'

Blood nodded and smiled and when he had engulfed a beaker of the fiery brown liquid, coughing like a dying beggar and feeling the burn all the way down into his belly, he opened his eyes fully, lifted his head and said: 'You are surely destined for Heaven, my son! The Lord will reward you.'

'Not just yet, I hope.' Father and son smiled at each other.

Blood gestured with his chin at the gaoler, who was watching them from the far side of the chamber, a tiny suspicious figure, pretending to clean the huge manacles with a blood-streaked cloth. 'Can you make him leave us alone for half an hour, son? I need to speak privily.'

Holcroft got up from his place on the floor beside his father's chair and strode over to the gaoler. Another bright coin passed.

He's grown, thought Blood. *His back is easily as broad as mine now – but, more than that, he is a man. He talks to other fellows like a man, as an equal. He knows his own worth. Why did I ever doubt it?*

When the gaoler had left, and Blood had accepted another welcome glass of the brandy, he said: 'Listen to me, son, we do not have much time. You have guessed that I did this business on Buckingham's orders – yes?'

Holcroft said, 'He sent me with a message to you: he says you are to stay silent. Keep your mouth shut and he will help you.'

'He lies. He always lies. He means to allow me to hang. But I shall not oblige him. I'll stay silent, yes, if I can find the strength to resist them. But I must have a royal pardon. Only a pardon from the King will save me. And I must see the King in person to obtain it. Now listen to me, son, remember my words: Buckingham gave me the order to make an attempt on the jewels, but he takes his orders from higher still. If he sanctioned this then his master – and by that I mean His Majesty himself – must have known about the attempt, at the very least, if he did not in fact order it. I was to turn over all the jewels to Buckingham, that was the arrangement we made, and we would receive a vast sum of money for all our pains – ten thousand pounds!'

Holcroft looked at his father with mingled incredulity and respect at the size of the sum. 'If the King ordered you to do this, even indirectly, then surely he must grant you a pardon.'

'I am sure the King would deny it to his dying day, if he could, and so would my Lord Buckingham. So I wrote a letter to the King and smuggled it out the day before they started beating me, praise God, for I do not think I could hold a steady quill now. In that letter I begged the King for an audience – and I made it blindingly clear that if I am to suffer death I shall tell the world everything that I know about both His Majesty's and Buckingham's role in this little affair. I also mentioned that I have been receiving funds – government funds from the Pay Office via his henchmen Sir Thomas Littleton and his brother James and that bastard Sir Thomas Osborne. I hope that will suffice to secure me an audience. But I tell you, too, so that you know the truth, in case everything should go bad. Also, I have an ace up my sleeve . . .'

At that moment, the chamber door opened a little and the dwarfish gaoler poked his head through the gap.

'We agreed half a crown for a full half an hour, sir,' said Holcroft, leaping to his feet. 'And not five minutes have passed!'

'Your honour, we did indeed. But here's another visitor for the colonel. I did not like to keep her waiting.'

He pushed open the door and Jenny Blaine walked in, looking pale and frightened, but still quite remarkably beautiful.

She took one look at Blood – even cleaned up by Holcroft he was appallingly bruised and battered – and rushed over to him and began exclaiming about the cruelty of his treatment, weeping in sympathy and kissing whichever unmarked parts of his face she could find.

Blood stopped her by grasping her arms. 'My dear, calm yourself. Have a drop of the brandy – get me another one, too – and allow me to finish this conversation with my son. A moment and I will be all yours, my love. One brief moment.'

Jenny looked uncertainly between Blood and Holcroft. But she had enough wit to realize that she was intruding. She stepped over to the table by the window and began noisily clinking bottle and glasses.

'As I said, I have an ace up my sleeve,' continued Blood then, looking into his son's puzzled face he said, 'By that I mean I have something to bargain with for my life. The jewels. They found some of them on me but the others – including our Tom – got clean away with the rest of them.'

Blood looked around the room. Jenny was out of earshot at the table on the far side of the chamber, looking hurt and sipping a glass of brandy.

Blood pulled Holcroft closer to him and whispered in his ear. 'Go to the Blue Boar Inn off White Chapel Street, ask for Matthew Warburton. He's a friend. Tell him who you are. He should have news of the others and the jewels. I mean to trade them with Buckingham and the King for my life. Go to the Boar and bring whatever message the boys have left for me there.'

'So it is blackmail,' said the King. 'This Blood fellow means to buy his freedom with threats against me. Do I have it correctly?'

'Yes, sire,' said the Duke of Buckingham. He was surprised by how calm the King was. It was near midnight, His Majesty had been readying himself for bed when he read the letter, thinking it was some private piece of correspondence, a love letter or something of that nature. He had immediately summoned Buckingham – the hour be damned! And now, wearing nothing but a nightshirt and walking up and down the royal bedchamber holding the letter from Blood in his hand, the King berated his chief minister in a stern icy tone. Sir John Grenville stood by the large brocade-swathed bed holding up a blue quilted silk robe, waiting patiently for the monarch to put it on. His face was quite expressionless.

The King looked again at the letter in his hand. 'It says here:

> May it please Your Majesty, this may tell and inform you, that it was Sir Thomas Osborne and Sir Thomas Littleton, both your treasurers of your Navy, that set me to steal your crown, but he that feeds me with money was James Littleton, Esq. 'Tis he that pays under the treasurers at the Pay Office. He is a very bold villain, a very rogue, for I and my companions have had many a hundred pounds of him of Your Majesty's money to encourage us upon this attempt . . .'

The King broke off and stared at Buckingham. 'Is this true? Did you have the wretched man funded out of the Pay Office? That is a public office – there are records, files, clerks who make a note of *everything*, a trail of papers that connects this murderous villain Blood all the way to myself. You have a reputation for being subtle as a serpent, my lord, but this is gross incompetence. There is no other word for it. You told me when I agreed to this outrageous scheme, against my better nature, I might add, that it would never be discovered and yet – here in my hand – I have a letter from this brass-necked old outlaw threatening to make all this business public. He is threatening to make me the laughing stock of Europe: the beggar King whose poverty forced him to steal his own Crown Jewels – and who made an appalling hash of it. It won't do, Buckingham, it really will not do!'

The duke was feeling distinctly uncomfortable. 'Your Majesty,' he began, 'all is not lost. We have recovered most of the jewels from that inn in White Chapel Street. Blood is in chains and the world knows he is guilty – after his past escapades in Ireland, the attempt on Dublin Castle, particularly, marks him indelibly as an enemy of the state and of your person . . .'

'Why on earth did you engage this dangerous rebel in the first place? He seems to be known more for his failures than anything else. You said it would be a reliable man who undertook the task. You *said* the jewels would be gone in the blink of an eye, they would be handed over to you and could be broken up and sold by your Jewish friends in Antwerp; you said I would receive no less than fifty thousand pounds and we would then persuade Parliament to vote us the money to buy more jewels. A King without Crown Jewels, you said, if I recall correctly, would be so lacking in dignity that both Houses must vote us money to replace them to avoid the shame.'

Buckingham's patience was near its end. 'I have said many, many things to Your Majesty in the past. But I think that now it might be wiser to concentrate not on the past but on the future.'

He whirled and glared at Sir John Grenville. 'And you can wipe that schoolboy smirk off your face!'

Grenville's face had, in fact, been entirely immobile. But the King remembered his groom of the close stool then and went over and allowed him to thread his arms in the sleeves, drape the robe around his shoulders and tie the belt around his waist.

'Your Majesty,' Buckingham continued, when he had regained his composure, 'all is not lost. We have the jewels, we have Blood – and I believe I can persuade him to keep his mouth shut until he is tried and hanged. A week or two should see it done. But I may need to make some outlays in gold – and perhaps if you were to make some gesture towards me in recompense for the expenses I shall undoubtedly incur, that would encourage me to manage this matter as swiftly and quietly as possible.'

'What do you want?'

'There is a sweet little estate in County Kildare called Straffan that would complement my lands in that county most charmingly.'

The King looked at him. 'I'll think about it. But can you truly get Blood to stay quiet and accept his own death without a murmur? How?'

'I have my own methods, sire, but I think it would be best if you were not party to them, don't you?'

For the first time the King looked discomforted. 'Yes, don't tell me. You're right. I don't want to know. But you should know this, my Lord Buckingham. If your methods are as incompetently managed as the rest of this risible shambles, I *will* make you pay for it. And you will never get your hands on Straffan or any other "sweet little estates" that are within my gift, that I can tell you. If I am in the slightest part embarrassed by this, whatever it is, and if you do not swiftly clear up this enormous stinking shit-pile you have created – you will be finished at court. Do I make myself clear?'

Monday 15 May, 1671

Holcroft had returned directly to the Cockpit after a brief visit to the Blue Boar. Warburton had been hostile and had claimed that he had no message for Blood but, grudgingly, he had shown the boy the room where the men had stayed and the bloodstains on the floorboards of the corridor where Parrot had met his end. He told him that the soldiers had taken Parrot's body and the glittering mound of jewels with them when they departed. Tom, he said, had jumped from the window and escaped. It was clear from his manner that he could not wait for Holcroft to leave his inn. Finally, Warburton asked him to tell his father that the favour was now more than repaid and that he would be most obliged if Colonel Blood never darkened his door again.

There had been no point in returning to the Tower to deliver this bad news so Holcroft had returned to the Cockpit from White Chapel Street, low-spirited, despondent and strangely exhausted by events. He went to bed.

The next morning after he had made his usual delivery and collection at the General Letter Office in the City, there was another shock awaiting him when he returned to the clerks' office in the Duke of Buckingham's apartments. When he looked in the little cupboard beneath his desk that held his few personal possessions, he saw that the lock had been crudely broken open with a knife or a chisel and that his belongings, usually meticulously folded and placed just so, had been rummaged through and were tossed into confusion. Holcroft felt sick. The intrusion felt like an assault on his person. Worse than that, when he looked again through his belongings, he found that his pack of Parisian playing cards was gone.

The cards might have been limp, greasy and past their best, but the feeling in his heart was akin to a bereavement. The queen of diamonds, and all the others, had been taken from him. He could feel an actual physical pain in his heart. Yet he also recognized with part of his mind that they were only fifty-two painted rectangles of cardboard worth no more than a shilling or two, perhaps less.

When they returned from their dinner, he asked Mullins and the other two clerks if they knew anything about the breaking of the lock on his cupboard, and they evinced surprise and horror and vowed they knew nothing about it, but there was something about their manner, they looked away from Holcroft when they offered their condolences for his lost belongings, that made him feel uneasy. Not that he was any judge of the subtleties of human expression, but he was almost sure that they were lying to him.

Then Mullins handed him a small letter that had arrived that morning from Lancashire, and he read with a sense of dull inevitability that his mother was dead. Granny Maggie wrote that despite the solicitous care of the local physician – whose fee was only affordable through Holcroft's generosity – his mother had been gathered unto God a week ago after a long, draining illness. She had been buried in the churchyard at Culcheth. Holcroft sat staring numbly at his desk and considered the twin losses of his Parisian playing cards and his mother. He wondered which he would rather have back in his life – then stopped himself from completing that thought.

When the little bell rang, summoning him to his master's study, it was almost with a sense of relief that he gathered up his papers and left his silent, awkward colleagues and made his way through the corridors and into the Duke of Buckingham's lair.

There was a palpable sense of gaiety in the duke's study as if some triumph were being celebrated. Sir Thomas Osborne, Sir Thomas Littleton and the duke were drinking port wine and it was clear when Holcroft entered that Littleton had been telling an anecdote. Oddly, when the confidential clerk came into the room, Littleton stopped mid-sentence and all three men stared at him as if they'd never seen him before in their lives.

'Should I come back later, Your Grace?'

'No, no. Come in, Mister Blood – we were just discussing your illustrious family.'

Holcroft had no idea what to say to that so he said nothing.

'Now, Holcroft – tell me, if you would be so kind, where have we got to on the matter of the Duke of Ormonde's letter?'

Holcroft looked meaningfully at Osborne and Littleton, then back at the duke with raised eyebrows.

'Oh do not worry about these two. You may speak freely in front of them; they have been fully appraised of the situation.'

'I have the letter on my person,' said Holcroft, touching the front of his coat and feeling the crackle of paper from the inside pocket. 'And I am prepared to give it to you in exchange for your word of honour that you will pay over the agreed sum of five hundred pounds within the week. You two gentlemen shall witness the duke's word, if you please.' Holcroft looked at Littleton and Osborne who merely smiled archly, then glanced at each other.

'Oh certainly,' said the duke, 'you have my word that I shall pay up like a lamb – if the letter is truly what it is purported to be.'

He held out his hand.

Holcroft reached into his inside coat pocket, pulled out the letter and passed it to him.

The duke opened the letter and took a long time in reading it. Holcroft looked out of the window. It was a cold, cloudy day, and though it was mid-May it had more of the chill of autumn about it.

'It's very good,' said the duke finally. 'Very good indeed.'

'You are satisfied with it then, sir?'

'I'm impressed. Who did Aphra use for this? Was it that playbill-writer Wilkinson? He's the best in the business and this is fine work. It's almost perfect: the signature is superb, if I didn't know it was as fake as a wooden farthing, I might well believe it. Tell Mistress Behn I congratulate her.'

Holcroft's belly felt as if it was filling with icy water.

'Are you not going to protest? Will you not swear on your honour that it is the real document?'

Holcroft shrugged.

'Will you not plead ignorance? Or say that you did not know that it was a fake? Weep bitter tears? Pretend that Aphra Behn hoodwinked you?'

Holcroft said nothing.

'Oh you are a sad bore, Mister Blood, a great disappointment to me. I promised my friends some entertainment today. I planned to have Westbury and d'Erloncourt come in and confound you with the evidence of their eyes – they followed you all over town, you know, and saw you meeting the Behn woman to plot this shabby little deceit half a dozen times. You were hardly discreet. So – nothing to say to me then?'

'If you do not want to buy the letter, may I have it back?'

Buckingham actually laughed. 'You are a cool one. Why not? I am a man of my word and I am certainly not going to pay you for this nonsense. Here. Take it.' He spun the letter from his fingers towards Holcroft. It reached about halfway between them and fluttered to the floor. Holcroft bent down and picked it up.

'I suppose you plan to sell it to Lord Arlington. Is that your scheme? You failed to dupe me so why not try again. Is that it?'

Holcroft said nothing. He was thinking of his wasted five pounds.

'I don't mind in the slightest if you do, actually; anything that blackens Ormonde's name is a joy to me. Make a fool of Arlington too, by all means. But do not dare to mention my name to him in connection with this.'

'Is there any thing else that you require of me, Your Grace?'

For the first time, the duke showed a trace of anger: 'Yes, God damn you. I require that you consider yourself dismissed from my service. I require that you take your miserable, conniving, ungrateful, cheating carcass out of my sight this minute. That is what I require of you, Mister Blood. And you should ensure that I do not lay eyes on you ever again. You are fortunate that I do not have you flogged through White Hall. I consider that I am being more than merciful in that I do not bring you before a magistrate and have you hanged. So go, consider yourself lucky, and do not trouble me again!'

Holcroft bowed, turned and headed for the door. Before he had got through it, he heard the duke say: 'Oh, and you should know, boy, that your father will be dead before the month is up. The King will not see him. Take that happy thought with you, ingrate!'

It took Holcroft less than five minutes to gather up his belongings from the clerk's hall, his papers and his clothes, and bundle them up in an old cloth fardel before heading out into the tulip garden. But during that short time, it seemed that word of his ignominious dismissal had spread like lightning throughout the entire staff of the duke's establishment.

The pages were all there to watch him go: Robert Westbury, with a superior smirk on his aristocratic face; Henri d'Erloncourt, who blushed and glared and seemed furious that Holcroft should have tried to dupe his lover; and Albert St John, who just looked confused and a little frightened. Mullins and his three clerks kept their faces artfully blank. Matlock the steward gave him an evil grin and a little comical wave goodbye. But it was Arnold the porter who administered the coup de grâce. As Holcroft passed through his gate and set off down the narrow alley towards The Street with his bundle over his shoulder, Arnold lashed out with his long leg and gave Holcroft a humiliating and surprisingly painful boot directly to the seat of his breeches.

Later that afternoon, in a mood of celebration, Arnold Smith and Robert Westbury shared a large jug of the duke's best burgundy in the cosy back room of the porter's lodge. The porter and the senior page had engaged in carouses before – over several memorable nights, Arnold had introduced the boy to some of the murkier houses of ill-repute in London, the kind of places where you could do anything, absolutely anything, you liked to the girls, up to and including murder, if you had the money to pay for it – and Westbury, while otherwise forgotten by his father, still received a generous allowance.

'I must say I was glad to see the back of that mad prig Blood,' said Westbury, idly scratching a louse in his groin. 'He's been like a stone in my shoe these past few months but, thank God, we've seen the last of him.'

'Trying to nip gold money out of our duke like that,' agreed Arnold, taking a deep swig of his stolen burgundy, 'he ought to be hanged at the very least. Old Bucky was too soft on him, in my humble opinion. Far too soft. Only encourages the other sharpers.'

'I suspect he fancied him. Blood probably sucked his fat cock most nights. Makes even the greatest nobleman feel mighty kind and forgiving, having his balls drained on a regular basis.'

'It's not right, though. Not right at all. He should have had more 'n a fare-thee-well and a boot up the bum after what he did.'

'I wouldn't have minded giving him a few good licks from my belt,' said Westbury, 'maybe even a proper old-fashioned horse-whipping. But it's too late now – the dim-lit bastard's gone for good.'

'It might not be too late, Bobbie,' said Arnold, shooting a glance at his friend. 'Might not be too late at all. Where do you suppose he might have fetched up?'

'Where would he go? To a friend's house, I suppose. His father is in the Tower, likely to be hanged any day. And I heard his mother was dead, too. So I suppose he would try to find lodging with a friend.'

'Didn't have too many friends, as I recall,' said Arnold slyly.

Westbury and Arnold looked at each other.

'He'll go to the Behn woman,' said Westbury.

'He's likely tucked up cosy with that little slut, sucking on her lovely titties as he cries his little eyes out at his great misfortune.'

'I wouldn't mind a bit of that myself,' said Westbury, laughing.

'How do you suppose our duke would feel,' said the old porter, 'if a pair of ruffians, knowing where Master Holcroft was roosting now, was to set upon him, say, in a darkened alley and give him a bit of a hiding – maybe that horse-whipping you spoke of. Maybe they might take a lash to that blonde bitch, too; maybe even give her a little something more besides.'

'I should think the duke would be delighted.'

'The ruffians would have to give it a few days, let the dust settle, so to speak. Make sure they knew where the bastard was staying. But then . . . Do you think a reward of some sort might be forthcoming from Old Bucky?'

'It might well be, for service above and beyond the call of duty. Ten pounds. Twenty, if the old boy was feeling generous. At the very least the, ah, ruffians would have the gratitude of our good duke – and that might be worth something one day – and o' course the satisfaction of delivering just retribution to those who most certainly deserve it.'

Holcroft heard the singing long before he saw the four men approaching. After six months in White Hall he was quite familiar with groups of drunken courtiers stumbling joyfully from one place of refreshment to another, but he had learned to avoid them since their rough horseplay and crude teasing could quickly turn to ugly violence – Albert St John had had his breeches pulled down by one such group of gallants not two weeks past and when he protested, the revellers, every man bearing some title of dignity, some even peers of the realm, had knocked him down and pissed all over him.

So, at the sounds of revelry, Holcroft got up from the stone seat before the sundial in the Privy Garden, where he had been sitting these past two hours, trying to quiet his frantic mind after his dismissal, and moved back thirty yards or so into the shadow of a yew hedge where in his dark coat he was reasonably inconspicuous. He recognized John Wilmot, Earl of Rochester, an intimate of the King and a notorious drunkard and one of the other men, a bluff fellow called Henry Savile. The bawdy singing, something about the King and his mistresses, broke down into confused barks of laughter as the four men drew near to the sundial. He heard Wilmot declaim: 'Restless he rolls from whore to whore; a merry monarch, scandalous and poor!'

His friends all honked like geese and clutched their hands to their stomachs with the agony of their glee.

Holcroft drew further back into the shade of the yew hedge.

Wilmot made a great show of peering at the enamel plaque that depicted the King holding his sceptre, which appeared to jut priapically from his lap, then he turned to his comrades, winked at them, looked back at the plaque and said: 'What's that, Your Majesty? Do you mean to fuck Time?'

His companions fell about, some laughing so hard they fell to the ground, praising his wit between gasps. Holcroft felt disgusted, even soiled, not just at the disrespect shown to the King's image but also at that shown to the sundial, that divine instrument, the incarnation of universal rectitude.

With a flourish, Wilmot drew his sword, a slim steel blade about a yard in length. 'I am afraid, Your Majesty,' he said, 'I cannot allow that unnatural congress. Kings and Kingdoms shall tumble, and so shall you!'

With that the Earl of Rochester began slashing wildly at the sundial; the glass spheres popping like pricked bladders, the metal arms clanging discordantly against the steel blade, slicing off the filigree works, bending the arms, the extremities snapping clean off. Holcroft stood rooted to the spot, frozen in horror. Wilmot's friends, hooting with joy, drew their own weapons and began to attack the sundial with a similar manic energy, hacking at its elegant limbs, cracking the enamel plaques, slashing at the central iron stem in a bizarre parody of the melee. When the others were puffing, red-faced, spent, Henry Savile hurled himself bodily at the ruined sundial, catching it with his beefy shoulder and knocking it down to crash against the gravel path on which it had stood. He picked himself up and looked at his companions: 'The tyrant is dead, long live Mother Time!'

If he had been expecting cheers, he was to be disappointed. Not a man said anything. The mood had changed as swiftly as the wind. Wilmot was looking at the nicks in the edge of his sword, feeling them with his thumb. The other two men looked shamefaced. 'This calls for a mighty drink!' said Wilmot. 'Come, my gang of merry revellers, let us celebrate our victory!'

'Let us stroll in St James's Park,' said Savile. 'There are wine-sellers a plenty to be found there – whores too, I'll warrant.'

As they staggered away, Holcroft saw Johnny Wilmot lay an arm over Henry Savile's broad shoulder and heard him say in a conversational tone: 'Much wine had passed, with grave discourse, of who fucks who, and who does worse . . .'

When they had gone, Holcroft approached the mangled remains of the sundial as if he were walking up to a fresh and bloody corpse. He looked down at the scattered, severed arms, the shards of broken glass and enamel, chips of gold paint, the twisted metal limbs, the hacked-off dials, the whole once-beautiful edifice lying on the gravel of the path like a fallen warrior, dismembered in the dusk of a battlefield, and he felt the acid tears burn his eyelids that had not come when he had heard that his mother was dead. Nor had he wept when the Duke of Buckingham had expelled him from the Cockpit that afternoon, dashing his hopes of ever becoming a soldier, nor had there been tears at the news of his father's imminent death.

The destruction of this beautiful object, however, the altar at which he had worshipped so long, had him gasping and snivelling like a little girl.

He bent and put a hand out towards a half-whole glass sphere, one he recognized by its yellowish paint as the moon. He felt an overwhelming urge to try to put it back together, to collect the strewn shards and somehow fix them back into position, to bring some order back into this shattered cosmos – to try to mend the breaking of the world. He withdrew his fingers at the last moment. There could be no remaking this. This man-made universe was destroyed, just as his personal universe was unmade by his expulsion from the Cockpit. All order had been turned to chaos. All of it. Chaos surrounded him, engulfed him, drowned him in black uncertainty. He sank to his knees, bowed his head as if in prayer and allowed the long-restrained tears to flow unchecked.

Sunday 21 May, 1671

Blood sat at the desk by the barred window in the prison chamber in the White Tower and sprinkled fine white sand over the letter he had just finished writing. It was a breezy note to his second son William, who was a steward aboard the frigate HMS *Jersey*, now cruising in the Caribbean, telling him that his father had some temporary difficulties with the law but that all would be well soon. He also mentioned, almost as an afterthought, the sad news that William's mother had died. Blood looked at the note – had he struck the right tone? It occurred to him that perhaps he should have begun with the news about his wife's death.

He shrugged. It was all one, he supposed. In truth he did not know if this son was even alive. He had not heard from him for more than two years and the Caribbean station was notorious for deadly fevers. He was writing to him now, he admitted to himself, because the shadow of the noose loomed large. His beatings had ceased more than a week ago and his body was on the way to recovery, his leg wound drying nicely, but the prospect of an ignominious end on the gallows had spurred him to write to all his children so that they should have some last communication from their father and might know that he loved them all before he was consigned to eternity.

He did not know why the beatings had stopped – although he was profoundly grateful for the fact – he assumed that either Wythe Edwards had finally admitted defeat in his attempt to make Blood speak or he had been recalled to his duty with the regiment in Flanders. Anyway, Edwards had not been seen for eight days now and apart from Jenny who visited him every day, and Holcroft who had come last Sunday, he had had no other visitors.

He folded the letter carefully, over and over, melted some of the blue wax in the flame of the candle, dripped it on the fold and pressed his gold signet ring into the spreading pool. At that instant the door to his prison chamber opened and the misshapen little gaoler looked inside.

'A gentleman to see you, colonel.'

'Thank you, Widdicombe. Please be so good as to show him in.'

Holcroft had left a decent amount of money with Blood on his last visit, his saved pay from his time in the Cockpit and some of his winnings at cards, and, since the end of his interrogation, Blood had managed to arrange his life in the prison so that it offered some comforts. Food was brought in from one of the many bake-shops to the west of the Tower and tobacco, wine and ale from the taverns there, too. He had managed to secure paper, quills, ink, a small folding penknife and sand; soap and a razor, decent bedding, several changes of linen and the services of a washerwoman. Life in the Tower was now about as civilized as it could be for a man who suspected that he was about to be hanged in the very near future.

Blood looked expectantly at the door. If his heart sank at the sight of Sir Thomas Osborne in the narrow doorway, he gave no indication of it.

'Ah, Tommy-boy, what a joy it is to see you again!' he said jovially. But the joke sounded stale even to him.

'I'm glad I bring you joy,' said Osborne, 'for I have little else to offer you except bad news. A date for your trial has been set for Friday the twenty-sixth of May, at eleven o'clock, at the Old Bailey. That is in five days' time. And I have more sad tidings: I am afraid that Sir William Morton will be the presiding judge.'

'Old "Murderous" Morton, eh?' said Blood, forcing himself to chuckle. 'He was the fellow who ordered that dandyprat Claude Du Vall to be strung up, the French highwayman, you remember, despite the outcry against it. You have picked a right hanging judge for the task, Tommy, oh yes indeed.'

'There can be no uncertainty about the outcome, I'm afraid.'

Blood and Osborne looked at each other soberly. Then the prisoner said: 'And you know – yes? – and Buckingham knows, that if I am brought to the Old Bailey, in front of the crowds, that I shall say my piece about what truly happened – who put me up to this. You know that I shall reveal all the names involved including yours and Littleton's and his brother right up to the highest in the land. You do know that, Tommy-boy, do you not?'

'We were rather hoping that we could persuade you not to speak of any of these matters. We hoped that you would accept the inevitable verdict and sentence of Judge Morton without kicking up an ugly fuss.'

'You want me to die quietly, like a gentleman, is that it? And why in the name of the Devil's hairy arse-crack would I want to do that? To protect you, to protect Buckingham?' Blood's voice had begun to rise. He knew that his temper was fraying dangerously but he was unable to command himself.

'Does the King know about this? I wrote to him, you know, and revealed your name. I made a veiled threat to implicate Charles himself, if necessary. I believe I have a good chance of receiving a royal pardon in due course. I may well write the King another letter. I might well write to that Muddiman fellow, the editor of the *Gazette*. So I may as well tell you now that I reject your offer of a quiet death – if I am to die on the gallows it will be as noisily as I can make it and I swear to you that before I dangle I will take down with me as many of you two-faced whore-sons as I possibly can.'

'I rather thought you might say that. For what it is worth, I think Buckingham was a damn fool to have used you for this task. He has been increasingly careless in recent months. Yet I do not consider you as much of an imbecile as perhaps I pretend. I realize that you were brought low only by the merest chance – if that young officer, Edwards, had not turned up at the very moment you were engaged in your business, we might have had a much happier outcome – and everyone a good deal richer. However, it *was* a failure and it has left a hellish mess; a mess that I am required to clean up.'

Blood frowned at the man. He let his right hand fall on the open penknife on the desk, feeling the cool steel of its two-inch blade beneath his casual fingers. Surely Sir Thomas Osborne could not be thinking of trying to silence him in that old sanguinary manner. He'd never manage the job, man to man, not in a thousand years.

'Let me tell you how it will happen,' Osborne went on. 'You will face trial, sentencing and death with all the fortitude and courage that I know you are capable of. Afterwards, you will be given a Christian burial and your name will be spoken of with respect across the land long after your demise. Three hundred years hence your story will still be told – and who then will remember Claude Du Vall? I will give you immortality in exchange for a quiet death. And during your trial you may speak or not speak to the court just as you choose, so long as, at any time, even alone in your death cell, you do not again mention my name, Thomas Littleton's name, nor that of his brother James. You will certainly not mention the Duke of Buckingham's role in this and, even more certainly, you will not mention the merest hint of a connection to His Majesty the King.'

'That's what you think is going to happen, is it?'

'Yes, because if you do not do exactly as you are told there will be two men, not one, on the scaffold that day: you and your eldest son Tom.'

Osborne took a deep breath and called, 'Widdicombe! Bring in the other prisoner.'

Blood rose slowly to his feet and looked on with horror as the dwarfish gaoler bundled a blood-soaked, raggedy figure, manacled wrist and foot, through the doorway of his chamber.

Tom Blood looked up at his father from the cell floor: he was almost unrecognizable. It was clear that he had been beaten with an equal ferocity to Blood's own ordeal and his face was a mass of livid cuts, dried gore and purple bruising.

'I'm sorry, Father. I told them everything I knew. That soldier, he kept on beating me. Day after day. I couldn't help it. I'm so terribly sorry.'

Blood smiled at his boy, but the tears were now spilling down his own bruised cheeks. 'Never fear, lad. Never fear. I know how I can mend this.'

'So you accept the arrangement?' said Osborne. 'A quiet death and Tom walks free. Otherwise, I'm afraid, 'tis two for the Tyburn jig.'

'A quiet death, then,' said Blood without bothering to look at the Treasury man. Then, much louder, to Tom: 'Don't you worry about a thing, son. Just keep the faith, my boy, and we'll all come up smiling yet!'

Aphra Behn was in her usual black habit. She was making the perennial pot of tea for them to share. Holcroft had been there almost a week now, sleeping on her floor at night and wandering the streets of London by day, racking his brains for some way out of the chaos he had found himself in.

He had no livelihood. His father would surely soon be condemned to die. His mother was already dead. His siblings were scattered across the world – maybe dead, who knew? He had two shillings and eight pence in his pocket and little hope of coming by any more. And he had squandered the finest opportunity he had ever had for advancement by chasing illicit riches.

When he had arrived unannounced on the evening of his expulsion from the Cockpit, he had swiftly explained to Aphra the situation and she had taken the terrible news with equanimity.

'It could have been worse. Buckingham could have had us up before a magistrate, slung into the Marshalsea to rot for months, even years, before a trial – he could have had you beaten to death. In these situations, one has to count one's blessings and move on.'

'Yes, but what are we going to do now?'

'We? We're not going to do anything. The game is over. We lost. We tried to take Buckingham and failed. He proved to be the better player. There is nothing left for us to do but move along.'

Holcroft had said nothing. He had become accustomed in recent weeks to presenting a problem to Aphra only to have her reassure him, calm him and solve it. Now she seemed to have nothing to offer. He had gratefully accepted her offer of a place to sleep for a few days but since then he felt he had been existing in a void.

On this night, the seventh under her roof, he stared mutely at the boiling water in the pan. He had been sitting there for two hours, continually rocking gently back and forth on a stool. He was thinking.

Aphra possessed a robust and buoyant nature that was rarely disheartened by adversity. But she knew that Holcroft was adrift in the sea of life and, tough as she was, she was not dead to compassion. She put out a hand and snuffed out the spirit burner under the pan of water.

'Listen, Holcroft. This is no time for mere tea. Let us go down to the Red Lion and order up a bowl of punch, maybe a slice or two of Madge's pork pie. I think I can afford to treat you. We will have a chat about our future with a full belly. That will make things seem better. How about it?'

Holcroft said nothing. He continued staring at the spirit burner and the cooling pan of water.

'Holcroft, come on. Let's get out of here. Come on.'

Aphra went to him and gently lifted him up by the arm from the stool.

They made their way down the decrepit wooden staircase, the smell of cabbage growing stronger as they descended, and stepped out of the front door and into St Thomas Street. It was full dark now, not a soul out of doors, and the only light was a big, cheerful lantern hung outside the Red Lion on the corner of Drury Lane a hundred yards away.

To the west of Drury Lane, on the far side of the road from the inn, was the great sprawling, stinking mass of the St Giles slum. Holcroft, of course, was oblivious to the fine social distinctions of London's neighbourhoods. Even had he understood the intricate hierarchy it is unlikely that it would have interested him. He had been thinking all day, for several days, in fact – and something, something was forming in his brain. A plan. He would need Aphra's help, of course. And that of another friend. But it could work.

A dark lump detached itself from the porch of a house near the end of the street about twenty yards away from the walking pair, and resolved itself into the forms of two men. Holcroft could see that one of them held a long thin pole or maybe a horse whip, it was highlighted from behind by the flickering light from the Red Lion's lantern.

'Aphra!' he hissed.

'I see them,' she replied.

They swung away from the two men, crossing the narrow street and making for the north side. The two men veered towards them. They were just yards away now. Holcroft stopped, turned to face them, standing in the middle of the deserted street. He could not make out their faces, with the lantern light behind them, but their shapes were familiar. He caught a flash of golden cloth in the darkness.

'You've had this coming a long time, Blood,' said the taller of the two, and he recognized Robert Westbury's patrician voice. The second man spoke then: 'And your pretty love-bird, your partner in infamy – maybe we'll have a little fun with you, *lady*, when we've dealt with this scoundrel.'

As he half turned to the light, Holcroft saw that the shorter, broader man was Arnold Smith the Cockpit porter.

'Go back to the house, Aphra,' he said, giving her a gentle push on the arm. 'Lock the door. Barricade it, if you have to. I will speak with these two gentlemen alone.'

'I don't think so,' she said. Out of the corner of his eye, down low by her right thigh, he saw a metallic gleam of reflected lantern light.

Holcroft sensed rather than saw the fist coming out of the darkness from Westbury, but his reaction was as swift as could be. He got his forearm up and deflected the punch past his left ear. At the same time his own right shot out and connected solidly with Westbury's chin. His opponent was knocked back a step but did not fall. Arnold swung the horse whip at Aphra, and he heard the sharp smack as it struck her shoulder. He had no time to intervene. Westbury came boring in with left and right hands punching wildly, the blows looping in one after the other. *He still can't fight,* thought Holcroft. He ducked the first right, blocked the next left with his elbow. Then he cut through the flurry of arms with a hard straight jab to the nose, feeling the cartilage snap, and smashing Westbury's head back. He was aware that Arnold had seized Aphra from behind, was now pinning her arms and holding her tight. He seemed to be whispering something into her ear.

Westbury was punching at him again. Very late, Holcroft felt the first acid rush of real anger, a sourness in his belly, a kind of roaring in his ears. His eyes felt clear and sharp, his head icy cool, his limbs infinitely powerful. He took one hard blow to the mouth and tasted blood, felt it wash around his teeth. He batted Westbury's flailing arms out of the way, stepped in, and smashed his forehead hard into the bridge of his opponent's nose. Westbury reeled. Holcroft hooked a fist deep into his belly under the ribs, and then another in exactly the same place. The man went to his knees, and Holcroft chopped a right into his jaw, a left into his cheekbone, then took a step back, lifted his knee and kicked him in the face, flipping him over on to his back. He walked to his side, looked down at the dazed and bloodied visage, raised his foot and stamped once, hard, on Westbury's cheekbone. He heard a loud crack and saw the eyes flutter and roll up into his skull.

Then he turned to deal with Arnold.

With the light behind him, Holcroft clearly saw what happened next. Aphra, firmly gripped from behind by the porter, jerked her head backwards, the rear of her skull connecting solidly with the porter's mouth. He cried out, arms loosening their hold. She raked her boot down the side of his shin, then stamped with her sharp heel on the toes of his right foot. Arnold released her with a roar of fury. She spun around, fast as a top, her right arm licked out, a fluid slash, and a red line appeared under the porter's chin; a line that expanded, filled and soon gaped blackly, pouring gore from below his astonished face. He fell to his knees, dripping hands scrabbling at his throat while the blood welled and poured down his body, spattering on the cobbles.

Holcroft watched in disbelief as Arnold's life flowed through his fingers. He whispered: 'You killed him. You murdered him.'

'It's not murder in my book,' she said grimly. 'He would have forced me if he could, maybe killed me too. Not murder – merely self-defence.'

'They will hang you anyway. They will string you up just like my father.' The shock was making him loquacious. 'They will know it was you. They will hunt you down and hang you. Me, too. Oh God protect us both.'

Aphra came over to him. She looked him in the eye and put a white hand on his arm. 'Nobody is going to be hanged. See that over there.' She pointed to the low, dark irregular mass of St Giles. 'There are bodies discovered every morning around here with their throats slit. No one questions it. No one will know it was us.'

'Buckingham must have sent them . . .' Holcroft's mind was still whirling with horror.

Aphra thought for a moment. 'I don't think so. He could have easily killed you in the Cockpit, if he had been so inclined. Besides, he would have sent a dozen men or more if he had wanted to take us alive. No, these two were after personal revenge, I would say, or a bit of vicious amusement.'

'What about him?' said Holcroft, indicating the unconscious form of Robert Westbury. 'He will surely tell them you killed Arnold and bring the magistrates to your door. Then they'll hang us.'

'You make a good point.'

She went over to the still body in the golden coat and knelt beside him for a moment, the squat knife glinting in her right hand.

'Wait! Stop! What are you doing?'

'You know what I'm doing. And now it's done.' Holcroft watched, frozen, as a pool of fluid began to trickle and form beside Robert Westbury's shadowed neck, ever-growing in size, gleaming black in the lantern light from the Red Lion. He saw that now she had her hands deep in the senior page's pockets.

'Search that one for valuables. And be quick about it,' said Aphra, nodding at Arnold's corpse. 'A pack of St Giles cutthroats would not leave a dead man with so much as a thin farthing. Get to it, Holly.'

Half an hour later, a dazed Holcroft was sipping hot tea from a bowl in Aphra's garret – she had laced it with a splash of brandy but Holcroft could barely feel the spirits working on him at all. He looked at the table, where a small stack of stolen gold and silver coins seemed to throb and glow in the candlelight. Beside the money was a package of dog-eared playing cards tied up with string, and Holcroft could see the cool, amused face of his very own queen of diamonds peeking at him from the top. It steadied him. She understood the plan he had made – all of it. And she approved.

'We made more in one night as footpads as we ever did as forgers and fraudsters,' said Aphra, smiling. 'Perhaps we should choose that as our new vocation.' She laughed a little. She seemed to Holcroft to be perfectly ordinary, just the same old Aphra, kind, sweet, understanding. He could hardly believe that less than an hour ago she had cut the life out of two men.

'Aphra, we need to talk about something . . . about everything.'

'There is nothing to talk about, Holly. Don't concern yourself. If it comes to the worst, I won't let them hang you. I'll admit the whole thing. Take the blame entirely on myself.'

Holcroft looked at her. 'It's not that, Aphra. I've had an idea. I know how we can get our reward from the Duke of Buckingham.'

'I think we are done with all that false letter nonsense, Holly. We need to move along. Find something new.'

'It has nothing to do with selling Buckingham that letter – although I do have a use for it. It's much more simple than that. I know, too, how I can help Father, maybe save his life. But I will need your help. Pass my fardel, over there, Aphra, and listen. I'll tell you what we must do.'

Tuesday 23 May, 1671

Holcroft stood outside the arch of the gatehouse that marked the entrance to the Palace of White Hall. He looked at the two sentries in their splendid uniforms and remembered his initial feelings of joy and wonder at seeing them the autumn before. He was a different boy now, he knew that – indeed, he felt he had finally become a man. He had made more money on the turn of a card than he had seen before in his life; he had witnessed the deaths of two men, men he knew well, seen their black blood flowing between the cobbles. He recognized the lusts that seethed in men's hearts – and women's, too; he had seen the King and learned that his court was a place of debauchery and treachery, of lies and deceit; he had become part of that deceit himself and been disgraced and expelled for playing the White Hall game badly. For it was a game, he now knew – and he *had* played it badly. But it was time for a change. He would play his own game: Holcroft's game. He would not meekly accept his expulsion from this place, he would return to the table and this time – knowing what he now did – he would play with all his heart and mind, with all his cunning. He would play to win.

First, however, he needed an ally. He needed a friend. He turned his back on the soaring arch of the White Hall gatehouse and marched over to the Foot Guards' House on the north side of the street. There was a single sentry on the door there, standing in a little upright wooden box not much larger than a coffin. He gave the name of the man he wished to see and was admitted, walking through the gates and into the old Tilt Yard with the soldiers' barracks on his left. He turned right and headed across the parade ground, past the guard hut where the duty officer sat outside drinking wine in the weak May sunshine, and trotted up the steps of a large white building with a row of Grecian pillars making a shady colonnade along the front.

He was stopped there by a pair of guards in crimson coats and blue turnbacks armed with muskets and, once again, he said the name and was allowed to pass. A soldier-servant showed him into a salon at the rear of the house, where a dozen officers were at tables playing cards or writing letters or were seated in deep leather armchairs reading the *Gazette* or drinking wine or coffee. Over by the empty fireplace, lounging in a chair with his long legs a-spraddle, reading a small leather-covered book, was the elegant form of Ensign Jack Churchill. His friend.

The servant led Holcroft over to him and they stood for an awkward moment before Churchill noticed and leaped to his feet.

'I do beg your pardon, Holcroft, I was miles away,' he said, shaking his hand. To the servant, he said: 'Bring us two cans of cooled ale, if you please. Some of those hazelnut biscuits, too.'

After he had settled Holcroft in a chair, and sat down again himself, he said: 'I do hope you don't feel that I have been neglecting you, Hol. I've been with my father in Dorset these past few weeks – staying away from court and London, I'm sure you can guess why – and I've been so busy with his affairs, the farm and lands, that I haven't had much time to write. How are you? I heard you parted company with the Duke of Buckingham. I'm so sorry to hear that. Do you need money? I'm rather short myself, as always, but I'm sure I could manage to lend you something – a few shillings to see you right for a little while.'

'I don't need money, Jack. But I do need a favour. Then I want to discuss a mutual venture. An extremely lucrative mutual venture.'

'A favour, yes, ah, of course, ah, anything I can do – within reason,' Churchill said slowly. He looked warily at his younger companion. Holcroft, oblivious to any shades of meaning, was moved by his friend's generosity.

'I need you to give this letter to Barbara Villiers, for her to give to the King. She must put it into his own hands – no one else's. Can you do that?'

He pulled out a folded square of thick white papers, tied with a ribbon and sealed with blue wax, and handed it to Jack.

Churchill took it, with some reluctance. 'Hol, I'm sorry but I'm not sure I can get in to see Barbara. It is, ah, a bit awkward these days. If the King found out that I was visiting her—'

'It is vitally important. My father's life hangs in the balance. I would not ask otherwise.'

Churchill frowned. 'Hol, I am truly sorry. I know that you love him, just as you should, but I cannot approve of what your father did. It was robbery pure and simple. The man set out to steal from the King. I would rather not risk my position here, and my prospects, bleak as they are, to help a notorious thief. Ask me something else, I beg you.'

Holcroft looked around the room, there was no one within earshot: 'Listen, Jack, and I will tell you how it is with my father. He is the Duke of Buckingham's hired man. He has been so for years. He was paid in gold by the duke to undertake the robbery at the Tower. It was one of Buckingham's schemes to find money for the King.'

Holcroft considered telling Churchill that the plan had the consent of the King but chose not to strain his friend's credulity.

'There is something else that I must tell you too about Buckingham.' Now he could not meet his friend's eyes. 'It was I who betrayed you to the King when you were with Barbara that time. I am heartily sorry for it. I cannot tell you how ashamed I am but Buckingham squeezed me, he forced me to it: he said that if I did not tell when you were meeting her, he would dismiss me from his service. I had no choice. He promised money, too. I hoped to make amends by warning you in time – but that did not work out. Forgive me, I beg you.'

Churchill stared coldly at him. The soldier-servant chose this moment to bring two tankards of ale over to them and, in the long, horrible silence, he laid down both pewter pots, already beaded with condensation, and a small plate of biscuits on a tiny round wooden table that he set between them.

When the man had finally left them, Holcroft forced himself to look directly at Churchill and said: 'Buckingham is the man responsible for your fall from favour. He urged the King to visit Barbara when you were there. Buckingham hoped to bring about her downfall – he cared nothing for you. But know that he is our enemy. Yours and mine. And I have a way that we can bring him down and gain a recompense for our troubles. We can best him, Jack, we can punish him, but only if you will help. Will you help me?'

Churchill looked at his friend for a long time without speaking. Finally he said: 'I suspected all along that it was you who informed on me but I did not like to admit it to myself. Only you knew that I was with Barbara at that time. Then when you turned up suddenly, bursting in on us, moments before the King arrived . . . But I have two things that I must tell you, while we are indulging in this most uncivilized candour: the first is that I lied to you just now – I must confess that I *have* been avoiding you since that day. I chose not to continue our friendship. I think it was because in a fashion, at some remove, I always knew you were the one who betrayed me.'

Holcroft looked hard at the plate of biscuits. He could feel his vision blurring, a fat, immoveable bolus forming in his throat.

'The second thing I must tell you is that when we first met, I thought of betraying *you*. You told me your father's name and I immediately thought of the handsome reward offered by the Duke of Ormonde for his head. I made friends with you, partially, I admit, because I thought that you might one day let slip something about your father's whereabouts, and that I might profit from it in a most shameful manner. So I say this to you now: neither of us is unblemished in our loyalty to the other – and if you can find it in your heart to forgive me for my avaricious designs when we first met, then I shall forgive you for succumbing to Buckingham's pressure. What say you?'

Holcroft could not at that moment say anything at all. His whole being was focused on penning back the tears that threatened to gush from his eyes and utterly unman him. He did manage to grasp Churchill's outstretched hand and shake it hard while smiling mutely and blurrily at his friend.

'So, we forgive each other,' Churchill said, taking a biscuit. 'Good. And we have a score to settle with my Lord Buckingham. Well . . . I will risk seeing Barbara – in truth, it will not be so difficult to be discreet – and I will ask her to deliver your letter to the King. Now, tell me, what is your plan of action? You used the word "lucrative" – which I confess is one the words I like to hear best.'

'Actually, Jack, I said "extremely lucrative",' said Holcroft, sniffing wetly and cuffing his smarting eyes.

Wednesday 24 May, 1671

Aphra Behn walked slowly up the slight hill of St James's Street towards Piccadilly. She was tired and wet and not in the mood to be trifled with by a hostile masculine world. Before her, at the top of the hill, she could see the massive gold-painted gates of Clarendon House and the figure of the porter in his moss-green coat, seated in his lodge through the window.

It had been a fine morning when she set out from her St Thomas Street lodgings, a few clouds and a brisk wind, but with the sun – indeed a hint of coming summer – definitely in evidence. She noted, as she passed the spot near the Red Lion at the end of her street, that there was now no sign of the two dead bodies she had made: scholars of anatomy, she knew, were avid for corpses, and many of the denizens of St Giles were happy to procure fresh meat for the medical men, no questions asked. So she was feeling quite calm and contented as she set off along Drury Lane. But, by the time Aphra had reached Charing Cross, purple clouds had come racing in from the west and a short, vicious rain shower had drenched her travelling cloak and hood, and transformed the street beneath her feet into a black river of filth.

She had bunched the cloak and her skirts in her hands and walked with them lifted above the flood. Her beautiful blue velvet shoes embroidered with white silk roses were in theory protected by a pair of galloshios; stout, backless leather overboots mounted on wooden blocks that lifted her three inches above the cobbles. But a particularly large wave of filthy water, gaining momentum and size as it ran down St James's, had washed over the tops of them and soaked her best shoes, her stockings and her feet in a pungent solution of old urine, fresh dung, mouldy food scraps and other repellent types of street waste.

She blamed Holcroft. She was undertaking this foolish errand for him, or rather for his ne'er-do-well father's sake – and she did not quite know why. It had amused her, more than anything else, to include Holcroft in her operation to gull the Duke of Buckingham: he was so very much the lonely outsider, so obviously in need of a friend, that the secret agent in her had had no difficulty in charming him and swiftly recruiting him into her scheme. At the time, she had no genuine feelings for him at all, just a mild interest in his extraordinary bluntness and the cold knowledge that he could be very useful for her purposes as her man inside the duke's household. But since that scheme had failed, she did not understand what now bound them together. And yet here he was, sleeping on the floor of her already cramped garret and asking her to run errands on behalf of his villainous father. She had no tenderness for him in the amorous line, although she could see that he was a handsome lad, well made in the body, with a lovely smile. He aroused no desire in her and she knew that he had no carnal feelings towards her either. So what was the bond? Was it maternal? Perhaps a little: he had a child-like innocence that aroused a surge of protective feelings in her. More accurately, she reflected – as she trudged up the hill, her footwear squishing in time to her footsteps, her heavy leather bag banging against her thigh – her feelings were sisterly. But they shared no ties of blood, kinship or affinity and given their differences in age, experience, skills and outlook, it was a stretch to call them friends – if men and women could truly be friends. So why then was she stepping out on this miserable day on his behalf, soaking her one good cloak, ruining her lovely shoes? Because he needed her. The bastard.

Aphra presented herself at the gates of Clarendon House, a somewhat bedraggled creature, but she lifted her chin and rapped imperiously on the iron bars with her small white fist and called out loudly demanding entrance. The lodge-keeper, a veteran of the wars called Brooks who was enjoying his usual morning nap, woke suddenly, full of fear and confusion. He leaped to his feet, believing himself to be under attack by hordes of Parliamentarian troops, knocking over the table on which lay his pot of ale, his pie and his pipe, as he blundered forward, tripping over the scattered debris, tangling his own legs with the table's before lurching out of the lodge at a full run, shouting out a warning about oncoming enemy cavalry and crashing his bald head noisily and painfully against the gilded iron bars.

If Aphra was surprised to see an elderly man in a moss-green coat rushing out of the lodge with a roar of fury and throwing himself face-first into the gate, she did not display the emotion. She said calmly: 'Good morning, sir, if it pleases you I should like to be admitted to see His Grace the Duke of Ormonde. I have something of great value to give to him.'

Brooks gathered himself; he stood upright, wiped a trickle of blood from his forehead and said with all the grace he could muster: 'Can't do it, miss. The duke's left orders: no visitors for him on any pretext whatsoever.'

Aphra drew herself up to her full height. 'I am a personal friend of the duke. He would be most angry with you if you left me standing out here in the cold for any longer than necessary.'

'Personal friend or not. The duke is not seeing any folk today. Can't let you in, miss, sorry. He'd have my skin off.' The porter seemed genuinely apologetic and he was also now bleeding quite heavily from his split scalp.

Aphra wiggled her cold toes inside her wet stockings, she felt the gritty filth of the street-water between them. She was not going to meekly walk home with her mission unfulfilled. She smiled at Brooks, a beautiful smile, one of her best. She fluttered her long lashes.

'Truth be told, sir. It's not really the duke I wish to see. I honestly do know him, for sure, we talked about him providing the funding for my new play. But, the truth is, I met a handsome young fellow the other day in the Bull's Head Inn, who told me he was the duke's private secretary, quite the charmer he was, a very well-set-up young man, tall, dark hair, lovely brown eyes, and I was hoping that I might take this chance to make his acquaintance again. James, his name is, James Pratt. Do you know him, sir?'

'Oh, I know old Jemmy Pratt,' the old man was beaming now and mopping at his bloody forehead with a filthy kerchief. 'But he's no secretary – senior page, is he. If you want him, you'd best go round to the side entrance. Down that street over there; there's a little red door a hundred yards on the right. Back of the kitchens. Knock there and say that I sent you – Brooks is the name – tell them you want Jemmy and they'll see you right.'

'Thank you, sir. Thank you most kindly.'

'Warburton at the Blue Boar says you are never to come to him for another favour again. He doesn't know what happened that day, doesn't want to know, all he recalls is that there were suddenly armed men everywhere in the parlour and running up the stairs and next thing poor Parrot was dead. Tom, as you know, jumped out the window, tried to flee on foot and was knocked on the head by a cavalryman waiting in Hounds Ditch.'

Holcroft was standing behind his father in the nearly capacious cell in the White Tower and taking a pair of none-too-sharp shears to the ends of his long hair, trimming them as neatly as he could. As he spoke, he noticed that his father's locks were now mostly grey, with only a few strands of chestnut mixed in with the overall iron hue.

'Does Warburton know what happened to Will and Smithy?'

'If he does he's not saying: they both disappeared on the first day, when you didn't show up after the job. Only Parrot and Tom waited for you at the Boar. Which was their undoing.'

'Hmmm.' Blood stared at the narrow, barred window, which was wide open, admitting a thick shaft of yellow and creating a warm puddle of sunlight on the wooden floor. 'What about you, son? How're you keeping?'

'I am very well, thank you, sir.'

'And how is my old friend the Duke of Buckingham? Is he treating you well? Allowing you decent food, a lavish stipend, a comfy bed, all that?'

'I have no complaints.'

Blood turned in his chair and looked directly at Holcroft. 'Son,' he said, 'I might be locked up tight in the Tower but I still have friends who tell me of the doings of White Hall: who's up who's down, who's been summarily kicked out of their post at the Cockpit for being simple enough to try to gull their lord with a *confect* letter.'

'If you know already, why do you ask?'

'Why did you not tell me?'

'You have enough to worry about, Father.'

'In two days' time, son, I'm going up in front of old Judge Morton at the Bailey. I was caught red-handed, the crown in my very pocket, jewels stuffed down my boots, I have no defence to speak of, and I doubt it will take him more than a long quarter-hour to pronounce me guilty and sentence me to the drop. A day or so after that, in less than a week, to be sure, I will be no more. And I care not a fig for that. Truly, I don't. I've had a grand old life. Never a dull moment. But I do care that you and your brothers and sisters have a secure place in the world. Elizabeth and Charles, up in Lancashire with Granny Maggie, will be just fine with her. Mary is married to that dull Corbett fellow in Northampton and she seems happy enough. Edmund and William are well berthed in the King's ships and placed to make their fortunes at sea, if they stir themselves. Tom, well, he's clearly got no talent as a rank-rider so I pray that maybe this spell in the Tower will set him on the straight and narrow. Anyway, they've promised to let him go the day I make the final journey to Tyburn and I still have friends who will help him if he wants to continue his calling as a filtching-cove. But you – I had high hopes for you, Holcroft. I thought you might make something of yourself – as a clerk with Buckingham or maybe even something in the ministry, perhaps a secretary to the King. I worried about you most of all, son. You are different from all of them. You always have been. Not a fool, I don't say that, just different. Until last week I thought that, at last, you were safely installed in a good position with Buckingham. But now, well—'

'I don't want to be a clerk or a secretary in the ministry or any cove who wields quill and ink for his bread.'

'What is it that you do want?'

'I want to be a soldier, Father, I want to be a gallant officer just like you were. I want a scarlet uniform, a black hat with a long white plume, a fine horse and a magnificent sword. I want to ride at the head of my company of brave men and conquer the enemies of my King and win glory . . .'

'I take it back: you are a fool – if you think that is what soldiering is. Soldiering is blowing a man's face off when he's half a dozen yards from you. Soldiering is stabbing the other fellow in the back while it is safely turned and before he gets the chance to stab you. Soldiering is burning women and children in their homes because some titled idiot gave you an order and you are too much of a coward to defy him. Soldiering is holding your best friend in your arms as he coughs up his life's blood and stares, weeping with terror, into the mouth of Hell. There is no glory on the battlefield, son. Not one single drop of it: but there is plenty of blood and shit and offal, and more than enough fear and pain – brave young men screaming for their mothers or just for the mercy of death, and other men looking in disbelief at their own shattered limbs and opened flesh. Headless corpses, pulverized bones, more gore than you ever thought possible . . . A battlefield looks like one gigantic butcher's yard, son, and smells like the worst jakes you ever had to hold your nose and take a piss in. It's not a place you want to visit twice. Trust me. My advice is stick to quill and ink. A quill never blew a man's leg off. But I have no doubt that you will do what you wish after I'm dead and gone. And good luck to you.'

'If you think quill and ink never killed a man, then you are the fool, Father. But listen to me, they are not going to hang you this week or the next, I promise you. I have started a train of events that will bring you before the King. Once you have an audience with His Majesty you will be able to plead for your life. I know that you, Father, of all men, can make the most of that chance. If you wish to live, it will be in your own two hands.'

Blood stared at his son. 'What have you done, Holcroft?'

'I cannot tell you, Father. Part of the arrangement is my silence. I can't tell anyone. But trust me. I am not the fool you think me. There is hope!'

Jack Churchill looked at the cards in his hand and frowned. He held the ace and the ten of diamonds, which were trumps, and both of them were winners, and he also had the king of spades, also a winner. And God knew what his partner Captain Fellowes had – a fistful of face cards and the last two aces, probably, by the way his luck was running tonight. There seemed to be no way he could lose this game without making it entirely obvious that he was deliberately playing badly.

Holcroft had been most insistent that he lose. Jack needed to be thoroughly beaten and to part with a significant sum of money. That was the plan. Not for the first time he wished he had his young friend's strange facility with cards. Holcroft would have known by now exactly where every unplayed card in the pack was and how to engineer a thumping defeat. Jack was too lucky, that was his problem. Too much God-damned good luck!

'Remind me, Sir Thomas,' said Jack, fingering his ten of diamonds. 'Why do they call this game Whisk?'

'It is not generally called Whisk any more,' said Sir Thomas Littleton testily. 'The name of the game is Whist – with a letter T at the end. And it is so called, I have been reliably informed by expert players, because it should be played in absolute silence.'

'Silence, you say? My humble apologies.' He let go of the ten and instead pulled out the ace of diamonds.

Littleton, who was on Jack's immediate left, saw the card and gave a sharp and, in the quiet of the deserted music room, surprisingly loud gasp. It was almost, but not quite, a whoop of joy.

'Whist!' said Jack to Littleton, wagging an admonishing finger at him, and the fat man, recognizing his opponent's wit, returned him a little smile and played a low diamond. Fellowes frowned at his partner across the table, obviously disapproving of Jack's reckless play, then he laid out the lowest diamond he had – the nine. The Duke of Buckingham smiled coldly at the other three and discarded an innocuous four of clubs – and Jack gathered up the trick and added it to the four that he and Fellowes already had.

Jack was pleased with himself. He had had no idea that Buckingham had a void in diamonds, not a single one of that suit, but even a card player as mediocre as he was able to determine that his ten must now lose to the king of diamonds, and perhaps, if he was lucky, he might be allowed to refrain from playing his king of spades until he was sure it could be beaten by the ace, which was still out there. God, he hoped Fellowes was not holding the ace.

The Duke of Buckingham looked round the music room on the ground floor of the Foot Guards' House: a tasteful, high-ceilinged, wood-panelled sanctum. He particularly admired the exquisite double virginal in the corner, which presumably gave the room its name, a beautiful walnut instrument with its pair of keyboards fashioned from ivory and ebony and a vibrant hunting scene painted on the inside of the open lid. The Churchill boy seemed to be taking an interminably long time to lead his next card, he thought. He probably still thinks he has a chance of winning this hand, even winning the game and match. He didn't, of course, but he might as well let this delightfully pretty young fellow work it out for himself – he really was quite extraordinarily handsome; no wonder that greedy old bitch Barbara Villiers found him so irresistible.

Buckingham raised his eyes from the table and examined the portrait of the King by Sir Peter Lely that hung directly in his line of sight over the fireplace, which was filled not with a cheerfully crackling blaze on this warm May afternoon but with an equally incandescent display of red and orange tulips. The King wore dark steel armour, and his left hand rested on a full-face helm, as befitted a portrait in this martial residence. He had the chain of the Garter around his neck, a sword at his left side and a marshal's baton in his right. In the background was a crown and sceptre of state, in case there should be any doubt about the subject's identity in this unusual attire. His expression was stern and wise, no hint of frivolity save for the thin black moustache under his long nose and white lace cravat at his throat, but that was to suggest to the viewer, Buckingham suspected, that the King was a gentleman of refinement and culture as well as a mighty warrior. What nonsense, thought the duke, what comical puffery. The King was one of the least martial men he knew. Despite a *de jure* declaration of war against the Dutch in the Treaty of Dover – the ridiculous sham that the duke had been involved in brokering last winter, to his lasting rage and humiliation – the King had done nothing since. It wasn't that he was a coward or lazy – far from it. The truth was he could not afford to go to war, not this year at least and possibly not the next either. His army numbered only a few thousand men – not much more than a substantial royal guard, in fact. His ships were still lying unfinished in the stocks at Chatham, the shipwrights idle or gone to seek more remunerative labour. All that was left to him was martial posturing in a portrait by a fashionable – and ironically Dutch! – painter. As for the majestic crown on the shelf behind him, that item or one very similar to it, had last been seen hammered flat and shoved into the coat pocket of one of England's premier bunglers as he made his botched escape from the Tower of London. They were a pair, Thomas Blood and Charles Stuart: overly conceited, dyed-in-the-wool buffoons, the both of them.

He wondered idly what Blood was doing now. Praying for salvation, he presumed, and may God have mercy on his soul for Sir William Morton certainly would have none, and in two days' time he would face his judge in this world and shortly afterwards his judge in the next. Good riddance, thought Buckingham, he'd been nothing but a nuisance recently. He was pleased, however, that Osborne had been able to convince him to die quietly, to keep his big Irish mouth shut. The threat to his eldest son had done the trick; he'd not had a peep out of Blood since. Osborne had a gift for that sort of thing – he would go far, no doubt, with a little help from his friends.

Churchill played the ten of trumps – a bad error, thought Buckingham, knowing that Littleton must have the king at least. The pretty young puppy had sealed his fate.

Indeed, so it proved. For ten minutes later, Churchill had his purse out and was cheerfully counting out guineas.

'Don't fret, Fellowes, old friend, I'll gladly cover your losses,' he said to his thunder-browed partner. 'I'm sure that it was entirely my fault that we lost. Damn this run of hellish bad luck.'

Captain Fellowes was mollified by Churchill's words. He put away his own purse with relief and began to calm down. However, the junior officer's next utterance brought his superior's simmering anger back to the fore.

'Your Grace, Sir Thomas – I thank you for a very pleasant and most instructive afternoon. Here are your winnings' – Jack gently shoved a stack of gold coins towards each man – 'but I must beg you to allow Captain Fellowes and myself to have our revenge. I am twenty-two guineas out of pocket and so I hope you will accept our challenge for a return match, same stakes, perhaps on Friday afternoon? If you are both at liberty, that is.'

Littleton chuckled and dropped the clinking pile of gold straight into his coat pocket. 'Certainly, sir, I should be happy to oblige, that is, if His Grace is also willing to play again . . .'

'Hold on there, ensign,' said Fellowes. 'After this display, I'm not sure I wish to be partner – that is I'm not sure I'm at liberty on Friday.'

'Ah, that is a dreadful shame, sir. But I expect that I can find a card-loving friend to take your place,' Jack waved airily towards the Foot Guards officers' mess that lay just outside the door of the music room.

'Your Grace,' he continued, 'I trust in your great sense of fair play: you will allow me a rematch, will you not?'

The Duke of Buckingham looked at the handsome young officer who was smiling so beguilingly at him. He looked down at the not-inconsiderable pile of gold on the table before his place.

'It will be my pleasure to relieve you of some more of your money on Friday. Shall we say two o'clock?'

The King rolled off his lover and lay on his back in the royal bed breathing heavily. Nell wiped herself with a corner of the sheet and sat up. She smiled down at Charles, who looked back at her with glazed, unfocused eyes, then she reached out a long arm for the goblet of wine on the table beside the bed. A moment later, red-lipped and refreshed, Nell slid off the bed, naked as a baby and stalked over to the stool closet on the far side of the room. Charles watched her walk, his eyes intent on her long, slim legs and round, almost boyish, buttocks. He felt a stir of lust in spite of his recent exertions. *I'll give myself half an hour*, he thought, *then we'll see.*

He became aware of a gentle knocking at the door of his chamber. 'Enter!' he called and a moment later the lean form of Sir John Grenville, groom of the close stool, slipped in and came to the foot of the bed.

'What is it, Grenville? You know that I'm otherwise engaged.'

'You have a visitor, sir, with a letter for you.'

'Well, accept the letter, then, and I'll read it in due course with the others. Do you really need to trouble me with this?'

'I am afraid the lady will not give up the letter: she says she will only put it into your hand.'

'I'm busy, Grenville. Tell her she can leave the letter or come back later or on another day. I care not. I merely wish to be left in peace—'

'With your new whore?' said a female voice. Barbara, Duchess of Cleveland, stalked through the open door and into the royal bed-chamber and stood, magnificent in a marvellously low-cut yellow silk gown and turquoise wrap, face powdered chalk white, full lips stained bloody with cochineal, kohl underlining her sleepy violet eyes, and staring down at the half-naked monarch, who was now scrabbling to cover his modesty with a bed-sheet.

'Madame, you cannot come barging into His Majesty's chambers,' said Grenville. 'I distinctly told you to wait outside until summoned.'

'Did you really think I would sit meekly out there while the father of my five children disports himself merrily with some cheap slut?'

'Who are you calling a slut?' Nell emerged from the closet, still without a stitch. She glared at the interloper, hands on hips.

'Madame, I am afraid I must ask you to leave immediately,' said Grenville. 'Guards! Guards, get in here right now—'

'I'm calling you a slut. Me. And you are a slut! A harlot! A whore! You think you can replace *me*, you trollop, you grubby little orange-seller.'

'Least I got nice firm oranges to sell, Grandma, not like your floppy old dumplings. Cover those hideous wrinkled things up, for God's sake. At your age, even if you've lost your bloom, do try to have some dignity at least.'

A pair of red-coated soldiers with half-pikes in hand had appeared at the door of the chamber. They stopped and stared goggle-eyed at the naked actress, the half-covered King in the bed, and the fully dressed duchess, who now stepped briskly across the room and delivered a slap across Nell's face that sounded loud as a pistol shot.

Grenville said: 'Guards, the Duchess of Cleveland is to be escorted from this palace this very minute . . .'

'Aaaarrhh!' screamed Nell – it was more a war cry than an expression of pain or outrage. She swung a short, hard and surprisingly competent punch at Barbara. The duchess ducked, just in time, and the powerful blow landed in the centre of the first soldier's face, who had just come up to take her by the elbow. He sat down hard on the carpet. Nell screeched in frustration, her long-nailed fingers raking out towards Barbara's eyes.

'Enough!' bellowed the King, shockingly loud. 'That's enough! Both of you!' Everyone froze. 'Everybody out, right now. Get out! Get out all of you! This is a royal bedchamber not some damned Cheapside tap room.'

'But I've done nothing wrong!' wailed Nell.

'Sire, if you will give me but a moment to restore order.'

'I'm not leaving this chamber till I've given you this,' said Barbara Villiers. And she pulled a crumpled letter from the sleeve of her silk dress and, walking calmly over to the bed, she handed it to the King.

Charles accepted the letter and watched, filled with more than a little awe and respect, as Barbara turned gracefully on her heel, lifted her immaculately powdered chin and swept out of the bedchamber, stately as a ship of the line, with the two red-coated pikemen trailing in her wake.

'This had better be worth my fucking time,' said Ormonde, 'or you, Mister Pratt, will be looking for a new fucking position.'

Aphra Behn dropped a neat curtsey and said: 'I do not think you will be the poorer for my coming, sir. Indeed, I think I can guarantee that you will be thanking me before the hour is up.'

The Duke of Ormonde grunted, and waved away James Pratt, whose face was now almost as green as his coat. He had known he was taking a risk by bringing the lady into the duke's presence against his express commands but she had persuaded him that his master would be extremely grateful.

'Say your piece then, missy,' Ormonde told her. 'After which you can take your simpering, self-serving cunt-smile out of my sight and leave me to the tranquillity of my own fucking garden.'

It was a beautiful and no doubt usually tranquil garden, there could be no denying that. The sun had returned in full force, the rain clouds swept away by a brisk, cooling breeze, and the ornamental garden which had been created behind the imposing block of the main building of Clarendon House looked magnificent. Aphra eyed Ormonde closely without saying anything for a few moments. She saw him shift on the wooden bench, and wince as he moved the position of his grossly swollen feet in their too-tight leather slippers ever so slightly. She recalled what Holcroft had told her about the man, all that he had gleaned from his conversations with Jenny Blaine.

'Move up a little,' she told him. 'I'm going to sit next to you.'

'The Devil you are – say your piece, wench, and be gone!'

'Move up and I will rub the soreness out of your feet.' And as the duke reluctantly shifted a few inches or so along the wooden bench, Aphra sat down next to him and hauled his massive left foot into her lap. She peeled off the slipper and began gently to massage the swollen flesh.

'Hhhhmmgh,' said the duke, closing his eyes. The sun shone down from a perfectly blue sky. 'God, woman, you're a witch,' he breathed. 'You remind me of a red-haired strumpet I used to know. Oh, ah, oh, you have the Devil's own skill in your fucking fingertips.'

'You are a very rude man – somebody clearly spoiled you as a child, but I'm going to overlook that for now,' said Aphra, working away with her hands. 'Later, of course, you will apologise to me for all the ugly things you've said but for the moment just be quiet and listen to what I have say.'

'Hhhhmmgh.'

'I have a letter. It's a fake, of course, but it purports to be a private message from you to the Prince of Orange. It contains treasonous indications, an offer of support for William, and suggests that you and other powerful men here would be willing to help him seize the throne of England by force.'

Ormonde's eyes snapped open. He struggled to sit upright, but Aphra held firmly on to his left foot, squeezing a little, just to show that she could harm as well as heal. 'Calm yourself, Your Grace, I shall give you this letter presently, I have it in my bag, and it is the only copy in existence. You are in no danger from me at all.'

'What do you want, witch?'

'For the moment, I want you to listen to me. Are you listening, sir?'

The duke said nothing.

'This letter was in the possession of the Duke of Buckingham and he was part of a plot to use this letter to discredit you with the King. I came to know of this letter – it doesn't matter how, and I will not tell you the exact details, save to say that the person who made the forgery is a very dear friend of mine – and I persuaded another friend of mine, a young man in the Duke of Buckingham's service to take the letter from the Cockpit, remove it from Buckingham's grasp. In doing so, however, my young friend was unfortunate enough to lose his position. We discussed what to do with this missive and decided that we should give it to you because—'

'Blood,' said the duke. 'The young man in Buckingham's service, your friend, is the younger son of Thomas Blood, is he not?'

'I am impressed, sir, your sources are excellent,' Aphra stopped kneading his foot. She *was* genuinely surprised. 'I had not expected that you would know his name.'

'I have people who tell me things. I heard the Blood boy was dismissed for gross ingratitude – but I can find out more if I need to. Keep on at your work, woman,' the duke gestured impatiently at his engorged foot in her lap.

Aphra continued her massage and silently gave thanks that she and Holcroft had stuck closely to the truth when concocting this tale.

'So, anyway, we decided that we would give the letter to you so that you might keep it, or destroy it, just as you wish – and with absolutely no conditions attached to the giving. All we beg, most humbly, is that you look kindly on Holcroft Blood, my young friend, who did you this great service at such great cost – and that you forgive his father Thomas Blood, now languishing in the Tower, for his many transgressions against your person. For myself, I only ask that you reconsider my proposal of some months past that you be the patron for my new play for the Duke's Company at Lincoln's Inn, a wonderfully fresh and witty comedy called *The Amorous Prince*.'

'For someone who says she is giving me a gift with absolutely no conditions attached, you ask a very great deal in exchange.' The duke laughed, a rough barking sound. 'So you're the young person who wrote that silly play that Betterton mentioned to me. What's your name again?'

'My name is Mistress Behn. My friends call me Aphra.'

'Well, then, Mistress Behn. I will take you at your word. No conditions. Now I will trouble you to hand over the letter to me.'

Aphra replaced the slipper over the duke's foot. She got up, went to her big leather bag, which was lying on the gravel beside the bench, took out the forged letter and handed it to the duke.

'Do my other foot, while I read it, Mistress Behn.'

They sat together in silence for a while, Aphra working the tender flesh of the right foot, the duke reading and then, when he had finished, sitting with the paper crumpled in his fist, his eyes closed and his head tilted back, allowing the late May sun to warm his face.

Eventually, the duke spoke: 'I enjoyed the way you did that, Mistress Behn. No conditions. No *quid pro quo*. Nothing overtly demanded. But I did also note that you made a point of telling me that the fellow who wrote this fraudulent letter was a dear friend of yours. Which presumably means that you could easily get him to cook up another letter just the same. That was delicately done, Mistress Behn, and despite what you might think of me, my crudeness, my cursing, I do enjoy delicacy in little transactions like these.'

Aphra slid the slipper gently back on to the foot, lowered it to the ground and stood up. 'I hope, then, that you will look kindly on the proposals I have made to you – concerning forgiveness for Holcroft's father and, of course, the production of my little play.'

'I'll put up the money for your play. I think you have certainly earned that. As for Blood, hmm . . . That villain has plagued me for years and I am not the forgiving type. But I will consider it. Do not expect too much of me.'

'Then I bid you good day and will take my leave.'

'There is one more thing.'

'Yes?'

'I would like to thank you for your kindness this morning – the letter, my feet – and also to, ah, apologise to you for my ugly language earlier.'

'I thought you might,' she said.

The King stared at the vast tapestry on the wall of the red audience room. The woven image depicted himself as the Roman conqueror Julius Caesar, complete with crowd of adoring servants and a pack of playful dogs in the background. Charles's own spaniels were locked in the adjacent room and the King could hear them whining and scrabbling at the door trying to return to their master. He longed to release them, and feel their unbridled affection, the joyful wagging of tails, but he needed to concentrate on the business at hand. He could not afford to be distracted by his darlings in the interview to come. He must be strong, regal, dominant: he had to resolve this awful situation before it became worse.

Caesar had it easy, the King mused. He told his legionnaires to do things and they instantly obeyed him. Capture this village, besiege that town, slaughter those rapacious Celts. Yet while he had his own Celt locked in the Tower, it now seemed unlikely that he could be summarily put to death despite the overwhelming evidence of his rapacity. That man had stolen the King's crown, the very symbol of the monarch; he had offered insult to the King himself and yet somehow this Irish lout still lived. It was inconvenient that Charles had known about the robbery beforehand, that he had, in effect, given the wretched escapade his blessing. But that was not the point here: the Celt had attempted to steal from the King. It was clearly *lèse majesté*. What would Caesar have done in those circumstances?

'I came as soon as I could, Your Majesty,' said the Duke of Buckingham, somewhat breathlessly 'your man said it was something of an emergency. Now I'm here, how may I serve you?'

The King swung around to face him. The duke looked a little ruffled: his cravat was badly tied, his wig was slightly askew. His waistcoat, an indigo silk wonder with swirling dragons picked out in green stitching, clashed violently with the long red coat he was wearing. His sallow face was creased, pinched, almost crumpled on one side. The King had the distinct impression that the royal messenger had hauled him from his bed in the Cockpit to bring him here, as well he might. It was only four in the afternoon but he knew the duke kept strange hours.

Charles held up the letter that Barbara Villiers had given to him earlier that afternoon. He had not bothered to read it till an hour ago and now that he had digested its contents he was struggling to hold back his rising panic. 'You, sir, can haul me out of the morass you have plunged me into!'

Before Buckingham could reply, there was a knock at the door and Sir Thomas Osborne came into the red audience room.

'I was told you needed me, sire,' he said, advancing towards the King and the duke, and making his bow. 'What is amiss?'

In contrast to the duke, Thomas Osborne was well-groomed, even polished, attire immaculate, face glowing with health and youth.

'That bastard Blood is still threatening me, or rather this time his son – one Holcroft Blood – is, on his behalf, asking me to grant his father a personal audience so Blood may plead his case and explain his actions.'

'I must confess that Holcroft Blood used to be one of my confidential clerks,' said the Duke of Buckingham. 'An ungrateful little viper, malicious and dishonest. I dismissed him from my service for trying to cheat me out of a large sum. Tell me, Your Majesty, of the nature of his threat against you.'

'I . . . I cannot say.' The King looked down at the silk bows on his shoes. 'It concerns the Treaty of Dover that you so deftly arranged last year, Buckingham. But I do not want to say more. Somehow your ungrateful viper has managed to find out something about the treaty. Something that would be most damaging to me personally, were it to become widely known.'

So that little bit of duplicity has come back to bite you, has it? thought Buckingham. *Serves you right for going behind my back.*

Instead he said, 'What does Holcroft Blood say he will do?'

'He says he will send copies of a pamphlet revealing the true story about the treaty to every parish in the land, and have them nailed on ten thousand church doors from Inverness to St Ives. He says he'll put one on every table in every coffee house in London; he'll give pamphlets to passers-by in the streets in every town in England, Scotland and Ireland.'

'So . . . it seems we cannot stop him telling the whole world,' said the duke. 'What exactly does Holcroft want for his silence?'

'I told you: he wants me to meet his father here at White Hall, listen to his plea and, by implication, graciously grant him a royal pardon.'

'Why not just agree to that, then?' said Buckingham.

'Because, Your Grace,' the King's voice had risen in pitch and volume, 'I would look like the fool of the world. A man breaks into one of my royal palaces, assaults my keeper of the jewels, makes off with my own regalia, precious, irreplaceable items worth thousands of pounds, and I just say, "Oh well, never mind," and forgive him? They would say I was mad – or afraid of him. And what would be worse would be having this Blood fellow wandering around London, with his pardon in his pocket, telling all and sundry that I was the one who secretly hired him to undertake this theft? You said you would mend this, Buckingham. You gave me your word. It is entirely of your doing – I told you that I did not care to be embarrassed. And what have you done? Nothing.'

'The only thing I can suggest, sire, is that you meet Blood, listen to him, pardon him, and swear him to silence,' said Buckingham. He looked old and careworn, exhausted by life. 'I can make some dire threats, if you like, to make him hold his tongue.'

'Might I say something?' asked Sir Thomas Osborne. Both of the older men looked at him. 'I have a man in my service. A useful man, a soldier and a man of his hands, and I believe he could help us in this matter, if we do not mind being utterly ruthless. I'm suggesting a permanent solution, sire, with the ends justifying the means. Do you understand what I mean by that?'

'I do not care what you do,' said the King. 'I only want someone to make this problem go away, and go away for good.'

'Then I propose that we send a message to Blood and tell him that you will see him personally, Your Majesty, on Friday, the day after tomorrow. The trial is set for eleven o'clock in the morning; I suggest you tell him that you graciously agree to an audience with him at nine o'clock. We'll tell the boy Holcroft to be here then, too, to witness your royal clemency. This capitulation should allay any suspicions Blood might have, and keep his wretched son from spreading his foul pamphlets all over the Three Kingdoms. I will arrange for my man to take care of Blood the night before the meeting. When the son presents himself here at the appointed hour, he can be seized and swiftly tried and executed for sedition. That Aphra Behn woman, the playwright, is his ally and she should be taken up and given the same fate. The other son Thomas is a known highwayman, quite apart from his role in the Tower business, and he can be dispatched at our leisure.'

Even Buckingham was a little shocked at the casual way in which Osborne disposed of four subjects of the realm in so few words. But neither he nor the King said anything to check him.

'With your permission then, sire, I will set things in motion. Will your people issue the formal invitation to the royal audience to Blood and his son? On Friday, at nine?'

The King nodded mutely but he could not meet the younger man's eye. As Osborne bowed and excused himself from the chamber, he thought: *What can it be about the Treaty of Dover that is so bad that our King would sanction the murder of three men and a woman to keep it quiet?*

Thursday 25 May, 1671

'A visitor to see you, colonel,' said Widdicombe, pushing wide the door of the chamber and admitting William Hunt with his hat pulled down low over his eyes but a big crooked smile adorning the lower part of his scarred face.

'William!' said Blood, rising from his chair at the writing desk. 'You are a sight for sore eyes. Come in. You'll take a gage of bingo, won't you? Good French stuff. My boy Holcroft brought in a wee cask for my comfort and there's a bottle already decanted.'

'Thank you, colonel, I will,' said Hunt, removing his hat and travelling cloak, hanging them on a wooden peg by the door and accepting a small measure of brandy in a glass from Blood's hand.

'What cheer?' he said, taking a sip.

'Excellent news, Will,' said Blood. 'The best I've had in months. I received a note from the King's chief bum-wiper, Sir John Grenville, inviting me to an audience with His Majesty himself tomorrow morning at nine. I think he will listen to me, and I have high hopes of securing a royal pardon. Would that not be splendid?'

'Splendid indeed, colonel, indeed most splendid.'

'Well, we mustn't count our pardons before they are signed, Will. I'll have to work the old magic on His Majesty, but I think he'll finally listen to reason. Cheers! Here, have another drop!'

Blood came over to his old friend with the brandy bottle.

'But tell me what happened to you? You heard about poor Parrot and the raid on the Blue Boar, I suppose? The jewels recaptured. Tom was taken – he's in a chamber on the floor above me. I can hear him pacing up and down, up and down, he's a nervous fellow, and little bits of dust and debris come sprinkling down on my head. There now, look, he's doing it now, look, look up there!' With his left hand he pointed up at the corner of the ceiling behind Hunt's head.

Quite naturally, Hunt turned his head to look. Blood hit him with the bottle; a cruel, full-strength blow to the side of the head, which immediately laid Hunt out on the floor in a puddle of brandy, shards of glass and blood.

Blood knelt beside him and flipped his slight unconscious body over with ease. He undid his linen cravat and used it to tie Hunt's unresisting hands behind him. Then he hauled his old friend over to the wall and propped his back up against it. While Hunt was groggily coming to, Blood searched him, pulling out two small pistols, primed and loaded, one from each coat pocket and a foot-long dagger shoved down inside his breeches.

'You are uncommonly well armed, Will, for just a friendly visit to an old comrade in the durance.' Blood placed the weapons on his writing desk and came back to crouch down next to Hunt. 'A man might conclude that you had bloody violence in mind, with an armoury like that on your person. And, you know, Widdicombe has orders to search anyone who comes to see me: it's to stop me receiving the means to make a mad break for freedom. So you coming in like that, armed for a scrap, well, that has to have been sanctioned by somebody – somebody very high up in the chain of command. So what am I supposed to think, Will? When you come to me like this? What should a rational man conclude?'

Hunt was now conscious again, although still bemused and muzzy. 'What did you do that for, colonel? I meant you no harm.'

'You see, Will, old friend, old comrade, I don't believe you.'

'I slipped the gaoler a few shillings to let me in with the ironmongery, sir. I was planning to help you make a run for it,' said Hunt eagerly. 'We can still do it, too, loose my hands and we'll fight our way out together. It will be just like the good old days. It's right dark out there and there's only a couple of simpleton buffcoats between us and our freedom.'

Blood sat back on his heels. 'You tell a pretty tale, Will. A very pretty tale, you always have. But that little knock on the head must have scrambled your brains – I can't run, not with this wounded leg, and I don't need to escape, anyway. I'm seeing the King tomorrow and he's going to pardon me. Shall I tell you what I think, Will? Shall I? I think someone gave you a big sack of gold to make sure that I *don't* get to go and see the King tomorrow. I don't hear a peep from you till the night before my pardon and – hello! – here you are, armed to the teeth and extending the hand of friendship. I think you came here to put me down, Will. That's what I think, old friend. That's what I'm suspecting as I sit here looking at your ugly old face.'

Hunt gaped at him. 'You got it wrong, colonel. All wrong. I came here to help you. If you don't want to chance an escape, well, that's fine and dandy. Cut me loose and I'll be on my way. No hard feelings about the ding on the head with the bottle. What d'you say, colonel? Let's part as friends.'

Blood looked at him sadly. 'I don't think I can do that, Will. I think I need to know just a wee bit more about what's going on out there before I set off to see the King on the morrow. Just for my own peace of mind.'

With only minimal resistance, which Blood quelled with one savage belly punch, he tied Hunt's legs and elbows and gagged him with a strip of torn bed-sheet. Then he lashed him securely to the chair. He went to the door, making sure that his large body blocked a view into the chamber. He paid a gold piece over to Widdicombe and told the gaoler that his friend would be lodging with him overnight and that, as they had much to discuss, he would be grateful if they were not disturbed until after dawn when it was time to make the journey across London to White

Hall to see the King. There would be another gold piece for Widdicome if they were unmolested all night, he promised. And he warned the little man that there might be the odd burst of raucous singing for Hunt was a very musical, if not a very tuneful fellow when the brandy was in him.

'I like a nice drop myself,' said Widdicombe, grinning at Blood. 'I may take this here guinea and see what delights it will buy at the White Horse. I will have to lock you both in, colonel, even though the whisper is that this is your last night as our guest.'

'I'd be disappointed in you if you didn't, Widdicombe. You are a man who knows his duty. Here's another hog, to drink my health,' said Blood handing the gaoler an extra shilling. 'Tell your mates what I said about Mister Hunt's singing. They mustn't be alarmed. No disturbances, mind!'

When the gaoler had left, and the bolts had slammed shut on the far side of the door, Blood returned to Hunt's side.

'Remember what we did to that fellow in Kent, Will? The cavalry-man we captured after the fight at Maidstone, Lord Somebody, one of Prince Rupert's aides, remember? Sir Thomas Fairfax told us to get any information we could out of him, and quickly, about where the King's men had run to? Remember, Will? I pushed a blade under his toenails and worked them off one by one. That brave man resisted answering all our questions until I had done seven of them, and you said you wondered whether the pain was really all that terrible for him. Well, good news, Will, it looks as if you're about to find out the answer to your question.'

Blood seized Hunt's leg, tucked it under his arm and pulled off his riding boot. His victim's screams were muffled by the bed-sheet gag in his mouth but the horrified expression on his face and the frenzied writhing of his body against his bonds made his emotional state perfectly clear. Blood pulled the folding penknife from his pocket and opened the two-inch blade.

'Let's start with an easy one, old friend. Why did you really come to see me tonight?'

Holcroft was entranced. He leaned his back comfortably against the sun-warmed brick of the inner wall of the Tilt Yard and watched as a company of the King's Foot Guards, under the stern eye of Ensign John Churchill, completed its drill. Ninety men in smart red coats with blue turnbacks and facings, muskets on their shoulders, swords at their waists, were moving as one man to the commands of a brass-lunged sergeant, who echoed Jack's far quieter directions. They marched across Holcroft's front, a hundred and eighty highly polished back shoes, crashing down in unison on the cobbles and at a shout of command they all stopped dead, pivoted neatly to face the opposite direction and marched back.

Holcroft could have watched them for hours. The perfect order, the uniformity of movement and dress, the machine-like quality of this body of men, all sang Hosannahs to his soul. He admired his friend's easy control of them, too. Jack was the brain that made this red-and-blue man-machine move according to his will. Now they were stationary in the centre of the Tilt Yard, and stamping, presenting arms. At Churchill's word, they saluted, stamped once more, stood easy and were dismissed, the formation crumbling and streaming away towards the barracks to the south of the Yard where food and ale was being served out for their noonday meal.

Jack sauntered over to Holcroft who was beaming at him and struggling with the urge to applaud the demonstration.

'What cheer, Hol?'

'I think your men are quite splendid.'

'Thank you. We do work pretty hard at being splendid but it is nice to hear it from a civilian. Come and have a glass of sack in the hut.'

When the two men were settled over their wine, Holcroft said: 'So, Jack, is it all set for the game?'

'Yes, I lost twenty-two guineas yesterday, which was more than a little painful, but he's agreed to allow me my revenge tomorrow at two, here in the Foot Guards' House, in the music room, as you suggested. Littleton and Buckingham against me and a player of my choosing. The game is Whist. No honours. First to nine points. And ten pounds a point. I've tipped the groom porter his usual fee to licence the game. Fellowes has declined to be my partner, as we hoped he would. He called me a reckless buffle-head.'

Holcroft looked at his friend for a moment, the childish insult stirring memories in his mind. He shrugged away the thought. 'So, Jack, I have raised as much as I can for our stake. I pawned some things. My friend Mistress Behn gave me seven pounds – all that she has in the world. And my father gave me ten – I do not know where he got it. You know he and I go to see the King tomorrow morning? We are rather hopeful, in fact: so would you please thank Barbara for her kindness in delivering that note.'

'I think she would like it if you were to thank her yourself. She has quite forgotten your little spat in the buttery, you know. She's a passionate creature, is our Barbara, she flies into a rage in the blink of an eye but it is all forgotten and forgiven the next day. She gave me fifty pounds to put towards our venture – which was more than generous – and sends you a kiss – a chaste kiss, she insisted I tell you. She says she wishes us all the luck in the world. I've managed to scrape up another thirty. I went to the Jews and put my best horse up as surety. God knows what I am going to do if we lose.'

'We're not going to lose, Jack. I promise you.'

'You have my credit in your hands, Hol, if not my actual life. But it does seem that we are fully prepared. By my calculation we should be able to take at least a hundred and fifty pounds to the table. It should be enough to take him. At least I pray it will be enough.'

'It'll be enough, Jack. Be calm, we're going to wipe his eye.'

Friday 26 May, 1671

Blood mopped the last of the soap from his face with a towel, wiped the razor, closed it and contemplated his freshly shaven reflection in the glass. Today was the day, he told himself cheerily. Today it would all be over. He would be a free man again. He looked pale, he thought, beneath the still-vivid bruises from Wythe Edwards's beatings, even old. My God, was he now an old man? No, surely not. He needed some fresh air, that's all, and exercise. The first thing he would do when he was free, if his wounded leg was up to it, would be to hire a good horse and take it for a gallop on Hampstead Heath, or maybe on a good heart-pounding run up to Epping Forest. He could stop in at the Lamb in Romford and see some friends, have a drink . . .

A shadow crossed his brow. He looked in the mirror and focused on the gently swinging corpse of William Hunt, hanging by a noose made from a torn-up bed-sheet from a roof beam in the corner of the chamber. *God be with you, Will. We had some good times, old friend. We had some rare old adventures, didn't we, you traitorous, back-stabbing little shit-weasel.*

It had only taken three toenails to get Hunt in a talkative frame of mind. He had admitted that he had been hired by Sir Thomas Osborne to kill Blood in his cell. The gaoler Widdicombe knew nothing about the plot but had merely been told by Osborne not to search Hunt when he came to visit Blood. Then Hunt had been foolish and had begun screaming for the gaoler, yelling at the top of his lungs for help.

Blood had punished him with another two toenails for that. And when Hunt became mulishly silent, it had taken another two to get him to open up again. That made seven and Blood was forced to remind his prisoner that while they might be running short of toenails there was a whole new world of pain available in his fingers. That broke him. Snivelling, sobbing and begging for forgiveness, the story had emerged. Hunt had been recruited by Osborne more than a year ago – he was not Buckingham's man, he had been adamant about that – Osborne knew his family in Yorkshire. Hunt's father had once worked for his grandfather and was now a tenant farmer on their huge estate, and Sir Thomas had used the usual admixture of persuasions – threat of punishment and promise of reward – to recruit him, saying that his father would be evicted if he did not comply and promising a reward of a hundred pounds in gold, if Hunt would just share a few details of Blood's plans. Hunt had been very stupid, Blood considered, because once he had supplied some details about his comrade he was for ever damned as an informer, and Osborne no longer mentioned the hundred pounds, instead the talk was all how Blood would react if he discovered that his lieutenant was a traitor.

There had been no more call for toenails. Hunt had confessed that he had informed Osborne, via a wherry man who took a note across the Thames to White Hall, when Blood was staying with Jenny Blaine at the Saracen's Head in Southwark last winter and Osborne had passed the information to Ormonde's son Ossory – aiming to curry favour with that powerful family. Hunt also admitted he had tried to shoot Blood as they were making their escape – hoping to claim the price on his head – but had missed.

Hunt had asked Blood only one question during that long night of pain and blood, snot, tears and confession: he asked how had he known he was coming for him? What mistake had he made?

'It was the soldiers coming directly to the Blue Boar four days after the attempt on the jewels,' he said, giving his bound friend a nice big jolt of the brandy from his own glass, just for old times' sake.

'Someone blabbed. Couldn't have been Parrot, or he'd just have surrendered to them instead of going out like a maddened bull when the dogs are set on him. It couldn't be Tom. If either of them blabbed they wouldn't have stuck around to face the soldiers.'

'I thought they'd run, too,' said Hunt sadly.

'More backbone than you, Will. Both of them. I reckoned Warburton was too afraid to betray me and, anyway, what would he gain from it? A lot of his customers do dark business in the Boar and he has a reputation to maintain as a closed-mouth man. So, really, it had to be either you or Smithy. And my money was always on you – despite all our years together. I suspected that Buckingham or someone would probably try to silence me the old-fashioned way, at some point, if I made too much of a fuss – it's the sensible thing to do – and when you turned up on the eve of my audience with the King, well, it all just fell into place.'

'It was nothing personal, colonel. I found myself in a tight corner and I couldn't get out of it.'

'I know, Will, I know. And neither is this personal.'

The sun was just appearing, painting the sky pink and washing away the dark shadows in the chamber. Blood pinched out the candle before moving behind his chair and putting his big arms around his friend's neck. Taking a firm grip on his right shoulder and his chin, he yanked once, very hard, and heard the little man's spine crack like a twig. Then he fashioned the bed-sheets into a rope and noose, cut loose all the restraints, replaced his riding boots to cover the damage to his toes and suspended his old friend from a beam, giving the small body a friendly slap as he went off to perform his toilet.

This was the day; it was a fine, warm, rosy dawn, and this was the day that he would be a free man at last.

Blood gave himself one final glance in the looking glass: fit for an audience with His Majesty? Yes, indeed! He nodded once, grinned at his reflection and then he went to the door and began to bellow as loudly as he could: 'Widdicombe, guards, help me! Come quick – there has been the most horrible accident. My poor friend Mister Hunt has hanged himself while I slept. Guards, guards, come quickly now . . .'

At every pillar along either side of the main hall of the Banqueting House stood a soldier from the King's Foot Guards as still as a statue. Holcroft's heart had risen when he saw their familiar red uniforms and he looked expectantly around to see if Jack should be their commanding officer. He was disappointed to spot Captain Fellowes lurking by one of the big wooden doors at the far end of the hall to the left of the King, who sat in majesty on a gold-painted throne on a low dais draped in scarlet silk between two elegant Grecian-style columns. On the right of the King stood a grim-faced Sir John Grenville, and beyond him His Grace the Duke of Buckingham, imperious in a towering black periwig and purple robes. To the King's left, partly obscuring the scowling guards officer by the door, stood Sir Thomas Osborne in an ordinary blue coat and linen cravat and looking dowdy, plain and business-like in these grand surroundings.

Holcroft looked up at the ceiling where a pair of huge chandeliers blazed, despite the morning hour, and shed their light on a series of extraordinarily beautiful paintings of noble kings and half-naked angels, Roman soldiers and cherubs. His father, freshly shaved, his long blue coat brushed, his hair neatly tied back, stood beside him, a pair of light manacles on his wrists and a serene smile curling his lips. A footman in scarlet livery with a short white wig announced their presence in a voice that boomed in the largely empty space – 'Mister Thomas Blood of Romford Market and his son Holcroft' – then the man whispered in their ears that they should bow as well as they could and approach the

King, but remain at a distance of no less than five yards from His Majesty at all times.

It was Sir John Grenville, who had been a justice of the peace in his native Cornwall, who opened the proceedings. He ignored Holcroft and addressed himself to Blood: 'You, sir, who call yourself Colonel Blood, stand accused of many gross crimes against the people of England, against the kingdom itself and against the person of His Majesty the King. Most recently, and perhaps most seriously, you have been charged with the attempted theft of the Crown Jewels of England from the Tower of London, a felony that carries with it the death penalty, also you have been charged with the assault and attempted murder of Mister Talbot Edwards, His Majesty's Assistant Keeper of the Jewels, who is still suffering the effects of the brutal attack on his person, and who may yet die. You have been accused of sedition, rebellion against your lawful King, of riotous assembly, of conspiring to overthrow the offices of state, of violence against the King's officers, of murder, robbery, rape, arson, horse-stealing . . . the list is as long as my arm. Do you deny that you are guilty of any and all of these crimes and is there any reason *at all* why it would not be a benefit to the whole country, indeed to mankind itself, if you were taken to the Old Bailey this very morning, tried, sentenced and hanged as swiftly as possible?'

'I've had a grand old time, I can't deny it,' said Blood. 'But I don't recall committing any rapes: they were all quite willing, as I remember it. Although no doubt they told a different story to their husbands.' Blood winked at the King and Charles found himself unable to suppress a smile.

'Nevertheless, you do not deny the majority of your crimes, any one of which would be enough to earn you the death penalty?' said Grenville.

'I've been a bad boy, sure. But I come here today to beg for a pardon from His Majesty for my mistakes – not to deny them. And may I take this opportunity to say how gracious it is of you, sire, how beneficent, to grant me an audience. The joy I feel to be basking in the radiance of your presence ... it is like a man who has been entombed in a cave all his life and who is finally released and granted a glimpse of the blazing sun ...'

'You did not give us a great deal of choice about the matter,' said the Duke of Buckingham. 'Your son there has been making gross threats to His Majesty, suggesting God-knows-what nonsense, spreading lies, stirring up seditious mischief ...'

'I only said I would reveal what I know to be the truth,' said Holcroft, 'if my father was not granted an audience with the King. The truth about the Treaty of Dover.'

There was a long, awkward silence.

'And what do you know, Mister Blood,' said Buckingham, 'that makes you think you can dictate terms to the greatest men in the kingdom – indeed, to His Gracious Majesty the King?'

'I know, sir ...' began Holcroft.

'Wait! Stop there,' broke in the King. 'You will be silent, Mister Blood. You will not say another word – for the moment.'

The King turned to his right. 'You, sir, Captain Fellowes, isn't it? I want you and all your men out of the hall, right now.'

'Sire, this man is a dangerous criminal. Indeed, when I went with my men to collect him from the Tower this morning we found a man, a friend of the prisoner, murdered in his cell, hanging by the neck from a beam. Blood almost certainly killed him ...'

'That poor fellow hanged himself – self disgust, I should imagine, at the treacherous creature he had become,' said Blood. 'Yet, Your Majesty, to ease your fears, I will give you my word as an Irish gentleman that I shall not seek to harm you, if you wish to send away your guards. Indeed, I may tell you now, since we are discoursing on the subject, that I did once seek to harm you, to my shame. I chanced upon your person while you were bathing in the Thames at Vauxhall one morning last summer. It was a beautiful day: a wide blue sky and a cheery rising sun. I had a pistol about me, as was habitual for me in those dark days, and I even went so far as to pull it from my belt and point it at your back. But in the end, sire, I could not fire. I was quite overwhelmed with a sense of awe at the majesty of your naked person, and I said to myself, I cannot remove this our Blessed Sovereign, anointed by God, from this world, only the Almighty Father has the right to do that. So I put up my pistol, gave thanks to God, and stole quietly away.'

'What?' exclaimed Sir John Grenville. 'You see, sire, he freely admits he once sought to murder you.'

'It is a charming story, Grenville, and doubtless a complete and utter fabrication but, even so, you have missed its point. He claims he did not shoot me down even when he had the chance. I think we can safely dismiss the guards. You give me your word, colonel, that you will not seek to harm me, nor attempt to make an escape.'

'I give you my word, sire. And, as a gesture of goodwill, might I ask for these irksome clankers to be struck from my wrists?'

Fellowes unlocked the manacles and led his men from the hall and Blood, grinning and rubbing his wrists said, 'Now that it is just family, so to speak, shall we indulge in a little more candour? My son was about to talk, I believe. With your permission, sire?'

'I should certainly like to hear what he has to say,' said the King.

Holcroft looked at the men ranged against him: Sir Thomas Osborne, the Duke of Buckingham, Sir John Grenville and, of course, the King himself, each of them infinitely richer, wiser and more powerful than he. He closed his eyes and pictured the queen of diamonds. She was smiling at him, urging him on, giving him the courage to speak in this august company. The diamond on the black choker around her neck winked shards of light. And then her face slowly changed; the crude flat, painted lines of the card became living human flesh. It was the face of Aphra Behn. She smiled at him, too.

He opened his eyes. 'I know that the Treaty of Dover, which was proclaimed in December of last year was a sham. It was the second treaty of that same name to be agreed between His Majesty and King Louis XIV of France. The first one was agreed, signed and sealed in June of last year a full six months before my Lord Buckingham arranged the false treaty with such strange ease. The true treaty was all but identical to the sham one, save for one crucial paragraph, which I shall come to in a moment . . .'

Holcroft faltered. The entire hall was deathly silent. He summoned all his strength and forged onwards, the phrases, long rehearsed in his head in Aphra's garret, coming out staccato, as if he were reading from a list on sheet of paper. 'The Duke of Buckingham was not told of the first treaty. This treaty was arranged by my Lord Arlington and his colleague Sir Thomas Clifford on a secret visit to France in May last year. Both of these men espouse the Catholic faith. The Duke of Buckingham, with the wide webs of informants that he has, soon discovered that his second treaty was false and he set himself and all his agents to uncovering the secret of the first.'

Holcroft stopped. He felt dizzy and sick.

'Is this true?' asked the King, looking at Buckingham.

The duke gave a small shrug but said nothing.

Holcroft continued: 'This secret, Your Majesty, was discovered earlier this year by my Lord Buckingham's new chief agent in Versailles, a fellow named Jupon. I shall now quote from the real treaty, the single paragraph that differs from the sham, which reads as follows . . .'

Holcroft closed his eyes again to block out the intimidating stares coming from the dais and said, 'The King of England will make a public profession of the Catholic faith and will receive the sum of two million crowns, to aid him in this project, from the Most Christian King, in the course of the next six months. The date of this declaration is left absolutely to his own pleasure . . .' Then he stopped and opened his eyes.

No one said a word. Holcroft saw that the King's expression had not changed, the Duke of Buckingham still offered him the same contemptuous glare. Sir John Grenville looked as grim as usual. Only Sir Thomas Osborne now looked surprised. His mouth gaped a little. Then he shut it with a snap and began shooting nervous little glances to his left towards the King.

'I came upon the secret report from Jupon while I was employed as a confidential clerk by His Grace. I made a copy of the coded report, which I have translated and had set as a pamphlet, and which I will distribute throughout all the Three Kingdoms, if necessary. On the other hand, if my father receives a pardon for his actions at the Tower – which all here know were ordered by the Duke of Buckingham with the full knowledge of His Majesty – then I will destroy all the pamphlets and give my solemn word never to speak of this matter to anyone, ever again.'

Holcroft let out a long, loud breath – his task complete; his shoulders slumped and he dropped his eyes to the floor. He felt utterly exhausted.

Blood said: 'Ah, Your Majesty, what *were* you thinking? To set such a promise down on paper, even in a secret treaty . . . such a rash course of action. I do not like to condemn a man for his religion but you must know the people of England will not stand to have a Catholic King. They have suffered under the rule of Papist monarchs before. Word that His Majesty had sold his soul to Rome would unleash a storm of fire and blood all across the land, a cataclysm far worse than all the wars of the last age. And, who knows, perhaps once again a King might lose his throne, perhaps his head.'

'Thank you, colonel, I think we all grasp the appalling implications of this information being revealed to the public,' said Osborne.

'Keep the Protestant faith, Your Majesty, and we'll all come up smiling yet.' Blood's innocent blue eyes twinkled.

'As I see it, sire, you have little choice,' said Osborne quietly in the King's ear. 'If this were to become generally known . . .'

'All right, Sir Thomas, I take your point. I understand the danger perfectly. So, now, tell me, Colonel Blood, what would you do if I were to grant you a pardon for your crimes?'

'I should endeavour to deserve it, sire,' Blood answered, with a broad smile.

'And you would be silent on this matter – all these dangerous matters?'

'I should ever be the King's most discreet and loyal servant – in so far as my dire poverty and lack of a proper livelihood would allow me to be.'

'Your poverty? Livelihood . . . Good God Almighty, man, that sounds like another threat. What else do you want from me?'

'My family had lands in Ireland, sire, at Sarney, in County Meath, such a beautiful little estate, and they were most cruelly taken from me by your man the Duke of Ormonde and given away to another. If there could be some small recompense for that deprivation . . .'

'By God, sir, you are a damned rogue – but, well, I imagine something might be arranged, if only to keep you on the side of the angels.'

'If I might suggest something, sire,' said Sir John Grenville, giving a sly sideways glance at the Duke of Buckingham.

'Yes?'

'I believe that little estate in Straffan, County Kildare, the one we discussed some days past, is of a similar size to the Sarney lands, sire. It yields at least five hundred pounds a year, if I remember aright.'

'What? No, no, sire. No! Hold hard just a moment,' the Duke of Buckingham had been jerked out of his silence. 'You promised me the title to those lands, Your Majesty. You gave me your word!'

'I said I'd think about it. But you most certainly did give me your word that you would arrange this matter of Colonel Blood without embarrassing me – and yet I find that, not only have you dragged me into one of the most painful episodes of my reign, but that your snooping into my affairs has led to your own clerk being able to extort pardons and favours out of me.'

Charles rose from his throne, standing to his full, imposing height, eyes glittering. 'So no, Your Grace, I will not hold hard, as you so crudely put it: nor shall I give the Straffan lands into your hand. You did this to me, and you shall not profit from it. I shall grant Straffan to the colonel as a fitting recompense for Sarney—'

'Sire, this is most unfitting,' said Buckingham hotly, 'this is all quite wrong. If I might have a private word, I am sure we can . . .'

'You will not interrupt me – and do not dare to tell me I am wrong. I shall grant Straffan to Blood and, furthermore, Your Grace, I believe that I shall thank you now to take your leave. Go! I have had quite enough of your odious presence at court. In your leisure time – and you will soon have a surfeit of it, I do most earnestly assure you – you may reflect long and hard on how badly you have served your King in this affair. Good day, sir!'

Buckingham stared at the King. His mouth worked but no words came out. Then, after making the most cursory of bows, and giving Blood and his son a look of deep malevolence, Buckingham began to stalk away, his footsteps echoing loudly on the wooden floor of the Banqueting House.

When he had gone, the King said: 'Well, gentlemen, that seems to have concluded matters satisfactorily.' He was actually smiling at the Bloods.

'You shall have your pardon, sir, my clerks will have it drawn up today – and I suppose we must include all the conspirators; you have another son residing in the Tower, I believe. And we shall also transfer the titles to those lands in Kildare. You can arrange all that, Sir John, can't you? And you, colonel, will swear to keep your mouth closed about this affair for the rest of your life. I hope that may satisfy you as well, young Holcroft – but wait! Since it appears that I am in such a forgiving mood today – tell me, Mister Blood, what is it that you desire from your King? What can I give you that will induce you to keep my little secret about this treaty business?'

'I require nothing, sire. I only wished to see my father pardoned.'

'Nonsense, it would please me to grant you some small mark of my favour. Name your boon, young man. I insist.'

'In that case, sire, I should like an ensign's commission in the King's Foot Guards. If you would be so pleased as to grant one to me.'

'Done! The King's Foot Guards have a new and, I have no doubt,' the King said with a certain hard emphasis, 'surpassingly loyal and closed-mouthed junior officer. Sir John, you can arrange that too, can't you? Have a word with Colonel Russell about the muster rolls, pay, billeting, and so on?'

Holcroft bowed deeply to the King.

'If you gentlemen will kindly come with me,' said Sir John Grenville, stepping forward with his arms spread wide and herding the two Bloods away from the dais and towards the far end of the hall.

Holcroft could barely feel his feet. He felt as if he were walking on the softest of clouds.

The Duke of Buckingham waited in the anteroom outside the main hall, pretending to admire an exquisite crystal vase in a niche on the wall. Henri d'Erloncourt, in his gold coat, stood in the corner of the room and two footmen waited by the door that led out to the wide White Hall street. The hall door creaked open and Sir

John Grenville ushered Blood and Holcroft into the anteroom and swiftly through another portal and into the maze of backrooms and service areas of the Banqueting House. Buckingham did not even deign to turn around as the Bloods and Sir John passed by, he merely watched their short journey in the reflection of the vase. Some ten minutes after that, when Sir Thomas Osborne finally came through the door, the duke turned, smiling, and said, 'A word with you, Sir Thomas, if you please.'

The two courtiers stood staring at each other. Both were tall, well-made men sporting fine, towering black periwigs, but one man was youthful, slim, pink-cheeked, crackling with energy, though plain in his dress; the other magnificent in purple robes, his face lined with age, yellowed by good wine.

'You disappoint me, Thomas,' said Buckingham at last. 'I had expected a little more zeal and imagination in this matter. Blood still lives. And, since you were not able to silence him for good, I would have expected a little more fight in that room to keep him from receiving his undeserved pardon and, incidentally, to support my own position with the King.'

'I'm sorry to hear that, Your Grace. But what's done, is done. And it is not a bad outcome, I think. Blood will keep silent – as I believe you once remarked to me, he is not a blab. And his son has received a reward that should ensure his future loyalty. He, too, seems to be a discreet fellow.'

'Not a bad outcome? I have been made to look incompetent. I have been chastised by the King, insulted and sent from his court like an unruly schoolboy being dismissed from the class.'

'I meant not a bad outcome for the King, for the stability of the Three Kingdoms. The secret is kept; there will be no disturbances, no rebellion, nor do we risk a return to the horrors of civil war. Not a bad outcome. That is the cross that we loyal men who strive in the service of the Crown must ever endure: we must always put our country's needs before our own desires.'

'How very pious of you. And what little *bon-bon* did you manage to inveigle from His Majesty just now, eh?'

'Since you ask, His Majesty felt that a mere knighthood was not a sufficient mark of recognition for a man of my talents. He feels that Baron Osborne or even Viscount Osborne would sound rather better. Lord Osborne does have a certain ring to it, wouldn't you say?'

The duke said nothing but his jaw muscles writhed under the skin.

'We also discussed my taking over the position of Lord Steward of the Household,' Osborne continued blithely. 'The Duke of Ormonde really is becoming quite advanced in years and these days he does not often venture from his house. And it seems there are no other men of great rank who are qualified for the role. Not one that His Majesty could think of, anyway. The King felt that someone younger, someone with more of a spring in his step, should take over the burden of that position. The complex business of state really is a young man's game, don't you agree, Your Grace?'

The duke was white with rage yet, despite his obvious fury, he seemed to have been struck dumb.

'I must not keep Your Grace,' continued Osborne, bowing very low. 'I'm sure you have many important matters to attend to – at your home, at least, if not at the King's court – and so I shall bid you a very good day.'

The music room in Foot Guards' House contained a good dozen men, both officers of the Foot Guards and civilians, when the Duke of Buckingham, followed by his golden-clad page Henri d'Erloncourt and two footmen, walked in at a few minutes before two of the clock. The hum of conversation faltered, then recovered, and His Grace noted silently that word of his humiliation in the Banqueting House that morning had already spread right across White Hall. A square wooden card table had been set in the centre of the room with four chairs around it. Ensign Churchill and Sir Thomas Littleton were already seated there, at the north and west positions of the table, chatting amicably and each shuffling a fresh pack of cards as they waited for their partners to arrive. Buckingham slid into his seat at the east position, opposite Littleton, signalling to Fox Cub to bring him wine.

'Have you found some reckless officer to partner you this afternoon, Churchill? If so, I hope he has brought a heavy purse with him. I have had a trying morning and am in the mood to relieve you both of a large sum.'

'I have found someone, Your Grace – and indeed a fellow officer. He is the newest recruit to the mess of the King's Foot Guards. I believe you are already acquainted with Ensign Holcroft Blood.'

Buckingham looked up slowly and saw his former confidential clerk standing behind the last empty chair. Holcroft had not had time to equip himself with the gorgeous scarlet of the regiment so he wore his drab clerk's attire. He tried to affect a military bearing nonetheless.

'Good afternoon, Your Grace.'

'Mister Blood, or indeed, Ensign Blood. I did not expect to see any more of you today. I cannot say that I welcome the sight.'

Holcroft sat down in his chair. The Duke of Buckingham was aware that many pairs of eyes were on him. It occurred to him that he might simply get up and walk out, with some remark about only playing cards with gentlemen, but he knew he would open himself to snide remarks about being too discomforted to play with a clever young man who had already bested him once that day. No, he decided rapidly, he would play the little sneak thief, would ensure that he won and he'd break the boy for good and anyone who was stupid enough to back him with their money. Holcroft Blood would be ruined – and if he could not pay his debts he would be shunned in this officer's mess before he even formally joined it. What could be more satisfying after this morning's debacle with the King? There would be no mercy for Holcroft Blood, the duke decided. No future for him either.

'The game is White Hall Whist,' said Sir Thomas Littleton, 'and just so that there shall be no misunderstandings between us, I shall briefly run over the rules of this variety of the game.'

Littleton rattled through the rules: trumps to be determined by the last card dealt by the dealer; one point scored for every trick over six won by the partnership – so, as there were thirteen cards in each hand and thirteen tricks, a maximum score in one hand would be seven points. The first partnership to reach nine points would win the game. The match to be decided by best of three games, so the first partnership to win two games would win the match and receive the bonus, which would be double the points they were leading by. The losers were obliged to pay their losses immediately.

'The wager per point is ten pounds, gentlemen,' said Littleton. 'Are we all agreed?'

Holcroft knew that between them, Jack and he had exactly one hundred and fifty-two pounds, which they had agreed was ample to play with even at these high stakes. Although the thought of losing that huge sum – and being unable to repay Aphra and his father, not to mention Churchill's loss of his horse and whatever else he had pledged – made Holcroft mentally squirm.

'Yes, we are all agreed,' said Holcroft.

'No, we are not all agreed,' said the duke. 'I do not want to waste my time with pin money. The wager per point should be something worthwhile – I suggest a hundred pounds a point.'

'What! That's preposterous,' cried Churchill. 'We agreed to ten pounds – it is already a ten times increase on the last game.'

'You wanted your revenge, sir. Are you not bold enough to attempt it?'

The duke's words were a hair away from calling Churchill a coward.

'We accept the new stakes,' Holcroft said quietly.

Jack gave him a what-the-hell-are-you-doing look but said nothing.

'Very good,' said Buckingham. 'Shall we cut for dealer?'

Holcroft frowned at his cards. He could not believe the run of bad luck he had suffered in the past two hands. In the first hand, he and his opponents had been almost evenly matched but Buckingham and Littleton had won seven tricks to Holcroft and Churchill's six to put them one point down. Holcroft had not been concerned. The luck was bound to fluctuate and he was confident that as long as he played his cards correctly in the long run he would come through. The second game his luck had been worse. Littleton and Buckingham trumped trick after trick. When all the trumps were played, Holcroft took one trick with his king of hearts, Jack took another with his ace of clubs, but Littleton and Buckingham had the rest and five points. That made six points to the enemy. Three more and they'd have the first game.

Holcroft fared a little better in the third hand. Once the trumps had all been played – which gave Littleton and Buckingham four tricks – Jack and Holcroft won the rest and they were finally off the mark with three points.

They won the next hand too, with Jack playing brilliantly and either by guesswork or some strange prescience, leading exactly the suit that Holcroft wished twice in a row. They won ten tricks in all and it was now six points to seven in their favour – two more points would give them the first game.

Holcroft picked up his hand and frowned in utter disbelief at his cards: he had nothing, no, not quite nothing – a knave of spades.

Holcroft made it a winner, trumped Buckingham twice and Jack won a trick with the king of spades, but that was it. Their opponents collected nine tricks in total, giving them three points and the first game. As they had won nine points to seven, Buckingham and Littleton were now two points up – two hundred pounds ahead – although these points would not count towards the next game.

By mutual agreement, the four men broke from the table then to stretch their legs, with Littleton disappearing out of the room to visit the officer's latrines at the back of the main building. Buckingham refilled his wine glass and began to talk loudly and confidently with Colonel John Russell about the state of the defences in the Dutch Republic and the likelihood of those doughty burgers being able to resist the might of Louis XIV's huge army.

Jack Churchill took Holcroft by the elbow and led him over to the Lely portrait of the King in his armour above the fireplace.

'What the hell are you doing, Hol?' Jack's face was pink. 'We're losing – we're already two hundred pounds down. It's more than we can pay. Do you know what happens to a guards officer who doesn't pay his gambling debts?'

'No, what happens to him?'

Jack paused for a moment. 'I don't know, as it happens, no one in the First Foot has ever welshed to my knowledge. But I warrant it would be worse than awful: stripped of his commission, drummed out of the regiment, thrown in the Marshalsea for debt – terrible, terrible things, anyway.'

'We haven't lost yet.'

'We're certainly not winning.'

'We just haven't had the cards, Jack. I can't win if they have almost all the top cards, no matter how well we play ours.'

'I trusted you, Hol. You can't let me down.'

'I won't, don't fret so, Jack, the cards will turn in our favour.'

But the cards did not turn in their favour in the next hand, the first in the new game and, to make it worse, Jack made a simple error discarding a ten of diamonds that might have been a winner.

They would have lost the hand anyway, but Churchill's mistake allowed Littleton to win two extra tricks that he might not otherwise have taken. In this second game their opponents were now four points up. *Two hundred pounds just thrown away*, Holcroft thought. *Maybe a whole lot more if we lose this game and therefore the match. Terrible, terrible things, Jack said.*

The second hand was better. By counting his own trumps and making an assumption about their distribution, Holcroft correctly surmised that Buckingham held the crucial ace of trumps but no others and forced him to over-trump Littleton's winning queen, wasting a trick. They ended up making ten tricks out of thirteen allowing them to score four much-needed points.

It was one game to their opponents, and four points each in this game. If the other side won five points in this next hand, it was game and match to them, and Holcroft and Jack would be seven points down, doubled for losing the match, at a hundred pounds a point: they'd owe their opponents one thousand four hundred pounds, nearly ten times the money they actually had.

Holcroft was dealer, he flipped out thirteen cards to each player, turned over the last card, his own, a seven of hearts, which indicated the suit that was to be trumps and then picked up his hand. At last, the luck was running his way. He could see five trumps and eight clear winners in his hand and if Jack had even a small amount of luck and a good fit with Holcroft they were going to make some points.

They did. Five points, which added to the four they already had made nine – and the second game was theirs. One game each. And Jack and Holcroft were now three hundred pounds up. The next game would settle the match.

The table broke again for refreshment. Holcroft summoned a soldier-servant and ordered a tankard of cooled ale. His mouth was dry and his head was aching slightly. He stood next to the double virginal and admired the painted hunting scene on the open lid. He felt a presence and turned to find the Duke of Buckingham by his side. 'Interesting game,' he said affably. 'It really could go either way.'

Holcroft said nothing.

'But it's not going to,' the duke said quietly. 'Thing is, my dear Holcroft, you *are* going to lose. And I will tell you why. You are going to make sure that you lose this match because, if you do not, if you do somehow manage to scrape a win, I shall immediately tell the Duke of Ormonde that it was your father who attacked him that night in Piccadilly last year. And while the duke himself might have mellowed in his dotage, I doubt his son the Earl of Ossory has. To put it bluntly, you will lose this match or your father is a dead man. As you seem so adept at applying pressure, I thought you might appreciate the irony of having to submit to it.'

'Then the rogue had the cheek to say to me: "Keep the Protestant faith, Your Majesty, and we'll all come up smiling yet!"'

'I am surprised you did not have him hanged on the spot,' said the Duke of York, sipping from his crystal glass of claret.

'My dear James,' said the King, 'if you ever ascend the throne of England – and recall that you are my heir until such time as my sweet Catherine can be induced to bring forth a son – then you can go about in that absolutist, continental manner hanging your subjects willy-nilly or chopping off their heads left and right, but sadly I have to be a good deal more circumspect. The whole country knows what this fellow Blood did at the Tower and Parliament would certainly punish me for it – they might stop my grant, God forbid – if I had him executed without trial. And trial means a public trial. Then there is the matter of the boy and his damned pamphlets. There was nothing I could do, brother, but smile graciously and pardon the old villain and his rascally progeny.'

'I would have proclaimed my faith – the true faith – to the world. You acted as if you were ashamed of the treaty. Never be ashamed of what you know to be right, brother. If Parliament ever gave me the slightest difficulty, over this or over any other matter, I should call on our Cousin Louis of France and have him send an army to hold the kingdom down by force.'

'That is what our father might have done, may he rest in peace.' Both men looked at each other sadly.

The King took a sip of his wine and filled his lungs with fresh air. It was a perfect May afternoon, not too hot, not too cool, and he and his brother were sitting in his personal withdrawing room, the Rose Room, with the glass double doors flung wide. A breeze blew in bringing the scent of the white roses that bloomed huge and heavy at the end of the garden.

'The difference between you and I, James, is that I would rather live in harmony with my subjects even if it means I must hide my faith, but you would put the salvation of your own soul above the security of the realm.'

'You are courting damnation, brother. Hell awaits you. You know the truth and yet will not acknowledge it.'

'Oh, I will make my peace with God and the Church at some point; before it is too late, I hope. In the meantime, I want to live in peace with my fellow man. And that . . .Yes, what is it?'

Sir John Grenville had appeared behind his chair. 'Your Majesty, the Duke of Ormonde is without. He craves an audience. Will you receive him?'

'Ormonde – this is indeed an honour. He's not been seen in White Hall for months. Show him in, Grenville, show him in.'

'What did the bastard say?' said Jack. 'You've gone as white as a lily.' He stood beside the double virginal and looked into his friend's face. Holcroft told him what Buckingham had said. 'I have to lose, Jack, I have to.'

Jack thought for a moment. 'Don't do anything foolish, Hol. Just play as normal. I must get a message to someone and a reply. Promise me you won't do anything rash.'

Holcroft watched Jack walk briskly out of the room. He saw that Littleton and Buckingham had resumed their seats and the duke was leering at him in a most unpleasant manner. Nevertheless, he went over to the table and joined them. A few moments later, Jack slid into his seat. Holcroft looked at his friend, eyebrows raised in a question. Jack just shrugged.

As Littleton dealt the cards, Holcroft looked around the music room. He had not noticed how crowded it had become since they had started their game. Word of the hundred-pound-a-point match had evidently spread fast. He wondered what he ought to do about Buckingham's threat. It seemed very likely that Ormonde, or his son Ossory, would kill his father if they knew that he was the man who had attacked the duke. He remembered Ossory's promise of murder at the playhouse last winter when he threatened Buckingham in the presence of the King. His father would have to go into hiding once more. And he was no longer a young man: those two weeks in the Tower under sentence of death had put a strain on his body and mind. Holcroft did not think he would survive another year on the run and, anyway, Ossory or his paid killers would find him eventually. More to the point, for Blood, returning to the life of a hunted man just hours after his moment of triumph would destroy his spirit. Buckingham's threat was real: he knew he must contrive to lose this game or his father would die.

Holcroft slowly fanned out his cards: an ace, a king, another ace, a queen, a knave, another king, and damn it, yet another ace – losing this hand was going to be as difficult a task as he had ever attempted.

With Jack frowning at him and making little grimacing expressions with his mouth, Holcroft contrived to win only eight tricks and two points from a hand that should have allowed him with ease to take every trick on the table: a grand slam. Buckingham under-stood early what cards Holcroft had and what he was about and gave him a pleased little nod that made Holcroft feel sick.

When Jack began to deal out the cards for the next game Holcroft's sense of shame was so great that he could not even look at him. Yet he knew he was right. Jack and he would lose a few hundred pounds – but they would find the money somehow, even if he had to play cards every day for a year, they would find the money. His father's life must be preserved.

The Duke of Ormonde hobbled into the royal withdrawing room and, after making his stiff bow to the King and the Duke of York, gratefully took his seat. After a round of tedious pleasantries and good wishes from all sides, Ormonde came swiftly to the point.

'I come on behalf of my son, Lord Ossory, to beg a command for him in Your Majesty's navy. He anticipates a largely naval war with the Dutch and is determined to be at the forefront of the action. You know the fellow well, sire, I am sure, and have no doubt rightly marked him as a hothead and a God-damned fool. But he does have higher qualities: he does not want for conduct under fire, indeed, he is as brave as a lion. Your Majesty will recall that he distinguished himself by his courage at the sea battle of Lowestoft against the Dutch in the fifth year of your reign, the year of the plague, and he longs to repeat that glorious experience. The war, I mean, not the plague. In short, Your Majesty, I am come to beg a ship of war for my son.'

'What do you think, James?'

The Lord High Admiral scratched his chin. 'Does your son know much about commanding a ship in battle?'

'He is a gentleman, Your Grace, he was born to command. As for the mechanical aspects of the ship, surely there are sailormen, tarpaulins, I believe they are called, who can undertake the menial business of raising the sails, hauling on the ropes and so forth. My son's task will be to lead them to victory from the quarter-deck.'

'Quite so,' said James with a smile. 'Well, the *Victory* lacks a suitably noble captain. It is being refitted at Chatham but if His Majesty agrees I could certainly assign the Earl of Ossory command of that vessel when it is finally seaworthy. What say you, sire?'

The three men were interrupted in their deliberations by the arrival of Barbara Villiers. She swept into the withdrawing room, completely unannounced, and glided over to the King. She curt-seyed prettily to the three men and said: 'I beg you will forgive my gross intrusion, gentlemen, but I urgently need to speak to the King and I am afraid the matter cannot wait.'

As the dukes of York and Ormonde got reluctantly to their feet and made insincere noises of forgiveness, Barbara whispered into Charles's ear.

'What?' said Charles. 'Now?' And then a few moments later. 'Did he indeed?' And then, 'Oh well, I suppose so – if I must.'

When Barbara had left, the King said to Ormonde. 'It is fortunate that you are here today, Your Grace, for it seems that I must speak to you about an entirely different matter.'

Holcroft had no difficulty at all in losing the second hand of the third game. Littleton had all the cards and Buckingham was able to support him strongly. As the cards were being collected, he cal-culated the points. Buckingham had won five points in the hand just played. Holcroft had two from the previous hand, and three from the game before. If Buckingham won four more points in the next hand, he would have the game, and the match. That would put Buckingham four points ahead of them – doubled for winning the match – so eight hundred pounds. They would owe the duke the colossal sum of eight hundred pounds! But that must be set against his father's life. He looked up from his deliberations to see a red-coated private soldier whispering in Jack's ear. Churchill nodded and said: 'If you don't mind, gentlemen, before we play the next hand I need to visit the jakes.' He rose from his chair. He stared hard at Holcroft, waggling his eyebrows up and down. *He looks perfectly ridiculous*, Holcroft thought. And frowned at his friend.

'Do you need to use the house of ease, at all, Holcroft?' said Jack. His eyebrows were jerking up and down like the arms of a marionette.

'No, thank you.'

'I believe your friend wants to speak privily with you . . . in the privy,' Buckingham told him. 'Why don't you run along like a pair of gossiping washerwomen and we continent gentlemen will wait patiently for you here.'

While Jack and Holcroft relieved themselves in the wooden trough in the building behind the Foot Guards' House, Jack said: 'I have fixed our problem, Hol. Do not be concerned for your father. You must play to win, play with all your heart and mind. Win.'

'What have you done?'

'No time to tell you now. You must trust me – play to win. Give this game all that you have and more.'

Holcroft sat back down at the table. Just as Buckingham lifted the cards to deal, he said: 'One moment, Your Grace. When we began this match you raised the stake from ten to a hundred pounds a point. You said you wanted to play for something substantial. I agree. I suggest we raise the stakes to something appropriate to this great contest: a thousand pounds a point.'

There was a loud collective gasp from the crowd – now as thick as the throng at a fair-day cock-fight.

Buckingham narrowed his eyes at Holcroft. *What does the little sneak have in mind, something that came of that gossip in the jakes, no doubt. But, no, they cannot not know what cards they will have.* He looked down once at the undealt pack of cards in his hand and remembered that he was five points ahead in this game. *Just four more and he would take the match. A thousand a point. That would break this silly little boy and no mistake.*

Holcroft glanced at Jack and saw that his friend was appalled. His face was bone white, beads of sweat popping in his hairline.

'How do I know that you are good for the money if you lose?' said Buckingham. 'You may have to pay several thousands to me within the hour – and you are both with hardly a penny to your names.'

'I will stand surety for my son's debts,' said a voice from the crowd. Colonel Thomas Blood stepped forward. 'I have here the title deed to a lovely little estate in County Kildare that I believe you are familiar with, Your Grace – they call it Straffan. As sweet a place as any on God's green earth. I will gladly set that deed against any losses my boy might incur.'

'Indeed.' Buckingham smiled. The chance to take down both father and son at a single stroke was too much for him to resist. 'In that case I shall gladly agree to the new terms.'

'Holcroft,' said Jack. 'I don't think—'

'Trust me, Jack. As I trust you.'

'Your Grace, I am most uneasy,' said Sir Thomas Littleton. 'I am not a rich man, sir. I'd prefer if we stuck to the original stake, if it please you.'

'It does not please me. I shall assume full responsibility for your debts, Littleton – if indeed you incur any. Play with a light heart, but play well, and you and I shall both be a good deal richer in an hour or so.'

'We are all agreed then,' said Holcroft. Three nods from around the table answered him.

Holcroft felt his gorge rise when he picked up the thirteen cards on the table in front of him and saw what he had done. He had nothing but the queen of diamonds, his old friend, a couple of low clubs, which were trumps, and a singleton heart that might win him a trick. But he refused to go down without a fight. He led the heart and to his delight Littleton, who clearly had the ace, played low and Jack won the trick with the king. Jack led a heart back to him and he was able to trump and win another. After that Littleton and Buckingham won trick after trick after trick. Jack then won with his queen of hearts and trumped Littleton's ace, and Holcroft made his lovely queen of diamonds work for him in the second from last trick.

But that was it.

Buckingham added two more points to his score. If he won only two more points, he would win the game, the match and Holcroft would owe the colossal sum of eight thousand pounds. Straffan would be gone: his father's dream of a life of gentlemanly ease would be swept away.

It was Holcroft's turn to deal and as he picked up the cards he noticed that his right hand was trembling. As he flicked out the cards to each of the four players, he was aware of a slight stirring in the crowd, a ripple of sound and movement, but he was too deeply into his deal to even lift his head. He turned over the last card, his own, and saw that it was the four of spades: trumps. Then he looked at the rest of the cards in his hand. It started well with an ace of clubs, a knave of spades and then the king of clubs, then a lot of mediocre hearts and clubs and another spade. He saw that he had a void in diamonds – not a single one of that suit – seven clubs to the ace, king, queen, and three trumps to the knave. It might not look like much but Holcroft felt a shiver pass through him when the import of his hand sank in. His void and the seven clubs in his hand meant that the normal distribution of the cards – usually three or four of each suit to each player – was badly skewed in this round, and sometimes, just sometimes, when this unusual event happened, with very careful play, great things might be achieved.

Littleton led the ace of diamonds, and Holcroft's heart began to rise. Jack played the two, Buckingham the five and Holcroft, possessing no diamonds, trumped with the four of spades and took the trick. One. He led the ace of clubs, saw that Jack had a void in clubs and that he was discarding hearts, won, and then led the king of clubs, and won again, noting that Littleton was forced to play the knave and thus had no more clubs. Three tricks. Holcroft played the queen of clubs, and Littleton ducked the challenge to trump it – knowing that Jack had a void and could over-trump him – and discarded a heart. Jack, realizing Holcroft's queen was a winner also saved his trumps and discarded a diamond. Four tricks. The same thing happened when Holcroft played his ten of clubs. Five tricks. Holcroft believed that Jack must hold some high trumps because otherwise Littleton would not have ducked trumping his clubs. Jack had also been discarding hearts, which meant that he might have a void now, and so could trump, or perhaps he had a very high card remaining. So Holcroft led the three of hearts. Littleton played the six, and to Holcroft's joy Jack tossed down the ace. Six tricks. Any more tricks they won would be points towards the game.

Jack, who was now sitting up straight as a poker, eyes starting from his head as he examined his cards, played a perfectly brilliant diamond, which Holcroft trumped with his five of spades. Seven tricks and one point to them. Holcroft played a heart, the eight, which Littleton ducked again, discarding the knave of diamonds, and Jack trumped it with the two of spades. Buckingham, now beginning to look nervous, played his knave of hearts. Eight tricks.

Jack led another diamond, which Holcroft trumped with his knave of spades. Nine. Holcroft led the nine of hearts. Littleton trumped it with the six of spades. Jack over-trumped it with the queen of spades. Buckingham was forced to play his queen of hearts. Ten tricks. The rest were all Jack's. He played the ace of trumps, then the king, and then when all the trumps were played except one, he played his eight of spades. Eleven. Twelve. Thirteen tricks.

A grand slam.

Holcroft looked down at the carefully stacked cards before him on the table. He was aware that the crowded music room was applauding with great fervour. He felt light-headed, almost as if he were in a dream. He had won.

'Thirteen tricks, seven points, I believe,' he said. 'Which makes nine points for us, gentlemen, and the game, and the match.'

He looked at Buckingham. The older man's face had fallen in, the lines were suddenly much more deeply etched, while Sir Thomas Littleton looked ready to weep. Jack's handsome face was a veritable beacon of delight.

'Five points, we've won by five points,' said Jack. 'Doubled for winning the match makes ten – a thousand pounds a point. I believe, Your Grace, that you must therefore now pay over to us ten thousand pounds.'

'A noble sum, for a noble victory,' said the King. And for the first time Holcroft noticed His Majesty, standing not two yards away and beaming at the four men at the table. Holcroft saw that beside him stood the Duke of Ormonde, scowling like an ogre. He looked as if he were in severe pain.

'I . . . I shall send round a draft for the money on my bankers before the end of the week,' said Buckingham. Holcroft had never seen him look so small, shrivelled and old.

'Nonsense,' said the King, 'you must pay up now. I believe that is the usual agreement, eh? Pay your debt promptly and cheerfully, my Lord Buckingham, you can certainly afford the loss.'

'But I do not carry that amount of gold with me, sire.'

'Then you should not be wagering it. But no matter, we cannot have you welshing on your bet. Do you know what they do to welshers in the King's Foot Guards, Buckingham? Terrible, terrible things, I hear. Tell you what: I shall have my clerks make out a draft this hour for the sum for these two gentlemen – ten thousand, wasn't it? – and you can pay *me* back by the end of the week. But do not keep me waiting for my money, Your Grace, I warn you I am not much minded to be patient with you today.'

The Duke of Buckingham got slowly to his feet. His eye alighted on the Duke of Ormonde and gradually, his spine uncurled, straightened, his chin lifted, he looked his fellow duke in the eye. Then he looked over at the far side of the room, where Blood was enfolding his son in a huge bear hug.

'Your Grace,' he said, with more than a trace of his familiar haughtiness, 'I have information for you, which I believe you may find interesting. It concerns the monstrous attack on your person last December in Piccadilly. I have uncovered the truth about the identity of the attackers.'

'If you are going to tell me Colonel Blood was the man who attacked me last winter, you can save your breath,' said Ormonde. 'The King told me the same not an hour past. He also urged me to forgive the fellow, as others have urged me, most persuasively – and, indeed, I am minded to do so.'

'You, sir,' Ormonde called out across the room to Colonel Blood who was now standing with his arm draped around Holcroft's shoulders and beaming like a trencherman sitting down to a feast. 'I know you have borne a grudge against me and my family for many a year for the settlements that were made of your lands. I know, too, that you were the man who waylaid me in Piccadilly, beat me and left me bleeding in the mud. But I tell you now, in the presence of all these witnesses, that I forgive you for that action. If His Majesty can forgive you making away with his Crown Jewels, I can forgive a few bruises.'

'That's handsome of you, duke. And I may tell you there are no hard feelings on my part either. I have lands once more.' He waved a stiff piece of paper. 'And a living; recompense has been made and I have no further cause for grievance. Let bygones be bygones. I say this to you: if we keep the faith with each other, my dear Ormonde, we'll both come up smiling yet.'

Holcroft watched as the Duke of Buckingham made his way out of the music room, followed by Littleton and his two footmen. The last person in his dismal train was Henri d'Erloncourt, and at the threshold of the door through which his noble patron had just passed, Fox Cub stopped, turned and gave Holcroft one final glance.

It was a look of undiluted loathing.

Saturday 10 June, 1671

The first performance of *The Amorous Prince* by the Duke's Company was a resounding triumph. The King remained awake throughout almost the whole performance and smiled continually when he *was* awake; he was even seen to laugh once or twice at some of the broader jokes. The play's new patron, the Duke of Ormonde, while possessing a temperament that was not much given to mirth, had praised the production to its author Mistress Behn and was also said to be pleasantly surprised at the takings by the ticket-sellers – for it had been a full house, with several dozen theatre-goers turned away disappointed at the door when the pit became dangerously full.

The leading lady of the play, Miss Jenny Blaine, had quite entranced the audience with her portrayal of Cloris the sister and, scandalously, the love interest of the titular prince; and John Wilmot, the Earl of Rochester, recalled to court after a temporary banishment following the incident with the sundial, had declared drunkenly at the fall of the final curtain that if he could not have her he would die. Miss Blaine, who might otherwise have been interested, and might yet too, one day, now feigned indifference to his advances at the party to celebrate the first night and flaunted a large ruby ring on the third finger of her left hand. She said she was promised in matrimony to the dashing Colonel Blood, the Irish landowner. But that gentleman was not in evidence that evening – urgent business, Jenny said, having called him and his eldest son Thomas to Romford, and he had been unable to say exactly when he would be back in London.

However, his younger son Holcroft had attended the performance – dressed in a splendid scarlet coat with blue turnbacks, blue breeches, white stockings and highly polished black shoes.

A brand-new sword hung from his side and a purple sash was wrapped around his waist indicating his new status as an ensign of the King's Foot Guard. He stood at the side of the stage chatting with the author of the play, a slight, pretty, blonde-haired lady dressed in widow's black from head to toe.

'I think they liked it, Holly,' said Aphra. 'I also think that with your new wealth and my success with the Duke's Company we may never need to return to our old, sad and criminal ways.'

'We might have been criminal but I don't think we were sad for very long. I think, in fact, I rather enjoyed the experience. I believe you did too.'

'Possibly, possibly. By the way, I heard something the other day that might amuse you. The Earl of Westbury has publicly accused the Duke of Buckingham of the murder of his third son Robert. He received an anonymous letter telling him that the duke liked to engage in sodomical practices with his pages, and that young Robert was a favourite bed-partner of his. The letter-writer informed the earl that his son grew tired of his employer's affections, tried to blackmail his older lover and was quietly murdered by the duke's henchmen for his pains.'

'You are a very clever woman, Aphra.'

'Some people might think so.' She put a hand to her throat, where a single large diamond gleamed in the centre of a black velvet choker. 'I want to thank you again for this,' she said. 'It was unnecessary but kind of you.'

Holcroft smiled but said nothing.

'Tell me, Holly, what have you done with your winnings – your five thousand pounds – apart from spending part on this vast bauble for me?'

'I took some advice that my former master gave me many months ago. I invested it. I bought an annuity.'

'Indeed? Are you going to retire then and live a life devoted to pleasure, a life of debauched luxury, regular degradation and daily vice?'

'No, of course not,' Holcroft frowned at her. After a pause he said, 'Were you by any chance making another one of your silly jokes?'

'I confess it,' said Aphra, smiling.

'Oh, yes, very funny. Ha, ha, ha. Well, since you ask, I may tell you that I'm going to sea.'

'Really?'

'Yes. Jack Churchill is still out of favour at court. The King suspects him of continuing his affair with the Duchess of Cleveland and, as a result, he will find no advancement if he remains in White Hall. So he has volunteered for foreign service in the Admiral's Regiment. He's going to be posted aboard a ship, in fact, his patron the Duke of York's flagship *Prince*, with a company from the King's Foot Guards. I'm going with him. We are going to fight the Dutchmen, Aphra. We're going off to war!'

'Just make sure you come back all in one piece.'

They fell into a companionable silence, watching the antics of the Earl of Rochester, who was whispering something filthy into Jenny Blaine's ears and making her blush, flutter her eyelashes and wave her fan enticingly.

'I must ask you something, Holcroft, although I am quite certain I'll regret it: did you like this performance any better than the written play?'

'You know, Aphra, I *did* like it. The actors gave it life. I found it very humorous, very witty but also sad and quite touching in parts, too.'

'Do you mean that? Did you really like it?'

'No,' Holcroft grinned at her. 'No, I did not like it. Not at all. I thought it was awful. A terrible play. But you see, Aphra, I can make jokes now, too.'

Historical note

When I was growing up, my mother, whose maiden name was Blood, told me that we were descended on her side of the family from a notorious character called Colonel Thomas Blood. This gentleman, she said, stole the Crown Jewels of England in Charles II's time, was caught red-handed, insisted on an audience with the King and, astonishingly, was granted one, pardoned, and even given a grant of lands in Ireland, despite his many crimes. That incredible (in both senses) story stayed with me over the decades and when I first started thinking of becoming a novelist, I knew that I wanted to tell it. So here, in your hands, is my version of that extraordinary story.

I have to admit that I don't know if it is strictly accurate that I'm descended from Colonel Blood. My mother now says that she is not so sure, just that she was told that when she was growing up, and it made an exciting tale for the children. But my late Uncle Tony (a GP in Cornwall – Doctor Blood!) apparently had a gold signet ring with the Blood crest on it and was adamant that it *was* true. I'm not convinced.

There are thousands of Bloods here in the British Isles and more across the Atlantic. The name is ancient, deriving in medieval times from the Welsh name Ap Lloyd, meaning son of Lloyd. So there must be lots of Bloods alive today who aren't related at all to the infamous seventeenth-century crown-stealing colonel. One day, if I am ever invited to go on one of those tear-jerking genealogy TV shows, perhaps I'll discover the truth. But, at the end of the day, it doesn't really matter. As we used to joke when I was a journalist: you should never let the truth get in the way of a good story. And, in my opinion, the tale of Colonel Thomas Blood and the Crown Jewels is a *cracking* story.

Thomas Blood was born in County Clare, Ireland in 1618, the son of a successful iron-master and grandson of a member of the

Irish Parliament. At the age of twenty, he married an English girl, Mary (or Maria) Holcroft from a family of Lancashire gentry, with whom he had at least seven children. When the English Civil War broke out in 1642, Blood initially joined the Royalist side and apparently fought bravely for the King. But when it became clear that the Cavaliers were losing the war, he switched sides and became a Roundhead. He rose to the rank of captain (his later colonelcy was self-appointed), and was duly rewarded for changing sides at the end of the wars with a gift of lands in Ireland. He settled down during the Commonwealth with his growing family to enjoy a gentlemanly life of moderate wealth and leisure.

All was well until the Restoration of Charles II in 1660, followed by the Act of Settlement of 1662, which stripped lands and properties from Cromwell's supporters and handed them over to the resurgent Royalists. Blood was ruined. His estates were confiscated and he blamed the government and particularly the Lord Lieutenant of Ireland, James Butler, Duke of Ormonde, for his sudden destitution.

Not the sort of man to take an injury without retaliation, Blood was part of a scheme in 1663 to storm Dublin Castle and kidnap the Duke of Ormonde and hold him for ransom. The plot was betrayed, however, and several conspirators were captured and executed. Blood had to flee Ireland and take refuge in the Netherlands, leaving his wife and family behind to manage as best they could. Blood vowed to have his revenge on Ormonde for this fresh indignity but was unable to take direct action against him for the next six or seven years, during which he lived the hunted life of an outlaw. At some point during this time Blood became associated with George Villiers, Second Duke of Buckingham and a rising power at Charles II's court.

By 1670, Blood was back in England, living in Romford Market, a few miles northeast of London, under the alias Doctor Thomas Allen. Despite having no medical qualifications at all, he made a good living treating the people of Romford for their various ailments. On December 6 of that year, on a rainy night, Blood and his confederates attacked the Duke of Ormonde's coach in St James Street as it was heading up the hill to Piccadilly. Blood and his gang pulled Ormonde from the vehicle but instead of killing him immediately, they decided to take him to Tyburn, west along Piccadilly, and hang him there like a common criminal. Ormonde was tied to the back of a horse but managed to wriggle free and he was rescued by footmen coming out with torches from Clarendon House. Ormonde, who suffered no more than a few cuts and bruises, and his fiery son Lord Ossory were convinced that it was their political rival the Duke of Buckingham who was behind the assault. Ossory openly accused Buckingham in the presence of the King and threatened to shoot him if his father was murdered. I've used Ossory's actual words in the scene in this book.

After the failure of the Ormonde assassination attempt, Blood lay low, probably in Romford, planning his next move. Sometime in April 1671, Blood, disguised as a well-to-do country parson, calling himself Thomas Ayliffe, and accompanied by his beautiful 'wife', an actress called Jenny Blaine, paid a visit to the Tower of London and asked if he might be allowed to see the famous Crown Jewels of England.

At that time, Talbot Edwards, the elderly Assistant Keeper of the Jewels, made a small income from showing visitors the King's coronation regalia, which were kept in the basement of the Irish Tower (now called the Martin Tower). He showed Blood and his charming companion the jewels and, when she feigned an illness and fainted, he kindly took them upstairs to his private apartments to recover under the care of his wife and daughter. A few days later Blood returned with a gift of four pairs of gloves – a thank-you for the Edwards' kindness. Over the next few weeks, Blood wormed his way into the affections of the family and dangling a rich 'nephew' as bait, he began negotiations with the Edwards's for the hand of their ugly daughter Elizabeth.

Early in the morning on 9 May, 1671, Blood and three companions arrived at the Irish Tower: his eldest son Thomas – an unsuccessful highwayman who had been posing as the rich nephew – and two accomplices called Hunt and Parrot (or Halliwell and Paris, according to some reports). Edwards unwisely allowed them to view the jewels and even went so far as to open the the cage that guarded them, whereupon he was struck on the head with a heavy mallet, knocked to the floor and stabbed several times. But Edwards, a former soldier in the service of the Talbot family, was made of stern stuff. While the thieves were cutting up the regalia and filling their pockets with jewels, he revived himself and began to scream for help. By sheer chance, Edwards's soldier son Wythe happened to return home on leave from his regiment in Flanders that day and he arrived with a friend called Captain Beckman at the exact time that Edwards was screaming from inside the Jewel House.

The thieves made a run for it, spilling jewels as they went, and were pursued by Wythe, Captain Beckman (who for simplicity's sake I have excluded from my story) and the Tower guards. There was a running fight as the gang tried to reach their horses which were tied up at the end of Tower Wharf at the Iron Gate. Blood was captured. As the soldiers seized him, he apparently said: 'It was a gallant attempt, however unsuccessful! 'Twas for a crown!'

Blood was imprisoned in the White Tower and questioned by the lieutenant of the Tower, Sir John Robinson, but he refused to give away any details of the plot or the names of the other people involved. Quite outrageously, Blood insisted that he would only give an account of himself in a personal audience with the King.

There is no absolute proof that either the King or the Duke of Buckingham were involved in the scheme to steal the Crown Jewels but there are some rather tantalising pieces of evidence that point in this direction. Firstly, the King was extremely short of money. Despite the subsidies from France (about which more later) and the money granted to him annually by Parliament, he lived far beyond his means and was always looking for ways to make ends meet. Secondly, Blood wrote a letter to the King, quoted in this novel, in which he claims that Sir Thomas Osborne and Sir Thomas Littleton, who were protégés of the Duke of Buckingham, persuaded him to make the attempt on the Crown Jewels and that Littleton's brother James, who worked at the naval pay office, had paid him and his gang hundreds of pounds to fund the preparations for the job. It is an extraordinary, almost preposterous claim – that he was hired by the Duke of Buckingham's men and paid with government money to undertake the robbery – yet I cannot see any plausible reason why Blood would make it unless it were in fact quite true. The last piece of evidence is that, even though he was caught *in flagrante delicto* with the Crown Jewels stuffed down his boot-tops, Blood was pardoned and even handsomely rewarded for his crimes with Irish lands.

Clearly something strange went on during that private audience with the King – of which there is no official record. Some historians have suggested that the 'Merry Monarch' was so amused by Blood's audacity, wit and charm that he just let him off. That doesn't ring true to me. I think it was blackmail, pure and simple. I think the Irish lands were a pay-off to keep him quiet. I think Blood let the King know that if he was to hang for the crime he would embarrass not only the Duke Buckingham, one of Charles's chief ministers at the time, but the King himself and, who knows, maybe he had more concrete proofs of their involvement that he threatened to use *in extremis*.

I should in good conscience mention here that I have changed some of the events of history to make the narrative run more smoothly. After all, while I do prefer to stick to the facts most of the time, I'm a historical novelist writing fiction, not an historian.

I have Blood incarcerated in the Tower for about two weeks, in truth he languished there for some months. I've made hardly any mention of Lord Arlington, who was a powerful player in White-hall (in maps of London of the time it was written White Hall) and who was deeply involved in Blood's case and who brokered his pardon and release from the Tower. It was Lord Arlington who delivered a written apology from Blood to Ormonde for attacking him that night in St James's Street.

For simplicity's sake, I wanted to portray the political landscape as divided into two camps, pro-Dutch and pro-French, and ruled over by two big beasts, the dukes of Ormonde and Buckingham. But politics in any age is never simple and, if I have neglected Lord Arlington, I have equally ignored Lord Lauderdale, Lord Ashley and Sir Thomas Clifford, who were the other political heavyweights of the day. While I am making my little confession, I should also say that, for plot purposes, I also have Blood as the sole member of the gang who was captured and slung in the Tower, when in fact Parrot was captured too, and later released, as was Thomas Blood junior. I have no evidence of William Hunt being a traitor either. *Mea culpa.* If you want to read up on the subject, *The Audacious Crimes of Colonel Blood* by Robert Hutchinson (Weidenfeld & Nicolson), gives a much fuller picture.

So while I have admittedly made some accommodations with the truth, I did learn something that filled me with enormous excitement about the Treaty of Dover when I was researching this book. There really *was* a secret treaty, sometimes called the Treaty of Madame because it was arranged by Charles's sister Henrietta, Duchess of Orléans, and signed on June 1 1670. In it, Charles agreed to make a public profession of the Catholic faith in exchange for a great deal of money from Louis XIV and the prom-ise to attack the Dutch. Six months later, the Duke of Bucking-ham, who was kept in the dark about the secret treaty, was asked to conduct negotiations with the French and he was amazed how smoothly the talks went. The public Treaty of Dover, which omitted the politically inflammatory paragraph about Charles professing his Catholicism, was signed on 21 December 1670. What is more amazing is that the Treaty of Madame remained secret for another hundred years.

Which brings us to Holcroft Blood, the Colonel's unusual third son. He is the hero of this series, and he was a real person born around 1655, but I have taken rather a lot of liberties with his character and life story. He was never a page in the service of the Duke of Buckingham, as far as I know. It is extremely unlikely that he would have known anything about the secret treaty, and even more unlikely that he would have been able to blackmail the King with his knowledge. Also, I have described him as someone with mild Asperger's syndrome – which may be taking more than just a liberty. On the other hand, we will never know, as that modern diagnosis would not have been possible in the seventeenth century. Someone with Asperger's would just have been considered a bit odd and probably rather stupid and I can easily imagine someone like that being bullied by other children and held in contempt by adults. The little we know of the real Holcroft indicates that he was rather shy and awkward as a young man, but also remarkably clever with a gift for numbers, indeed, a pronounced mathematical bent – he went on to become a celebrated gunner in the British Army, and a brilliant artillery general under the Duke of Marlborough (the man Jack Churchill will become). The real Holcroft may not have been anywhere on what we now call the autistic spectrum but I think giving him this slight disability makes my fictionalised hero a good deal more interesting. That's my excuse, anyway.

Holcroft Blood's military career will be the focus of future books in this series, as will Jack Churchill's. And the story of the future Duke of Marlborough's rise is, I think, an instructive one. He was the son of Sir Winston Churchill, a Royalist from an old Dorset family of gentry, who was impoverished when the war was lost. It may have been this early experience of poverty that fuelled Churchill's later urge to accumulate wealth, which his detractors described as excessive greed. The family fortunes turned with the Restoration and, through his sister Anne, young Jack secured a place as a page in the household of James, Duke of York, King Charles's brother.

Such was his great personal charm and beauty that young Churchill was described as 'irresistible to either man or woman' and it was not long before he caught the eye of the King's mistress Barbara Villiers, who was also a distant cousin. Barbara had borne five children to the King but was being eclipsed by the actress Nell Gwyn, who was ten years younger. Barbara took Churchill into her bed around this time (she gave birth to a daughter by him in July 1672) and was very supportive of the impecunious but handsome young man, giving him a present of £5,000 in cash – with which he bought an annuity from Lord Halifax worth £500 a year.

There is a story that the King paid an unexpected visit to Barbara Villiers's apartments while she was entertaining Jack Churchill. The young gallant was forced to hide naked in a wardrobe when the King arrived (in some versions he had to jump out of the window). The King discovered him hiding there but when Churchill fell to his knees begging mercy, Charles laughed and pardoned him saying: 'You are a rascal but I forgive you because you do it to get your bread.'

There is another story about this incident, which I have appropriated in this book, which says that the Duke of Buckingham, hoping to bring Barbara Villiers down, paid a servant £100 to tell him when Churchill and his mistress would meet. When he had this information, he urged the King to visit her at precisely this time.

Jack Churchill might have been forgiven by the King – who had basically called him a male whore to his face – but he was out of favour at court and unlikely to receive any advancement in his career from the monarch. His patron the Duke of York, who had arranged for him to receive a commission as ensign in the First Regiment of the King's Foot Guards (much later to become the Grenadier Guards), now had him transferred away from White Hall to the Admiral's Regiment for service with the fleet. We know that Holcroft also fought at sea in the Anglo-Dutch war and so at the end of the book, I have them leaving London together to serve on the same ship.

One of my favourite characters in the book is Aphra Behn, who was another extraordinary figure of the time. Aphra was the widow of a Dutch (or possibly German) merchant who traded with Surinam and was lost at sea. She was a spy for the British Crown in Antwerp (not for the Duke of Buckingham) and spent some time in a debtor's prison on her return to England, which suggests that she was not well paid for her espionage. She was also one of the first women ever to have made her living as a writer, which endears her to me. She wrote plays for the Duke's Company which were performed at their theatre in Lincoln's Inn Fields, including the two plays mentioned in this book, although they were rather better and more successful than I have described them. Indeed, she was a prolific playwright, occasionally using the pen-name Astraea, but was mocked for writing in a masculine style. She also wrote a bestselling novel which expressed surprisingly progressive views on gender, race and class. She was buried in Westminster Abbey in 1689. As a British spy, successful writer and proto-feminist, Aphra was a character that leaped out of my research and forced her way into the book. I hope I've done her memory justice.

The code that Astraea uses to communicate with the Duke of Buckingham, which Holcroft finds so easy to read, is in fact a real, if rather simple code, used during the English Civil War. The vowels A E I O U are the numbers 1 to 5 with an apostrophe against them. V is also 5', W is 5'5' and Y is 6'. The letters B to L are the numbers 1 to 9; and the letters M to Z are also 1 to 9 but with an asterisk beside them.

I suspect that Buckingham would have used something a bit more challenging to the code-breakers of the day, but I wanted to allow the readers who like that sort of thing to be able to work out what was written in the letter Holcroft discovers in the duke's desk. Likewise, the card games Holcroft plays – Slamm, Trump and Ruff and Honours – are real games of the period, all variants of Whist, which emerged as the most popular variety at the end of the seventeenth century. The extraordinary final hand in the Whist game with Buckingham is finessed from 'The Quality of Evil' by Gustavu Aglione in *More Bedside Bridge* (Collins Willow) edited by Elena Jeronimidis.

I have to confess to one last bit of historical jiggery-pokery when it comes to the sundial in the Privy Garden of White Hall. The sundial, erected in 1669 by the Jesuit priest Francis Hall, was the mechanical wonder of its age, the King's pride and joy and a Royalist symbol of authority. It was attacked and ruined by the poet John Wilmot, Earl of Rochester, and some of his friends in a drunken frenzy in June 1675. I moved the date of Rochester's infamous action to May 1671 because I wanted the sundial to stand as a physical symbol of Holcroft's orderly worldview and to be wrecked when his personal life falls apart; after his mother's death, the capture of his father and his own ignominious dismissal from Buckingham's service. For this and my other historical transgressions, many abject apologies. But I am no longer a journalist. I am a storyteller, a writer of fiction, one who uses history to weave tales, and if those pesky historical facts threaten to get in the way of a good story, well . . .